THE HOUSE IS DARK

BY REBECCA JAMES

THE HOUSE IS DARK
STORM'S END

Rebecca James

THE HOUSE IS DARK

DOUBLEDAY & COMPANY, INC.
GARDEN CITY, NEW YORK
1976

All the characters in this book are fictitious, and any resemblance to actual persons, living or dead, is purely coincidental.

Library of Congress Cataloging in Publication Data

James, Rebecca Salsbury.
The house is dark.

I. Title.
PZ4.J28478Ho   [PS3560.A394]   813'.5'4
ISBN 0-385-03135-1
Library of Congress Catalog Card Number 75-21230

208605

For Francis G. Cleveland
and all "The Barnstormers"
through the years.

CONTENTS

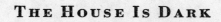

THE HOUSE IS DARK

OVERTURE

Chapter One

The curtain has gone up on the last act.

I can hear the voices of the actors out on the stage saying their lines, each word bringing them closer to my entrance. But my costume has disappeared and I am standing there in my slip. There doesn't seem to be any way through the heavy black velvet drapes to the stage. I realize now I have never learned the lines for the final scene, do not even know how it will end.

There is silence as the other actors wait for me. Then, somehow, I am out on the stage. The lights are bright on me. My mouth is dry, I cannot open my lips . . .

It was the night before I started for Vail's Point that I first had that dream. And unlike other dreams, it did not fade and disappear in the morning. It stayed with me, clear and whole, all through the awkward breakfast with my father, through our farewells, the bus trip into the city, the cab ride to the train station, and the settling of myself and my luggage on the nearly empty train to Connecticut.

Actors have told me since that it is the most common nightmare of their profession, coming from a fear of being unprepared, unequal to their work. But I had never, in my twenty-seven years, been an actress. I had never appeared in a school play or made a public speech or even played an instrument in a recital.

And yet the dream stayed with me, so terrifying that even to remember it made my skin clammy and my hands tremble.

There were reasons for the dream; I could list them rationally. Anxiety about going to a new place, to new people, all involved in a profession I knew nothing about. And since their profession was the theater, that could explain the setting of my dream.

But not why I had dreamed it.

That Sunday afternoon in June, I stared out the rain-streaked window at the Connecticut countryside going slowly past. It had been raining for days now, up and down the eastern seacoast, and the few scattered houses and heavy barns outside looked soaked.

2

The land was as gray as the sky above it. We were two hours out of New York and I still had miles to go before the train would reach the town of Westaven and then, beyond that, the house at Vail's Point.

The house and the *theater* at Vail's Point.

I looked at the nearly empty train car, the seats lined up on each side of the aisle in front of me. I had taken my seat in the last row of the car, placing my luggage and the thick Sunday *Times* on the seat beside me. I had no desire to make conversation with a stranger that afternoon, not that it was likely that anybody would sit beside me even if the train were full. I have learned I am not the sort of woman to whom strangers talk.

Still, I had taken the seat deliberately, to protect myself. I knew what I would find in the second section of the paper, the picture of Dilys and the announcement of her engagement. And if I should cry . . .

I have never liked people who cry in public, any more than I have liked people who indulge in self-pity, but I was thoroughly prepared to do both when I read the article.

DILYS HAINES TO WED PETER LEYDEN

It was there, all right, page 55. With that picture of Dilys in the jonquil satin gown she had worn for her debut. We had all rather laughed at that debutante party. It represented one more victory for Dilys' mother over her quiet father, Professor Haines. For one evening at least, Mrs. Haines had managed to get Dilys out of her tight blue jeans and into a conventional dress; had wiped off most of the heavy makeup and brushed the unruly hair back into a neat arrangement of curls . . . and photographed the moment for posterity.

The article accompanying the picture recorded the details with appropriate dignity: *Dilys Catherine, the only child of Professor and Mrs. Stephen Haines . . . to be married to Peter Leyden, associate professor in her father's department . . .*

My Peter. Only he wasn't mine any more. Perhaps he never had been mine.

Still, the tears did not come. There was no one to see me now. The car had emptied as we passed through the suburbs and exurbs of New York. I could have indulged myself with privacy . . . and some justice. Instead, the dream of the night before came back, and always at the one last moment before I woke up. Only now there

3

were more details to remember, adding to my fear, like bits of a jig-saw puzzle that make the picture more complete.

There are people staring at me out there in the darkness. No, not people. Eyes. A thousand of them, but all belonging to one body. And now the other actors look at me . . . but I know some-how they can't see me, they are looking through me. And the silence grows longer and longer, but still I cannot speak. I do not even know who I am supposed to be . . .

My name is Alison Howard, the only daughter of Professor Grant Howard. In November I will be twenty-eight. I'm sure to some people I seem much older than that already. But Father thinks that women should still look as they did when Mother was alive, and so my dark blond hair is strained back into a neat knot at the nape of my neck, I do not go out of the house without putting on stockings, and I am probably the only woman left in America who does not own a pair of slacks.

Not that I have objected; at least, not too strongly. I have been Father's only real companion these long years since Mother died. I was twelve then, thin and gangly, and to me Mother was the most beautiful woman in the world. Even now, looking at her photographs that are in every room of our house off the college quadrangle, she still seems remarkably lovely. She had high cheekbones and long, graceful hands and violet-blue eyes. "Lilac eyes," my father called them. Her eyes are all I have inherited from her.

Her eyes.

And, of course, her money.

I must have been eighteen when I first realized how much money Mother had left the two of us. I had known, from the vague jokes that she had made with my father, that she was much wealthier than he with only his professor's salary. And I knew that there were no other relatives, that we were her only family; I'd learned that forever the day of her funeral, the two of us alone in that great black limousine following the hearse to the cemetery.

But I had never realized how large a fortune Mother had left until that afternoon I had come home from sophomore registration. The house was quiet (except for Martha humming one of her end-less hymns down in the kitchen). The hall was cool after the hot September sunlight outside, cool and dark. The bare wood floors had been polished to a high gloss, as was the Sheraton sideboard and the curving railing of the stairs that wound up to the second floor.

And then I heard Father. The door to his study was beyond the stairs. It was open and I could hear him muttering with growing intensity the multiplication table. In French. It is far from his native language, as any Frenchman would have been able to tell instantly, and it was something he did only in moments of great irritation as a substitute for swearing.

I dropped my books on the sideboard and went to the open doorway. "What is it, Father?" I asked, looking at him with some amusement. He is a handsome man most of the time, but that day he had been running his hands through his fine gray hair so often that his head looked as if it were erupting.

He looked up at me from his desk and indicated the papers that covered every inch of space in front of him. "Alison, it's money," he groaned. "There's so much of it."

It was that afternoon I had my first lesson in family finances. I knew that Mother had set up a sizable trust fund for each of us. And that the Federal house that she and Father had so lovingly restored with its signed antiques and gleaming silver was his completely. But the other third of her fortune was to be used to form a foundation to aid the arts, and it was the awarding of grants to the most worthy of the applicants that was driving my father to distraction.

From that day on, I worked with my father. And I was no longer eighteen. I was twenty. Twenty-five. Twenty-seven.

It wasn't an unpleasant life. Father was good company, when I could raise his head out of a book—capable of shrewd perception and a dry, light humor, rather like the old sherry we would have each night at six. The foundation work was interesting, separating the sham from the valuable. During the years, we built a small museum for local artists. We brought out a new edition of Father's beloved English poets, with some exciting illustrations done by a Chilean girl, and established a school for native crafts on a reservation in South Dakota.

And there were people to entertain, although social life on the campus of a small Pennsylvania college can be as narrow as a coffin. But as my father's hostess, it was my duty to see that there was at least one small dinner party each week during the school year. It was at one of these dinners that I first met Peter. I had heard that there was a new teacher in Professor Haines's History Department, and at Father's instigation I had sent him an invitation.

That evening, for once, I was late. The first guests were already arriving as I came down the staircase. Peter was standing with his back to the stairs, talking with my father. My father made some sort of gesture and Peter turned toward me just as I walked down the last steps.

In a conventional sense, you could not call Peter handsome. Tall and angular, with deep hollows under his strong cheekbones, he had thick, rather coarse black hair and high, thin shoulders. But there was strength in his face and an intriguing hint of a ruthless quality that I was to learn so well in the following months. Compared to the quiet scholars I had lived among all my life, he seemed the most fascinating man I had ever met.

Then the front door opened.

Dilys wore orange that night, a thin silk jersey that every woman in the room knew was a size too small and that every man thought was perfect. Even my father eyed her with obvious pleasure.

And Peter was no longer looking at me.

I sat back against the train seat, forcing myself to examine the months since the previous September. There were no tears in my eyes and I ignored the rain still streaming down the window at my side. What actually *had* been between Peter and me? Quite a few evenings together, yes. A few kisses, yes. But he never had actually said that he loved me. But even as I tried to look at it sensibly I knew that I was lying to myself. He *had* loved me. I wasn't mistaken about that.

Until after Christmas . . .

Dilys had planned to go south in January; she had announced it gaily at all the holiday parties. But she wrecked her car New Year's Eve, and her parents, in one of their few attempts at discipline, refused to pay for her vacation. So there she was in January: bored, discontented, and not beyond making a little mischief.

6

It started then, that January, that she began to notice Peter and me. And casually, for lack of anything better to do, she decided to take him for herself.

I didn't know that, of course. Not for quite a long time. Even when I finally realized what was happening, I wouldn't let myself think about it. Peter loved *me,* I was sure of it. Even when he began to spend as many evenings with Dilys as he did with me.

And then he was spending more evenings with her.

I felt the tears in my eyes now, but I forced them back, making myself focus on the antique watch pinned to my gray linen suit. Four o'clock. It would still be at least another half hour before we got to Westaven. How far is Vail's Point from the town? I wondered. I must find something to fill the time, I thought. I will not reread the article announcing Dilys' forthcoming wedding. I will do the crossword puzzle or walk up and down the empty aisle or stare out the window at the rain; but I will not think about Dilys.

I tightened the knot of my hair. What was I doing on this train? I thought bleakly. Going to a small town in Connecticut to collect the papers of a dead writer. A fairly obvious maneuver of my father's, so that I would not have to sit in the college chapel and watch Dilys in triumph become Mrs. Peter Leyden. An escape for a limited number of weeks. And then what was to become of me? I felt the same panic I'd had from the dream, and deliberately forced myself to think of what I knew of the work ahead.

"Dilys has asked you to be her bridesmaid?"

My father and I were seated in the dining room over our coffee. It had been a quiet dinner, even for us. In fact, I'd had time in the long silences to think of how many dinners the two of us had shared in the past, and the thousands of dinners that lay ahead of us in the years to come. But now, suddenly, Father was looking at me, his gray eyes shrewd behind his glasses.

"Yes." I tried to smile at Father but it wasn't very successful. "I suppose Dilys means it kindly."

"Nonsense, Alison!" It was as close as I'd ever heard my father come to anger. "Stop being angelic about it."

7

"Should I take to my bed in tears?" I asked him, my voice drier than I expected. "The Maiden Deserted?"

"You should take an ax to her." He sat back in his chair, carefully checking to see that the door to the kitchen was closed. Not that Martha didn't know what had happened between Peter and me. Not that everybody on the campus didn't know by now, I thought bleakly.

"It's not Peter's fault, Father. There was no . . . tie between us. And if he wants to marry Dilys . . ."

"He'll have his hands full," my father replied crisply. "The only thing I can say in his favor is he's not a fortune hunter."

Or he would have chosen me, I thought. Even with money, I couldn't . . . But Father was still speaking:

"Although after a year of paying Dilys' bills, he'll wish he had been."

The conversation was becoming uncomfortable. For three days now, ever since Graduation Day, when Dilys arrived wearing Peter's ring, her arm draped through his, Peter with a somewhat dazed expression on his face, Father and I had not discussed the two of them. I think I behaved as I always had, my voice quiet, my face controlled. But if Father was going to pry into the matter, I was not sure I could keep from tears.

I started to leave the table, but Father waved me back into my chair and went on. "Alison, I have no desire to pry into your life. But I don't particularly relish seeing Dilys rub your face in the mud." I started to protest automatically, but he again waved me to silence. "I think you should be away from the campus for a while. Maybe for the whole summer. The wedding's not until July?"

I nodded my head, not trusting myself to speak.

"Yes," he said. "This just might do it." He wasn't looking at me then; his eyes were thoughtful and he stroked his chin with one long finger, a habit he had when he was plotting something.

"What?" I managed to say that without letting my voice quaver, and then curiosity made me go on. "What might do it?"

"I've had a letter. An appeal to the Foundation, actually." I again started to interrupt, but he went on quickly, looking at me now. "Yes, I know, I promised to turn them all over to you. But this is something different; I wanted to think it out. Now I'm beginning to feel it might be perfect for everybody." He paused and took a sip from the thin cloisonné coffee cup at his side. He looked at me again, his eyes studying my face carefully.

"Alison, what do you know about the Vails?"

For a moment I didn't know what he was talking about. My mind went quickly back through years of students and teachers, and my first instinct was to answer, "Nothing." And then I realized, from the way he had said the name, whom he meant.

"The Vail family? Haidee Vail, the actress? And her brother . . . it *was* her brother, wasn't it? Lionel Vail, the playwright?"

"Is that all you know about them? That they existed?" He sighed a little and settled back into his chair. "Ah, well, I forget how young you are."

There was a curious expression on his face, as if for a moment he was remembering his own age. But he was barely sixty and I felt embarrassed at my ignorance.

"I know she was a great actress. Haidee Vail, I mean. Mother took me up to New York just before . . ." I took a deep breath and hurried on. There was no need to remind him of Mother—not tonight, when he was disturbed already. "Haidee Vail was starring in a revival of *The Corn Is Green* at the City Center . . . Mother felt I ought to see her."

"Did you like her?"

"She was wonderful . . . even as a child I knew that." I tried to think of something further to say, anything to continue the conversation. "Is she still alive? She seemed quite old to me then."

Father chuckled a little. "Don't tell her that. In my limited knowledge of actresses and women . . . neither of them like to be reminded of the years."

"And the brother . . . wasn't there something strange about him? Something to do with his death?" I was trying to search my memory, but nothing seemed to come together.

"Lionel committed suicide." Father tapped his fingers on the table idly. "Haidee and Lionel were the most famous of the family, but there were others. They had a sister, May. Nobody seems to have heard much about her the last few years. I remember she was very quiet when she was young. And very kind."

"You knew the Vails?" I stared at him now. The idea of my

quiet Father having been involved with one of the most famous theatrical families in America was as strange as if he had said he had once lived on the moon.

He looked at me with some amusement. "I haven't always been buried in books, Alison. As a matter of fact, Lionel Vail and I were in school together. For one semester. Before he was expelled." He smiled with dry amusement. "Lionel was expelled from quite a lot of schools in his time."

"What has this got to do with the Foundation?"

He straightened in his chair slightly, aware my curiosity was calling him back to the present.

"They've written to us. Or at least somebody named Corin Vail has." He narrowed his eyes thoughtfully, figuring out the years that had passed. "That could very well be Haidee's grandson. Julie's boy." Then he looked back at me again. "You must have heard of Julie Vail. Even I've seen her on television."

"They're all named Vail?" I found myself smiling with some amusement. "Didn't any of the ladies of the family marry?"

Father laughed. "I'm sure they did. But you do not give up a name like Vail easily. Not if you're working in the theater. At any rate, I received this letter about a week ago. Would the Foundation be interested in the papers of Lionel Vail? There's never been a biography of him, although I'm sure people must have tried. He died right after the War. Over the years there must have been hundreds of eager young students anxious to do a thesis about him. But the family has never given anyone permission to examine his papers. Not until now."

"Isn't that a little . . . peculiar?" I was finding myself becoming interested. All these years of living Father's quiet academic life, I had become familiar with the drive of students to find a new, unexplored subject for the work that meant their degrees and ambitions. Students do not discourage easily.

"They're a very private family, for all their fame."

"And now they want somebody to write about him?"

"The family is approaching me directly. Naturally, a biography of such an important playwright . . . well, it's not my field at all. But it might be something the Foundation should take a hand in." Father rubbed his chin again reflectively.

"Where are the papers?" I asked.

"At the family home, Vail's Point. One of those great robber-

10

baron mansions on the Connecticut shore. Haidee's father built it for the family in the early 1900s. I guess it's as close to a home as any of them has ever had."

"They all live there?"

"On and off. I know Lionel wrote most of his plays there. I suspect the house has something to do with this letter. There's mention of a theater on the Vail estate, and the possibility of its opening this summer. They might have an idea that the Foundation could pick up some of the bills."

"But that's absurd!" I felt my back stiffen as I looked across the table at my father. He knew the rules of the Foundation as well as I. "You know the way the grants have been set up . . ."

"I know, Alison. Still, the Foundation *is* to help the arts in America. And Lionel Vail was one of the most important playwrights this country has ever had." He stood then, but the conversation wasn't over. He started for his study across the hall, knowing I would follow him. Once in his small, book-lined room, he went straight for one of the far shelves and began to look for a volume. "Have you ever read any of Lionel Vail's plays?" he asked, not looking at me.

"Once in Contemporary Literature," I answered. "Didn't he write *The Basilisks?* About an old lady being held prisoner by her greedy family?"

He nodded absently. "That won him his second Pulitzer prize. For a time there in the thirties he was considered the equal, if not the superior, of Eugene O'Neill." He gave up his search then and turned back to me. "No, I can't find it. He autographed a volume of his work for me once, just before the War."

"What was he like?" I sat down on the low bench by Father's desk. Lionel Vail was merely a name to me, but a conversation about him would keep Father from discussing Dilys and Peter, and I was prepared to listen for hours about any subject in the world rather than think about the two of them.

"Lionel? A strange man. Never married. Dark. Lean. Not what I'd call handsome, but women found him irresistible. Deep, brooding eyes. A heavy drinker. Every woman he knew thought she could change that."

"Women can be very foolish about men sometimes," I said, and regretted it instantly. That was too close to what I was thinking about myself.

Father went on without comment. "It might be an interesting project for you, Alison. You could stay at Vail's Point; they mention that in the letter. See what papers there are. See if it's something the Foundation should interest itself in. Maybe you could even recommend the right biographer."

"And stay away from here until August." My voice was sharper than I intended. Father gave me a quick glance and then turned back to studying the bookshelves once more.

"I'm not sending you away, Alison," he said quietly. "But it might be interesting to have a change. Think about it."

I got up then and started for the door. I made no answer. I knew he was expecting none.

Dilys called the following morning to ask me, very sweetly, if I would go shopping with her for the bridesmaids' dresses. But by then the telegram had already gone to Vail's Point announcing my arrival the following Sunday. I don't think Dilys was deceived for a moment about the urgency of the project.

But this time there was very little she could do about it.

"Westaven."

I looked up at the conductor standing beside me. I realized suddenly the train was gradually slowing down. Scrambling my luggage together, I had barely a moment to glance out the streaked window. It was raining harder now. I could see a few buildings, gray in the dark wet afternoon, then more buildings closer together, the trees sodden and heavy along the embankment to the highway. The train stopped and the conductor began helping me down.

I managed to get my suitcases onto the platform, out of the rain. And then as the train started to pull out again, I straightened and looked at the station. It was a small building, with the paint peeling, as so many of the stations along the line were. Even on a sunny day it would have looked grim and deserted. Worse, the doorway to the small waiting room was locked.

I walked to the far end of the platform. Apparently I had been the only passenger to get off. The rain was too heavy now to see much of the village across the highway from the station. There were no signs of people, no signs of anybody waiting for me. But at the far end of the line of parking spaces that edged the station stood a battered car with the word "Taxi" painted on the side.

There was even a man in the front seat, his head buried in a newspaper.

I hurried down the empty platform, and, pulling up the hood of my pale-blue raincoat, I made a dash for the car. The driver never raised his head until I tapped on the car window. I could barely see him through the wet glass, so I signaled him to roll the window down. The rain kept splashing my forehead, and I could feel my hair straggle loose. Finally the man lowered the car window a few inches.

"Please," I said, "I've got some luggage. Can you take me to Vail's Point?"

The window came down a few inches more. I could see the driver clearly now. He was a big, middle-aged man, with a hard face that could have used a shave.

"What did you say?" His voice was surly.

"Vail's Point. Do you know where it is? Can you take me there?"

He looked at me for a long moment, his eyes cold under his thick eyebrows. I had never seen such dislike in a face before. "I don't go to Vail's Point, lady," he said. "Not ever."

And then, before I could stop him, he rolled the window back up, leaving me standing there in the empty parking space, the rain sliding down my face.

Like tears.

CHAPTER TWO

For a moment, I could only stand there, the rain hitting my face, dripping down my coat, splashing my legs. I could not believe the man intended to ignore me, but when he made no further move I felt a surge of anger. Without thinking, I yanked open the door to the back seat of the taxi and climbed in.

There must have been something about my appearance that had not prepared him for this, for I am sure if either of us had guessed what I would do he would have snapped the lock shut on the door. As it was, he turned to stare at me, his face open and vulnerable with surprise.

"What do you think you're doing?"

"You're supposed to be running a taxi. Well, I'm a passenger. And I have to get to Vail's Point." I was calmer now that I was actually inside, out of the rain. I made myself look at the driver steadily. There must have been something about that look that convinced him there was no way he could get me out of his car unless he removed me bodily. And I didn't think he would quite dare that.

The coldness disappeared now that I had called his bluff, but his mouth was still grim.

"I told you. I don't go to Vail's Point."

"Are there other taxis?"

He turned forward again, shaking his head no. But I could see him watching me carefully through the rearview mirror.

"You could rent a car, maybe." He said it grudgingly.

"I don't drive."

He gave a short laugh. "Wouldn't do you much good if you did. Only place to rent is Eastman's. And they're closed Sundays." He leaned back in his seat as if he had made up his mind to a course of action (which was clearly to outwait me), and picked up his paper again.

There was no partition between the front and back seat, there was nothing other than the one word "Taxi" painted on the door outside to suggest this was different from any other car.

"Please . . ." I tried to make the word sound more helpless than angry. "Please . . . can't you help? I don't even know where

14

the house is. There's no one to meet me. There's no way I can even phone . . . the station is locked."

He made no answer, just turned the page of his paper defiantly. My coat, which had been too thin for the weather outside, now seemed hot and steamy as I sat there surrounded by closed windows.

"Look," I said, starting with what I hoped was a sensible tone. "Surely the requirements for a taxi license must be that you take people where they want to go? *All* people?" I added firmly, "I could call a policeman . . ."

He twisted around then, a strange grin thinning his lips. "Wouldn't do you any good," he said. "I'm the police."

Something of the shock I felt must have shown on my face. He grinned again. It was, oddly enough, not unpleasant. He may not have shaved, but he had clean white teeth and I could see, when he was younger, some people might have even considered him handsome.

"State trooper at least. I only moonlight with the cab to make a little extra. Two college-age kids, you take what you can get."

I sat back. If this was to be some sort of bargaining process about his fee, that I could handle. "I'll pay whatever you ask," I said quietly. For a moment I saw in his eyes the same anger as when I had first mentioned Vail's Point.

"Lady, I'm not looking for handouts. I don't go to Vail's Point. And that's final. Now, get out of this car!"

As he lit his cigarette, I realized getting angry wasn't going to work. I looked out the streaked window. The train tracks and station seemed to form one side of a village square. The other three sides were lined with buildings huddled together in the rain. They all looked closed from here, and there was no one on the sidewalks. If I wanted to get to Vail's Point, this man was my only chance.

"Tell me something," I said conversationally. "Vail's Point . . . is it far from here?"

He hesitated for a moment. "Four or five miles maybe," he said finally. "Out by the beach."

"Is there a road out there? A highway?"

He nodded briefly, still keeping his face forward as if he could see something through the rain streaming down the windshield. I noticed a muscle on his jaw twitching.

I smoothed back the damp hair that had escaped from my

15

hood and leaned forward again. "Couldn't you at least take me down the highway? Toward Vail's Point? You haven't got anything against the highway, have you?" I could see that he was watching me through the rearview mirror again, and I put on my most helpless smile.

"You one of them actors?" He sounded more like a policeman now; that tone of voice that makes you feel guilty even when you know you've done nothing.

"No, I'm . . . And then I stopped, not quite knowing what position I did have. "I guess you could say I'm here to do research."

"A newspaper?" He was becoming interested now.

I wondered if that would impress him, but I decided to tell the truth. "No, I'm . . . from a college." I could see he was not so hostile now and I went on quickly. "Please? Just give me a lift down the road. You wouldn't have to go into the place. I'm sure I could find my way once I got there."

He considered this for a moment, chewing his lower lip. Then he gave me another swift glance through the mirror and I could see he had made up his mind.

"Where did you say your bags were?"

He got out without even waiting for my answer. He was taller than he had seemed sitting in the car, his shoulders broad and heavy. The rain splashed steadily on him but he paid no attention; he didn't even move under the station roof for cover until he reached the corner where the platform ran parallel with the railroad tracks. I suppose I should have been curious about his anger, but I wasn't. I was only grateful to have persuaded him.

It was a quiet ride. Mr. McNaughton (I had noticed his name on the driver's permit taped to the dashboard while he went for my suitcases) asked no questions, and I was afraid to say anything further for fear he would change his mind again. As we left the station, he drove the car down a tree-lined Main Street and then we were out on the highway. The rain was softer now, the afternoon full of June warmth, and I could see mist—or maybe it was steam —clinging in low, white layers to the soaked fields.

When the town was behind us he started to drive faster. He was a good driver and the narrow, black road was empty before us.

Then, before I was even aware there was anyone else driving

on the road, a car raced up from behind, a low white sports car, a blur of chrome and metal curves as it drove beside us for a second and then pulled sharply ahead. Mr. McNaughton stiffened. He swerved his wheel swiftly and I could hear him curse under his breath.

"Damn fool!" He pushed his foot down hard on the accelerator; I think for a moment he forgot he was making this trip as a taxi driver and not as a policeman. The sports car was twenty feet ahead by now, roaring through puddles so fast that a spray of water rose up on each side like wings.

"That idiot ought to be arrested," McNaughton muttered. And again his foot went down on the pedal for more speed. But the white car was too fast for us. It pulled farther and farther ahead, not even slowing for the curve that came up swiftly.

With another roar it disappeared out of sight. And before us on what had been an empty road there lay a dark, limp object . . . a squirrel perhaps, or a rabbit, still as only the suddenly dead can be. Mr. NcNaughton slowed as we came near it, but he did not stop. He circled his car around the body of the animal carefully. I wanted to see if the poor creature was still alive, but I knew it was too late to do any good.

I must have made some sound, for Mr. McNaughton was looking at me again in the mirror. "You all right?" he said.

I nodded, not trusting myself to speak.

"It was so . . . ruthless," I said finally. "Just to kill something like that. And not even to care."

"There's a lot of that in this world," he said, his voice as stern as any Puritan preacher. "Probably one of that theater crowd. A bad lot, all of them."

I stared at him, no longer even trying to hide my reaction. Could his hostility be nothing but old-fashioned, New England prejudice against the theater? It was hard to believe a bias like that could still survive in this century. I thought of what had been implied in the letter the Foundation had received from the Vail family, about their hope of reopening the theater on the estate. If Mr. McNaughton's reaction was typical of the people of Westaven, the project was already doomed to failure.

We drove on in silence. The white sports car must have turned off the road, as it was no longer ahead of us. The highway was not straight now. We curved through what looked like a forest, the trees thick overhead, dripping the last of the rain on the roof of the car. To my left, I noticed, we were running alongside a low wall of gray stone, dug from the hard Connecticut earth years before. Then, even from inside the closed car, I could hear the sound of waves splashing against a shore. The road curved once more. We were at the gates of Vail's Point.

"This is as far as I go."

Mr. McNaughton was out of the car before I could stop him. Yanking open the door to the back seat, he started to remove my suitcases. I got out on the other side. For a moment, as I stood there on the wet highway, I thought he was playing a sour joke on me. All I could see was the gray ocean ahead of me, waves pouring steadily onto a strip of beach, and beyond, the same color as the water, the low, sullen clouds, still full of rain. Then I noticed, beside the parked taxi, a break in the stone wall to allow for a gravel driveway to enter the highway. A metal arch curved high above the drive, connecting the two stone gateposts. Squinting against the soft mist that I hoped was the last of the rain, I saw iron letters had been twisted to form the arch: *Vail's Point*. But Mr. McNaughton's car was parked in front of the driveway and the trees bent low and dripping over the stone walls on either side, so I could see nothing beyond.

"Your bags are by the gate there."

I turned to look at Mr. McNaughton. I am not a short woman, but he loomed above me, his face gaunt under his battered cap. There was no trace of anger in them; they seemed sad and distant, as if he were no longer aware of me.

"The house . . . ?"

I realized I had no idea whether it was miles from the road or only a short walk. McNaughton nodded briefly toward the driveway. I had money in my hands, but he brushed it aside impatiently and strode back to the open door of his car. Then, for a moment resting his hands on the door, he turned to look up the driveway, seeing something that from where I stood was still invisible.

"Tell them I brought you here," he said quietly. "Tell them Ed McNaughton didn't take any money for it."

Then he got into his car, slammed the door, and with a quick swerve of wheels, turned the taxi around and started back up the wet highway toward the town.

I started toward the gateposts, where he'd placed my suitcases. There was no sound now except the raindrops dripping from the trees and the slow whisper of the ocean less than thirty feet away. When I reached the entrance to the drive I looked up as McNaughton had.

The house was not far from the road, perhaps less than a city block. It stood alone on a low rise of land, the trees on each side and in front having been cut away as if to give the building room to breathe. From the front steps down to the wall that edged the highway there was a sweep of long-untended lawn, the wet grass bent low toward the house as if in subservience. From the corner of my eye I could see that there were a few rusting iron benches scattered up the slope, signs that someone once had lived here in comfort and enjoyed the ocean view.

But it was the house beyond that fascinated me. It was the ugliest building I had ever seen. Enormously wide, stretching great arms across the top of the rise, all of it was covered with gray shingle the color of elephants. It had clearly been built at a time when American architecture was at its most grotesque. Deep verandas girdled the whole building, imitation Moorish turrets emerged from the steep eaves of the roof, and thin little Gothic windows, all framed in gingerbread fretwork, broke out in unexpected angles. Over what seemed to be the center of the house, a great bubble of shingle swelled as enormous as the roof of a Turkish mosque. And on each side, as if to make some attempt at symmetry, there was a wide widow's walk. Below these I could count perhaps a dozen balconies. It seemed less a house than a deserted summer hotel that no one had lived in for the past seventy years.

I stood without moving, as depressed as I have ever been in my life. Then a breeze from the ocean chilled my shoulders and I started through the narrow gateway up the drive, leaving my heavy suitcases where they were. The rain started up again, spitting great drops on my face and coat, but it no longer seemed important that my hair hung limp or that my neat shoes squished deep into the wet gravel.

It was a longer walk than I had expected, and with each footstep I could feel my spirits sinking further and further. If McNaughton had waited with his cab, I would have turned around and fled.

As it was, there was no way out but to go on. The house was closer now, still grim and ugly. Not much attempt had been made to keep it up and I found myself wondering if the Vails had fallen on hard times. Rain dripped from the overflowing gutters. All around me I could see the signs of neglect: uncut grass, shingles missing on the corners of the building, cracked and peeling paint on the balconies. Tired curtains covered every window.

The place looked deserted. It was too early for lights, perhaps, but there were no other signs of life either. No sounds, the noises that tell a house is lived in . . . voices or a radio playing or someone in a far kitchen preparing supper.

The wide front steps that led down from the veranda ended abruptly on the lawn. There was no path from the driveway to what must have been the main entrance of the house. To the left, as I approached the house, there was a high porte-cochere wide enough to hold two cars. Only today it too, was deserted. At least I could be out of the rain there, for it was coming down heavier now. I started to walk faster.

From behind me I heard a car. I turned just as it sped up the drive from the highway. It was a white sports car and it moved recklessly over the wet gravel.

Like most people who do not drive, I do not know the separate makes of cars. And while I could not have sworn that it was the same car that had pulled past us on the road, it *was* white and it *was* moving much too fast. I stood where I was, ignoring the rain that was coming down steadily now. All I could feel was disgust rising inside me, driving out my depression.

The car braked to a stop barely three feet behind me. The front door banged open and, before I could move, the driver was out of the car, around the front of the vehicle, and standing in front of me. He was a tall man, nearly as tall as McNaughton, with thick black hair that the rain was already starting to plaster over his forehead. In the one instant I had to look at him before he started shouting, I judged him to be in his early thirties. He had a strong face that might have been called handsome if it were not at the moment furious with rage.

20

"Who the hell left their damn bags by the gateposts?" he yelled, his fists planted squarely on the hip pockets of his bright plaid sportscoat, his feet wide apart. He paid no attention to the rain that was soaking his jacket and tan trousers. The tone of his voice and the way he glared left no doubt what he expected my answer to be.

Suddenly, all of the anger and frustration I'd felt this day—had indeed felt for weeks—came out in a fury that surprised me and, I think, even him. "They're my bags!" I shouted over the rain. "And I didn't put them there, the cab driver left them there because he wouldn't come into this place." Conscious I was finishing more lamely than I had started, I added, "And from what I've seen, I can't blame him!"

"Damn near had an accident," the man answered, but I thought he was a little taken aback by the vehemence of my reply.

"It wouldn't be the first one you've had today, would it?" I jerked my chin up at him, wishing I were taller so that I could look him square in the eye.

"What's that supposed to mean?"

"Or don't you consider killing animals important?"

"Are you crazy, or is it me? What the hell are you talking about?"

I turned away, with as much dignity as I could, aware that the rain had soaked through my new coat, that my hair was straggled and wet and my shoes were probably beyond repair. I didn't have to stand there in the pouring rain listening to this ruffian.

He grabbed my arm and twisted me around so quickly that I would have fallen if his grip had not been so tight.

"Who are you, anyway?"

"My name's Alison Howard . . . ," I began, but he pulled me toward the shelter of the wooden porte-cochere.

"Let's finish this out of the elements, if you don't mind."

He hurried me forward, ignoring the open door to the car behind him, ignoring the fact that he could stride faster in one step than I could move in two, ignoring, in fact, everything but that he was determined to continue this where it most pleased him to be.

I struggled to free myself from his grip, but I might have been a child for all the attention he paid. Before I could get my breath to protest, we were under the sheltering roof of the carriage entrance of Vail's Point. He released me then and strode up the two stone steps to the front door. The door was of some heavy dark wood, rising almost as high as the porte-cochere above us. Inserted in the door were long panels of frosted glass and, below them, a round brass bellpull of the type that hasn't been made in fifty years. He gave the metal handle of the bell a sharp twist and then, still on the steps, turned around to look down at me.

"Now . . . who are you?" he said, his voice only somewhat calmer. The color was receding from his face, or perhaps it was the half-light we were in. His eyes were dark green and, even in the gloom, penetrating. For a moment he reminded me a little of Peter, although he was a bigger man. But Peter's features were fine; this man's nose and jaw and chin could have belonged to a truck driver. I tried to smooth my hair, but it was too heavily soaked, and all I managed to do was shove the hood back onto my shoulders.

"I'm Alison Howard," I began, as coldly as I could manage. Angry as I was, I knew my attempt at dignity was not a success. He came down the two steps before I could go on, and then, with the impersonality of a man buying a coffee cup, he took my chin lightly in one hand and turned it slightly to the left and then to the right.

"Too innocent," he said, his hand finally letting go of me. "I told Julie what I needed. Didn't she even listen?"

"What . . . ?"

"Look, I'm sorry you made the trip for nothing, Miss Howard, but don't blame me. That's Julie's problem. She knows who I want."

"Look, Mr. . . . ?"

"Reives. Jeb Reives." He said it scornfully, as though I were playing some sort of trick on him. "Don't pretend you don't know who I am."

Without even waiting for my answer, he left me and went back up the steps to give the bellpull another twist. "Somebody should be up. It's almost time for the 'Comfort Hour,'" he muttered. By now I had got my breath back as well as my anger, and I no longer cared how I looked to this barbarian.

"Listen, you insolent . . . will you stop bounding around like a monkey and tell me who you are and who you think I'm supposed to be?"

He paid no attention to me. The words might have stayed inside my head for all the notice he took. Marching down the steps, he went past me as if I were no longer there. He was out in the rain now, walking firmly toward his car. And then, as if he had thought of something, he stopped and looked back.

"There's a train at six-fifteen, if you want a lift," he yelled. He continued to pay no attention to the rain that splashed heavily down on him.

I didn't say a word, but turned my back, keeping my shoulders stiff. He shouted something I could not hear and the car door slammed. I kept my back to him as the motor started. There was a long screeching sound as the car swiveled on the wet gravel. His voice was closer when he shouted again.

"Tell them I've gone to the inn for a drink. And they'll be damn lucky to see me at dinner," he shouted. I heard the car roar off. When the sound grew fainter, I sneaked a look over my shoulder. It would be just like him to run over my suitcases deliberately. But he maneuvered carefully through the gateway, not touching my luggage and, with a final blast, the car disappeared in the direction of town.

Then I heard a voice close behind me, a cheerful, female, unmistakably cockney voice.

"Don't just stand there, ducks. Come in or you'll have *la grippe* before nightfall."

I turned to get my first look at Esme Laughton.

ACT ONE
(THE THEATER)

CHAPTER THREE

She stood a step behind me, a woman of about sixty, so short that the top of her head barely came to my shoulder. She had a soft round body, the sleeves of her mulberry dress hardly containing the great padding of flesh on her arms, and her bosom as shapeless as if she had stuffed it with pillows. Above all of this, in a face as white as if it had been powdered with flour, were the tiny features of a child: a button of a nose, small brandy-colored eyes, a little cleft chin, and a mouth as pursed as a keyhole. Her hair was dark red, or had been once; it was hard to tell in the fading light of the afternoon whether it was badly dyed or aging in some strange and inexplicable fashion. A large crocheted shawl had slipped off her shoulders, but as I looked, fat little hands pulled it up again and clutched it closer to her throat.

"Come along, luv, you're soaked to the skin." She stepped back onto the steps and gestured toward the open doorway behind her. She had turned on a light inside, and what I could see behind her looked warm and inviting.

"My name is . . ."

She stopped me before I could go any further.

"It's Miss Howard, isn't it? And it looks like you've had a bit of a time of it!" There was no mistaking the ghost of Bow bells now. "Come along, dearie. We'll soon have you nice and cozy." She didn't wait for an answer but, pulling the shawl tighter, moved heavily into the house.

I followed her up the steps and inside. After closing the door smartly, she stepped back to give me a shrewd look, her head cocked slightly, like a speculative robin.

"Wet clean through, aren't we? And I doubt if those shoes'll ever come right again. You should have put in your wire when you were coming. We would have met you."

"I did."

"Bless us all! What must you think!" She reached out and touched the limp hood of my coat. "And you were wearing no more than this. I don't know what they're making clothes out of these days, no thicker than a bit of tissue . . ." She dropped her hand, returning it automatically to meet her other one over her solid stomach, the fingers clasping together companionably.

"But you *were* expecting me, Miss . . . Mrs. . . . ?" I stared at her, still confused.

"Esme, dear. Everyone calls me Esme. Oh, yes, you're expected right enough. Here to look at Lionel's papers, aren't you? You're to have the yellow room and *she'll* be happy to see you at the Comfort Hour."

She dropped her voice a little at the end of the sentence as if the "she" referred to was royalty. I knew instantly who was meant. Haidee Vail.

"My luggage . . ." I thought of my suitcases, still out in the rain.

"Not to worry, ducks. Frankie will have fetched them by now. I sent him out as soon as I heard the bell."

"That wasn't me. It was some sort of madman . . ." I could see him still, lunging out of his white car and, oddly, I found myself trembling. Esme put out a soft little hand and patted my shoulder gently.

"That was Jeb, dearie. Jeb Reives. You mustn't mind him. Never knew a good director yet that had any patience. Or manners. The stories I could tell!"

But she cut herself off and moved away, leaving me to have my first real look at the inside of Vail's Point.

We were standing just inside the tall front door, but this was no safe little vestibule to keep out the elements; the mansion had been clearly designed for summer heat in an era when there was no air conditioning and fans were slow and ineffective. The ceiling was high in shadows above us, and on both sides the main floor of the house stretched wide and open as a hotel lobby, as if the family had never needed or desired walls to enclose them and give them privacy.

To my right the house curved in a great half circle of windows draped in thick folds of dusty gold brocade. All of the walls above the dark walnut wainscoting seemed to be covered with the same faded material. Not that much was visible: every conceivable space was filled with huge dim portraits. The area to the right was up a step from the rest of the floor, rather like a platform for a concert or a small stage. I could see in the dimness a long piano and some great Chinese vases filled with tall strands of dried leaves and dusty

27

peacock feathers. Edging away from the door that led to the front veranda beyond were stiff white wicker chairs, their backs rising to impossible heights with great swirls and curves, placed around the doorway to the porch as evenly as courtiers around a throne.

To my left, Esme was carefully turning on lamps against the twilight. This seemed to be the main drawing room of the house. Here there were low soft comfortable sofas in faded velvet, wide easy chairs (some with their seats slumped almost to the floor) and squashed leather hassocks. Long refectory tables ran behind the sofas, each one covered with what looked like a jumble of dusty manuscripts, cigarette boxes, and sepia photographs in tarnished silver frames. The floor, as far as I could see, was of dark wood, badly in need of waxing, most of it covered with wide Persian rugs, their brilliant colors dimmed by the years. There was even the yellowing skin of a massive polar bear—head, claws, and great glass eyes—thrown down before an enormous stone fireplace. In this huge room, if room it could be called, it seemed as insignificant as a bathmat.

The far wall captured my eye. A great staircase rose to the floor above. Two wooden knights in armor, taller than I, stood as stair posts, holding, instead of spears, great metal branches that erupted into a cluster of frosted globes. Between the knights wide steps covered in chocolate brown carpet led to a landing deep enough for the catafalque of a queen.

Filling the whole back wall of the landing was a massive, cathedral-size organ. The staircase split at the landing and twin stairs rose steeply to the left and right alongside the tiers of dusty organ pipes.

Suddenly I felt embarrassed; I had stared at it all with such open curiosity. I glanced quickly at Esme to see if she had noticed. She was just turning on a lamp at the far end of one of the sofas and for one moment her face was above the Tiffany glass, a glow coming up under her double chin as if she were lit by footlights. There was a wise twinkle in her eyes.

"I know, ducks," she said. "Hits everyone that way the first time they see this place. A bloody great set for *The Prisoner of Zenda*, that's what it is. And hell on wheels to clean."

With a crook of her finger, she started for the staircase, and I followed her obediently. Something puzzled me, but it wasn't until we reached the landing that I knew what it was. Heavy or not, Esme could move as quickly and silently as a young girl.

Once on the landing, she turned to the left. Looking up, I could see nothing of the second floor. The two staircases disappeared behind a wall, which, oddly, had been painted to look like old stone, complete with artificial ivy. The only break in the wall was a miniature iron balcony overlooking the landing below, a balcony so theatrical it seemed lost without Juliet standing in a pink spotlight.

But there was no Juliet, no spotlight. Only the late-afternoon shadows growing darker and darker.

When Esme reached the second floor she turned back to wait for me. "You'll probably get lost the first couple of days," she said, glancing around at the open area behind her. "Don't let it worry you. Viola designed the house, and whatever else she was, she wasn't an architect. Just tucked in rooms anywhere, big ones, little ones. And the old man so besotted with her, he couldn't say no." She let out a vast sigh. "Of course there were servants to be had then . . ."

"The old man? Viola?" I felt hopelessly confused by now, rather like an Alice who had tumbled into a very strange Wonderland.

"Dearie, don't you know anything about the Vails? You that's here to do research?" But there must have been something woebegone about my appearance, for Esme patted me kindly on the shoulder again and smiled. "Never mind. We'll get you all caught up once you're dry."

"I'm sorry to seem so stupid . . ."

I stood awkwardly in the half darkness. Esme had turned on no lights on this floor, and from what I could see we were in a square area where several dark corridors seemed to converge. But I didn't continue, for Esme made a swift gesture, putting her finger to her lips for silence, her head twisting slightly as she listened to something I had not heard.

In the dark caves of one of the corridors there was movement. Before I could question Esme, she called out in a voice gentler than I could have imagined her to possess.

"May, dear, is that you?"

There was no answer. And then I sensed, rather than saw, another movement, and slowly a woman came out into the open area where we stood.

She was a tall woman, taller than most men. It was hard to tell her age in that half-light (although I guessed she was in her sixties). What I could see of her face had been painted like a mask. She had high, proud cheekbones and a scarlet slash of a mouth. Her jet-black hair had been pulled up so tightly to the smooth roll on the top of her head that it seemed to draw her long eyebrows and sallow skin upward with it. Her eyes fascinated me. They were absolutely black as we stood there in the gloom, large and shining, but with a glint somewhere behind them, like a live coal at the bottom of a dying fire.

She came nearer, moving slowly with a fluid grace that a queen would envy. She had a dark green robe of some sort of heavy crepe. It swept the floor, the full cowl of the dress framing her head. It had the severity of a nun's habit; indeed, her hands were folded in front of her, out of sight behind some loose panel of her long gown. She came straight toward me, her eyes never leaving my face. A few feet away, she stopped, the green draperies of her robe falling naturally into graceful folds around her as if she were a statue.

And still she said nothing.

"May, dear," said Esme, "this is Alison Howard. Remember we told you? She's come to look after poor Lionel's papers."

So this was May Vail. I thought of what my father had said, but she seemed more like an oriental empress than the kind and quiet girl he had described.

"I believe you knew my father once," I ventured, my voice loud to my ears in the silence. "Grant Howard?"

She continued to stare at me. It was not an impersonal look, or cold, but, rather, as if she had heard a thousand secrets over the years and had no interest in hearing more.

"That was long ago," she said finally. Her voice was deep, and each word was as clearly shaped as if she were speaking in a foreign language. "Very long ago," she repeated.

She turned her back on us and, moving swiftly with a litheness I would not have expected, disappeared down the corridor from which she had come. I turned to Esme. She must have seen something of my surprise even in the half-light of the hall.

"May has her little ways, dear," she said comfortingly. "You'll get used to them. In time."

She beckoned to me again and started off down a corridor away from the one that May had taken. More afraid than ever of getting lost, I trotted quickly after her.

After passing two closed doors, Esme turned sharply and we faced a doorway that led to a balcony and the rain outside. To the right of this was another door. Esme turned the knob and it opened easily. She stepped aside and with a brief smile signaled me to go in ahead of her.

To my surprise, I found quite a pleasant little room. Not so small as bedrooms are built today, but in comparison with the rest of the house it had almost a cozy, intimate quality. A massive rosewood bed stood against the wall to my right, the headboard rising to the low ceiling. Cheerful lemon-yellow chintz covered the thick mattress and the pillows. A tiny needlepoint footstool stood on the near side to give anyone who needed it a step up into the bed. Opposite the solid footboard was a small fireplace and, although it was late June, a fire was burning, drying the dampness of the afternoon. The chintz drapes, of the same material that covered the bed, had not been pulled and I could see, through the thin curtains, the rain splashing the balcony outside. There was a sturdy bureau by the bed, its marble top vacant except for an old-fashioned lamp with a glass globe riotous with painted peonies. A door by the fireplace led to what must be a closet, and another door, on the far side of the bed, stood half open. Through it I could see part of a Victorian bathroom. A rocking chair swayed slightly by the fireplace, and at its side, stacked neatly, was my luggage.

"Now, ducks, think you'll be happy here?"

I smiled at Esme gratefully and moved toward my suitcases.

"Here, let me help." She picked up the heaviest of my bags without any obvious strain and deposited it on the bed.

"While we're getting you tucked away, I'll tell you about the house."

"It all began in 1900," she started, after we'd opened my suitcases. Clothes were strewn all over the room by now, as I continued to find places for my wardrobe, Esme settling herself comfortably into the rocker. Her hands had found each other again and were woven once more together over her stomach.

31

"The house, you mean?" I said it absently as I searched for my bedroom slippers. Esme had been right. My shoes looked completely ruined by the brief walk from the road.

"Oh, no, dear. The house came later. No, it was the Vail family that started in 1900. Matthew Patch . . . ever heard of him?" I shook my head. I'd found my slippers at last and it was good to slip them on my cold feet.

"Millionaire, my dear. Pots of money." There was no criticism in her voice. Clearly I was not expected to know about Mr. Patch.

"Came East, he did, from some godforsaken place. Colorado, something like that. Not a young man either, and closemouthed about his past. Dead before my time, of course." She started rocking in the chair. Even with her great weight it made no squeak of protest. "At any rate, that's when he first saw Viola. Barely twenty she was then, and pretty in the style of the time." She paused as she considered the style of the time. "They liked a woman of flesh in those days," she said, almost with regret.

"Viola was making her first big hit that season . . . one of the six *Pompadour* girls." She stopped her rocking abruptly and leaned forward toward me. "You *have* heard of *The Pink Pompadour?*"

I stood where I was with an armful of clothes, trying to search my memory. "It was an . . . operetta, wasn't it? And all the chorus girls married millionaires?"

"Ladies of the Ensemble, my dear." She chuckled. "Chorus girls were another breed entirely. Still, the six *Pompadour* girls all did rather well. Not quite in Viola's class, of course. There weren't too many men like Matthew Patch around, even in those days. But he was mad for her and she knew a good thing when she saw it. So they got married." She stopped for breath then. And when she went on again there was a different note in her voice, almost one of awe.

"And produced Haidee Vail."

I looked at her, the tone of her voice catching my attention again. "And Lionel and May as well," I added to fill in the pause.

One fat little hand flickered as if brushing away a fly, and Esme sat back again. "They came later. Haidee is the eldest. It was because of her that Vail's Point was built. Viola was carrying her and she couldn't take the summer heat. You can imagine what it must have been like in the city in those days, July, August. Haidee

32

was born in August." She was rocking comfortably now. I could see, whatever her position in this house, Haidee was her favorite topic of conversation. But I was here to learn about Lionel.

"And this house?" It seemed the most tactful way to change the subject.

"It's cool here by the shore. And Viola originally came from Westaven. It was quite a thing: 'Local Girl Returns in Triumph.' Matthew was happy to give her anything she wanted. Didn't even get the place named after him, the poor dear." She smiled and shook her head sympathetically. "So that's how we have Vail's Point. Been home for us all ever since."

"For Lionel, too?"

But, for some reason, she decided to end our conversation then. She sat forward as if to heave herself out of her chair.

"Don't stop now. There's so much more I don't know." I gave her what I hoped was an inviting smile. Lionel would have to wait: "I understand there's a theater on the estate. How did that happen?" Esme settled back in her chair again.

"Viola," she said instantly. "She kept up with her career after her marriage. A new play every season. Light stuff, the way they liked it in those days, not like what we did here before the War." I could see Esme was about to be sidetracked again.

"She was a star? Viola, I mean?"

"She was popular enough for her time," Esme said, considering her words judiciously. "And Matthew's money helped."

"But why did Mr. Patch build a theater here?" I knew the more I learned about the theater, the better able I would be to cope with a request for foundation money. For I was sure by now a request would come. My brief glimpse of the house had told me that the Vails' days of grandeur were long gone.

"Regular Broadway theater it is, too, except for the size of the auditorium. Only seats a couple of hundred," said Esme, not answering my question. "But the rest of it . . . all the equipment . . . same as the Lyceum or the Empire—New York houses Viola might expect to play in the winter. Making it the same, you see, she could bring her whole company up here, out of the heat, and rehearse. And then as the years went on and old Matthew wasn't getting about so much, he could just stroll down the garden path and have his own private performance."

33

"But wasn't it ever opened for the public? I'd heard . . ."

Esme broke in quickly. "That was us, dear. In the thirties. Before the War. Grand theater we had then, even if some of it wasn't what you'd call 'commercial.' Haidee ran it every summer. World premières even. A new play by Bernard Shaw once." A muscle twitched on the side of her fat white face. "I never took to that play. But Haidee looked ever so lovely. She wore pale green in one scene . . ."

She was silent for a moment, a pleased smile on her face. I sat down on the cleared bed, wondering where Esme fit into this household.

"I know Haidee Vail was a great actress," I began tentatively.

"*Is*, dearie, *is*. We've never retired and we never will." The reprimand was unmistakable. I tried again to get the conversation back to the reason for my being here.

"And Lionel Vail? Were his plays also done in the theater here?"

Her eyes shifted quickly, searching my face for a second. Then she glanced down to study her fat little hands. But she was not quite fast enough. I'd seen her look and it was one of complete hatred.

"No," she went on carefully. "We never did his plays here. Lionel was . . ." She hesitated, clearly trying to pick an impersonal word. "Lionel was always . . . very difficult, dearie," she finished finally.

It didn't sound angry, the way she said it. But I'd seen her face at the mention of his name. She shifted her great shapeless body out of the chair and onto her tiny feet with one motion. I stood as well.

"Have yourself a nice hot bath, luv," Esme said as she moved toward the door. "You've got time before the Comfort Hour." Then she caught my puzzled glance and smiled benignly, anticipating my next question. "That's when we start serving the drinks. We gave it that name during Prohibition so the public wouldn't get upset . . ." She was almost out the door by now.

"Please . . . I'm still a little lost. Who, actually is here in the house? The letter we received from someone named Corin . . ."

"You'll meet them all later, downstairs. Haidee, of course. And May. And me. Corin and Julie. Jeb for the night, I expect. I must find a bed for him. The bathroom's through there. You share it with the next bedroom, but don't fret. I won't have to put anyone in there tonight . . ." She gave a quick supervisory look at the room and started for the hall.

"I suppose if the theater reopens you'll need all the rooms . . ." I didn't quite know why I said that. It would have been wiser for me to stay away from any mention of the theater, and yet somehow the sentence came out before I knew it. It couldn't have affected Esme more if I'd slapped her.

A slow, frightened flush started to rise under her powdered white skin.

"Who said it's going to open?" Her voice was quavering. I started to sputter something, but she went right on as if I were not there. "Closed it's been all these years, closed it must remain."

But she said it as if she was afraid.

CHAPTER FOUR

She left then, shutting the door behind her quietly. I sat down on the bed and for a few moments went over the strange bits and pieces I'd learned since I'd entered this house.

Clearly there were two factions about reopening the theater. And as guardian of my mother's Foundation, I would be wise to stay out of the conflict. Only, how much power did Esme possess? Was she related to the family? She'd used the word "we" when speaking of Haidee the way a curator might speak of the museum to which he had dedicated his life.

I smoothed the soft chintz under my hand. You're here to collect Lionel Vail's papers, I reminded myself. Nothing else. The theater shouldn't concern you. If the family is peculiar and the house an enormous monstrosity, it is none of your business.

As abruptly as if someone had turned on a light switch, sunlight came through the windows, splashing across the rag rugs to touch the bed where I sat. Sometime during my talk with Esme the rain must have stopped and the clouds cleared. There were still drops spattering down from the eaves onto the balcony outside but the gray afternoon was over. We would have an hour of clear sky before sunset.

I walked across the room and, pushing back the organdy curtains, opened the windows wide. Stepping onto the narrow wooden balcony, I was startled to feel it sway a little under my feet. But nothing in this house appeared to have been repaired for years, and wood this close to the ocean would rot quickly.

I held onto the inside of the window frame and looked over the shaky railing of the balcony. My room was on the west side of the house. Directly below was a large clear space, paved in concrete, for the cars of Vail's Point. To my right I saw a row of what were obviously garages, all covered with the same shingle as the house. They looked deserted, their doors closed, their windows broken and dirty.

Below me to my left was the roof of the porte-cochere. Beyond the parking space the woods pressed in close, the trees thick with summer green. There seemed to be some sort of path into the woods, but it was hard to tell, for the grass and underbrush were as untended as the house.

The sun, as it came over the trees, was warm on my face. I looked up, pleased that my balcony at least had no roof over it. The house was not as high as I had first thought; directly above me were the white wooden railings of one of the two widow's walks. The paint was peeling off the railing and one of the spokes was lost. And above that, clouds broke in the late-afternoon sky.

I took a deep breath. The air after the rain was sweet. Although it was past time for lilacs, there still seemed to be a whisper of their fragrance in the soft air. Oddly enough, I could not hear the sea from this balcony, and yet I know it could not be more than fifty feet away.

But I did hear something. It had a steady beat, as if it might be a motor of some kind; only, this was lighter, more of a ticking sound. More like a clock. And yet I somehow knew it wasn't.

For a moment I thought again of the dream I'd had the night before. There had been a sound in that as well, but I couldn't remember now what it was.

Then I stopped trying to remember and went back inside. It was time to get ready to meet the Vails.

The Victorian bathroom turned out to be more comfortable than I had expected, and a hot bath made me feel ready for the evening. My hair was still damp, which made it darker than I liked, but it also made it easier to twist into the usual neat loop at the nape of my neck. Picking what to wear was more difficult. Haidee Vail was not only a woman of importance but one of another era, in which formality was highly regarded. Reluctantly, I put back the simple linen dress I'd placed on my bed before my bath and took out a long patchwork skirt of blue-and-white cotton. It was easy to wear as well as attractive, and with a long-sleeved white silk blouse I would at least look respectable. The blouse clung tighter to my body than I liked and, remembering that the angry man I'd met on the driveway was also expected for dinner, I pulled over my shoulders a dark blue suede vest.

As I pinned on my mother's gold watch, I noticed it had been almost forty-five minutes since Esme left. I had no idea when the "Comfort Hour" (as they called it) began, nor did I know whether they had a bell or a gong to call their guests for meals. It would be simpler, obviously, to go downstairs and wait there for whatever was to happen.

I went out into the hall and closed the door behind me. For a moment I found myself wishing that there was a key in the lock. Instantly I felt foolish. Locks were unnecessary. I had brought nothing with me of great value and I had no secrets to hide. I started for the stairs and I did not look back.

I found my way easily enough, despite Esme's warnings. The area where we had seen May was lighted now. Two antique tables stood opposite each other against the walls that separated the corridors, and on each of these tables, twin gilt lamps with satin shades had been lit. They gave a rosy-pink glow to the hall. I started down the great staircase carefully. The full patchwork skirt swirled down to the floor, so that the stairs were a bit treacherous. But there was no one below to notice my cautiousness.

Standing at the foot of the stairs, I tried to adjust to the space around me. The lamps that Esme had lit were still on, although with the late-afternoon sunshine streaming through the long windows they were no longer needed.

I walked across the wide rug toward the great stone fireplace. Two long sofas jutted out like supplicating arms in front of a low granite step, the polar-bear rug between them.

There was golden lightness in the air at that moment. Everything in the room as I moved forward seemed to be touched by light: glass ashtrays and crystals hanging from table lamps, odd silver boxes and silken threads in old cushions—they all caught the last of that Sunday afternoon, twisting and glowing in the sun before it faded. The room was alive with color and a sense of time both past and present.

The fireplace was dark gray stone, sulking in the shadows of the two glowing windows on each side. Somewhere in the practical part of my head I realized the mantel, the chimney, and the low step leading up to where the huge logs rested must have all been pulled out of some older house and moved, stone by stone (probably from across the ocean), to please the builder of Vail's Point.

But it was the painting over the mantel of the fireplace that drew me. It covered the wide space of the chimney and showed its four figures in dimensions far larger than life. There was a brass fixture over the top of the painting, but at this one moment there was so much light in the room that the spotlight seemed unnecessary.

It was a family portrait, the painting over the mantel. The artist (I could barely read his name in the lower right-hand corner) was "Buisseret" or something close to that. There had been a date after his name but crude hands had rubbed it out with paint remover.

But no one could remove the era the artist had painted.

I knew at once the central figure must be Viola Vail. She was seated on a satin love seat . . . the same I spied in a far corner of the room, the material now split and faded. Viola was, as Esme had described her, a woman of some flesh. Not fat—the corsets of the period contained her to a waistline any woman my age would envy. But over the soft chiffon of her powder blue tea gown billowed ivory-white curves, and the artist clearly had enjoyed painting the soft skin of a well-fed woman.

Seated beside her on the love seat was a sallow girl. Although over half a century had passed, I knew at once it was May. She seemed dim in the painting, a quiet, rather plain child of twelve or so.

Behind the love seat stood a tall young girl, and I knew, as I had recognized May, that this must be Haidee Vail. The adolescent figure was in a severe version of a school uniform: cream middy blouse and dark blue silk tie, the body angular, the face far too old for adolescence and already a little haughty. Her dark brown hair had been cut, obviously against her will, into thick bangs in an unsuccessful attempt to make her seem more of a child, flattering her mother's age.

But it was the small boy seated on a cushion at Viola's feet that caught and held my eye. This, I knew, must be Lionel Vail, and though as far as I could remember I had never seen a picture of him before, at any age, there was something about him that seemed familiar.

He was not dressed as a boy of the early part of the century should have been dressed. It was almost as if the artist painting the family portrait had given up on Lionel and said (I could almost hear the exasperated sigh): "Let him wear what he wants, so long as he appears."

The boy was small, out of proportion with the women in the painting, and clad in a white shirt and dark trousers. He must have been under ten at the time the portrait was painted. He was curled up, like an animal in a burrow, on a plum velvet cushion. But he, of all the figures, looked straight out of the painting: young Haidee stared stonily away from the artist, May was turned toward her mother, and Viola, in a pose calculated to present her at her best, was glancing coquettishly both at the world and the children at her side.

I have no feeling for people who sense omens and portents about places or people. I do not believe in ghosts or witches or "things that go bump in the night." Indeed, I have a barely concealed contempt for such pretensions. But I *have* known feelings I cannot describe, during certain moments.

They are never good feelings. They are of a sudden kind of coldness that occurs only when I am near something truly evil. It has happened perhaps three or four times in my life. And it has nothing to do with the age of my surroundings. Once I was in a very modern motel room near Scranton, visiting a college friend and her brother, whom she hoped I would marry. I felt a chill in that room, so bitterly cold that I had to move in the middle of the night. The following morning the desk clerk, with a very sophisticated smile, talked of a murder that had recently occurred in my original room. There was an implication in his voice that I, too, had heard of it.

Only, I hadn't.

I am sensible enough to realize that if I had some special gift or intuition I would have known much earlier the truth about Peter and Dilys. Perhaps whatever instinct I have cannot be applied to the living . . . or at least the living of my own world. Still, staring at the painting over the mantelpiece that first night at Vail's Point, I knew there was pain behind those painted faces; pain and tension and a kind of anger tying the four figures together that was outside anything I had ever known. So many of the secrets of life that I had missed might be there, if I could only understand them.

And then, as I stood there, I knew someone was behind me, watching.

But not watching the portrait.

Watching me.

I knew who it was even before I turned. But in the second before I saw Haidee Vail, my mind dismissed any thoughts of intui-

40

tion. The woman who had come down the stairs so quietly had dominated theater audiences for over forty years. It should be no surprise that I was aware of her presence even before I saw her.

She stood on the bottom step of the great staircase. It was a trick, I was to learn, she often used to make herself even taller and more impressive. The artist had exaggerated her height in the portrait. On the same level, Haidee and I stood eye to eye, both of us considerably shorter than May.

She came toward me, threading her path through the furniture gracefully, the last rays of the sun illuminating her as clearly as if she were moving into a spotlight.

I knew, from what I'd heard of the Vails, that Haidee must be at least seventy. And I suppose, somewhere in the back of my mind, I had expected a rather grand and domineering figure: white hair piled on top of her head, a flowing robe in rather theatrical colors slightly out of date, maybe even leaning on a thin ebony cane. Or, conversely, a sweet little old lady, all cameos and dimples, everybody's favorite grandmother.

But whatever Haidee might turn out to be, she must definitely be old.

But the woman who came toward me with a welcoming smile on her face could be called anything but that. Her body was as thin and supple as a high-fashion model's, reminding me the first second I saw her that Haidee's first great successes had been in the era of boyish women. She had on what looked like black slacks, the top of her thin body covered by a simple black silk turtleneck. Over all this hung two long panels of black satin, fastened at the shoulders with small diamond clips and swinging free to the floor, revealing her lean body. Soft black suede slippers, like ballet shoes, covered her tiny feet, and a diamond choker circled the high black throat of her sweater. The diamonds, I saw instantly, were large, old-fashioned, and badly in need of cleaning; they had that dim glitter of objects stuffed unnoticed into a drawer for years and pulled out to wear as casually as I might put on a sweater.

Her head fascinated me. It was large and out of proportion to her slight body. As she came closer, I could see the fine lines of age etched in her pale face. But there was no folds under her tilted eyes, and her strong jaw line was almost as clean as that of the young girl in the painting behind me. The passage of years had softened it perhaps, but only slightly, so that it gave her a more femi-

41

nine look than she had had as a girl. Her thick, shining silver-gray hair was brushed back off her forehead and curled under in a long pageboy bob at her shoulders. All this I saw in the one instant before I caught her eyes.

After that I could look nowhere else.

Haidee had large, aquamarine eyes, their curiously clear blue emphasized by the only makeup that I could see she wore: thick black false eyelashes. The lashes did not seem artificial, although I knew they must be, but rather a necessary frame for that brilliant blue.

"You must be Alison Howard," she said as she reached me. She took my hand, her grip firm.

"Yes, Miss Vail." It seemed the wrong thing to call her, and it struck us both at the same moment. She threw her head back and laughed, revealing small, rather uneven teeth.

"Haidee, my dear. You can't possibly live in this house and call me 'Miss Vail'; I'd think you were asking for an autograph." She released my hand and bent over a low table by the sofa, reaching with quick fingers for a cigarette in the tarnished box. Her hands were graceful and she used them well, plucking like a magician a cigarette holder from an unseen pocket in one of the loose panels that draped her body. But although her hands were beautifully manicured, they revealed her years in a way her face and her body did not. The fingers were mottled with ugly spots, and arthritis was twisting them into claws. She lit her cigarette quickly and, flicking back her silver hair, sank into a deep sofa.

"Come and sit down," she said, patting the place beside her. I did as she asked. The light from the windows was in my eyes now and behind her, and I knew, even as I took my place, our positions were not accidental.

"I gather everything was in a muddle about getting you here. I'm so sorry." She inhaled deeply and, without looking for an ashtray, tapped her cigarette to one side. A fleck of ash dropped to the dusty carpet. "It was right in your telegram when you'd arrive. I told everybody to make some sort of arrangement."

"It was all right. I managed to get a cab." I remembered then the strange ride. "Finally."

Even in the shadows I could see her incredibly blue eyes narrow slightly. She leaned forward, her cigarette forgotten.

"A cab? Who drove it?"

42

"A Mr. McNaughton." I heard his voice once more. "He was quite . . . strange. He said to tell you he took no money for it. He seemed to feel it was important I tell you that." Her eyes continued to stare at me, but I had a feeling they were not, just at the moment, seeing my face. I went on, somewhat lamely: "I don't know what that means."

"McNaughton's our local troublemaker," Haidee answered crisply and leaned back again. "Damn nuisance, since he's the town policeman. But there it is." She smiled again, as cheerful as when she had first come into the room. "Anyway, he doesn't matter. You're here. And we're going to do our best to make you welcome."

"It's very kind of you to put me up," I said politely. "If it's an inconvenience . . ."

She broke in quickly, putting out a friendly hand on my arm. "Nonsense child. We've dozens of rooms. If you don't like where you are, just roam around the second floor and take your pick."

"Where I am is fine, thank you." I wanted to be less formal. She was so clearly trying to make me feel at home. "It's just that I don't know how long it will take. To go through your brother's papers."

"Oh, yes. Lionel's papers . . ."

She got up then, like a restless cat, and threw her cigarette into the dark fireplace. After a moment, her back still toward me, she said, "You seem awfully young to be writing biographies."

Shifting slightly, the sun still in my eyes, I felt suddenly embarrassed. Obviously she had the wrong impression of my visit. "I'm sorry," I said. "I thought I'd made that quite clear in my telegram. I couldn't possibly be qualified to write such an important work. I'm just here to see if there's sufficient material for the Foundation to sponsor a proper biographer."

She made no answer. She did not even turn around. Instead, she raised her head slowly and looked at the painting over the mantel.

"A biography of Lionel Vail . . ." She said it quietly, without any particular inflection. "So that's what you're here for. I thought . . ." She swiveled around, that same radiant smile back on her face. "You see, when Corin mentioned the letter to me . . . and the Foundation, I thought . . . well, we had been talking about reopening the theater here for the summer . . ."

She let her voice stop then, the unspoken words a wall between

43

us. My back stiffened. Great lady of the theater she might be, this was an out-and-out appeal for funds, and I had already made up my mind not to be drawn into it.

"I'm afraid the Foundation could not possibly support such a private enterprise," I said. My voice sounded priggish even to my own ears.

"Of course it can."

We both turned. A young man lounged just inside the open French windows to the driveway.

"I looked up the charter before I wrote you. Foundation charters have to be registered, you know. It's the law," he said cheerfully.

Corin Vail must have been thirty, but he looked younger, his body short and slender. His face was clever rather than handsome, with bright brown eyes and thick russet hair cut low over his forehead. He wore faded blue jeans and a white sweatshirt that was much too large for him. He looked at me.

"There's absolutely nothing in the Howard Foundation bylaws that says you can't hand out pockets and pockets of cash for anything that's even vaguely for 'the cultural good of the community.'" I felt the blood coming to my face. Corin had done his homework: that phrase was indeed part of the charter.

"And we *do* plan on letting the locals in." He came forward then.

"So don't go terrifying my poor old Gran. She has her heart set on one last season, haven't you, luv?" He draped an affectionate arm over Haidee's thin shoulders. She glanced at him warmly. "So, dear Miss Howard, please say you've brought a nice thick checkbook with you. Or you'll be treated to the fabulous Haidee Vail doing four verses of 'Over the Hills to the Poorhouse.' Or else her own rather original version of a female *King Lear*." With a wry twist of his voice he managed to mimic Haidee's cello tones: "How sharper than a serpent's tooth is a misleading grandchild!"

I would not have been surprised to see Haidee step back and slap him for his impertinence. Or even to shove him to one side and exit indignantly. Instead, she touched his tan face with gentle fingers, her voice rippling with amusement. This seemed to be an old game between them.

"Dearest Corin, is that any way to ask money from a pretty

44

girl? Here I've been giving her the benefit of decades of practiced charm and you come in with all the subtlety of a highwayman. What will she think?"

"That my grandmother obviously adores me," he said promptly, giving her a swift peck on the cheek. "As well my grandmother should. For I am bright and talented and thoroughly irresistible."

"To think in my declining years I've fallen for this aging juvenile," Haidee said with a fake sigh, and reached for another cigarette. Corin had the match ready before she even found her holder.

"'Declining,' my toenails!" he said, as she bent for the light. "You who could play Juliet tomorrow. And if you're that young, how can *I* be aging?" She started to answer, her eyes sparkling with happy malice, but he put up a hand in semiprotest. "Not another word in front of the ingénue," he said, nodding toward me. "Besides, Mother's still passing for thirty, which makes me twelve no matter how you figure it."

"Ah, well, soap opera," Haidee shrugged. "The ladies who watch Julie would believe your mother if she said she came from outer space." And then she became aware of me again, staring at the two of them like an awkward teen-ager. "Now, come over here, Corin, and meet Alison properly. And not another word about getting money out of her until she's been fed."

He walked toward me, changing before my eyes from a Pan-like jester into a suave diplomat. Taking my hand, he bowed low, bringing his heels together in a neat click.

"*Enchanté, chère mademoiselle. C'est une grande plaisir.*"

His accent was flawless. His hand was warm and dry and I could feel my fingers tremble slightly as he held them. There was a wicked twinkle in his eyes, as if he knew quite well the effect he was having.

"Thank you," I said, withdrawing my hand, not without effort.

"Now," he said, relaxed again. "What can we do to amuse you? Dance naked on the lawn? Strew roses on your path? Get you a drink? We live but to please."

He was determined to make me laugh, or at least smile, confident that he could charm anyone. And, perversely, I was determined not to be charmed. I sat up a little straighter.

"Actually, what I'd really like is to see Lionel Vail's papers."

There was a second of silence. Corin glanced swiftly at his

45

grandmother, but Haidee had turned aside to put out her cigarette. I went on before he looked back: "That *is* what I'm here for, after all."

"Of course. It's just that . . ." He faced Haidee directly now. "Do we have time before the 'Comfort Hour,' Gran?"

"I suppose so. Lord knows when everybody will show up. Your mother's still in the city in some sort of conference about that wretched television series of hers. You'd think they'd at least let her alone on Sundays." Haidee's voice was as calm as it had been before, but there was a curious flicker in Corin's eyes as he stared at her. As if some unspoken question lay between them. "Of course you can show Alison around, Corin. Just don't take too long."

"We won't." His voice was lazy, and he did not move. "There isn't time for a real search." He emphasized the last words so carefully that even I caught it.

His grandmother refused to be drawn. She moved to the back of one of the sofas and started to flick idly through a pile of manuscripts. "Dear Corin . . . ," Haidee said finally, still not looking at him. "You and your fantasies of a search. You'll have poor Alison hopelessly confused. Run along and show her Lionel's rooms." Her voice was still beautifully controlled, but the warm amusement was gone. There was something else now—anger, or at least irritation just beneath the surface.

I stood then. Corin, his eyes still on Haidee, held out a hand.

"I'll need the key," he said. He kept his hand out until Haidee finally raised her head and looked at him. From where I was standing I could see only her face at that moment. Her clear blue eyes were cool and impassive, the way I imagine a gambler bluffing at a high-stakes card game might look. And then she dropped one hand into the concealed pocket of her robe and pulled out a long key. She handed it to Corin, one eyebrow rising slightly. It gave her a look of sardonic amusement.

"Here you are, Corin. At last." He reached for it, but she still held on to the other end, so that for one moment the key was a link between them. "But I warn you . . . you'll find nothing."

She turned away from us abruptly and stood staring up at the painting once more. There was no question now. We were dismissed.

CHAPTER FIVE

I wanted to ask what she meant by a "search," but Corin's shoulders were stiff as he walked up the great staircase. It was only when we started from the landing to the second floor that he turned.

"Did Esme explain about this?" he asked, indicating the wall painted to look like stone and the iron balcony above us.

I shook my head, happy to have the silence broken. "Was it the outside wall of the house at one time?" I asked politely, knowing it could not have been.

"It was Great-Grandfather's idea. Old Matthew Patch himself." Corin stopped for a moment on the carpeted stairs, looking up at the balcony. "Seems he always wanted Viola to play Juliet. She, having a fairly good idea of the limits of her talent, had the sense to refuse. So he had this built and on certain nights he'd have her get into costume and recite the Balcony Scene. Just for him."

He pointed to the bench in front of the organ on the landing below. "He'd sit down there . . . an audience of one." There was a wry smile on his face, but it was not contemptuous of Matthew's whim. "Makes it one of the most expensive stage sets ever built, I should think."

He continued up the stairs. We had turned to the right on the landing, the stairs leading us into the open area behind the balcony near one of the corridors. I could not be sure if this was the hall down which May Vail had disappeared, nor did I have a chance to ask as Corin moved ahead of me quickly into the dark passage.

"Did Lionel live here all the time?" I asked, hurrying after him, hoping that he would slow his pace.

"Questions later," he threw over his shoulder. "Let's see his rooms first." He stopped now in front of a door, allowing me to catch up with him, but it did not turn easily and I heard him mutter something under his breath.

"Here . . . let me try."

He stepped back without protest. I wriggled the key in the lock gently, relying on my experience with the old doors in my father's house. For a moment the key stuck and then I felt the bolt give way and the door unlock. I looked at Corin, reluctant to push the door open myself.

"The lock doesn't seem to have been used for a long time."

"It hasn't," he said. "Not since Lionel died. That's almost thirty years."

I stepped back, puzzled. Even in the shadows he must have seen the expression on my face. "Haidee's orders," he drawled.

Without giving me a chance for further questions, he turned the handle of the door and pushed it open.

The room faced east, and even with the windows closed I could hear the slow pounding of the waves on the shore below. The sunset was over now and the sky outside gray, not that much light could have penetrated the streaked and dirty windows. Corin reached out to the wall inside the door, feeling for a light switch. He found it, but after clicking it a few times, dropped his hand.

"I guess we can't expect bulbs to last forever," he said. He stepped aside, letting me walk into the room.

There was still enough light for me to see that this must have been Lionel Vail's study. A great wooden roll-top desk stood facing the bay window, and the walls were covered with bookshelves. There were no curtains. A green blind, torn halfway across, hung limply over one window.

Cautiously, Corin moved farther into the room. I could see now the reason for his hesitation. Whatever virtues Lionel Vail had, they obviously did not include neatness. The floor was filled with cardboard cartons bulging with papers: newspapers and photographs and typewritten pages that could be letters or contracts or even manuscripts. If all these were concerned with the life and work of Lionel Vail, there would be more than enough to satisfy the most avid biographer. Standing there in the gloom, I thought that if I had been expecting the workroom of one of the major playwrights of the twentieth century to be sterile and formal and museum-neat, I should have realized by now that nothing in this house could be predicted. For at that first moment I felt we had wandered into a storeroom by mistake.

There was a door in the wall to the right, and Corin stepped his way carefully through the cartons toward it, with me following. There was a little more space there and we could stand side by side and look into the far room. It was small, hardly bigger than a closet, somewhat circular as it was part of one of the towers of the house. This had been Lionel Vail's bedroom. The walls were mostly tall, thin windows as streaked and dirty as the ones in the room behind us.

The bedroom was at the front of the house. There were no cartons there, just a low narrow cot and a rather battered table beside it with a cheap lamp. The sheets were rumpled as if someone had left the bed impatiently. A shabby brown robe had fallen to the bare linoleum floor, and from underneath the robe protruded the tip of one worn slipper.

Over everything lay a thin perfect layer of dust, as in the room behind us.

And on the bedside table stood a whiskey bottle, long empty.

"Poor bastard," Corin said softly. I turned to look at him. Even in the weak light I could see the grimness in his face.

"Did he die here?" Without meaning to, I had lowered my voice to a whisper.

"No. At the theater." Then he turned to look at me, frowning a little. "Don't you know anything about him?"

"Only a little," I said apologetically. "I wouldn't be the one to write his biography, in any case." I stepped back from the doorway. For some reason, I did not want to go any further into Lionel Vail's bedroom.

"He . . . he killed himself, didn't he?" I asked, avoiding Corin's eyes even though I knew as I stood there that he wasn't really seeing me.

"That was the verdict."

His voice was curt. He moved then, suddenly restless, as if the bedroom beyond held no further interest for him. Making his way casually through the cartons, he went to the windows that faced the sea. "It makes sense, I suppose. He was an alcoholic after the War. Or so they said."

"'They'?"

He glanced back at me for a second. "The newspapers. The family. The town." His face was in darkness as he looked at me, but I knew it wore the same cool look he had had downstairs. I liked him better now that he was not trying to be charming. "The town especially," he repeated. "Everything that belonged to him was just left here." His voice was dry. "With the door locked . . . for thirty years."

"He must have been very unhappy to kill himself."

Corin twisted away. "Lionel? He was the happiest person I've ever known. Patient and kind . . ." He stopped, letting the words

49

hang in the air between us. For a moment we stood in silence, looking out the dirty windows at the sea below.

"Do you remember him? After thirty years?" I said finally.

He gave a short laugh. "I'm older than I look. And it wasn't quite thirty years. I was two or three at the time." Once more his voice had that mocking ring, but his eyes in the half-light were sad. When he began to speak again, his voice was calmer, more matter-of-fact.

"The Vail's Point Theater was going to reopen the first week in July, that summer after the War. The opening play was to be Lionel's new one, his first in years. He'd been in the Army . . . the War . . . there were a lot of reasons for him not to have been writing. He spent most of the winter up here, by himself, working on the play. Or so he said."

"Where were the rest of you?"

"Let's see . . . Mother had replaced the ingénue in one of those long-run comedies on Broadway. May had come out of retirement during the War and was still teaching dancing in the city. Haidee was on tour with an all-star Shakespearean revival, Esme of course trotting right along with her."

"I don't quite understand about Esme. I thought at first she was the housekeeper . . ."

Corin laughed again. "Never let her hear that. Esme is Gran's shadow. Haidee picked her up as a dresser her one season in London, and she's been with us ever since. The house keeps itself, you'll find. And not very well."

"Tell me about Lionel," I said. "The last winter . . ."

"Some of the time I was in the city," he said slowly. "Some of the time I was here. Successful ingénues like Mother weren't supposed to have children in those days; it spoiled the image. I was just a baby . . . but it's funny, the things you remember." He fell silent again, still staring out at the gray sea, the room growing darker behind us.

"None of us were here that last night," he said after a moment. "It was about this time of the year . . . the night before the first rehearsals. There was a terrific thunderstorm . . . or so I've been told. Telephone wires down, some of the roads washed out . . ." He rubbed a hand over his forehead as if he could make himself remember.

"They found Lionel the next morning in the theater. The coroner's report said alcohol and sleeping pills, taken together. Since he wasn't in his bed, the conclusion was it had been a deliberate suicide."

"And his last play?"

"Never found. A myth, everybody said. A lie he had made up because his talent was gone and he couldn't face it. Until the night before the first rehearsal, when there was no time left for lies. So he killed himself." He looked down at the closed roll top of the desk in front of us, idly rubbing one finger down through the thick dust that covered it.

"You don't believe it?"

"Maybe. Maybe there was a play. Or maybe it's just one of my fantasies. Like Gran says. Only, she'd never let me in here to look. She's never let anybody in here. Not since he died."

I began to understand something then. "Was that why you wrote the Foundation? To get somebody in here? To go through the papers and see if there could have been a play?"

He raised an eyebrow as Haidee had downstairs. "You're very clever, Alison," he said. "Do you have any idea of what an undiscovered play by Lionel Vail might be worth?"

I shook my head dumbly.

"Maybe a couple of million dollars. Granted, Lionel's a little out of fashion these days, but so was Eugene O'Neill before they started reviving him. And Scott Fitzgerald. Lionel was of the same caliber, one of our few genuine American geniuses." His eyes were bright now in the dark room. "'A new play by Lionel Vail,'" he said softly, as if he were reading a poster. "That *would* be a coup for a young producer."

"Is that what you do? Produce plays?" The question sounded rude as I asked it, but I couldn't help being curious. We were standing close now, closer than I liked, and even though we were not touching I could feel a warmth radiating from his lean body. It made me uneasy, but there was not room enough to move away.

He smiled as if he knew what I was thinking. "You really are an innocent about us, aren't you? I'm an actor, my dear. All the Vails are actors, whether they hate it or not. Even Lionel served his term."

I wanted to ask Corin if he was one of the Vails who hated acting, but something made me hold my tongue. After a moment he went on as if he had noticed nothing.

"That's why I mentioned reopening the theater in the letter. Haidee would agree to anything to start the theater again." He gestured to the dark room about us, the dusty cartons, the shelves of books. "Even to letting a stranger poke through all of this."

"Maybe she's been trying to protect him—his reputation, I mean," I said thoughtfully.

"Perhaps."

Corin moved away from me, touching one or two of the packing cases lightly as he made his way to the door to the hall. I started after him, remembering the question that had bothered me ever since I had entered this house. It was a question that in the polite world in which I had been raised would never have been asked of anybody and, if asked, would certainly never have been answered. And yet, somehow, with Corin it did not seem rude.

"Isn't there enough money in the family to reopen the theater for the summer, even without outside support?" I asked. Instantly I regretted what I had said, but Corin laughed casually. "I merely meant . . . well . . . you've all been so successful," I finished somewhat lamely.

"Oh, we're successful, all right. Only, what we earn, we spend. 'The Curse of the Vails,' my dear. Holes in our pockets. It never really mattered, as we've always had Matthew Patch's fortune behind us. Only, none of us can lay our hands on it. That was one thing Great-Grandfather was very stubborn about. I think he had an idea that one of us might go wild and back some superextravaganza and blow the whole wad. And he could have been right. So it's all carefully tied up in trust funds. We live well, but we can't get our hands on any really big money. And it would take that to open the theater here again."

He swung wide the door to the hall. Someone had turned on the lights in the corridor outside, and for a second Corin was silhouetted in the doorway.

"Don't worry, Alison," he said. "I didn't really expect you to come up with the cash for a summer season. I just wanted to get in here."

I moved closer. "And now that you have . . . ?"

He shifted slightly, the light from the hall splashing across the side of his clever face. He held out the key to Lionel Vail's rooms to me.

"Now it's up to you," he said. "Hang on to this key. It's the only one. Don't give it to anybody. Not to Haidee, or Julie, or even me. Let's see what you find."

I took the key from him. I began to understand now what he

had meant by a "search," but the whole idea seemed totally implausible.

"You really think I'm going to discover a lost play of Lionel Vail's in all this?" I could not keep the skepticism out of my voice as I looked at the cartons on the floor.

"You don't believe me? That it exists?" It was hard to see his face in the shadows of the room, but there was something different in his voice now, a sense of repressed excitement.

"I . . . I find it a little difficult," I said.

"Then let me tell you a secret, Alison. There *was* a play . . . I saw it. Remember I said I was up here part of that winter?" Corin's voice was quiet, but there was no mistaking his conviction. "Lionel didn't mind having me around . . . He'd let me play in this room while he was working. I remember the floor covered with discarded pages . . . he'd rip them out of his typewriter if something went wrong . . ."

He stepped back into the room now, looking straight ahead at the old desk by the windows, remembering that winter so long ago.

"That doesn't mean he finished the play," I said. Corin was standing as if he had forgotten I was there.

"Perhaps not. But I can still see the neat pile of pages on the desk. I wasn't allowed to touch those." Then, with a lightning change of mood, he looked at me, his eyes glittering, his thin lips twisted into a mocking smile. "Maybe I'm wrong. Even if he finished it, maybe he tore the whole thing up the night he died." He stepped back into the open doorway and gestured for me to follow him. "Only, maybe he didn't."

"You really think I might find it? Here?"

"I don't know." Corin's face was serious again. "It's worth a try, isn't it?" Before I could question him further, a gong sounded from the floor below. "The 'Comfort Hour,'" said Corin, relaxing again. "Come along, you look like you could use a drink." He started for the staircase without waiting, and then turned as I closed the door to Lionel Vail's study behind me.

"Lock the door," he said quietly.

And I did.

CHAPTER SIX

We heard the sound of the argument even before we came down the stairs. Haidee's voice, trained over the years to reach the last row of a third balcony, was clear; the man she was quarreling with responded only in a low mumble. Corin turned to me just before we started down to the landing.

"Jeb," he said quietly. There was an amused glitter in his eyes. "Wait till you meet him."

I remembered the angry man yelling at me as I stood in the rain. "I already have," I answered crisply. I could tell my reaction surprised Corin, but before he could question me further I went down the stairs ahead of him.

They were all gathered in the main room, and for a moment, as I came toward them, something seemed to echo in my head. I remembered the dream of the night before, the ominous feeling of walking onto a stage not knowing who I was supposed to be or what I was supposed to say. But this moment was real and none of the people gathered were paying me the slightest attention.

Haidee sat on one of the long couches near the fireplace. She had a glass of champagne in one hand and a cigarette in the other, both of which she ignored as she leaned forward to argue with Jeb Reives. He stood directly in front of her, his hands buried deep in his pockets, his tall drink neglected on a table nearby. He was calmer than when I had first seen him, but he wore the kind of maddeningly superior expression on his face that always makes me think of someone addressing a backward child. Esme stood at the table behind the sofa where Haidee sat. A large silver tray, heavy with bottles and glasses and ice buckets, was in front of her. Apparently she was, among other things, the bartender of the "Comfort Hour."

There was a fourth person in the room, but I did not notice her until I moved closer to the figures gathered by the fireplace. Seated in a huge wing chair in the corner was May, quietly watching the others. She still wore the same heavy robe. At her side was a pitcher of what appeared to be plain water. She held a heavy cut-glass tumbler in her long hands, but she made no move to drink from it.

Haidee had not seemed to notice us as we came down the stairs, but as we approached, she turned, sweeping one hand wide in our direction. It was the hand that held the champagne glass, and Esme instantly bent forward to refill it.

"Ask them," Haidee cried out. "You're so full of rules and regulations, you should be directing traffic, Jeb, not actors. Ask them if there shouldn't be a theater here this summer."

"'Shouldn't be'? Don't you mean 'Is it possible'? Gran?" Corin moved behind the sofa, where Esme was standing. Without asking, he started to mix us both martinis.

"Don't tell me you're on his side? It's your theater, too, Corin!" Haidee's eyes flashed as she looked at her grandson.

"'My' theater, indeed! All that means is I'd have to act in it."

"And why shouldn't you act?" There was steel in Haidee's voice now. She took a deep swallow from her glass and leveled her eyes at her grandson. "You're a Vail. You're an actor. You'd be a good one, too, if you weren't so lazy."

"Come on, Gran!" Corin's protest was automatic. He handed me my drink without looking away from his grandmother.

Oddly, it was Jeb who was studying me instead. I took a quick swallow and sank into the sofa opposite Haidee, trying to ignore the director's steady gaze.

"I've just had seven straight months playing a crazed dope addict on Mother's soap opera. Aren't I entitled to a little time off?"

"To do what?" countered Haidee. "To go racing out every night God knows where and smash up your car like you did last summer? To read obscure plays by a lot of people nobody ever heard of, where the second-act curtain is the entire cast taking off their clothes? A lot better you spend your time doing the classics."

"The classics generally have large casts, Haidee." Jeb had picked up his glass and was leaning casually against the mantelpiece. It gave him a clear view of all of us, including (unfortunately) me. He bent forward, his eyes directly on my face, interrupting the quarrel effortlessly. "I'm sorry about our first meeting, Miss Howard. I had you mixed up with somebody else. My apologies."

I nodded coldly and took another sip of my drink.

"I should have known you couldn't be an actress."

His tone was indifferent and it was possible he did not mean to be as insulting as he sounded, but I found myself irritated all over

55

again. I glanced at Corin to see if he had heard. But Corin had finished his drink and was mixing a second.

"And what's the matter with a large cast?" said Haidee, not to be deterred from her argument. "There's a whole university not ten miles away with a theater department that's supposed to be one of the best on the East Coast. They're having a summer session and the new campus theater isn't finished yet. I checked. You could get all the apprentices you want."

"You still need an Equity cast to play the principal parts, Haidee," Jeb said patiently. "And that means Equity salaries and an Equity bond. You couldn't budget a season for less than six thousand dollars a week. And unless you charge ten dollars a seat and fill every one of them every night, you can't pay that off. Not with the less than three hundred seats in the Vail's Point Theater."

She snorted at this, but it was obviously an argument for which she had no answer. Jeb saw this and pressed his advantage, still in the same infuriatingly reasonable tone of voice. "Not to mention what it would take to get the theater back into shape. When was the last time anybody went inside?"

"Thirty years ago," Haidee admitted grudgingly. Suddenly the anger left her. She seemed frail as she sat there, and for the first time close to her real age.

"My God, Haidee!" Jeb's voice was infuriatingly practical. "The seats are probably falling apart. The wiring would have to be done from scratch. You'd never get past the fire laws with what's there now. You need all new equipment backstage . . ."

She started to protest, but he waved her to silence. "I mean *new*. There couldn't be a piece of scenery there that would last through one performance. Not to mention the whole place would need a paint job, inside and out. You couldn't open for less than twenty thousand dollars, more likely thirty." He slouched back against the mantel again and took what seemed to be a triumphant swig from his glass.

We were all watching Haidee now. She had slumped back against the sofa while Jeb was talking, her champagne glass forgotten, her face gray. But then she set her jaw stubbornly and I saw a flicker of anger rise in her eyes.

"I could probably get the Equity bond suspended," she said, almost too quietly. There was a snort from Corin as he twirled the ice in his squat glass.

She turned on him defiantly. "I could, Corin! After all, I earned my gold star, that should be worth something."

She twisted around, the mask of polite sociability suddenly back on her face. "This probably doesn't make sense to you, Alison dear," she said, recognizing me for the first time since I had come into the room. "But when the union went on their first real strike, in 1924, every actor who walked out on a play at the time for the cause of Actors Equity was entitled to have a gold star placed forever on his card. I was having my first big success that season, and it hurt to close." She barely nodded over her shoulder to the heavy woman behind the sofa. "What was the play, Esme?"

"*Trinket*," said Esme promptly. "Al Wood's management . . . 193 performances. You got four hundred a week."

Haidee ignored this recital and turned back to Corin and Jeb. "Anyway, that should entitle me to *some* consideration. After all, no actor who worked a Vail show ever lost one penny of his salary."

"And the rest of it, Gran?" Corin moved forward, a little flush glowing under his tan, his voice as practical as Jeb's. "This is the end of June. We'd have to open in July if we're going to accomplish anything. That gives us barely three weeks to raise roughly twenty-five thousand dollars. We've no subscription list, no money for ads, no cast, no crew, no plays, no usable theater . . . and no chance." He smiled, but it had a chilly quality to it. "It's only in movies they say, 'Hey, gang, let's put on a show' . . . and manage to save the orphanage."

"The community wants us," said Haidee stubbornly. "I told you the Westaven selectmen came to see me. The town's been dying on the map. It needs the publicity of the theater to bring in summer visitors."

"Great!" answered Corin, the same superior look on his face that Jeb had. "Only, I don't notice any of those tightfisted Yankees coming up with the cash to get us started. They know about the family trust funds. Matthew Patch's will is right on file at City Hall."

Haidee sprang to her feet at this, lithe and young again in her anger. She clutched at the diamond collar at her throat. It was a melodramatic gesture that should have made her ridiculous, but her passionate sincerity turned her into a strangely moving figure.

"All right, then," she said, close to shouting. "The diamonds go! I don't care whether we pawn them or sell them or what! But I'm going to reopen the theater. There's going to be at least one more season here before I die! With the Vails acting! On a real stage! Not doing motorcycle movies or suffering as amnesia victims between spaghetti ads on TV . . . but acting before real, living people!"

She started to claw at the catch of the heavy choker, the rest of us watching fascinated.

I wondered later what Haidee would have done if she had not been interrupted by the slamming of the front door. She had been caught in such an outrageously dramatic position, nothing less than the fall of a theater curtain could have kept her from eventually seeming a little foolish. She could hardly have ripped off the heavy collar of jewels. Even from where I was sitting I could see the clasp of her diamond choker was much too intricate to unfasten in the careless, sweeping gesture she had started. I suppose she would have either collapsed or swept grandly from the room.

But she was saved from such embarrassing decisions by the arrival of Julie Vail. The front door banged open and we all turned as Haidee's daughter hurried into the house.

I knew who she was instantly. I had never watched her very popular daytime television serial, but one look and I could recall so many other times I'd seen her face over the years . . . publicity photographs in the paper, magazine stories, movie ads.

Julie Vail had never been a major film star, but she had been signed with the biggest Hollywood studio for over a decade and had appeared in most of their important pictures. Usually she played the sophisticated society wife who kept the hero from marrying his simple and more worthwhile secretary. Occasionally she was the heroine's best friend with the driest of comedy lines or else met a fatal end halfway through the picture (generally off camera) suffering from whatever sins the heroine was being tempted into: infidelity, alcohol, or being overambitious about a career. Julie was never as sexually beautiful and consequently never as popular as the girls who starred in her movies. But she always gave the best performance.

While she was closing the front door with a solid thump and coming toward us, I did a little quick figuring. Haidee Vail must be seventy and her daughter Julie very close to fifty but, truthfully, I had to admit neither of them looked it. Julie wore a full, spinach-colored rain cape that set off her tangled auburn hair, and her arms were loaded with packages. The rain had stopped long before, but there was still a quality about her as if she'd just come from a long walk through a twilight mist. It was a quality I was to realize in time was a permanent part of her, like her wide, startled eyes and her heart-shaped face. She started talking the moment she came in the door, her words rushed, her voice clear, with that intriguing little break in it that made everything she said sound as if there were laughter bubbling just below the surface.

"Sorry, darlings. I know I'm terribly late. Esme, ducks, I've brought some things for cold supper, so don't cut off the Comfort Hour. I'm dying for a drink . . ."

She dumped some of her packages in Esme's hands and then, tugging at the buttons of her cape, planted a kiss on Corin's forehead. "Corin, dearest, I know you love that sweatshirt madly, but it *is* Sunday and you've got a dozen brand-new shirts up in your dresser drawer. I know because I put them there. Haidee . . ." She turned to her mother and tossed a small package to her, which Haidee caught deftly. "Caviar, and don't ask me how I managed to find it today with the stores closed."

She waved to May as Jeb grabbed her cape just before it slipped to the floor. "May, dear, I got your pills . . . oh, thank you, Jeb . . ." She turned to the director and patted him on the arm before sinking into the long sofa beside me, smoothing the full skirt of her paisley dress. "You must be Alison. I'm so sorry I wasn't here to greet you . . ."

"Julie, take a breath!" commanded Haidee, still holding her package. "I haven't seen an entrance like that since dear Billie Burke last played summer stock."

There was a minute flicker in Julie's eyes. I don't think anyone else caught it, but it was almost as if her mother's comment had made her flinch. But then she was smiling again, her dark blue eyes wide and innocent. "Sorry, Mama. Did I interrupt something?"

"We were talking about the theater . . . and opening it this summer." There was no mistaking the tartness in Haidee's voice now. Julie's entrance may have saved her from an embarrassing moment as she struggled with her necklace, but it *had* broken the older woman's control of our attention. Corin caught the acid in Haidee's voice, as did I, and laughed openly.

"Ma, you just destroyed one of the great *tirades* of all time. Gran was about to sacrifice the family jewels so that we could all be troupers again."

"You are entirely too flippant sometimes, Corin," said Haidee. It was not just her words that were cold: the look she gave her grandson would have shriveled any other mortal.

"But Mama knows we can't sell the jewels," Julie answered mildly. "All of Viola's things are entailed. We're stuck with them, even if we haven't got a dishcloth to our name."

Now it was Haidee's turn to flash a look at Julie, which her daughter returned with bland equanimity. At that moment Jeb stepped directly between the two women, handing Julie a glass, breaking the tension between them. I had not seen him or Esme mix her a drink, so absorbed was I in the conversational duel, but apparently he knew what Julie liked, for she took a grateful sip from the glass and murmured quietly, "Thank you, Jeb."

"Actually, with all the money in the world . . . jewels included" (Jeb bowed politely to Haidee, who turned away frostily), "I don't think you could pull a season together. Not this summer."

"Oh, no, Jeb!" There was no doubt of the genuine concern in Julie's voice. "That's what I've just had the meeting about. The network finally agreed to let me have a whole month off from *With This Ring*."

"And how come I wasn't included? In an executive meeting?" Jeb's back was rigid. I remembered now someone had mentioned he was Julie's director on her television series.

"Jeb, you know perfectly well I get along much better with Anderson if I handle him all by myself. I can't very well bat my eyes at Doug with you glowering in the corner." Julie stretched out one hand and touched Jeb's arm. It was the gesture of a woman in love, and I wondered how many others had noticed it. Or perhaps this was a common secret. Only Corin seemed interested.

He leaned back against the couch and regarded his mother and her director thoughtfully, his face without expression. Julie removed her hand and took another sip from her glass, and Jeb was smiling once more. There was no denying that of all the Vails, Julie had the most charm and (I realized) perhaps the most desire to use it. Attractive as she was, Jeb must have been over ten years her junior.

"So what were Anderson's terms? A new contract?" he asked.

60

"I was going to sign that anyway, Jeb. But I told him the theater would be wonderful publicity for all of us. The series, you, me, even Corin if he wants to come back."

Corin, glass in hand, regarded his mother with a sardonic eye. "No, thank you, Ma. I've had seven months on *With This Ring* and that is more than enough. Besides, you might remember that the writers killed me off last week."

Julie waved Corin's remark away lightly. "Darling, your plane went down, but your body was never found. We can bring you back any time we want to . . . we've done it with lots of characters."

"Could we possibly bring back the main subject of discussion?" Haidee cut in coolly. Without waiting for an answer, she went on: "We were talking about reopening the Vail's Point Theater."

"No, we weren't, Gran." Corin leaned forward on the sofa beside her. "We were talking about money. Without money there's nothing else to discuss."

A little crease appeared between Julie's eyes as she turned to her son. "How much would it take, Corin? I mean, I've a little bit put away . . ."

Corin smiled at her with amusement. "Ma, it would take over twenty thousand dollars. And you've never had that much money at any one time in your entire life. Not with trying to keep this old barn over our feckless heads."

"I could raise half of it," said Julie doubtfully. "And maybe I could get an advance from the network."

"Julie, that's insane!" Jeb sat on the arm of the couch and looked at Julie indulgently. "You wouldn't have a chance of getting it back. Not to mention that the network expects you to take your month's vacation for exactly that . . . a rest. You know how hard we work on the show."

She shrugged lightly, wrinkling her nose. "I can handle it, I'm healthy. And if the community wants a season. And Mother . . ." She let her voice drift off.

"No," Jeb said firmly. "Reopening the theater is out of the question."

It was then I caught sight of Haidee's face, the skin gray, lines that I had not noticed before now carved deep. She looked old and

61

lost. She knew that Jeb and Corin had won, and a quick glance at the dresser standing quietly behind her told me that Esme knew it, too. And while it was as Esme had predicted, I could not see that the news had made her happy.

I cannot romanticize what I did then. It had nothing to do with the theater; it probably even had very little to do with the pitiful old woman in front of me. I think perhaps it was a desire for once to fight all the practical, sensible people who always know all the facts and figures. The Dilyses and the Peters . . . and yes, perhaps even I had been one of them. But I didn't want to be. Not if it meant living in league with the Jebs of the world, always so smug and sure in their common sense. At any rate, I sat forward a little. "It might be possible," I began, picking my words carefully, "for the Howard Foundation to contribute to the theater."

They were all staring at me now. May's eyes were bright, Haidee looked as startled as if I had suddenly ripped off my clothes, even Esme was regarding me with new respect.

"Of course, there would be certain conditions," I went on, turning to Julie. Her eyes were warm and understanding, but there was something more in them, something that puzzled me. Behind her, Jeb crossed his arms and glared sullenly. This was one person who was not pleased with my offer. And in a curious way, I was glad.

Then came a babble of excited voices: Corin let out a cheer, Haidee swooped over instantly to hug me, Julie started in with dozens of questions. It was as if I had released the room, the whole house, from some kind of spell. But in the middle of the congratulations, Jeb's voice cut in coldly.

"Does the Howard Foundation have this kind of money on hand?" he asked.

It was a challenge, everyone in the room knew it, no one more than I. I returned his look, my eyes as icy as his. "We not only have it on hand," I said distinctly, "but I am the hand responsible for giving it out." There was a suppressed snicker from one of the others—Corin, I think—and then I went on, keeping my voice as cool and controlled as before. "I'm sure we can match anything the family raises." For a moment I saw the startled expression my father would surely wear when I told him the sum required, and then I concentrated on staring Jeb down.

For a moment his face was blank, and then his mouth twisted

into an unwilling smile. "Julie," he said finally, "it seems we're in the presence of an heiress."

"An angel, that's what she is! In every possible sense of the word." Haidee raised her glass to me and finished the contents in one gulp. Julie leaned forward, touching my arm gently.

"And the other . . . 'conditions'?" she asked, her face a little troubled.

"I *am* here to look into the life of Lionel Vail," I answered. "I'm sure if the theater were to revive one of his plays this summer the Foundation would consider that an important cultural contribution." Not to mention, I thought silently, that it would make discussing the money with my father somewhat easier. "Perhaps you could do *The Basilisks?*" I said to Haidee, who had returned to her seat, adding tactfully, "Isn't there a wonderful part in that for you?"

And then there was a sudden silence in the room.

I heard a stifled gasp, but I could not tell who made it. Haidee's eyes were fastened on me and I could not look away. The clear, cold blue was suddenly clouded with pain as if I had struck her. And before I could recover from the shock, her huge eyes began to fill with tears.

I had never seen anyone cry so quickly, or so quietly. The great drops poured down her pale cheeks, and yet not a muscle in her face moved.

Still no one spoke.

I forced myself to look at the others, my neck stiff as I turned. What on earth had I said that had chilled the room so completely? None of them would catch my eye; either they turned away or they busied themselves studying the glasses in their hands.

Haidee rose and moved quietly for the staircase. She said not a word. She did not look back, but went slowly up the stairs, her shoulders straight, her head high. By the time she had reached the open landing, Esme had reached her and the two old women continued together up into the darkness of the floor above.

For the first time since I had entered the room, May spoke. She, too, had risen, her long green robe draping her large body with dignity. There was a bitter twist to her scarlet lips, and her eyes were hooded. "It's time for supper," she said, moving past us toward the far end of the room. "The 'Comfort Hour' appears to be over."

CHAPTER SEVEN

The meal that followed was surely the most uncomfortable I have ever sat through. Beyond the sliding doors at the far end of the great hall was the dining room, large and gloomy, paneled with dark wood all the way up to a heavily encrusted plaster ceiling. The table was long, with tall, ugly chairs placed down each side—far more chairs than the five of us needed. I was still stunned as we entered the room. I tried to pull Julie aside to ask what I had done, but she refused to listen. With a quick smile she showed me to a place next to her, opposite Jeb and Corin. May then took the throne at the head of the table, where she sat through the meal in impassive silence.

My face was still burning as I sat down, but the others paid no attention. Almost as if they had come to some unspoken agreement among themselves, they began to talk . . . arguing the merits of various plays it might be possible to include in the season, discussing actors who might be available, the work that would have to be done before the theater could open. It became a hopeless muddle to me, as I had never heard most of the names. However, I did notice that neither Haidee nor the works of Lionel Vail were mentioned again.

Haidee never reappeared.

After a while Esme came in silently and, without joining the conversation, crossed the long room and went through a swinging door into what I presumed was the kitchen. Shortly afterward she came back carrying a covered tray and went out the way she had come in. Neither time did anyone speak to her or seem to pay her the slightest attention.

The supper, if that is what it could be called, was served by a young girl wearing a pink cotton maid's uniform. She provided in silence what little service was required, darting back between times into the dark rooms beyond. But I noticed she was watching us all carefully and there seemed to be a flicker of a smile on her face whenever somebody—usually Corin—made a particularly outrageous remark. I also noticed that from time to time after she left the room the swinging door did not quite close but stood slightly ajar as if someone was behind it, listening.

Although I could not feel comfortable after what had happened, I did observe that whatever financial straits the Vail family might be in, they managed to eat in luxury. It was a cold supper, but it had been as carefully arranged as if it were a banquet. Homemade breads, soft little butter rolls, cut-glass containers of jellies and jams and pickles, great platters of cold meats: pink slivers of ham, the soft white breast of turkey, squares of spiced tongue, paper-thin cuts of fresh salmon garnished in dill sauce, rough country pâté, salad in a huge china bowl, tall bottles of white wine in the two silver buckets on the sideboard, potato salad and deviled eggs and pitchers of iced tea . . . a perfect summer supper. But I could not feel hungry.

I stared down at the old-fashioned linen tablecloth, so carefully embroidered years ago, and toyed with the heavy silverware, still lost and confused in my embarrassment and not made any more comfortable by the thought that the conversation going on around me may have been half to cover the uneasiness everyone else at the table was feeling.

Finally, the supper was over. The last of the fresh raspberries, glistening with powdered sugar, had been eaten, there was a wide gap in the homemade angel-food cake on the porcelain stand, the coffee cups were empty. And still the conversation between the others went on. I had long since stopped trying to follow it; all I wanted to do was escape.

As we rose to leave the dining room, I spoke to Julie for the first time since the start of the meal, explaining that I was tired and thought I should go upstairs. She nodded absently, almost as if she had forgotten who I was. I left them as they gathered around the fireplace in the large open room. Corin was pouring brandy for them all, and it looked as if their theatrical conversation might continue for several hours more. Only May seemed to notice as I started up the great staircase, but she turned sharply back to the others, as if even my departure was something she did not wish to consider.

Once I reached my room, with the door closed firmly behind me, I took a deep breath. Sinking down on the bed, I tried for a moment to think what I had done to have caused such a reaction. Had Haidee been offended because the part I had recommended in *The Basilisks* was that of an old woman? I had heard about actors' vanity, but this made no sense . . . the one play I had seen her in, years before, when I was a child, she had played a woman of at least sixty.

I lay back on the bed. Obviously it was something between her and the dead Lionel that had brought the tears to her eyes. Something the others also knew, which caused their embarrassment.

My mind began to work again. There was no possible way I could continue in this strange house. I would cheerfully have gone through a dozen weddings between Dilys and Peter rather than suffer the agony of another meal like this evening's. If I wanted to stay the summer here, I supposed I could move in the morning to the local inn (there must be one . . . hadn't the director said something about going there for a drink?) and continue my work here each day. But as soon as I thought of that, I realized it was impossible. Not knowing how to drive, I would have no way of getting from the town of Westaven to the house each day, and I could not possibly face another experience with that angry cab driver.

No, the thing to do was to leave Vail's Point as quickly as possible. My job, after all, had been to discover if there was material enough to interest a writer in a biography of Lionel Vail. A quick glance at the cartons in his rooms in the morning should satisfy that. I could then in honesty report what I had found to my father and let him make a choice of writers after that. As for myself, I had the money for a summer in Europe if I wanted to spend it. Father could take over the Foundation's involvement with the Vails, even including supporting the theater if he thought it worthwhile. As for Corin's wild hopes of finding a last play of Lionel Vail's, the whole thing seemed to me now completely insane. With any luck, I could be out of the house by tomorrow afternoon and never see any of them again.

I sat up then and slowly started getting ready for bed. Curiously, my decision did not make me feel any better. I did not like thinking of myself as a coward, and yet I knew I could not face another scene such as had occurred this evening. To leave was a sensible, adult decision, the kind my mind told me was right to make.

Only, it didn't *feel* right.

I took off my patchwork skirt and found myself almost angry as I hung it at the back of the closet. For some reason, I never wanted to see it again, as if the skirt were to blame for all my problems in this house. I turned down the bed and slipped into my lavender silk nightgown. After I had brushed my hair, I turned off the overhead light and opened the French windows to the balcony. The sky above was clear, the full moon touching the trees outside and the top of the porte-cochere below me, bathing the balcony on which I stood with a clear silver light. It was cool now, a ghost of a breeze ruffling the thin curtains.

Restless, I turned back to look at the room behind me. It had been a long day and the bed should have been inviting, but it wasn't. I thought of the dream I'd had the night before. For the first time, it seemed distant, no more frightening than any other dream vaguely remembered. I was leaving the Vails. By tomorrow I would be gone and I knew as I stood there I would have no more nightmares of appearing on a stage lost and bewildered

And yet I could not force myself to go to bed. Perhaps if I read for a while . . . Then I realized there were no books in this cheerful room and I had brought nothing with me. I could see in my mind the manuscripts and magazines scattered over the tables in the large room downstairs, but nothing could make me go down to the others again this evening.

The key to Lionel's rooms lay on the bureau by my bed. I had taken it out of the pocket of my skirt as I undressed, and it glittered under the lamplight as if it were made of solid silver. Surely in his rooms there would be a complete edition of his plays. Perhaps if I reread *The Basilisks* I might get some idea of what I had said that was so wrong. It had been years since I had read the play; little more than the basic plot came back to me. And perhaps it might be well to re-examine his works thoroughly before committing the Foundation to a book on his life. How very satisfying it would be to write (in the name of the Foundation, of course!) that on consideration we had decided that Lionel Vail was far too unimportant an author to sponsor his biography.

It was a bitter and childish thought, which I instantly regretted. One moment of embarrassment and I was ready to strike back at all of them! But still, I *was* curious about Lionel's plays and I *did* have the key to his library. If I was quiet, no one need ever know.

I slipped on my lavender robe, knotting the sash firmly. If I moved quickly, I could go to his room, find his plays, and be back here before anyone found out. I thought fleetingly of fastening my hair back into its neat knot—I looked so childish with it hanging loose—but with any luck, I would not meet anyone. Besides, if I was going to venture out, the time to do it was *now*.

I had the door to the hall open when I suddenly realized there would be no lights in Lionel's rooms. Corin had tried the switch unsuccessfully when I was with him early in the evening. I remembered the shaky lamp on the table by his cot. The last thing I wanted to do was to go into that deserted bedroom, but if it was either that or condemn myself to a sleepless night, I would have to chance it.

I went over to the lamp by my bed. Using the full skirt of my robe for padding, I lifted off the ornate globe and then detached the thin glass tube that covered the bulb. The light bulb felt hot through the thin silk, but I managed to unscrew it and drop it into my pocket. I would have to count on the moonlight giving me enough illumination to find the lamp by Lionel's bed.

The corridor was empty as I made my way quietly toward the large area above the main staircase. Far below, I could hear the voices of the others still deep in their conversation. I had a moment of panic when I realized I could not be sure which corridor we had taken to the suite of rooms, but then I remembered we had come up the far branch of the great staircase, and I started boldly down the dimly lit hall nearest to it.

I could no longer hear voices; the house was quiet, my footsteps in my slippers made no sound on the carpet. From outside came the soft muted roll of the waves on the shore. The door ahead on the right seemed familiar. I moved toward it, the key held firmly in my hand.

I hesitated for a moment before placing the thin key in the lock. It would be awkward if I had picked the wrong room. Suppose I should find myself confronted with a tearful Haidee or, worse, the hurt white face of Esme? I tried the handle gently. The door did not open; it was locked. This was the entrance to Lionel's rooms.

The lock turned easier this time. I removed the key and, slipping it back into my pocket, opened the door carefully. The only sound was the clicking of the key against the bulb in my pocket as I moved inside the room.

The moonlight was coming through the dusty windows here as well. It stretched a white carpet across the cartons on the crowded floor, touching my slippers under the hem of my robe. But I knew it

68

was not bright enough for me to pick a book from the shelves along the dark walls. I would have to get the lamp from Lionel's bedroom after all.

I left the door open a crack and started carefully for the far room. There was nothing to be afraid of, I told myself. Lionel had died nearly thirty years ago and his death had not taken place here. I stopped at the threshold, looking at the room beyond. How quiet it seemed in the moonlight! If perhaps I had expected some moment of uneasiness, some sense of pain long past that had been suffered in this room, as I had felt earlier downstairs looking at the portrait of the Vail family, I was disappointed. I felt neither fear nor unhappiness here. Perhaps it was the moonlight that made everything clear and cool and a little unreal.

Like a stage set, I thought wryly. Everything about this house seemed to remind me of the theater: the dramatic behavior of the Vails, the dusty grandeur of the rooms they lived in, their highly charged manner of speaking that made even the most ordinary of sentences crackle like dialogue. Now even the moon seemed affected by them; it lit Lionel's bedroom as artificially as if spotlights had been trained on the windows.

I crossed to the bed and changed the bulb in the shaky lamp. The shade, flimsy enough when it had been bought years ago, fell completely apart in my hands as I removed it, but the lamp itself worked when I twisted the button. Luckily the cord was long enough to stretch to the entrance of the other room.

The bare light of the naked bulb fought back the moonlight and made the rooms ordinary again, throwing enough light on the far shelves in Lionel's study for me to see the titles clearly. I started at the bookcase nearest the door.

By the time I reached the second set of shelves I had a deeper appreciation for the mind of the dead man. I had never seen a collection of books covering such a wide range of interests: there were volumes on religion, philosophy, poetry, several (oddly enough) on copper mining, biographies of every conceivable sort of person from seventeenth-century theatrical managers to Episcopalian divines. Plus detective stories, complete sets of Poe and Dickens and Thackeray, plays (by other playwrights), atlases, scrapbooks . . . I sighed in sympathy for the poor soul who would have to arrange a bibliography of the library for scholars of the future.

But I did not find a copy of Lionel's plays.

I had reached the last bookshelves, the ones nearest the roll-top desk by the windows, when I heard someone in the hall outside. The door, which I had left open a couple of inches, moved slowly back and I had a moment when I realized how I must look in my thin robe, my hair hanging loose, the naked bulb of the lamp I had placed in the far doorway showing me as startled as a surprised thief.

"Who is it?" I said, trying to sound calmer than I felt. The door opened completely and Jeb Reives stepped into the room. He threw up his hand over his eyes instantly, shielding them from the bare light of the lamp on the floor.

"Who's there?" he said. Then his eyes adjusted to the harsh light and he put down his hand. Stepping farther into the room, he stood between me and the lamp on the floor. "What on earth are you doing here? At this hour?" His tone was more curious than I had heard it before, without the smug authority that had so irritated me when he had spoken downstairs.

"Looking for a book, obviously," I answered. "And you?"

He moved in a little closer. The light was behind him now, outlining his broad shoulders, making a fiery halo behind his thick black hair.

"I thought you might be a little upset about this evening," he said easily. "I *was* rather . . . rude. Julie felt another apology might be in order. I was trying to find your room when I saw the light."

He's lying, I thought instantly. Even though I couldn't see his eyes or his face, I knew he was not telling the truth; the words had come too smoothly. Almost instinctively, I put up one hand to close the robe tighter at my throat.

But he was not looking at me. He had turned to stare at the shelves that filled the walls of the study and then at the bulging dusty cartons on the floor, moving his head slowly from side to side. And when he spoke again there was a new note in his voice, almost one of awe.

"So this was Lionel's study," he said finally. Then, as if ashamed of revealing so much of his feelings, he turned to me and said briskly, "What book were you looking for?"

I was reluctant to tell him why I had come here, but since I would be leaving the house the following day it hardly mattered what he thought. "A copy of *The Basilisks*," I said. He turned

70

slightly toward me and I could see his eyes steady as they searched mine. "I thought perhaps if I read it again," I went on, keeping my voice level, "I might discover just what it was I said that was so wrong this evening."

"It wasn't wrong, exactly." He tugged his lower lip thoughtfully. He hunched down on one of the cartons on the floor and stared up at me. I could see his face now; the light hit the side of his strong cheekbones and the black arrow of his widow's peak, making him look rather like an Indian chief. "Actually, it was a good suggestion. Haidee would be wonderful as the old lady. If she'd play it." He hesitated for a moment, then went on carefully. "She's never appeared in any of Lionel's plays. Did you know that?"

I shook my head dumbly. Suddenly I was aware that my thin summer nightgown and robe were not much protection with the light shining directly on me. I stepped back into the shadows near the bookshelf I had been examining.

"Do you know what the title means? *The Basilisks?*"

"I believe so," I said, turning away from him. I had no curiosity about the real reason he had come to this room. I simply wanted both of us out of here and the door safely locked behind us. "Basilisks were supposed to be fabled monsters, weren't they? Who could kill with one glance?"

"Not a bad talent for theater people to have," said Jeb idly. He made no move to leave. "Think of all the critics we could destroy that way." He stood again. "At any rate," he continued, moving nearer, "Lionel meant it as a collection of monsters. In this particular case, his family."

He had said it deliberately to shock me, and he succeeded. He raised a cynical eyebrow. "Didn't you know that? Lionel's plays were always about people he knew. *Red Mountain*—that was his first big hit—that was about his father. *The Basilisks* . . . well, roughly speaking, it's about Haidee and Viola, their mother. And May."

"What did he write about them?" I didn't like asking this rude man anything, but my curiosity was too strong to stop now. "I mean . . . even mentioning the play seemed to hurt Haidee so much."

"When you name a play after monsters and make Haidee one of the leading characters, you can be sure it isn't going to be a simple little bedroom comedy." He gave a short laugh, but it was not one of amusement. "God knows what he would have written in the third play of the trilogy if he'd ever gotten around to it."

"The missing play? Corin told me about that." I moved to the window and looked out at the sea rippling softly along the moonlit shore below.

He smiled sardonically. "What did he tell you? That he saw the pages on Lionel's desk?" He went on in the same superior drawl. "Julie told me about that years ago. It's all nonsense, of course. Corin was only a baby." He laughed. "There is no last play."

"Perhaps Lionel was disappointed with it," I said. "Perhaps he destroyed it before he killed himself." I found myself wondering under what circumstances Julie had told the director her son's secrets.

"Not a chance! Believe me. I know writers. They don't kill themselves if they've just finished a brand-new play." He laughed again. "Maybe if it's a flop they might. Or if everyone hates it when they first read it. But not when it's still their own special baby." I heard a ripping sound then and turned in time to see him pulling off the top of one of the cartons.

"Leave that alone, please," I said, happy to have a reason to be curt with him. That infuriating superiority had come back into his voice again. At that moment, quite unreasonably, I could cheerfully have slapped him.

"Just taking a look," he said, but he put the cover back on the box.

"I'm responsible for these papers. At least until a proper biographer takes over. Now I think we'd both better leave things as they are, Mr. Reives." I started toward the door, but the path between the cartons was too narrow for me to pass him. He stood, looking down at me, blocking my path.

"You *do* have a temper, don't you?" he said, almost clinically. "If you're going to get this angry at me all the time, hadn't you better start calling me Jeb? It's much shorter."

"I don't think we'll have to worry about what I'm to call you. I don't intend to stay beyond tomorrow." Lifting the skirt of my robe, I managed to step over a low carton and reach the lamp on the floor. If we were to continue this argument, moonlight was sufficient illumination.

"So you're going to run away," he said quietly. "Just because Haidee was upset? She'll be over it by morning, I promise you."

"Perhaps." I knelt and deliberately turned off the lamp. Instantly the room was cool in the moonlight again. Oddly, it made his presence even stronger than when I could see him clearly. "Now, if you don't mind, I'd like to lock up these rooms for the night."

"In a minute." He stepped over to the bookshelves by the window. While his back was turned I unscrewed the bulb and slipped it into my pocket. I would take the first book I could reach on my way to the door and be content to let it bore me to sleep.

But then I heard the snap of a cigarette lighter, and in its red glow I saw Jeb reach for a thick volume on one of the shelves.

"It's hardly the wisest thing in the world to use a lighter in a room full of important papers," I said from my dark corner.

"Do be quiet," he said, almost absent-mindedly. "Here's what you're looking for . . ."

The lighter went out and he started toward the door to the hall. I let him pass me in silence and then followed him out, closing the door firmly and locking it with what I hoped was an air of some authority. He stood watching me and I could almost have imagined he knew what I was thinking, for his lips had twisted in a smile.

"*The Complete Plays of Lionel Vail*," he said, handing me the heavy volume. "Authors always keep their own works right by their desks. I think it's to remind them when they're working that they really exist. You see, I *do* know how writers think."

I took the book from him. "Thank you," I said, trying not to make it sound as grudging as I felt.

"You're welcome," he replied, the amused glint back in his eyes. "I won't say good-by. You won't be leaving in the morning." He strode away. Before I could think of a sufficiently sharp answer, he had already disappeared.

Nor was there any sign of him when I reached the open area above the stairs. I do not know whether he had gone to rejoin the others, for there was still a murmur of voices from the floor below; but the hall to my room was deserted, and I was happy not to have to face him or anyone else for the rest of the night.

My room was in moonlight and I did not bother to turn on the overhead light. Dropping the heavy volume on the bed, I went around to replace the bulb in the lamp on the bureau. But as I

73

passed the open window, something outside caught my eye and I stopped and pulled back the thin organdy curtains.

The moon was lower now, the forest beyond the open driveway should have been solidly black in the night. And yet, somewhere among the trees there was a flickering of light, rather like the glow of the cigarette lighter Jeb had used. I stood there, just inside the balcony, watching it, somewhat puzzled. As far as I knew, the forest stretched down the hill toward the main road. Why would anybody, at this hour of the night, be out among the trees with a lighter, or, rather, a candle? For by now I was sure that was what I was seeing.

I realized I had no idea of how far the Vail property ran. There could easily be another house, somewhere among the trees, that belonged to someone else. I was about to step back from the window when I sensed, rather than saw, someone in the driveway below my balcony.

I pressed closely against the thin curtains. I didn't know why, but it seemed important I should not be seen by whoever it was that had just left the house. The moonlight was still clear and I could see a figure drift out from under the porte-cochere and head through the long grass toward the woods beyond. The figure was wrapped in a long cloak, a hood covering the head. I knew from the height and the slow grace with which it moved that it must be May.

I watched her as she crossed the silver lawn. Then she disappeared among the trees. I could not be sure she was headed in the direction of the candle that still flickered far beyond in the dark forest. I stepped back then and, crossing deliberately to the lamp on the bureau, replaced the bulb. I would not concern myself over where May was going. I had had enough of the Vails and their mysteries for one evening.

The room glowed cheerfully into light, and I took great care in fitting the glass shell and the ornate globe back onto the lamp. Then I went to the window and pushed aside the thin curtains. If anyone was watching, I did not care if he knew I was still awake. Contrary to Jeb's predictions, I was through with all of them.

There was no sign of May now.

The flickering candle was out and the forest lay dark and silent in the moonlight.

74

It was after midnight by the time I finished reading *The Basilisks*, and close to two in the morning by the time I completed *Red Mountain*. The rest of the plays would have to wait for another time, for I knew by then that Jeb was right. I would not be leaving Vail's Point with the daylight. I would not be leaving it for a long time to come.

They accused me later that tragic summer of having fallen in love with the dead Lionel Vail that first night. I denied it then and I deny it now. I had seen no picture of him (other than the small boy in the family painting), what I had been told of his life was not attractive, and I was far from being a stage-struck adolescent mooning over a dead man. I simply knew after reading two of his plays that I had been exposed to a great writer. And nothing I had done in the twenty-seven years of my life was as important as the project I was about to begin: protecting his name and reputation and bringing his work back to the prominence it deserved. The task my father had assigned me so lightly was worth all the dedication and ability I had to offer.

Later, when I did know more about the real Lionel Vail, I sometimes wondered how I would have felt about him if we had ever met. He was handsome enough to attract any woman and, judging from the letters I was to read in the long summer days after that first night, he could be charming when he wanted to be. But there was a coldness in him, a distance he kept between himself and other people, a bitterness that was bone-deep that I think would have repelled me.

One thing I *do* know: he would not have liked me, at least not the Alison Howard I was that first evening, priggish and self-pitying, quick to embarrass and even quicker to take offense. But fortunately Lionel and I were saved from confrontation and mutual disillusionment by the unchallengeable fact that he had died nearly three years before I was born.

So I did not love Lionel Vail, no matter what the others said. He did not come to possess me or fill my mind with fantasies; he was not a Brontë "demon lover," nor even a writer particularly sympathetic to my own tastes. I remembered, after I had put down his plays, a remark I'd once heard from a student of my father's. She had spent nearly four years on a doctoral dissertation of a seventeenth-century poet she had grown to loathe. I had asked her why, then, she went on with the work, when she so disliked the man himself. She looked at me somewhat puzzled for a moment and then said with a sigh, "Because he's so damn *good.*"

And that is how I felt, and shall always feel, about the plays of Lionel Vail.

I had read *The Basilisks* before, in college, but it had made no particular impression on me then, and in rereading it I could see why. It was not a work that would be attractive to anybody of college age. It was not a play, nor were any of his others, that hopeful people would enjoy. This was perhaps Lionel Vail's greatest failing as an author; certainly it was his most commercial failing. You could not be exposed to his words and come away unchanged, not if there had ever been unhappiness in your own life, or disappointment or failure. Especially if you had ever known deception from other people. He wrote for adults, forcing them to see the vicious and the mean, the tragic and the cruel sides of life. In the Depression—the years of his major plays—when there was already more than enough hard reality in the streets outside the theater, he gave his audience no escape, no pleasant "happy endings," no reaffirmation that the human spirit could conquer adversity.

So he was not a popular writer. But he *was* a great one. His was a narrow view of life; he made no pretense of showing the good or the cheerful. His virtuous characters (and he had some) were invariably weaker than the evil they faced, and, inevitably, they were doomed to lose, to be trampled, crushed and destroyed. In *Red Mountain* he showed how a ruthless mine owner—I began to understand now the books on copper mining on his shelves—forced various corrupt and vulnerable senators to change the laws of the land to preserve the mine owner's fortune. The mine owner was clearly based on Matthew Patch, Lionel's father, a stinging, brutal portrait of a crude and grasping man. The gentle side of the man—who yearned to see his beloved wife recite the Balcony Scene from *Romeo and Juliet*—was nowhere in evidence.

The Basilisks, the play I had so innocently mentioned before dinner, took the millionaire's family a generation further (although

Lionel kept it a period piece set slightly after the turn of the century). The millionaire's wife was a widow now, a sweet, rather vague old lady. She lived in a house in the country (clearly Vail's Point, from the detailed descriptions that Lionel carefully wrote), protecting a nearly mute cousin, an affectionate portrait that I was sure Lionel had based on his sister May. I saw now why my father had spoken of May as vulnerable and kind when she was young. Lionel saw her the same way.

The house is invaded at the beginning of this second play by another "cousin," a character Lionel called "Helen." Flippant, selfish, greedy and very close to a murderer, she is after the old lady's money. I understood now why I had brought Haidee to tears and the rest of the family to stunned silence when I had mentioned that she should appear in a revival of the play. Lionel had painted a vicious portrait of his sister in the character of Helen.

Gradually "Helen" and her confidantes turn the old lady into little more than a servant, weakening her mind and reducing her will, preparing to have her declared incompetent so that "Helen" can seize control of her fortune. The climactic scene has the villains working on the fragile cousin until the old lady comes slowly in, bringing a glass of warm milk, which has been the symbol throughout the play of the love between the old and the helplessly young. "Helen" tries to persuade "Emily" (as the character based on May is called) not to drink it, but in a desperate attempt to fight the evil influence, the nearly mute girl swallows the contents of the glass, tears up the confinement papers the others had been after her to sign, and with the single cry "Never!" dashes up the great staircase and out of sight.

It is a chilling scene, one, I was to learn as I started research on the life of Lionel, that has been called one of the great moments in the American theater. Highly theatrical, of course, for Lionel was aware that the bitterness in his characters alienated audiences. So he tried to compensate by structuring his plays in a melodramatic fashion that dated back to that of a previous generation, the theater of his mother, Viola Vail. He was not beyond using thunder and lightning to increase the power of a scene, as well as flickering lights and slamming shutters, dramatic gunshots, confessions of drug addiction, and dying curses—all to keep his audience's attention.

And, at the same time forcing them to look deep into the evil of their own natures.

I got up from the bed then, leaving the book behind. The night was still black outside, although I knew it was later than two by now, closer to three. For even though I am not an actress, and have never particularly liked the sound of my own voice, after I had finished reading the two plays I had to go back and read some of the passages aloud; they cried out on the page for the human voice, the words hard and glittering, the anger and the pain leaping up from the printed words, demanding to be spoken.

The world outside was quiet now, as I stood by the window. The sky was clear of clouds and bright with stars, and a cool breeze continued to move through the curtains. There were no lights to be seen in the forest, nor could I notice any on this side of the house when I stepped carefully out onto the balcony.

I thought then, for the first time in hours, of what lay ahead of me. Yes, I would have to help them with the theater. And no, I could not desert the project now. I would fight anyone, even my own father, to get the right biographer for the life of Lionel Vail, and I would not leave this house until all of the dead man's papers were in perfect order. There must be no errors, no omissions in the man's life to weaken the work of future students. For there would be more than one biography of Lionel Vail; I knew that now. He was too important a person and he had been too long neglected. With a dry laugh, I realized as I stood there on that moonlit balcony that the poor soul I had pitied only a few hours before, the person who was going to have to compile a list of Lionel's library, was going to be . . . me.

And if there could be, as Corin thought, one last undiscovered play!

I stepped inside and closed the drapes. I would need a good night's sleep for the work that lay ahead—the work and the problems that I knew would develop with the people of Vail's Point. These people and their secrets—Good Lord, I thought, suddenly weary, what have I let myself in for? But I knew it made no difference. I was committed to them now and I would have to make my way among them with as much grace and tact as I could manage.

The first I would have to handle would be Haidee. She must have thought me unbelievably cruel to have mentioned *The Basilisks* in front of her. For great writer though Lionel was, I had no doubt as I lay there in the darkness of my room how deeply he had maligned his sister.

Still, I thought, as I turned over to sleep, she *would* be marvelous in the part of the old lady.

That night, for the first time in weeks, I slept easily, with no thoughts of my own personal problems, and I did not dream. It was close to nine when I awoke, much later than usual for me. I must get an alarm clock today, I thought, and realized I should start making lists of the things I would need for my work. Suddenly there seemed so much to do, and I realized, without hesitation, that I was as committed to the project this morning as I had been the night before.

I hurried out of bed, wondering if the others were all awake yet. The house seemed quiet, but the thick walls of the old building would hide anything less than a shout. I pushed back the chintz drapes and looked out at the morning.

The sun was golden on the trees of the forest, the sky a bright, cloudless blue. The long grass beyond the porte-cochere was still wet with dew, but it was going to be a hot day. I washed in a hurry and slipped on a cotton dress with a cheerful pattern of tiny pink roses. I might as well look as attractive as possible when I faced Haidee and the others.

I fastened my hair back into a neat bun as usual, but somehow this morning it looked out of place and much too formal. I took out the pins and tied my hair back with a pink silk ribbon. It looked more natural with my summer dress. After all, no one here knew or cared that I was the proper daughter of the eminent Professor Howard. I could wear what I wished.

There was no one downstairs in the great hall, and when I pushed open the sliding doors to the dining room I found no one there either. For a moment I thought perhaps I was too late for breakfast, but then I saw that the table was neatly laid and none of the places had been disturbed. I smiled at my haste. I should have realized actors get up later. I noticed as I walked along the long table toward the door to the kitchen that seven places had been set.

Obviously Haidee and Esme would be joining us. That was an interview I was not prepared to face without coffee.

But before I could open the door to the far regions of the house, it swung back and the pretty young girl who had served us in silence the night before came hurrying into the room. She held a heavy tray in her hands, full of covered silver dishes, and for a moment when she first saw me I thought she was about to drop it.

"Here, let me help," I said, taking the far side of the tray.

"Oh, thanks," she said gratefully. "That's all I need . . . starting the day by dropping this. But I didn't know who had come down." Together we managed to set the tray on the old-fashioned sideboard. She grinned at me companionably. "I should have known it wouldn't be any of the Vails."

"Actors get in the habit of sleeping late, I imagine." I smiled back at her. She was younger than I'd thought her the night before, still in her teens with a pixie face covered with freckles that made you warm to her instantly.

"Not all of them." She was placing the heavy dishes carefully on the sideboard now. "Miss Julie's sometimes up at dawn to get to the city for her TV show. And May . . ." She gave me a quick look, as if wondering how much she dared to say, and then, thinking better of being too confiding she went back to arranging the dishes, finishing the sentence lamely: "She's likely to be around all hours."

"Who are you?" I asked. Young as she was, I could tell she had a common-sense practicality that I had not found in some of the others. "Are you a Vail, too?"

"Me? Gosh, no!" She let out an infectious giggle. "My name's Yvonne. Yvonne McNaughton. Frankie . . . that's my older brother . . . and I, we're just working here for the summer."

Something about her name puzzled me, but before I could speak she looked at me with a wise smile, suddenly mature. "That's right. It was our dad who brought you here yesterday."

I stepped back, startled. This bright young girl the child of that strange taxi driver? "I . . . I'm afraid I don't understand. He was so . . . vehement about not setting foot in this place—"

Yvonne broke in then, taking the tray off the sideboard and getting ready to disappear back into the kitchen. "I know . . . he's got a real thing about Vail's Point. Don't ask me why . . . and don't ever try to ask him. He gets very closemouthed if you do. Course, he was born in town, so he's known the Vails all his life. Who knows what some of them may have done? Anyway," she flipped the empty tray under her arm lightly, "it's a deep, dark secret."

I was still hopelessly confused. "But then . . . why . . . would he let you and your brother work here?"

She grinned then, a skinny little slip of a girl with all the confidence of seventeen. "We need the money for college. And money means more to a Yankee than a feud. So he lets Frankie and me work here. We just don't talk about it." She hesitated in the doorway and then came closer, her voice dropping conspiratorially.

"Is it true?" she asked. "You're going to reopen the theater here?"

"Yes," I answered firmly.

"You know, they say in the village that the theater is haunted." She grinned again, as if to tell me she for one didn't believe it. "Ever since Lionel Vail died."

She rested her tray on the sideboard, her eyes sparkling, and I could see she enjoyed the chance to gossip. "The theater used to be a real popular place to come late at night . . . you know, kids necking in their cars. It was kind of romantic. But after Mr. Vail killed himself there, people started saying something funny was going on —that they could see lights sometimes, even in the middle of winter." She lowered her voice solemnly. "And there's been no electricity in that building since before the War!"

I thought of the light in the forest I myself had seen the night before.

I would have liked to hear more of her stories, but she was looking over my shoulder, her eyes suddenly cautious.

The heavy sliding doors pushed open behind me, and Corin, still in the same jeans and sweatshirt he had worn the night before, came in.

"Yvonne, my gorgeous, dappled beauty, how's chances for some coffee?" he said.

"It's all made," she said calmly. "I figured you'd want that first thing, after I straightened up the living room this morning. Did you go through a whole bottle of brandy last night?"

"Snoop," he said equitably, as he poured himself a tall glass of orange juice.

"There's eggs in the big dish," she said, starting for the kitchen. Corin made a face as she passed him. "I know . . . but you can't

81

live on just coffee and brandy." And she disappeared into the kitchen.

"Want to bet?" he called after her, and then, for the first time since he had come into the room, he turned to me. "Well, good morning! Don't you look fresh and pretty and ready for church!"

"Sunday was yesterday," I said calmly. I went over to the buffet to help myself to the poached eggs warming on the silver tray. There was crisp bacon in a separate dish, soft English muffins and buttered toast steaming hot under a third cover.

"So it was." I knew Corin was still watching me as I made my way to the table, taking the same place Julie had shown me the night before. "I don't have to ask how you slept. You look wonderful."

"Thank you."

"You also look like you're settling in." I glanced up at him. He stood across the table from me, his bright brown eyes full of curiosity.

"That's right." I smiled at him innocently, as if I had no idea what he wanted to know.

"I thought maybe after last night . . ." He hesitated, toying with the empty glass in his hand. I was determined not to finish the sentence for him, and after a moment he realized it. "I mean . . . well, you seemed upset. I wasn't sure you'd be staying."

"I made an innocent blunder," I replied coolly. "I'll apologize to your grandmother about it later. But it's not serious enough to call off a project as important as the biography of Lionel Vail. Or a summer season for the theater."

"Good for you!" Corin looked at me with amusement, but something else was in his eyes as well, almost a look of respect.

"I heard that," said Haidee, coming in through the open doors.

She wore a white sharkskin pants suit that morning, a bright red turtleneck covering her thin throat. There was a warm smile on her face and she came quickly over to me and touched me gently on the shoulder. "There's no need for an apology, my dear. Except perhaps for me to make one to you. *The Basilisks* always hurts me . . . Lionel wrote it at a time when he and I were squabbling like cats and dogs and I always felt he took an unfair advantage. But he *was* a great writer, and I *would* be good in the old woman's part. I think it's a very definite possibility for the season."

With that she gave my shoulder another little pat and moved

82

around the table to the sideboard, Corin staring at her with total amazement. "The whole family's going crazy," he said finally, and slumped into his chair in mock surprise.

"Not in the least, Corin," said his grandmother, helping herself to the orange juice. Her face was clear and unlined this morning, and although it was not yet ten o'clock, her thick false eyelashes were firmly in place. "And I think you've had quite a long enough run in that costume. I shall expect to see you in a shirt and tie for dinner tonight."

"Yes, Gran," said Corin. His voice was subdued, but he looked at me and his eyes were twinkling. "Any other orders for the day?"

"I want you to be as helpful to Alison as you can. She may need certain things in town for her work. You could drive her." Haidee turned to me, her face pleasantly composed. "I believe you said you can't drive yourself?" she added.

I didn't think I had told that to anybody in the house, but it seemed simpler to nod acceptance than to question where she had received her information.

"Good; that's arranged. We should have a group discussion about what funds we'll need for the theater. Perhaps we can schedule that for around one. You'll find us very casual about lunch here . . . if you want anything, Yvonne or Esme can make you a sandwich. The Comfort Hour will be at six, as usual." She settled herself at the head of the table, in the chair May had taken the previous evening, and opened her napkin with the authority of a general planning an attack.

I glanced at Corin, but his eyes were still bright with wickedness and I was afraid if I continued to look at him I would break into laughter. Whatever pain or indecision Haidee had felt the previous evening, she had obviously recovered and was clearly the head of the family again.

Yvonne came in then to pour the coffee, instantly subdued by the sight of Haidee at the head of the table.

"Gran," said Corin, with a humility that did not quite sound sincere, "wouldn't it be more sensible to show Alison the theater before I take her into town?"

Haidee looked up at him, her bright blue eyes clear, and then she turned to me. "Of course," she said. "How foolish of me. Corin will take you down after breakfast. After all, you should see what you're going to be spending the Foundation's money on." She signaled the waiting Yvonne to pour her coffee and, like properly behaved children, Corin and I ducked our heads and began to concentrate on our breakfast.

When we came out the main door under the porte-cochere, Corin started ahead, turning not toward the driveway to the main road as I expected, but down toward the thick woods where I had seen May disappear the night before.

"Is this the way to the theater?" I asked him as I followed him through the long grass. There was still enough dampness from the night before to make my white shoes glisten.

"Shortcut," he said. He looked back at me. "I suppose I should take you down the road to the main entrance. It's more impressive, but you might as well learn about this path now. We'll all be using it." He pushed aside an overgrown bush and started into the forest. I remembered the light I had seen from my balcony the previous night and May's strange excursion.

"Is all this . . . Vail property?" I asked, following him into the woods. There was a path between the trees, but it did not look as if it had been used for years. Rain had washed away much of the gravel, and the bushes grew so close to each edge that in places it was hard to see any path at all. Only rarely did the sun penetrate the thick foliage above us. After a few moments it felt as if we were making our way through virgin forest.

"All Vail property, down to the road," said Corin, glancing back briefly. "Old Matthew liked his privacy. I suppose it'll have to be sold someday, the taxes are ruinous. But not while Gran and Aunt May are alive. Old Matthew tied it up for their lifetimes. He tied up everything—money, jewels and land." He held a branch back so that I could move up to walk beside him, the path having become a little wider now. "Anyway, I hate to think of all this being flattened out and made into some kind of a development."

"There's nobody living in the woods now?" I was trying to phrase it cautiously, but Corin stopped and stared at me and I knew he was puzzled by my question. "I mean . . . no buildings?" I added, somewhat lamely.

"Just the theater. Why do you ask?"

"No reason." It was not a satisfactory answer and I knew it, but I did not want to mention the candle I had seen the previous night.

Nor did I want to mention having seen May. If I was going to stay at Vail's Point, it might be wise to keep other people's secrets to myself.

"I thought you might have heard some of the local gossip," said Corin looking at me steadily.

"Gossip?" I repeated innocently.

"About the theater being haunted. By Lionel." He broke off a low branch that blocked the path. "Some tramp probably slept there a couple of nights once years ago and since then the whole town's convinced they've seen a ghost. Pure rubbish." He seemed almost angry.

"Is it much farther?" I asked, trying to change the subject, "the theater?"

"Right ahead," said Corin. He stopped again and looked at me, a strange smile on his face, rather like a magician who knows he is about to produce a trick that will astonish. "Brace yourself."

He pushed aside another low-hanging branch and stepped to the left, leaving room to walk into the open ground directly ahead.

And there in front of me was the theater of Vail's Point.

CHAPTER NINE

It was a low, curved building, shaped somewhat like a circus tent, settled deep in long grass. As far as I could see, as I stood there at the edge of the forest, the theater was surrounded with a wide, deep veranda. A slate roof came to a peak at the top with a rusted weathervane that still managed to glitter a little in the bright morning sun. The theater had obviously been built by the same architect who had designed the great house, but the family mansion had a heaviness to it, with its odd rooms and jutting balconies, that made it grotesque. The theater was different; here the turn-of-the-century décor made the building light and gay. It might have been an enormous concert pavilion in a town square or the home of a permanent merry-go-round.

It wasn't a large building, or at least it didn't seem so at first glance, and perhaps that was what kept it from being as pompous and ugly as the main house. It was covered in brown shingle, but the gingerbread trim still held faint traces of once cheerful colors: pinks and apple greens and yellows. When it was new and freshly painted it must have looked as gay as a children's toy box.

"Welcome to the theater," said Corin, standing at my side. And then he added, looking at me quite seriously, "Do you like it?"

"Of course!" I smiled at him. There was something about that oddly shaped building in front of us that would have delighted anybody. It sat there in the middle of the forest as happy a surprise as the cottage in "Hänsel and Gretel." "Can we go in?"

"I've got the key," he said. "Of course, the electricity won't be on and I don't know how strong my pocket flashlight is . . . maybe we can find an oil lamp."

It seemed strange, as we stood there in the morning sunlight, to be talking about needing light to see the inside of the theater but I knew Corin was right. Trees hung low over the roof of the theater, and the verandas were far too wide to let more than a minimum of sun into the building even if we were able to open the long, shuttered windows that ran around the porch.

"We should call into town today and get the electricity turned on," I said practically. "Some things don't have to wait for the 'group discussion' at one."

"Right," said Corin. He moved ahead of me across the thick

grass to the theater, with me right after him curious to see the front of the building.

Once around the first gentle curve of the building, I found we faced the entrance to the theater—three wide steps leading up to the deep wooden porch. Below the steps was a driveway that had once been covered with gravel. But tall weeds and straggling grass had pushed their way through, destroying the graceful curve that swept up to the front steps. The driveway completed its circle, disappearing into the far edge of the forest some forty feet beyond.

Corin stood on the first step to the porch, picking through some keys he held in his hand. Swallows were chirping gently somewhere nearby, and a little breeze ruffled the leaves of the two ancient trees that stood on either side of the wide front steps.

"Where actually are we, Corin?" I asked him. He looked up from the jumble of keys he had been studying. "I mean, I know the main road must be somewhere near here . . . but *where?*"

He pointed toward the trees that almost obscured the far curve of the driveway. "There's a side road," he said. "Leads to the highway. There used to be a sign up, pointing toward the turnoff for the theater. That'll have to be replaced." He glanced around the area in front of us squinting his eyes against the sun. The grass was long and untended, the tall summer green broken with the sharp yellow of small dandelions. "This should be cleared, too. For parking space." He turned back toward the great double doors that led into the theater. "Come on, we'll just have to try all of these. I'm not sure which one works."

I followed him up the steps. Although it was still not eleven, the sun was hot in the clear sky, and it was a relief to walk into the shade of the porch. Corin stood by the doors, the keys forgotten in his hand, a frown on his face. As I walked nearer, I realized what was puzzling him. One of the double doors was slightly ajar.

"This shouldn't be open," he said almost to himself. Then he shoved the keys into his pocket and pushed the door wide. "Anybody in here?" he called out as he stepped over the threshold. There was no sound but the birds in the trees behind us.

Corin disappeared ahead of me into the darkness. When I saw the thin beam of his small flashlight, I followed him into the theater lobby.

For a moment my eyes were still dazzled by the sunlight, and then Corin turned his flashlight toward the floor in front of me.

"Watch your step," he said. "The lobby hasn't been cleaned in years."

I could barely make out in the gloom how cluttered the area I was standing in was with boxes, odd folding chairs, even a tall standard lamp fallen on its side. Corin flashed his beam ahead of me. The far wall was filled with an ornate ticket window framed with heavy swirls and curves all painted in faded colors, so that to purchase a ticket would have been like staring into the center of an enormous wooden flower.

"How's that for *art nouveau?*" chuckled Corin. And then I felt him tense, as did I. There was somebody moving in the auditorium beyond.

I thought for an instant of what Yvonne had said about ghosts, but before I could laugh at myself for being foolish, Corin moved forward.

"Is anybody in there?" he called out sharply, sweeping his flashlight from one side of the ticket-window wall to the other. There were two paneled doors on each side of the ticket window. Suddenly the far one slammed open. I gasped and stepped back, nearly falling over a crate filled with dusty paper flowers. Corin focused his beam on the open doorway and a figure emerged, hand up against the light.

It was Julie.

"Corin, put that down!" she said sharply.

"What on earth are you doing here, Ma?" Corin's voice was testy, but as he lowered his flashlight we could both see that Julie was not alone.

Jeb Reives stood in the darkness behind her.

We went back out on the porch again, all four of us, Julie chattering as naturally as if it were perfectly ordinary for her to have been caught in the empty theater with the young director.

"We were both up early, so we had breakfast at the inn," she said, settling herself on the wide steps just out of reach of the sunlight. She looked at her grimy hands and brushed them together absently. She was wearing a loose, flower-embroidered Mexican blouse over dark green slacks, and with her hair hanging free down her back she looked closer to thirty than her real age. Jeb, in jeans and a black T shirt, lounged against the pillar by her side, but other than a brief nod at me, he seemed to pay no attention to the conversation. "The theater's filthy, Corin," Julie said, giving up trying to clean her hands.

"How'd you get in?" he asked, his voice carefully controlled. He was making a point of not looking at Jeb, I thought. And I wondered if any of the others had noticed. "Gran gave me the only key."

"The door was unlocked." Julie looked up at Corin standing over her. "Truly, Corin! We were just going to take a look at the outside. And then Jeb tried the door . . ." She let the sentence trail off. Corin glanced at the director briefly and then, his voice deliberately casual, said, "Well? What do you think?"

"Of the theater?" Jeb didn't move, but I could tell he was not as relaxed as he appeared. "It's in better shape than I thought. Needs a lot of work, of course. And that will take money." He looked at me pointedly. There was a moment of silence, and then Julie smiled at me gently.

"Alison, I know things weren't exactly . . . well, *easy* last night," she began, "so if you want to change your mind . . ."

I broke in then. I was reluctant to admit that Jeb had been right in his prediction of the night before, but there was no point in delaying what I had to say.

"I want to go ahead with the project," I said firmly. "Both projects. I've already talked to your mother this morning; she seems quite willing to do *The Basilisks* as part of the summer season." Julie flicked a glance at Jeb, but his face remained impassive. "I think she'll be wonderful in it," I finished, looking directly at Jeb. If he wished to gloat over my decision, let him. But his face betrayed no particular emotion.

"I hope you don't regret this," he said quietly.

Julie obviously was relieved. "I don't know how you managed that, Alison, but bless you," she said. And then she turned to Corin with a vivacious smile. "Darling, what do you think? Jeb has agreed to direct. And design the sets."

"Wonderful," said Corin flatly. The way he said the word was just this side of insulting, but Julie chose not to notice, bubbling on.

"We've already seen some carpenters in town," she said. Then, realizing that might have presumed too much on my co-operation, she put out her hand and touched my arm. "Just in case," she added, with a warm smile. It was impossible not to smile back.

"And what else has been decided?" asked Corin. The thin edge of hostility in his voice was becoming more apparent now. "By the two of you?"

"Now, Corin, don't be cranky," said his mother. "We were just talking about the other plays for the season. We'll need at least three—a comedy perhaps, and a classic. No matter how highly you think of Lionel's works, we can't count on just *The Basilisks* to bring in people, not for a full season, even a short one. Jeb thinks . . ."

"'Jeb thinks,'" Corin repeated flatly. But there was no mistaking his anger. "I thought we were all to decide this as a group."

"Darling," said Julie placatingly. "It doesn't hurt to have a few ideas in advance of the meeting. You're going to have to pick something to use the college apprentices. They're not going to give up their whole summer to painting scenery unless they get a chance to appear on stage."

Jeb said lazily to Corin, "If we make it the last play, they'll stay."

I wondered, watching the two of them, how they had ever managed to work together on Julie's television series, the antagonism was so strong between them.

"What else got decided this morning?" said Corin. He, at least, was not to be soothed by his mother's charm. She patted the wooden step beside her.

"Come and sit down, Corin," she said. "Jeb, you run along and show Alison the theater." I knew he was no more eager to give me a tour of the building than I was to go with him, but he detached himself instantly from the pillar he had been leaning against and started for the doors to the lobby. Corin slumped down sulkily on the steps next to his mother, and I had no choice but to follow Jeb inside.

Once in the lobby, Jeb pulled out his flashlight, much larger than the one Corin carried. "If I can get the shutters open we should be able to see all right. Even without electricity," he said, flicking on the flashlight. "Watch your step. I'll go first."

He went through the door to the auditorium ahead of me, his broad shoulders filling the doorway. Once inside the theater, I could see nothing.

"Stand still for a second," Jeb commanded. "Let your eyes adjust to the dark."

I did as I was told. It would have been foolish to resent his authority; he and Julie had obviously already explored the theater. After a few seconds, I began to realize the building was not totally dark. All along each of the side walls there were thin lines of sunshine where the shutters covering the French windows did not quite meet. Jeb flashed his light ahead of us, sweeping the auditorium. Even in the semidarkness I could see it was not an enormous area; perhaps there were twenty rows of seats, covered with canvas sheets, but if the theater was not long, it was surprisingly wide. There were several aisles, straight black lines cutting through the huddle of covered seats toward the total darkness ahead that must be where the stage was.

"Stay right where you are. I'll see if I can open the windows." He passed along the last row of seats to the far side of the theater, the flashlight splashing a yellow beam in front of him. Then he stopped and I could hear him fumbling with a rusty metal latch in the darkness.

Suddenly, light spilled across the back of the theater as he pushed open the first window. He walked down the far aisle, opening each window in turn, until I could see almost as well as I had outside. But he kept his flashlight on.

"Come down the aisle," he called to me. He turned and flashed his light at the far darkness ahead of me.

I knew the stage would be there, and I had remembered Esme telling me the night before that it had been built on the scale of a major Broadway theater, but the first glimpse of it as Jeb moved his flashlight from side to side stunned me. It seemed so *big*. I could hear Jeb climb up on the stage itself, moving deeper into the great black cavern that lay at the end of the covered rows. "Come ahead," he called back. "It's perfectly safe."

I moved forward then, down the nearest aisle. It was carpeted, and I could see in the half-light that my feet were making footprints in the thick dust. Still, the stage seemed a huge black wall in front of me. There were no windows up ahead as far as I could see.

I reached the first row of seats, to be stopped by an ornate wooden railing, the gold paint on it peeling and cracked and thick with cobwebs. I was reluctant to move any farther; there might be an orchestra pit beyond the railing—it would be suitable for a theater of this period.

"Where are you?" I called out. Jeb and his flashlight had disappeared and I felt completely alone in the building.

"Right here." He flashed his light on me from the far side of the stage, blinding me for a moment. "There are steps up to the stage on your right."

He moved his light, making a path for me to follow to the far end of the first row. I walked along the space between the railing and the covered seats. I could almost taste the dust around me as I moved, and smell that curious dead air that belongs only to buildings that have long been closed. If ever a building could be haunted, I thought, this was it.

There were steps up to the stage over the dark orchestra pit. There was no railing, but by clinging to the wall I managed to climb up without stumbling. The flashlight beam turned away from me and I heard the creak of a heavy wooden door at the far side of the stage. A square of sunlight appeared in the darkness, and I could see blue sky and green trees outside, as sudden a shock as if I had been watching a movie in black and white that had abruptly turned into Technicolor. I heard footsteps to one side of me and Jeb walked across the path of light from the open doorway.

"What do you think of it?" he asked, not coming any nearer to me. He stood instead looking out at the auditorium.

"I . . . I can't see very much," I said. I noticed a long trough for footlights bordering the stage in front of me and the deep black of the orchestra pit beyond. Thirty years the building had been closed! "It's very big, isn't it?"

He pointed his flashlight upward. Near the roof, a balcony railing hung out over the darkness. He swiveled around, still holding the flashlight up toward the ceiling. High above the stage I saw a confused blur of rafters and metal pipes and hanging ropes. "We can hang scenery up there. That's a help when you're doing repertory. There's also a trap door—a big one, too."

The light explored a far corner of the dusty stage floor. I could see a square roughly ten feet by ten feet outlined along the boards. "So we can bring furniture up from the cellar below."

He played his flashlight against the wall some thirty feet behind us. "Come along, let's take a look at the rest of the place."

For the next ten minutes Jeb showed me around the backstage area of the theater. Even though we were alone, he made no attempt to challenge my change of plans, my overnight decision to stay on at Vail's Point and help with the theater and the biography of Lionel Vail. It was as if our meeting and conversation of the night before had never occurred. Jeb was not sullen, as he'd been before, but curiously impersonal, as if he were a guide showing me through a palace. I gradually realized that was indeed how he looked upon the theater.

The building was much larger than it had seemed when I first saw it. The stage was not only wide, but deep. There was another great door, as big as one into a barn, on the opposite side from the one Jeb had opened.

"Also for scenery," said Jeb, opening the second door. A slight breeze swept across the bare stage between the two open doors. "This way it can be taken in and out in case we can't hang it. In the days they built this theater, every act had a different set."

I noticed then a spiral iron staircase at one end of the back wall. "Where does that go?" I asked. Jeb had moved over to something by the edge of the proscenium that I could see was a primitive light board.

"What?" He looked at where I was pointing. "Oh . . . I guess that's a walkway across the rafters, for hanging lights and tying up the scenery. The stairs also go down to the basement . . . extra dressing rooms. There's a place for a paint shop down there, rooms for props and furniture." He returned to studying the equipment at the side of the stage. "Lord, even thirty years ago this was pretty meager," he said, almost to himself.

I wandered away from him, curious about the back wall of the stage. It curved slightly, following the circle of the outside of the building, and along the wall at regular intervals were closed doors.

"Where do these doors go?" I asked.

Jeb left the light board and started along the black wall, opening each of the doors as he came to them. "Dressing rooms," he said. I peeked into the first small room. There was a wide shelf that stretched along one wall, holding three dim mirrors, with empty light fixtures between them. The far wall had a little window and a glass door that opened onto the veranda outside. Everything was covered with dust.

"Actually, it's not a badly designed building," said Jeb. He had come up behind me quietly as I stared into the first dressing room. "With all the doors and windows open, backstage and front, the whole place becomes like an open tent. Must have kept it cool on summer nights."

I moved past him, down the row of little rooms. There was one door at the very end that was still closed. "What's in here?" I asked. I tried the handle. The door appeared to be locked.

"Leave that alone!"

I looked at him, somewhat startled. For the first time since we had come into the building he had dropped his indifference. He stood a few feet behind me, his sturdy legs planted wide apart. As soon as he caught my eye he tried to resume his previous indifference, but he was not very successful. However much talent Jeb might have for the theater, he would never be an actor.

"Isn't it just another dressing room?" I asked. And then I took a guess. "Or was this where Lionel Vail killed himself?"

His eyes were carefully impersonal now. "I wouldn't know. I . . . I think it was downstairs someplace. Anyway, if there's a closed door in a theater, you'll do well to leave it alone. There could be electrical equipment in there, or maybe the flooring isn't too secure. This is an old building, remember. And we're the first people in here in thirty years." But he added this lamely. He's lying, I thought. Almost as if he were aware I'd caught him, he turned sharply on his heel and started for the spiral staircase, near where we were standing.

"I'm going to check the cellar. Don't go poking around."

It was an order. And without waiting for an answer, he clattered down the metal stairs. As Jeb's dark head disappeared, I moved obediently away from where we had been standing. But then I stopped and looked at the closed door. Somehow I *knew* that behind that locked door Lionel Vail had spent the last moments of his life.

The stories I'd heard of ghosts did not disturb me. I wanted to know more about how and where Lionel had died. Walking back to the closed door, I tried the handle again. The dressing room was not locked: the door was only stuck. With a little effort I managed to open it.

The room beyond was like all the other dressing rooms, empty and dusty, the little window and the glass door in the far wall streaked with dirt. But there was something different about this room; I felt it as strongly as I had when I looked at the family portrait over the mantel the night before. I knew this was a room of Lionel's. Hadn't Corin told me that even the dead playwright had served his term as an actor? There were gray strings of spider webs high up in the corners of the ceiling, woven long ago.

Suddenly I shivered. I could feel a coldness in the air, a coldness alien to this hot June morning. But I could not walk out of the room; it was as if something held me there, something that said, "Look . . . see . . . understand . . ."

I heard a sound behind me, something like what a heavy footstep might make on an old floorboard, and instantly I was back in the doorway. But there was no one on the bare stage beyond. The open doors at each side of the building gave all the light I needed to see that. Jeb must still be in the cellar. I turned back to the dressing room. I could still feel the strange coldness in the air, the presence of *something*. The rest of the theater may have slumbered in enchanted sleep all this time, but in this room something was still alive, something had survived the years.

I looked at the room again, more carefully now. It was as bare as the other dressing rooms. A couple of shoeboxes and an old open wooden box sat on one corner of the makeup shelf, filled with odd tubes and sticks of dried makeup. There was an empty ashtray, one rickety chair. Lying under one of the gray mirrors was a small, badly mildewed book bound in crumbling leather. Without picking it up I could see it was a copy of *Macbeth*.

I walked across the linoleum floor to the glass door to the porch. The door was locked. The glass in the door and in the small window next to it, like all the others in this building, was streaked with dust and rain-caked dirt. There was a crack in the bottom of the window that had let in the wind through the years; the dust on the sill below lay swirled in an uneven pattern. I rubbed a small circle on the window pane and looked out.

The trees were close here, bending over the veranda beyond, but through them I could see the edge of the woods . . . and beyond the woods, barely clearing the top of the trees, were the roof and cupolas of the main house of Vail's Point. I pressed my face against the dusty glass. Yes, there was the edge of the widow's walk above my room. I could even see part of my balcony.

I thought again of the flicker of light I had seen the night before. It could have been somebody in the woods. It could also have been somebody exploring the theater, exploring this room . . .

It was then that I found the tiny drops of wax near the window sill. They had not been there for thirty years; they had not even been there for twenty-four hours. For in all the theater, the stiff wax drippings in front of me were the only surfaces not covered with dust.

CHAPTER TEN

By the time Jeb came up from the cellar of the theater, I was standing by the far open door, looking out at the sunlight on the green grass beyond. The door to Lionel's dressing room was closed once more, and I had had time to think.

It would be useless to pretend that there were no questions that puzzled me about the people of Vail's Point. But I thought to myself as I stood there it would be wise to avoid looking for mysteries and secrets, and concentrate, rather, on facing the problems of the summer ahead as sensibly and realistically as possible. The house and the theater had seen three generations of a highly dramatic family; I would be a fool if I thought I could decipher all the tangled threads of the past . . . at least in the few weeks that I would be living among them.

And so, standing there that June morning, I firmly resolved to try to ignore the fancies that were plucking at my brain. Candles in the night and "missing" plays and ghost stories . . . I was becoming much too impressionable. Even the coldness I had felt in Lionel's dressing room and while staring at his portrait in the great house seemed to me now, in the light of that warm Monday morning, melodramatic nonsense. And my visits to Lionel's study had shown me I had more than enough material to work on as it was.

So when I heard Jeb's footsteps coming up the iron stairs, I took a moment to arrange a look of placid innocence on my face; for, in addition to my other decisions, I had determined again to keep my thoughts to myself this summer. I noticed Jeb gave a quick look at the closed door of the last dressing room, but he did not ask if I had obeyed his order, and I volunteered no further information.

"Let's join the others," he said crisply. "I've seen enough for the 'group discussion.'"

The next two hours were spent in the most furious conference I have ever been exposed to in my life. It was hardly a "discussion," veering at times closer to mere argument, but I came out of it with a reluctant admiration for the common sense of theater people.

Over a platter of sandwiches brought silently into the main hall by a frozen-faced Esme (followed by an equally subdued Yvonne carrying pitchers of cold milk and iced tea), the schedule for the summer season was hammered out, plans for the reconstruction of the theater were made, arrangements for rehearsals, casting of the company, even the types of advertising to be used, were decided. Quite early I had become the secretary of the meeting, for I noticed with a smile, with all their energy and ideas, none of the others had thought to attend the gathering with anything so practical as a pad and a pencil.

It was decided, since it was now the end of June, that it would be impossible to run a full season of two months, the way the theater had in the years before the War. Instead, three plays would be done, opening the end of July, each play running one week; and then, for the fourth and final week, either running all of them in repertory or else bringing back the most popular of the three for extra performances.

The season would open with *The Basilisks,* as it had a fairly small cast. The second week would be Ibsen's *Ghosts,* a title I alone found wryly amusing. It seemed to me a rather heavy selection for summer stock, but the reasons for doing the great tragedy were surprisingly practical.

"Five characters, one set, a star part for Julie," said Jeb briskly. "And Corin, you were born to play Oswald."

"The disease-ridden son who goes insane in the end," answered Corin wryly. "Thanks ever so much." But I noticed he gave Jeb no argument. Whether or not Corin really hated acting, he was obviously as interested as the others in the parts he would be going to play.

The final play would be Oscar Wilde's *Lady Windermere's Fan,* which would give both Julie and Haidee excellent roles as well as providing a number of small parts for the college apprentices who would be working as the theater crew.

May took no part in the discussion, wandering in and out of the room, occasionally getting a glass of iced tea before returning through the French windows to the garden outside, where we could see her weeding the straggling beds of flowers along the walls of the house. She was wearing a tentlike garment of something that looked like oatmeal sackcloth and, with a wide-brimmed hat on her head and sunglasses, it was impossible to see from her face what she was thinking. But I had a feeling as she worked outside that she was paying closer attention to the conversation than she appeared to be.

After the plays were set, the next part of the discussion was money, and I realized it was time for me to call my father. I had no anxieties about getting the funds from the Foundation (although I could see the others did), but I was concerned that he should not think that I was behaving foolishly.

Yvonne led me out through the deserted dining room to the butler's pantry beyond, where the phone was, and then tactfully went on into the kitchen. The conversation was easier than I had expected, Father making no protest when I told him the amount I would need from the Foundation and that it was very possible that I would have to ask for more later. But he was curious about the household at Vail's Point, and although I knew there were two closed doors between me and the group in the main hall, I was reluctant to talk.

"I'll write you all about them," I promised. There was a pause, as he obviously tried to find some tactful way of asking what he wanted to know.

"Are you all right?" he said finally. It was only after I assured him that I was and had hung up that I realized he was still concerned about the reason I had left him for the summer.

I must be a very shallow person, I thought as I walked back to the great hall. I hadn't really thought of Peter and Dilys for the past twenty-four hours.

Soon after that, the "group discussion" broke up. Since time was going to be harder to find than money, each of them left the meeting with specific projects to start. Rehearsals would have to begin in three weeks, which meant the theater must be in working order by that time. Jeb would be in charge of the stage, planning the designs for the scenery and borrowing an apprentice crew and, he hoped, some modern equipment from the nearby college, where, oddly enough, he had once gone to school. Somehow I had thought if he had been educated at all it would have been in some rougher background than an East Coast university.

Corin and Haidee were to supervise the rehabilitation of the theater itself, and Julie was to go back into New York to arrange for the casting of the professional actors who would fill in the real company. Even May, still as silent as before, agreed, with a nod of her head, to attend to the look of the grounds around the theater itself. There was suddenly a feeling of energy in the house, as if windows long closed were being thrown open; silent rooms were starting to echo with excited conversations, and old dreams were once more coming back to life.

I left them then, aware with perhaps a little sadness how out of their world I really was. My job, as far as reviving the theater was concerned, was finished. I had provided the money they needed. Now I could only be a spectator, as unable as anyone else sitting in the audience to contribute to the magic of their work. But as I climbed the great staircase that afternoon, I realized that the important part of my summer was still ahead of me.

It was time for me to begin on the life of Lionel Vail.

I opened the door to his study and, slipping the key back into my pocket, went into the room. It seemed different today, as if even these long-deserted rooms felt some of the excitement that was spreading through the rest of the house. The sun shone through the dirty windows and I could see Lionel's study more clearly than I had the day before. The windows should be washed first, I thought. I'll need to get some light bulbs. I smiled as I looked around. The dust was thick on everything. Before I even started on Lionel's life, a job of housekeeping would have to be done. And I knew it would have to be done by me. The teen-aged brother and sister who apparently ran this house had more than enough to do, and I suspected from Esme's conversation that she would not lift a hand for Lionel Vail.

I decided to go into town that afternoon to purchase my own supplies. Quite apart from the cleaning that would have to be done to Lionel's rooms, I would need certain necessities when I started on his papers—card cabinets and files, pencils and pads, a good solid lamp or two. With the family performing each evening in the theater, it would be well for me to have work to retreat to after dinner. It might seem dull to most people, but years of living with my father had taught me the joys that can be found in research. Suddenly I was anxious to get started.

I thought of finding Corin to drive me in, but the house

99

seemed quiet now and I did not want to go in search of him. Perhaps I could borrow a bicycle (for I had seen one that morning by the kitchen door) from Yvonne and go into town that way. It would be impossible to bring much back with me, but if I could not have what I needed delivered, at least I could order it and perhaps Corin could bring it back to Vail's Point later.

Within half an hour I was on my way. I got from Yvonne not only permission to use her bike, but instructions on the shortest way to the village. She and Esme were hard at work in the butler's pantry off the dining room, polishing silver—great, huge set pieces that had obviously not been used in years: epergnes and ornate tea services, flat square trays, and plump little bowls and pitchers. Yvonne looked as if she would gladly come with me, even if she had to walk, but there was a grim expression on Esme's face that stated silently but firmly that the afternoon was going to be devoted to housework. Clearly the decision to reopen the theater meant the start of a new regime at Vail's Point.

The ride into town was easier and shorter than I had expected. The afternoon was hot, the first of the real summer we had that year, but the highway was practically level and the trees along the road screened off most of the sun. I felt surprisingly young and free, perhaps because I had not been on a bicycle since I was a child.

The town of Westaven was smaller than I had thought it, seeing it the day before in the rain, and as I pedaled down Main Street toward the village square I noticed something I had missed before. Set back from the sidewalk was a one-story building of maroon brick with the words "Westaven Library" carved in the granite arch above the entrance. On impulse, I stopped the bike and wheeled it up to a rack near the front steps. I had a sudden desire to see if the library had any newspaper files that might date back to the day of Lionel Vail's death.

You're being foolish, I argued with myself as I went up the stone steps. This is exactly what you promised yourself you were *not* going to do. You're here to concern yourself with Lionel Vail's life, not his death.

Besides, quite practically, a library this small would hardly have back-date newspapers on file. Only a city would have facilities for that. But still I felt a desire at least to try to find out something about the circumstances of his death. I knew by now that no one at Vail's Point would tell me.

The library was cool after the heat outside. There was one fairly large main room, with a long table down the center. On it were stacks of the more recent books, while along the walls were shelves with older volumes divided by subjects: Science, Biography, Fiction, and the rest. Oddly for such a small community, there was also quite a large section marked "Drama." Beyond this room I could see through an open doorway a room for children's books. The library was shining clean, the bare floors highly waxed, and totally quiet. I seemed to be the only one in the whole building.

"May I help you?"

I turned, startled. Standing in the doorway to the children's section was a woman in her late fifties, her silver hair rigidly waved in a style long out of date, wearing a neat navy-blue dress. Bright eyes shone behind her glasses, and I found myself thinking in that first moment that she resembled a very wise sheep.

"I . . . I was looking for something . . ." I found myself suddenly embarrassed to tell her exactly what I was hoping to find. I knew it was ridiculous, but her eyes were so steady on me that I felt as if what I had hoped to find was something immoral. "Perhaps I should start by asking if I could fill out a card." I went on. "I'll be living in the area for the next few months, Mrs. . . . ?" It seemed a practical way to start a conversation with this woman, who continued to study me with quiet amusement.

"Treble. Miss Lucy Treble. And aren't there enough books at Vail's Point?" she asked pleasantly. Now it was my turn to stare. She smiled briefly and started for her desk in the corner, not bothering to glance back as she continued talking. "You're Alison Howard, aren't you? We'd heard you'd come to do some research on Lionel Vail." She sat down behind her desk and started to fill out a blank library card.

"How on earth did you know that?"

She looked up, her eyes twinkling with good humor. "My dear, you've obviously never lived in a small New England town. Word gets around faster than if we still had the town crier." She stopped writing and folded her hands on the desk in front of her, looking up at me quite seriously. "Tell me, will it be a *good* book on Lionel? Or will it be an attack?"

That last word seemed strangely sharp in this quiet room, but there was no doubt about her concern. I wanted to meet her honesty with my own. "I think he is one of our few genuinely great American writers," I said, not without some defiance. If this woman was to be as antagonistic to the Vails as the local taxi driver, it might be well to draw the battle lines right at the start. But, not exactly to my surprise, the woman at the desk smiled warmly.

"I couldn't agree with you more, Alison. You don't mind if I call you that, do you?" I shook my head. "I've been waiting for someone to do a biography of him. He's been too long neglected." She leaned forward, lowering her voice slightly, although there was still no evidence that there was anyone other than the two of us in the building. "Tell me, is it true that Haidee has agreed to do *The Basilisks* this summer at the theater?"

I gave her a rueful smile. "Word certainly does get around, doesn't it?"

She nodded cheerfully. "We're all interested, you know," she said. "Not just economically, although Lord knows we could use the tourist money that the theater will bring."

"Even with talk of ghosts?" I said, curious as to what her answer would be.

"That's just an added attraction," she said, smiling again. "Besides, they're *our* ghosts. The Vails have been part of this town for years. Not just since they built the great house. Viola was born here . . . did you know that?"

I nodded.

Miss Treble evened a stack of cards on the desk in front of her. It was as automatic a movement as if she were a professional card dealer; she never took her eyes off my face. "Viola's father's family had been here for years. They're all buried in the old graveyard. And when Viola married Matthew Patch . . . well, they became our first family for quite a long time." She sighed a little and looked away from me. "Maybe they still are," she added softly.

"Did you know Lionel Vail?"

She looked back, suddenly on guard. Slowly a softness came over her face. As a young woman she must have been remarkably pretty. "Yes," she said, "I knew Lionel." She hesitated for a moment, but then she obviously decided to volunteer nothing more. But as she reached for the pen to fill out my library card, her hand was trembling.

"Could you tell me about his death? Nobody at the house seems willing to talk about it."

Miss Treble's back stiffened, the skin on the fingers holding the pen suddenly turning white. Then she relaxed and sat back, looking up again. She studied my face for a long moment.

"What is it you want to know?" she said slowly.

"I've heard he killed himself in the theater. Was it in one of the dressing rooms?"

"That's where they found his body." She said each word carefully, but without expression. I could see that Lionel's death had some personal meaning to her.

"There seems to be some dispute whether it was suicide or an accident. I know he'd been drinking . . ."

"He wasn't drinking!" Her words were ice-cold, and her pale eyes snapped. "I don't care what the coroner said! Lionel Vail didn't have one single drink that whole winter." Her soft face was suddenly hard, her little chin jutting forward stubbornly. I started to apologize, but she went on without paying attention.

"I know what they reported, but it wasn't true. Lionel was here that whole winter. He didn't have a car, he had to walk into town. The inn hadn't reopened yet and there was only one place in Westaven that sold liquor." She looked at me defiantly. "And my brother ran that. Lionel never set foot in the place. He never had a drink those last six months, whatever the death report said." Her shoulders began to tremble and the hardness went out of her eyes, but she showed no embarrassment.

The library was silent around us. For a long moment I could think of nothing to say, but then Miss Treble smiled again, her eyes still suspiciously damp. "You don't know very much about Lionel, do you?"

I shook my head and started to explain that I would not, in any case, be the biographer of the dead playwright, but she cut through my explanations.

"He was a wonderful man, a very great talent," said Miss Treble. "I'm not saying he hadn't had problems with the bottle before, but not that winter. He was working, and that was more important to him than anything else. That's why he stayed here, shut up in that great house all by himself: he wanted no temptations while he finished his new play."

"Then . . . you think there *was* a last play?" I asked gently. Even as I listened to her I could see the flaw in her argument. A house as big as Vail's Point was bound to have a wine cellar sufficiently stocked to satisfy even the most hardened drunkard. But it was obviously important to her to believe that Lionel Vail had been sober that winter so many years ago.

But my question seemed to trouble her. The soft pink that flushed her cheeks while she had been defending him faded, and once more her hands trembled. "I don't know," she said finally. "It wouldn't be like him to lie about that." She sighed again. "Still, he lied about . . . other things." She stood up. "What, actually, did you expect to find here, Alison?" she asked looking at me directly.

"I . . . I thought perhaps you might have the local newspaper on file. With the reports of his death. I'd like to read them."

"Files from thirty years ago?" She gave a rueful smile. "I don't think even the newspaper itself has files that far back. And the paper's not here in Westaven, anyway. It's in Conley, the county seat."

I felt worse than foolish then, having been caught prying. If the town already knew about my arrival in less than twenty-four hours, I could only wonder how soon it would get back to the Vails that I had been poking into the circumstances of Lionel's death. Something of what I was thinking must have shown on my face, for Miss Treble reached out a tentative hand to touch my shoulder.

"However, *I* have some news reports here," she said quietly. Her eyes were steady on mine, as if she was asking some question which only I could answer. "Shall we call it . . . my own personal collection? I'll be glad to let you look at it." Before I could answer, she went over to a cabinet under the shelves of the section marked "Drama." "I've kept the clippings all these years," she went on as she took a cardboard box out of the cabinet. "I knew someday somebody would want to write about Lionel. I thought it only right that his own town should keep some record of the end of his life."

She brushed the top of the cardboard box off absently, not noticing she had transferred the dust on the lid to the sleeve of her dress. She put the box down on the long table and started to unfasten the string that held it together. "He left a suicide note, did you know that?" She said it as calmly as if she were reporting that he had had two eyes. "At least they called it that. It was a page torn from a book. Some people say it didn't mean anything, but he'd marked some lines on the page. You'll find it mentioned in the clippings."

She removed the lid of the box and pulled up a golden oak chair to the table. "Take your time," she said as she moved away from the table toward the room beyond. "I've plenty to occupy me in the children's section." Then she paused in the doorway to give me a rather wistful glance. "Only, . . . you *will* be careful with the clippings, won't you? Thirty years . . . they're rather delicate."

"Of course, Miss Treble." I was very grateful to her for this unexpected bonus. For whatever reason she had saved the reports on Lionel's death, it would save me a long trip into the city. For I had faced the fact by now that my curiosity about Lionel's death would not be satisfied until I knew as much as the others. As I sat down, I thought of something, and even before I touched the first clipping in the box I looked at Miss Treble, who stood quietly watching me in the doorway.

"What book was the page torn from? The one that was supposed to be his suicide note?"

"It was a copy of a play," she said before disappearing into the far room. "*Macbeth.*"

CHAPTER ELEVEN

As I started going through the top layer of newspaper clippings, I found myself thinking of Lionel's dressing room as I had seen it that morning, and especially the thin volume on the makeup shelf. That must have been the copy of *Macbeth* from which he had torn his suicide note. Several of the newspaper reports in the box failed even to mention the existence of the piece of paper.

Lucy Treble had been thorough. There were clippings in the box from papers all over the country, even one or two from England. In addition to the actual reporting of Lionel's death, there were several lengthy obituaries complete with pictures of Lionel at various stages of his career. For the first time, I saw what Lionel had been like as a man. He had a strong face; his long, bony forehead usually half covered with a heavy lock of hair, the chin firm, the mouth surprisingly sensitive under his straggling mustache. But it was his eyes that held me. They photographed as dark as night, and even in the most relaxed of poses they had a piercing intensity and haunting sadness that reminded me of someone. And then I realized his sister May had the same eyes.

Most of the news reports could tell me nothing I didn't already know. As Corin had said, Lionel was found in what was called "his" dressing room at the theater (although I could find no mention that Lionel had ever actually appeared on the stage of the Vail's Point playhouse). The reports were unanimous that the cause of death was the mixture of alcohol and barbiturates. He had been alone at Vail's Point that last night. There had indeed been a tremendous storm, which kept the rest of the members of the company from arriving until the following day, when rehearsals for the season were to begin.

Haidee had found him, coming up in the morning with May by car; Esme and Julie, the baby Corin and the other members of the company arriving an hour later from New York by train. Several of the newspaper reports mentioned the fact that Lionel had supposedly been working on a new play, but only two clippings made any reference to a note being found with the dead body. The first merely stated that a piece of paper had been discovered clasped in his clenched hand.

It was the second clipping that told me what I wanted to know.

This, I could see by the date, had been printed several weeks after Lionel's death and burial in the Vail family plot, and was obviously a "Sunday Supplement" piece of the kind that was once popular. It had a lurid headline: "HAS THE CURSE OF MACBETH CLAIMED ANOTHER THEATRICAL VICTIM?"

According to the article, *Macbeth* was known among theater people as a "bad luck" play. The feature writer had done some research on his theme, and the article was filled with quotations from well-known theatrical figures of the period about the accidents and unfortunate fates of people who had somehow been connected with productions of the Shakespearean tragedy.

One of the most universal of superstitions was that no actor ever quoted from *Macbeth* unless rehearsing for the play, and that in British theatrical circles the tragedy was not even referred to by name, but merely called "the Scottish play."

I found myself smiling at some of the stories. Too many great actors had made successes of their appearance in the title role of that tragedy for me to believe there was anything to the superstition. Still . . . it *did* seem strange that, of all plays, Lionel should have selected this one to grasp in the last moment of his life. I would have thought he would have ripped something from his own works if he had intended to leave a message for the world.

It was at the end of the article that I found what I had been looking for: a reproduction of the actual suicide note. It was a page torn from the fifth scene of the fifth act. Most of the page was filled with one of Macbeth's most famous soliloquies, the "sound and fury" speech. The newspaper had printed what looked like a photograph of the note, clear enough to show the wrinkles in the page after it had been smoothed out. And there *were* several lines marked with what seemed to be a heavy pencil. The page looked something like this:

SEYTON: The queen, my lord, is dead.

MACBETH: She should have died hereafter;
There would have been a time for such a word.
Tomorrow, and tomorrow, and tomorrow,
Creeps in this petty pace from day to day,
To the last syllable of recorded time;

> And all our yesterdays have <u>lighted fools</u>
> <u>The way to dusty death</u>. Out, out, brief candle!
> Life's but a walking shadow, a poor player
> That struts and frets his hour upon the stage
> And then is heard no more; it is a tale
> Told by an idiot, full of sound and fury,
> Signifying nothing.
>
> *Enter* a MESSENGER . . .

And that was the end of the page.

I read the speech again, saying it to myself in a whisper as I sat there, wondering what the words had meant to Lionel at that last moment of his life. Why had he deliberately underlined from "recorded" to "death"? The sentence "And all our yesterdays have lighted fools the way to dusty death" could conceivably be the farewell of a man who had fought against giving in to liquor and had lost the battle; a trifle theatrical, perhaps, but none of the Vails was without that quality. But it made no sense for him to have also marked the preceding words: "recorded time." I could not believe his pencil had merely slipped in his drunken and drugged state. The two words were on the line above; he would have had to make a specific effort to mark just those words and no others. Rereading the speech, the marked lines seemed less a lachrymose note of self-pity than a specific message.

Only, of *what?* And to whom?

"Does it puzzle you, too?"

I glanced up. Lucy Treble had quietly re-entered the room and was standing behind me, looking at the last clipping over my shoulder. I handed it to her silently.

"What do you think of it?" I asked, adding cautiously, "It doesn't seem like a suicide note to me."

"I never thought it was. In fact, I've always thought . . ." But then she stopped and put a warning hand on my shoulder. The door to the street had opened and a man came striding in.

He was tall and straight-shouldered, wearing the uniform and hat of a state trooper, and it took a moment for me to realize that this was the same man who had given me the reluctant ride to Vail's Point yesterday. However, now Mr. McNaughton (for I had remembered his name) looked completely different. He was clean-shaven, his uniform starched and pressed, the shield on his blue shirt glittering like sterling silver, his boots a shiny dark brown. But one part of his rudeness remained: he made no attempt to remove his wide-brimmed trooper's hat.

"Lucy," he said as he came in the door, "Carl wanted me to remind you there's a selectmen's meeting tonight."

"I know, Ed," said Miss Treble calmly. She removed her hand from my shoulder and took a step toward the state patrolman. I had a feeling it was less because she wanted to talk to him directly than that she was trying to prevent him from seeing who I was. Or was it the box of faded clippings on the table she was trying to hide?

"Not much point in having a meeting," grumbled McNaughton. "I voted against giving town money to that damned theater in the spring, and I'm not going to change my mind now." Lucy deliberately stepped aside, and for the first time McNaughton could see who was sitting at the library table. "Oh. So it's you," he said coldly, but I could see that he was surprised.

"That's right, Mr. McNaughton." I looked at him levelly. I had no need to act helpless today. I had my own way of getting to Vail's Point.

"Well, you can go right back to the Vails and tell them they're not getting one penny of Westaven money. Not while I'm a selectman." He said it defiantly. It was exactly the kind of challenge that has always brought out the worst in my temper. I stood up. After all, the news would be around town soon enough; I might as well make the announcement myself.

"I don't think the Vails will be appealing to the town for money again, Mr. McNaughton. They've received a foundation grant to reopen the theater." There was a sudden flush of color in his tanned face, and wickedly I hoped he would ask me which foundation had come forward to flout his authority; it would be such a pleasure to tell him.

"What bunch of idiots has gone and done that?" he asked, snapping at the bait.

"The Howard Foundation," I answered, keeping my voice cool. There was a small gasp from Lucy, and I could see the question forming in McNaughton's eyes. "Yes," I went on, not giving him a chance to interrupt, "it's my family's foundation. And we're going to do all we can to revive the reputation of Lionel Vail."

He stood there glaring, the small muscle on the side of his firm jaw twitching slightly. I had made an enemy of him at that moment, if not before, and I had sense enough to realize that he could be a dangerous adversary.

"Surely it will be good for the town for the theater to reopen," I said placatingly. "For the stores and the inn? Won't tourist money be an advantage to everybody?"

"We don't need outsiders."

He turned sharply on his heel and started for the door to the street. "And we don't need anything from the Vails. They never had anything to give but trouble." He swung the door open violently, slamming it against the wall.

I was determined not to get angry, and equally determined to try to make him less hostile if I could. I'd had my moment of surprise and it would be of no help to the Vails or the theater if I made a personal and permanent enemy of the town's only police officer. Not to mention that he (and apparently Lucy) were on the board of selectmen, who ran the town. I remembered Jeb's words of the night before about passing inspection laws, and I moved forward quickly with what I hoped was an ingratiating smile on my face.

"Please, Mr. McNaughton," I said, stopping him just before he went out the door. "I don't want us to be enemies. And I'm sure all the Vails need as many friends as they can get." He continued to look at me stonily, his face as stiff as an engraving of a disapproving Pilgrim Father. I smiled again, and then, trying to move the conversation into safer waters, went on: "By the way, I didn't know your daughter was at the house. I think Yvonne's charming."

But this, too, seemed to have been the wrong thing to say, for without another word he went through the door, banging it behind him loudly. I stood where I was, bewildered, watching him go down the short sidewalk to the street and his patrol car. I turned back to look at Lucy. She stared at me, her soft face without expression, a curious look in her eyes.

"I didn't handle that very well, did I?" I asked after a moment.

"Ed's a hard man, Alison," she said quietly. "I don't think there was any way you could have made it any better." She turned away then, as if she didn't want to face me, and began to put the clippings back into their box.

"Why does he hate the Vails so much?" I asked, moving closer to the table. "Do you know?"

She refused to look at me, and when she spoke her voice was impersonal. "You don't know much about New Englanders, Alison.

We've a lot of interest in other folks' business, but we're mighty tight-mouthed about our own." Then, before I could press her further, she glanced at her wristwatch and with a perfunctory smile ushered me firmly toward the door to the street. "I have to close now," she said. "You'd better be going along."

Then she hesitated. There was a new expression on her face now; cautious, guarded, and it seemed to me as I stood in the doorway, almost a little frightened.

"Be careful," she said in a voice softer than a whisper. "It can be very dangerous at Vail's Point."

Before I could ask what she meant, I was outside on the porch, the library door firmly closed behind me. And to make sure I could make no further attempt to intrude on her, the yellow shades were hastily pulled down over the windows.

I walked the rest of the way into the village, leaving my bicycle in the rack by the library. To be honest with myself, I had to admit my visit had been a mistake. I had learned the facts of Lionel's "suicide" note, but I had made a permanent enemy of McNaughton (and I was sensible enough not to treat that lightly). And Lucy's cryptic warning had set my mind once again on family secrets that were none of my business.

The next hour, I tried to shut off the questions in my head by being as businesslike about my shopping as possible. Deliveries were out of the question, but all the stores agreed to hold my purchases for me. I noticed with some interest that when I mentioned I was staying at Vail's Point nobody seemed to care. Apparently the Vails were simply another family to most of the town of Westaven, and to mention them was to create no reaction one way or the other. After I had bought the office supplies I needed, as well as cleaning equipment and light bulbs, I took the time to get some clothes for the summer. I realized by now that most of what I had brought with me was not appropriate for the days ahead. Sorting through the dusty cartons of Lionel's rooms and pedaling into the village were not activities for which starched, full-skirted cotton and slim linen dresses were designed. So I purchased sleeveless blouses and bermuda shorts, knit shirts and cotton slacks. The colors were brighter than I was used to wearing, but in a small town there was not much choice. And after all, no one from my father's college would be likely to see me.

It was after I finished the last of my shopping and was walking out onto the porch of the old-fashioned country dry-goods store that I saw Jeb Reives. Ever since I'd left the library, some part of my mind had been puzzling over the last clipping I'd read. What, actually, was the *Macbeth* superstition? Jeb would know, I suspected. Only, how to persuade him to tell me?

He was standing in front of a truck on the other side of the street, piling in lumber with the help of a young man. Even before I crossed the street, I knew the boy with Jeb must be Yvonne's brother Frankie. He had Yvonne's coloring: bright red curly hair and a freckled face that seemed always about to break into a grin. I wondered for a moment as I walked toward them how such a surly man as McNaughton could have fathered two such cheerful, exuberant children. Jeb saw me first. He looked up as I crossed the street, squinting his eyes against the afternoon sun.

"I heard you came to town," he said by way of greeting. "How'd you get here?"

"I borrowed Yvonne's bike," I said amicably, nodding to Frankie. He smiled back but made no attempt to introduce himself. "I've had to buy some things . . . I was wondering, would you be able to take them back in the truck for me?" If I could also get a lift, it might give me the chance to talk to Jeb that I needed.

Before he could answer, Frankie spoke up. "Sure, we got plenty of room. Where are your things?"

Jeb leaned with exaggerated laziness against the side of the truck. "I don't know that the lady should trust herself with us," he drawled, eying me with barely concealed amusement. "There might be an accident. Like yesterday."

I'd almost forgotten our first meeting and my suspicions of the white car he'd been driving, but I had the sense to look him straight in the eye and say, "Perhaps if I'm riding with you there'll be no accidents."

He smiled at that and made no further comment.

Within a quarter of an hour we were on our way. The packages of my shopping expedition were in the back of the truck with the lumber. We made one final stop at the library to pick up the bicycle. Frankie piled it in the back with the other things and then climbed in to ride on top of them, leaving me in the front seat with Jeb. Whether he was being perverse or not, Jeb seemed to take his deliberate time in driving back to the house.

"What were you doing at the library?"

It was the first thing Jeb had said since we had left Westaven, and I was not eager to answer him. I was the one with questions that needed answering.

"Just . . . checking something," I said evasively. "Tell me, . . . Jeb." I hesitated over using his first name, but he didn't seem to notice. "What do you know about theatrical superstitions? I mean . . . do actors really believe them?"

"Oh, they believe in them all right. Or if they don't really believe, they're not about to take any chances. And considering how crazy the theater is, who can blame them?"

I was a little surprised at his answer. Somehow I had expected this rather surly and stubborn man to have dismissed the whole idea of superstition as nonsense. He gave me a quick glance, as if he had read my thoughts, and went on, his voice dry with amusement.

"Actually, if you examine any superstition, theater or not, you'll usually find some basis for it in good hard common sense," he said.

"Such as what?"

"Well . . . the color green, for instance," he answered after a moment. "Always considered bad luck on stage. That dates back from when a green curtain was lowered if an actor in the company had died. And even before that it was a sign to the audience that tragedy would be played that night." He laughed a little. "I think that particular superstition died when they painted the sets for *Life with Father* green. Longest-running play we've ever had in the American theater."

I wondered how to start him on the superstition of *Macbeth*. I did not want to ask him directly, for I suspected Jeb knew a great deal more about what I was after than he was admitting. "Tell me some more," I said, trying to look innocently curious.

"More? Well, did you know there's a superstition about whistling in the dressing room?"

"You're joking!"

"Nope. Don't ever do it when some of the old-timers are around. Like Haidee. Or even Julie. If you whistle in a dressing room it's supposed to mean the person nearest the door will be fired. The only way to stop it is for the person who whistled to go outside, turn around three times, and spit over his left shoulder. That's supposed to take the curse off."

I smiled at the thought. "And where is the core of common sense behind that?" I asked, wondering if I could ask him next about *Macbeth*.

"I don't know about the spitting over the shoulder, but about the superstition, well, in a way it makes sense. In the old days, traveling actors would pick up extras and small-part players in every town they played. Naturally these civilians wouldn't have theater discipline; they'd probably been pulled in off the streets and promised a ticket for that evening for their families. So they might be a little restless and noisy waiting in the crowded dressing room to come on for their scene. Can you imagine someone like Edwin Booth or Sarah Bernhardt trying to work out the lights for their death scene and hearing a lot of noise in the wings? They'd send the stage manager to get rid of them if he couldn't quiet them down. The stage manager, being in a hurry, would stick his head into the room and point at the first person he saw . . ."

"Which would be whoever was nearest the door," I filled in.

"Exactly. 'You're fired,' says the stage manager. And a theatrical tradition is born." Jeb was not looking at me now. He was checking the side of the road to his left. "Do you mind if we stop at the theater first? I want to get rid of this lumber."

I nodded and watched as he swerved the truck into a small road, hardly wider than a path, cut through the thick trees that lined the highway. It was not surprising I had missed it on the day before, driving along this road in the rain. The truck bumped on the ruts of the road, and Jeb slowed down as branches scraped the roof of the truck. In another minute we would be at the theater.

"And the tradition about *Macbeth?*" I didn't like asking him directly, but I had no time now to be subtle.

"What?" Our conversation had apparently been forgotten. Jeb frowned a little as he maneuvered the heavy truck along the narrow dirt road.

"Isn't it supposed to be a 'bad luck' play? I mean . . . that's what I'd heard," I added quickly, hoping he wouldn't ask where I'd heard it.

"Any play with a lot of sword fights is bound to have more than its share of accidents. Dangerous ones, too." He looked over at me and, while he was still smiling, there was a different look in his eyes. They were cold . . . and cautious. "Besides," he went on, "there are very few women in the cast of *Macbeth*. That always causes tension among actors. And if the only way to work the tension out is in an on-stage duel . . . well, that can lead to an actor coming back from a tour of *Macbeth* minus an ear or something. And another superstition starts going around."

In a way, I was oddly disappointed. Jeb had made everything seem so . . . practical. I don't know whether I had expected glorious legends or tales of dark secrets, but certainly what he had said gave me no further clue as to why Lionel Vail had picked a page from "the Scottish play" for his suicide note. Something of what I was thinking must have shown in my face, for Jeb stared at me pointedly, his eyes still cold.

"What's the natter?" he asked. "Disappointed?"

"No . . . I just thought there was some sort of superstition about *Macbeth* and death."

"You mean Lionel's suicide note?" He said it quietly, no longer looking at me but concentrating on steering the heavy truck through the bushes that grew on both sides of the narrow track through the woods. "Oh, yes, I know about it. It's one of the great mysteries of the theater. I just didn't expect you to find out about it so fast," he went on. "I guess that explains what you were doing at the library." He swerved the truck sharply and we were in the clearing in front of the theater. Pushing his foot down on the accelerator, the truck jumped forward along the wide curve up to the porch of the building.

"Is there anything wrong about my knowing the circumstances of Lionel's death?" I tried to say it with as much dignity as possible, but it was obviously the wrong time to be correct. Jeb's mood had changed abruptly and he had the same surly look on his face that he had worn the day before.

"No. Only, I don't like people playing games with me. If you want to know something, ask me directly. You don't have to be cute about it."

I could feel my face turning pink, for there was truth in what he had said. And yet, after his curtness and his evasions this morning about Lionel's dressing room, how could I have approached him directly? "All right," I said, trying to keep my voice even but knowing my anger was beginning to show. "Why did you lie about Lionel's dressing room?"

He braked the truck to a halt and then turned toward me, his green eyes snapping with irritation. "Because there are some things that are none of your business! And poking around an old building nobody's been in for years is one of them!"

"Lionel is my business," I said, making no attempt to keep the anger out of my voice. "His life, his death, his rooms . . . and whoever is trying to pry into them!"

He spat out a short angry word. From the corner of my eye I could see Frankie had left the back of the truck and was standing alongside, staring up at us wide-eyed. Jeb glanced at him and then pushed open the door and jumped to the ground. "You don't know what you're talking about," he flung back at me.

I got out of the truck then and went back to where Jeb was lowering the metal panel. "Don't I?" I said. He refused to look at me, but started pulling off the lumber from the truck. "Then, will you explain to me why a theater that's supposed to have been locked tight was standing open this morning? And why there's fresh candle wax in the dressing room that's been closed for thirty years?"

He stopped then, the anger leaving his face and something else replacing it; a look of caution, and something more, as if he'd been waiting for me to make a mistake and I had just made it.

"So you went into the dressing room this morning?" he said calmly. "I had a feeling you would. All right. Let's see what you found."

He started up the steps to the theater with me right behind him, and Frankie, eager as a puppy, trotting along in silence after us. The side shutters of the theater were still open, as were the great barnlike doors on each side of the stage, so I had no trouble making my way to the stage and Lionel's dressing room beyond.

Jeb stood to one side in silence as I pushed open the door. Even though I was anxious to show him what I had seen that morning, I hesitated on the doorstep. Angry or not, I could still feel that curious coldness of the room, that strange quality of something waiting, something strange and more than a little frightening. But I refused to let Jeb see what I was feeling and forced myself to walk over to the window I had looked out that morning. Jeb lounged into the small room after me, Frankie staying out on the stage, a puzzled frown on his young face.

I looked down at the window sill. Jeb was standing so close I could feel his heavy shoulder touching me.

"All right," he said quietly, "let's see what got the lady all worked up about death notes and superstitions and mysterious candle wax."

But the window sill was bare.

The candle wax was gone.

Something of what I felt must have shown on my face as I turned to Jeb, because for once he had no sarcastic remark to make. He stepped back, looked casually at the walls of the small room, and then moved out onto the stage.

"Whatever you saw," he said as he moved away, "it seems to have disappeared. Pity we can't get the rest of the theater cleaned that easy. Thirty years . . . it's going to take a lot of work." He looked at Frankie, the two of them framed in the doorway to the stage. "I'll start taking the lumber off the truck, Frankie. You'd better help the lady close up."

He disappeared, whistling cheerfully as he started for the front of the theater. Frankie stood in the doorway, waiting for me to tell him what I wanted. I could see his thin shoulders shudder for a second as he stepped over the threshold. I knew that he, too, felt the same coldness in the room that I did.

"So this is where it happened," he said quietly.

"You knew about it?" I was surprised. Lionel's death had probably occurred a dozen years before the boy had been born.

"They still talk about it. In the village." He looked at me again, his eyes troubled. "All except Dad. And yet, he was in charge at the time."

"Why does your father hate the Vails so much, Frankie? Or is it just Lionel?"

Frankie showed no more embarrassment than his sister had at the same question. He frowned a little and took a moment to think before he answered.

"I don't know. Yvonne and I have talked about it lots. He didn't always, I know that much. But when he came back from the War, everybody said he was different. Once, he almost got into a fight with Lionel. Did you know that?"

I shook my head. Even when people gave me answers, I thought, it only seemed to lead to more questions.

"It was a couple of weeks before Lionel, . . . Mr. Vail . . .

killed himself. I don't know what the fight was about, but it must have been important. Dad never uses his fists, not even when he's really boiling." He smiled again and faked a shudder. "Let's get out of here. Place gives me the creeps."

"There *was* candle wax on the window sill this morning, Frankie," I said stubbornly. "And it wasn't from thirty years ago either."

"Maybe. But it doesn't look like there's any way you can prove it. Not now."

He went off then to help Jeb at the front of the theater. I closed the door of the dressing room, my head still full of questions. If someone had been in the theater, why did he feel he had to hide all traces of his being there?

I knelt and studied the lock on the door. On impulse, I pulled out the key to Lionel's room in the great house. Whatever else Corin imagined, his advice to keep the key with me at all times was good and I had followed it. I tried the key in the dressing-room door. Lionel Vail wouldn't be the first eccentric to have arranged for all the locks in his life to be opened by one key. My guess was right, and I heard the lock turn.

I stood and stared at the closed door. If I had the only key to the rooms where Lionel had lived and died, whoever had been here the night before would find it impossible to disturb his possessions any further.

That is, if I had the only key . . .

Only, . . . *Who* had been there the night before?

And why?

ACT TWO
(THE PLAY)

Chapter Twelve

The next three weeks went by faster than I could have believed possible. The weather had definitely turned to summer, and I found it easier working in Lionel's suite of rooms in cotton shorts and sandals, my legs bare, my hair during the daytime in a thick braid.

The excitement I'd felt in the house after that first conference continued; Vail's Point never seemed to be quiet now, not even late at night. Even when the sound of voices stopped, there seemed to be a rhythm ticking through the house, somewhat like what I'd heard that first night on my balcony. Jeb had moved in permanently, but luckily his room was in a far corridor from mine and I saw him only at dinner, in the evening. Julie returned from the city with two actresses who also were to stay in the house for the summer. One of them, Rita George, was to play major parts during the season. She had a vaguely familiar face, dark hair and snapping black eyes. The energy and strength of her personality left no doubt that she had talent, but there was an impatient quality about her that seemed to give her handsome face a look of almost permanent irritation. But soon she was deep in conferences with Jeb and Corin, and after the first days I probably said no more than six sentences to her.

The other girl was more of a problem. The house was beginning to fill up now, and Esme had placed this actress in the room adjoining mine, so we shared the connecting bath. Her name was Wendy Troy, and she seemed barely twenty. She was to play small parts, and I sensed even they might be beyond her. If she had been content to sit back quietly and keep her mouth shut, I would have considered her one of the loveliest creatures I had ever seen. She was my height, with beautiful soft blond hair, classic features and a truly remarkable figure. Unfortunately, her voice was thin and whiny, and she never seemed to stop talking. If her conversations had been about the theater, as were most of the others', I might have had more patience, for I found myself gradually becoming more and more fascinated by this strange world I had entered so innocently. But Wendy's conversation was exclusively about herself: which way to wear her hair to make herself more attractive, which fingernail polish to put on for dinner, which earrings went best with her face. I found myself avoiding her, spending most of my time concentrating on the work for which I had come to Vail's Point.

And the work was fascinating. Not that Lionel Vail could have been an easy man to know; in character I suspect he was rather like the irascible Jeb Reives, only, of course, with much more talent. But the chance to go through his papers, to examine his life in detail, made my days as exciting as if I were living through a detective story.

The process of correlating a dead writer's papers may seem dreary to many people, but I found it as stimulating as any work I had ever done. By this time I had read all Lionel's printed works, and I started by dividing those papers that dealt specifically with his plays from those that concerned his personal life. Naturally, certain letters crossed the line and had to be doubly indexed, all of which went on small cards, neatly numbered and dated, all filed in appropriately labeled catalogue boxes.

I learned a lot about Lionel those first weeks, not all of it attractive. He had a truly prodigious romantic life, involving, among others, a lady who later became the wife of a very important senator. There had been a six-month affair with an enchanting movie star about whom, as far as I knew, there had never been any gossip whatsoever. There was also a female novelist who seems to have lost all of her not inconsiderable literary talent whenever she wrote him, and one series of letters, written on heavily scented green stationery and signed by someone named "A," threatening with monotonous regularity to kill herself if Lionel didn't see her again. There was no record that he ever bothered to answer.

The first weeks, I carefully stayed away from the theater. The check from the Foundation had arrived and was placed in a special account in the Westaven bank, and periodically I would sit down with Julie and Haidee and pay the necessary bills.

But I chose not to see what was being done.

However, I knew work was under way. From early morning until the Comfort Hour I could hear the sounds of hammers and saws from the theater, rising through the forest up the hill to the great house. Julie was often in the city, tying up the current plot of her soap opera to be free for rehearsals, which were to begin the middle of July. Corin was absent from breakfast till late in the evening, but when he appeared he was dressed in crisp shirts and new trousers. I did not know whether this was because of Haidee's insistence or because he seemed determined to flirt (equally) with Rita and Wendy.

And me.

Jeb seldom made it to the house even for dinner. Once, I saw him in the village surrounded by a group of young people, apparently the summer students from the nearby college who had signed on as apprentices for the theater, all of them laughing over ice-cream cones as they piled into the Vail's Point truck. He did not seem to notice me as I went by on Yvonne's bicycle. And at the library there was always someone other than Lucy behind the desk when I stopped in.

It was Haidee I got to know best during those first weeks at Vail's Point. Perhaps this was because Esme was busier than usual, taking care of the increased domestic chores of a houseful of people. Even May was occupied with the theater, clearing and arranging the landscaping. So Haidee often had no one to talk to at lunch or during the quiet twilight hour before dinner.

No one to talk to but me.

She was by far the most interesting, exciting person I had ever met. After that first evening there was no hint of the grand star about her; I was accepted as one of the family. No, more than accepted. She seemed genuinely to warm to me, telling me ribald stories of theatrical history, some of them none too flattering to her. One of the most amusing was her chronicle of Julie's father, a handsome English actor who considered marrying Haidee and siring a daughter sufficient work to last him a lifetime and who was then content to make the principal concern of his days the choosing of a proper necktie.

When I asked Haidee whatever had happened to him, she dismissed him with, "Went on tour to South Africa, my dear, and was never heard from again. Shouldn't be surprised if one of the natives ate him." She gave me an enormous wink that left me helpless with laughter.

By this time I knew how unfair Lionel had been in his portrait of Haidee in *The Basilisks*. He was a brilliant writer, I had seen nothing to change my opinion of that; but he was also a man of unreasonable prejudices who had obviously translated his personal angers into the bitter (and often unfair) venom of his plays. Genius as a playwright or not, Lionel was not to be trusted as an accurate reporter.

And so I grew to love Haidee, rather like a wonderful grandmother who could be counted on to beguile and charm you with an amusing story for every occasion. My own grandparents had died before I was born. Haidee made me realize how much I had missed.

She was always attractively dressed at no matter what hour I might see her, and although she expressed interest in my work, I never had a feeling that she was prying into what I may have discovered. Oddly, it was Julie who asked the most questions, the few times that I saw her.

Julie and Corin. But there was a light touch to Corin's questioning, and he asked as much, if not more, about my previous and personal life as he did about his great-uncle's papers. As the time went on, I had the feeling I was unwillingly winning his attentions from Rita and Wendy.

And so the weeks passed and it was time for the first rehearsal. There was to be a reading of *The Basilisks*, the opening play, at the theater that evening, with regular rehearsals to begin the following morning. By now the great house was full, Julie having driven up shortly before noon, clearly exhausted from having taped scenes for her television show in advance. With her she brought Oliver Montague, who was to play the kindly doctor in Lionel's play, as well as character parts through the rest of the summer. Mr. Montague was a heavy man with the look of a contented elephant, his body comfortably sloping downward with the years, his pale blue eyes wise in his sagging face. He took one look around the large living room (we had gathered there before lunch) and came straight toward me.

"And who is this enchanting girl?" he said with a booming voice. Haidee, amusement in her eyes, made the introductions while Oliver continued to stare at me with the lack of embarrassment of a man who enjoys the frankness allowed old age. I was glad I had changed from my working clothes into a fresh lemon linen dress.

"Good heavens, Haidee," he went on, still staring at me. "The child's blushing! I haven't seen anybody do that since Elsie Ferguson played in *The Varying Shore*."

"Nonsense, Oliver," said Haidee. "You're much too young to have seen Elsie Ferguson in that; it was even before my time. And stop making Alison uncomfortable."

"No such thing, Haidee. Actresses adore being stared at," he answered, and smiled warmly. "Don't you, my dear?"

"I'm afraid I'm not an actress, Mr. Montague. But thank you for the compliment."

"Not an actress? Nonsense!" He turned then. Jeb was just coming through the French windows that led to the lawn. For once he was presentable, in a clean white shirt and madras trousers, with even his hair combed, as if he had made some effort at the theater to clean up for lunch. "Jeb, my boy," continued Oliver, "can't you find something for this pretty girl to do on the stage? Anybody as attractive as this ought to be seen."

Jeb looked at Oliver, raising one eyebrow sardonically. "Haven't you heard, Oliver? She's our backer."

Oliver turned back to me then, an exaggerated look of respect in his eyes. "Money, too," he said cheerfully. "Alison, you and I should have met years ago."

"Don't take him seriously," said Haidee. "As long as Oliver has the Players Club to go home to, no woman stands a chance."

Oliver considered that with mock gravity. "Haidee's right, of course. Still, you never know. Now, Alison, you're to sit next to me at meals. I'm making that a clause in my contract. If I'm going to have to learn three enormous parts in the epics planned for this summer, I demand something lovely to look at."

"Don't get taken in, Alison," said Corin cheerfully. "All he wants is someone to cue him on his lines."

"Of course, my boy," said Oliver, not in the least disturbed. "I've always said it's the only valid reason for an actor to marry." Then he looked at me again. "Still . . . a pretty girl with money . . . I'm surprised one of these young bucks hasn't staked a claim on you." He glanced at Corin, his old eyes suddenly shrewd. "Or have they?"

"I've been waiting for you, Mr. Montague," I said demurely. It was impossible not to like the old gentleman, although I was quite sure over the decades he had broken more than his share of hearts.

124

"Oliver, my dear," he said absently. The rest of the others had begun to talk again and Oliver lowered his voice as he turned back to me. "Actually, Julie *did* tell me something about you as we drove up." His eyes were very steady as they looked at me now. "And how is the work coming on Lionel's life?"

"Fairly well." His eyes continued to hold me, as if he were making up his mind about something. "Did you know him?"

"Lionel Vail?" he asked, his voice very low. "Yes, my dear. I knew him. I knew him very well. Someday we must have a long talk about that. And about the last year of his life." He glanced around at the others. None of the family were standing near us, nobody seemed to be paying any attention. Then Oliver Montague said something very strange.

"The last year of his life was the most important, but I suspect you've found that out, haven't you? In your research?"

He continued to study me, his old eyes on mine as if there was more to what he had said than the words implied. I found myself frowning, but before I could ask him what he meant, Esme came in to announce that lunch was ready. With a hearty laugh, Oliver left my side and went over to take Haidee into the dining room.

During the luncheon that followed, Haidee and Oliver seemed to be competing as to who could tell the most outrageous theatrical stories, pulling all of us into their merriment to the point where I saw even May smile from time to time. I was still puzzled by what the old man had said, but there was no opportunity to question him further; for afterward he disappeared immediately to his room to nap before the first reading, which would take place that evening after supper.

It was Jeb who stopped me after lunch, pulling me aside to let Rita leave the room first, followed by the querulous Wendy.

"Actually, Oliver was right." I stared at him, puzzled. Could he have heard what the old man had whispered to me? But I remembered that Jeb had been on the other side of the long room at that moment. I looked at the director uncertainly. "We could use you at the theater. At least tonight, until I figure out who of the crew I can delegate as my assistant."

"Assistant? To what?" I asked him, still not understanding him.

Frankly, I was eager to get back to my work in Lionel's rooms, for what Oliver had said had suddenly put a question in my head.

"Assistant to me," said Jeb. He stood there looking down, his face the usual cool, expressionless mask. "I'll need someone to hand out scripts, take preliminary notes . . . It would be a help. Would you mind? Just for tonight?"

I was so surprised to find Jeb asking instead of commanding that I found myself nodding in agreement. "If you need me, of course. I'll be glad to do what I can."

"Good." He smiled, the same mocking smile I'd seen so many times before. "Besides, you really should see how your money's being spent." With that he turned coolly on his heel and walked out of the dining room.

I had no more time to think of Jeb that afternoon, or even of his curious offer. I went quickly up the great stairs of the house, but instead of going to my room to change back into working clothes, I turned immediately in the opposite direction and hurried to the door to Lionel's study.

I had placed the key to Lionel's room on a thin chain that I kept about my neck, and I found my hand trembling a little as I took it off to unfasten the lock. I felt I knew what I would find that afternoon, or, rather, what I *wouldn't* find, but I was still eager to prove my suspicions correct. Only, once I had the door open, I stopped for a moment on the threshold and looked at the room beyond, almost as if now that I was there I was reluctant to know the truth of what I had guessed.

Lionel's study had changed in the weeks I had been working on his papers. The books still crowded the bookshelves (I had not had a chance to start on them yet), but the rest of the room was already beginning to fall into order. The study was clean now, the cartons had been placed in the bedroom, and I had set up my boxes of card catalogues on a small table near Lionel's roll-top desk. The papers I had been examining that morning were on the desk. Warm afternoon sunlight came in the open window facing west, and a slight breeze brought in the salt smell of the ocean below.

After carefully closing the door behind me, I walked over to the desk. Oliver's words kept repeating themselves in my ears . . . "the last year" . . . "the last year" . . . I sat down on the swivel chair in front of the desk, realizing how stupid I had been. Or perhaps "stupid" was too hard a word. At least, I hoped it was.

You prying little fool, I told myself. Having such a delightful time reading Lionel's love letters! Did you even bother to notice there was *nothing* in *any* of the boxes that related to the last months of his life?

I opened the card catalogue and flipped through my cards, but I knew even as I did there was nothing that had any date more recent than the fall of 1945, when Lionel had been discharged from the Army.

Of course, there were still boxes I had not examined thoroughly, but I had at least looked into all of them, enough to be sure that each box or trunk contained material bulked according to a separate year.

And there was nothing for the winter of 1945–46.

Yet there should have been *something*. Whether or not he had finished that last play, Lionel *had* talked about it. Lucy Treble told me that. The family had planned to produce the play. Corin remembered seeing the pages on his desk. There should have been letters to friends, to his agent (now dead). He had always used them before in working on his plays, as a sounding board. Surely there must be something related to his last winter in all these boxes!

But I knew, sitting there in the afternoon sunlight, that I would find nothing. Whatever had been written—letters or notes or even an outline for the play—was gone.

"Did you finish it, Lionel?" I said in a whisper. "And was the play so dangerous it had to be destroyed?" Another thought struck me. "And did you have to be destroyed as well?"

A breeze came through the open window, and I heard again the two words that Lucy Treble had said to me that first day in the library. They echoed in my brain: "Be careful."

Only, what have I to be careful about? I thought wryly. It had all been arranged long before I came to Vail's Point. I need not have worried about locking the doors to Lionel's rooms; whatever was important to find had already been removed. How foolish they had been, to be so thorough! If they had just left some notes from that last winter, some letters, even a rough outline of the proposed last play, I would have filed it away neatly and conscientiously and left Vail's Point with no further questions.

But now I couldn't stop the questions from coming. It was unbelievable that a man like Lionel Vail would not have received letters that last winter, would have written none, would have made no notes or kept no carbon copies of his business correspondence. And yet that was what someone expected me to believe.

There must be *something,* I thought, as I swiveled the chair around to face the roll-top desk. I'll start all over again, and I may as well begin with this. I had gone through the desk the first morning I started to work on Lionel's papers. It held nothing of any particular interest—typing paper and carbons, scratchpads, pencils, erasers, rubber bands and paper clips—the sort of things that might be found in any office desk.

But now I looked at the desk more carefully. I had no "feeling," or hunch. No chill wind brought shivers down my back as I had felt in the theater dressing room. I did not have any fancies that the dead Lionel was guiding my search; there was no such nonsense as that. I simply knew that somewhere there must be a hint or clue . . . and his desk was the logical place to begin.

I found it an hour later. By then my yellow dress was streaked with dust; it covered my hands, and I was sure there must be some on my face where I had brushed my hair back impatiently. I had taken all the drawers out and examined the contents of each, going through the piles of blank stationery page by page, shaking each pad of paper for something loose that might have lain forgotten these past thirty years. Something that might have escaped the prying eyes of whoever had searched before me. But there was nothing. The sun was lower now, skimming across the tops of the trees to the west. Soon it would be time to get ready for the Comfort Hour and the first rehearsal of the season. I might as well accept Jeb's request, I thought dully. I would have no desire to come back to this room tonight.

It was then, as I was fitting the last drawer back into the desk, that it caught on something.

CHAPTER THIRTEEN

I pulled the drawer out again carefully and reached into the dark vacant space under the desk top. I could feel nothing that might have stopped the drawer. Getting down on my knees, I looked into the opening. I could see two thin strips of wood crossing what would have covered the drawer if it had been in place; these supported the top of the desk. The strip farther back had something stuck to it. It looked like a bit of torn paper. Moving my fingers carefully, I managed to pry it loose.

I realized before I spread the paper open what had happened. Lionel had obviously stuffed papers into this drawer until it was full, and this last page, a thin tissue paper used for carbons, had been on top. When someone had pulled the crowded drawer out, it had been snagged by the wooden ridge; and when the drawer had been replaced, it had been shoved permanently out of sight. I unfolded the page gently and spread it out on the desk to read.

It was a copy of the last sheet of a letter, so I had no idea of the date or to whom it was addressed. But a quick glance told me I had found what I was looking for: the only writing in these rooms that dated from the final winter of Lionel's life. The page started with the end of a sentence:

> . . . *finally finished. The last act has a "murder" scene that's going to cause trouble. Let it. I cannot be concerned with what people think, not the town nor the family. What I have discovered must be told, if only to avenge a terrible wrong, one you have never guessed.*
>
> All Our Yesterdays *is set as the title, the hell with actors worrying about quotes from* Macbeth. *As for the script, it's better than anything I wrote before the War. I have taken the usual precautions, but what can happen now? Rehearsals start Monday.*

There was no signature. I could not expect one on a copy of a letter. But there was no doubt in my mind that Lionel had written it.

I sat back in the swivel chair and read the letter again. There *had* been a last play after all, better than anything he had written before the War, Lionel said, and he was a harsh judge of his own work. But despite the "usual precautions," something *had* happened to the manuscript before that Monday rehearsal: Lionel had died and the play had disappeared.

Bits and pieces of facts that had confused me began to fit themselves into a pattern. Lionel had died in the theater. Why would a man who had taken sleeping pills wander from his own bed? An impulse? Perhaps, but I dismissed the idea as soon as I thought it.

Suppose Lionel had not taken the pills deliberately? Suppose somebody, knowing his weakness, had led him back into drinking? And the lethal combination of barbiturates and alcohol had already been mixed together in the bottle of whiskey? I remembered the first night Corin had shown me Lionel's bedroom, and the empty bottle by his bed. I left the swivel chair and went over to the door to the far room. I had filled it with boxes of papers as I had gone through them, but his cot had not been touched and the bottle was still on the bedside table. I picked it up. The empty bottle was thickly covered with dust. I sniffed at the top of it, although I knew there was no chance that there would be any odor to prove my suspicions. I could not even be sure that this *was* the bottle used, and I knew even the most technically proficient laboratory would never be able to establish contents that had been emptied thirty years before.

I put the bottle carefully down on the table. If what I suspected was correct, Lionel had not killed himself; someone had deliberately murdered him or, at the very least, made him unconscious so that whatever terrible truth he had revealed in his last play could be destroyed. And had waited until the night before the first rehearsals.

Only, rereading the torn page in my hand, I wondered who had the most to fear? The town?

Or the family?

I left Lionel's study shortly after that. It was time to get ready for dinner and the first reading at the theater. But where to hide the scrap of paper I had found? I'll have it copied, I thought, as I walked down the long hall to my room. The next time I get into town. But where can I hide it until then?

I checked the antique gold watch my mother had left me. It swung from a small gold bar pin, and I remembered as I looked at it there was a space behind the watch designed in that more sentimental era for a lover's picture. The thin sheet of paper would just fit in there if I folded it tightly enough. At least I could keep it with me until I could think of a safer place.

Wendy as usual was monopolizing our bathroom. I stepped out of my lemon-yellow dress (now completely covered with dust from the afternoon's search) and slipped on a robe, the piece of paper fitted neatly into the watch.

Then, while I was laying out my clothes for the evening, I began to think about what I had discovered. There was no doubt in my mind that what I suspected was true. However, I realized the Vail family, and even my own father might have a dozen sensible objections to my conclusions. Lionel *could* have taken the pills himself, he *could* have been drinking all that winter, he *could* have been lying even in this last letter about finishing the play.

But I knew he hadn't. Weeks of going through his papers had revealed enough about the man that I knew he would never lie about his work. His deceptions (and I had found proof of many) had always been to avoid becoming entangled with people—their demands, their needs, their desires.

"Bathroom's all yours, Alison."

Wendy's voice came as a surprise, I was still so deep in my thoughts. I hurried in and started my bath. Something else had come back to puzzle me: the page found in Lionel's dead hand.

Why had Lionel underlined the two words *before* the line "And all our yesterdays . . ."? He had done it deliberately. As I sank into the hot water of the bath, I started considering what might have happened, not to Lionel, but to the play. It had never been seen after that last night, destroyed by whoever had mixed the sleeping pills with the liquor.

Or had it been destroyed?

Lionel mentioned in that lost page that he had taken the "usual precautions." Could that mean he had *hidden* the script of his last play? And that the two words he had so carefully underlined—"recorded time"—could that be some sort of hint as to the hiding place for the script?

I got out of the tub and started to dry myself. The whole thing was becoming more and more complicated and (I had to confess) more melodramatic as I thought about it. Still, the Vails were a melodramatic family, given, as I had seen in just these few weeks, to fits of laughter that could end in tears, sudden angers and even swifter affections.

I heard Wendy in the next room preparing for the evening. Finishing drying myself, I went back into my bedroom. I had placed a periwinkle-blue cotton jumper and a short-sleeved white blouse on the bed. It was not my favorite outfit, making me look rather like a student nurse, but the skirt had deep pockets. I suspected Jeb would expect his assistant to carry pads and pencils, a copy of the script and perhaps a dozen other things. The only other skirt I had with pockets was the long patchwork one I had worn the first night at Vail's Point, and I had no intention of sweeping around the dusty theater in that.

For once, the Comfort Hour was brief; nobody seemed interested in drinking, and within twenty minutes we had all taken our places in the dining room. A half hour later we were ready to start for the theater.

We went down the path through the forest, now carefully cleared. Rita and Corin went ahead, Wendy and I behind them. Wendy was wearing a tight black cocktail dress; with her high-heeled black satin pumps, she was finding it difficult to walk. The rest of the company had gone on before while I prepared myself with pencils and pads.

"Wait a minute, Alison. This darn heel . . ."

Wendy stopped and, leaning on me for support, bent down and slipped her foot back into her shoe. Corin and Rita were out of sight now, having made the last turn before the open space in front of the theater. There was still evening light in the sky, clear enough to see our way, and I was eager to catch my first glimpse of the remodeled playhouse before it faded.

"Why on earth did you pick shoes like that to walk through the wood, Wendy?" I said with some exasperation.

She looked up at me, her lovely face sad as a child's for a second. "If I don't wear heels my legs look short . . ." She let her voice trail off. Standing erect again, she smoothed down the tight black crepe of her dress. "Let's face it . . . all these people are real actors. All I've got are my looks."

For a moment I almost felt sorry for her. Wendy seemed so out of place in the middle of a forest. She should be in a city, high in a penthouse, with successful men offering her cigarettes from expensive cases, protecting her as carefully as a hothouse orchid.

"Come on, Wendy. It isn't far now," I said, starting on again.

"I was doing fine as a cigarette girl," she grumbled behind me. "I never would have taken this job except for . . ."

She stopped short, and I turned to look at her, puzzled by what she had left unsaid. She smiled a sly little smile and covered her mouth with a beautifully manicured hand. It was a deliberate gesture, and I found myself not feeling quite so sorry for her now.

"I'm not supposed to tell. It's a secret," she added. She moved triumphantly past me down the path, pushing aside a branch from one of the bushes. And then I could see the theater in front of me.

In that first look I realized the enormous amount of work that had been accomplished in the previous weeks. The walls of the theater had been freshly painted a rich chocolate brown, and all of the merry little gingerbread trim had been restored to its original colors. The railings of the veranda were cream spiced with bright pink, the cornices and pillars of the porch white, the outlines a cheerful apple green. The trim was butter yellow, picking out the curlicues and fretwork that supported the roof of the building. Even the weathervane, at the very peak of the roof, glittered with a fresh splash of gold in the last of the evening sun. The theater was as cheerful as a circus tent. And with all the doors and long windows open, it seemed to be waiting impatiently for an audience to enter.

May had achieved miracles with the meadow that surrounded it. The long grass was neatly cut, the dandelions gone. The circular driveway up to the front porch had been graded and covered with fresh white gravel, and flowers of varying shades of rose and white grew along the walls of the building.

"How lovely!"

I said it more to myself than to Wendy, who also stared at the building.

"What's lovely about it?" she said impatiently. "It's just another summer theater." She wobbled on her high heels across the grass. "Come on, let's get this over with."

If what had happened to the outside of the theater had stunned me, it was nothing to the work that had been done on the inside. The lobby was clean of rubbish, the walls a soft tan, the woodwork glistening white. The ornate box office had been repainted, but in more delicate pastels than before. It looked like an enormous spring flower about to bloom. Inside the theater the canvas had been taken off the seats, and they had been re-covered in garnet velvet that glowed softly in the shadows.

The lights were on in the theater. Ahead of me I could see the bare stage, filled only with folding chairs placed in a semicircle, a small table and two other chairs, backs to the auditorium, facing it. Lights from high above the stage lit the area, and the cast was already gathering along the dressing-room wall of the theater. Jeb turned as Wendy and I came down the aisle.

"I wondered where you were, Alison," he said. "Hand out the scripts, please."

I climbed up the steps onto the stage, Wendy behind me. Of the group on the stage there were many I didn't know. I gathered that the younger ones were apprentices.

"Alison, everybody gets a script."

Jeb did not bother to look up as I came near the table. The books were in a neat pile. I picked them up and started around among the actors. Oliver Montague waved one at me as I offered him his copy.

"Lionel gave me a copy years ago, thanks. I figured I'd better get started on the lines early. Hell of a long time since I had to perform stock," he said.

Haidee, who was standing near him, pulled a packet of pages from the pocket of her full purple caftan.

"You don't need to give me one either, Alison dear," she said. "I had Esme type up sides."

"Good heavens, Haidee. I haven't seen sides in years." Oliver took the pages from Haidee and flipped through them.

"You won't need a script, Haidee?" I was curious about the pages Oliver had taken from her. The pages were about the size of note paper, black with typing.

"No, dear. I never could learn from anything but sides," she said. "This way I just have my own lines on the paper, with the cue words. Saves my having to hunt through the script to find out where I speak. Don't see why actors ever gave up sides . . . they're so much easier."

Oliver chuckled quietly. "Haidee, it wasn't for the sake of the actors that they used sides. It was supposed to prevent actors from duplicating a hit script and going off with it on their own."

"Never worked, of course," said Haidee crisply. "Still, once you get used to learning lines this way, no book helps."

I was suddenly aware of complete silence on the stage. Jeb and the rest of the company were staring at me. They were all in their places by now, except for Jeb, who stood in front of the little table, his back to the shadowy auditorium.

"If you're through talking, Alison, we'd like to get started."

I felt my face flush. He made a gesture to the folding chair at his side, and without looking to see if I had understood him, he turned to the actors and crew who sat quietly watching him. I slipped over to the table and sat down, hoping the others were too absorbed in what the director had to say to notice my awkwardness.

"First, a few basics," he said. "Rehearsals will be every morning and as many hours as Equity will allow in the evening. That's before we open, when the house, the theater, is dark each night. Once we open, Sunday and Monday will be our dark nights, and we'll need those for dress rehearsals.

"*The Basilisks* is a costume show. Alison, I'll want you to have everybody's measurements before they leave tonight. Also, make sure everybody fills out their health insurance cards, and see that the company chooses a union deputy. Wendy"—he glanced at the young girl fingering her script nervously—"check with May about rehearsal sessions on the pantomime."

He turned to May Vail, seated at the far end of the semicircle, her hands folded quietly in the lap of her long gray robe. She looked more like an abbess than ever, but her eyes were bright and alive. "Most of what she has to do on stage as Emily is without words, but that doesn't mean she won't have to work at it." May nodded.

Jeb's tone was one of authority, but without the arrogance I was used to hearing. "Now, everybody, please print your name on your script right now. That's for cast, crew, all of us . . ." He made a point of doing it on the cover of his own script, borrowing a pen from me. "*The Basilisks* is out of print. So if one of you loses your script, it means a day wasted while we try to get another copy from New York. So write your names on your scripts and hang on to them."

I sat back then, making notes, my own embarrassment forgotten. Jeb was clearly in charge and, even more clearly, knew what he was doing. I looked at the faces in front of me . . . the young college students getting their first chance to work in a professional theater. Next to them, the cast, all of them sitting forward at attention. Even the oldest and most experienced members of the company, Haidee and Oliver, had that same look in their eyes, a look of complete and total concentration. More than that. It was a look of what I can only call joy. This is where they wanted to be; they were about to start the work they were meant to do, and there wasn't one of them who would have traded his chair in that charmed, listening half circle for all the money in the world.

Except, perhaps, for Wendy.

CHAPTER FOURTEEN

"What have you discovered?"

"I . . . I don't know what you're talking about."

"Come on, Alison, you don't fool me. I've been watching you all evening. At dinner, at the first rehearsal. Your eyes give you away, did you know that? Something's happened since lunch, something exciting, and if it has anything to do with Great-Uncle Lionel, I want to know about it."

I looked up at Corin. He stood in front of me, as if to shield my face from the prying glances of the rest of the people in the room. But no one was looking at us, no one was paying any attention.

The whole company had come back to the great house after the reading, all of us threading our way through the dark woods, flashlights painting strange shadows on the old trees. It was after eleven by then, but Esme had the house brilliantly lit, and the long dining-room table was covered with dishes and platters of food. Golden scrambled eggs thick with country cream simmered in twin chafing dishes. Tiny sausages and crisp bacon were being kept warm under covers, and the chicken curry, neglected at dinner, had been reheated and wrapped in the thinnest of crepes. There were pitchers of cold milk, buckets of ice for drinks, cans of frosty beer stacked high on wide silver trays and, on the sideboard, coffee bubbled in a huge urn. The company from Haidee down to the youngest apprentice fell on the food as if they had not eaten in days.

I had filled my plate and wandered into the great drawing room next to the dining room. Sitting on the step leading to the section of the room closest to the porch, I was content to be alone in the shadows. I wanted to think about the piece of paper I had found that afternoon, now safely folded and hidden in the antique watch I wore pinned to my dress. The company was spread through the two great rooms, for once filling them with laughter and the sound of eager, excited voices. Haidee was holding court in the dining room, Julie at her side. Perhaps I was the only one to notice the wistful look in Julie's eyes when Jeb, his hands full of plates and glasses, left the dining room to sit with the younger members of the company clustered about the great stone fireplace in the drawing room. But if Julie was disappointed in Jeb's defection, she said nothing and, turning back to Oliver, she joined his laughter over some theatrical anecdote.

I had not been aware that Corin had followed me out of the dining room, so to see him suddenly standing in front of me was startling. He continued to stare down at me as if he were willing his eyes to read in my face what he wanted to know. He lowered his voice, although no one was sitting near us. "Is it about Lionel? About the last play?"

"You told me the day I came here I shouldn't trust anybody. Not even you."

I was hedging, and he knew it, for he made a swift impatient movement with his free hand. "That was about the key to Lionel's rooms. I didn't mean it about what you might find." He pursed his lips and continued to study my face. "You *have* found something, haven't you, Alison?"

I made up my mind then and stood up. "Let's go out on the porch, Corin." He let me lead the way. No one in the far dining room saw us leave the room, and if I thought I saw Jeb look up as we went out, it was only an impersonal glance before he returned to the laughter of the young students sprawled at his feet.

The thin moon was hidden that night, and beyond the lowest step the lawn stretched far out into the darkness, almost as if we were standing on a lighted pier beside an endless, silent ocean. Above us, mosquitoes and tiny moths circled the two bare bulbs that lit the porch. Some of the great wicker chairs had been pulled onto the porch, and I sank down into one of them, placing my half-empty plate on the floor beside me. Corin sat opposite, his eyes never leaving my face.

"Suppose I told you I have proof there *was* a last play?" I began quietly. "And that what Lionel wrote may very well have caused his death?"

"Are you sure?" All the laughter had disappeared from Corin; his face was grim, but there was something else—a glitter in his dark eyes as if he could barely contain his excitement.

"I think so. But other people might not be."

I told him then what I had discovered, leaving out only the cryptic words that Oliver had said at lunchtime that had started my search. When I had finished, I unfastened the watch from my dress, opened the catch at the back of it and removed the carefully folded piece of thin paper. Corin read it in silence and handed it back to me. He slumped down in his chair, no longer looking at me but at the darkness beyond.

"So he did finish it," he said at last.

"It's the title of the play that's important," I said. "Corin, it makes a whole different thing out of that page from *Macbeth* that was supposed to be his suicide note."

Corin snorted impatiently. "He never committed suicide. I never believed that."

"Then it was . . . murder." The word seemed to hang in the silence between us, far too melodramatic a word for the quiet summer night around us.

Corin scratched at an insect that had landed on his arm, and somehow that small gesture made everything real again. "No, I don't think it was murder," he said thoughtfully. "Whoever got him drunk may just have wanted him to be unconscious, start him on another binge. Lionel used to have monumental ones, from what I heard. By the time he came out of it, they might have been able to persuade him that he had destroyed the play himself."

"But the sleeping pills . . . ?"

"Could have been an accident. Lionel might have wanted a good night's rest before that first rehearsal. We don't *know* they were mixed with what he drank that night."

He scrunched farther down into the old wicker chair, making it creak sharply, and stretched his legs out in front of him. "The 'murder' scene, Lionel called it," he said quietly. "I wonder what that was about?"

"Corin, the important thing was he wrote that he had taken 'precautions' about the script." I tried to keep my voice quiet, but now I was seized with the same impatience that had gripped Corin. "Doesn't that mean that the words he underlined in the last moments of his life take on another meaning?"

"He may not have known they were the last moments of his life. He may just have suspected someone was plotting against him. And the play." Corin's voice was controlled, but I could feel his excitement rising again. "And he may have suspected whoever got him drunk might be coming back to see if he was out cold. If he really thought he was going to die, he would have left some clue about the killer."

" 'all our yesterdays have lighted fools the way to dusty death' . . . that sounds to me like he knew." I folded the paper again slowly and put it back inside my watch. A breeze had come up from the unseen ocean to our left. It made the lace curtains of the open windows tremble behind us, and I felt myself shiver slightly.

Corin paid no attention. "Recorded time," he whispered, still staring at the dark night beyond the porch. "I always thought that was a clue of some kind. One summer, when I was about twenty, I even went through every clock in the house, just on the chance that Lionel meant that as a hiding place." He smiled wryly. "And all the phonographs and record players. Didn't find a thing, of course."

I smiled. "I thought of that, too, this afternoon," I said. "Only, I didn't know how to go about making a search. There are so many rooms in this house. And I can't quite see your family letting me poke into everything."

"Recorded time," Corin said again, as if he had not heard me. "It has to mean something, Alison. If we can only figure out what."

I went up to my room shortly after that. The party was beginning to break up, Jeb reminding everybody that rehearsals would begin promptly at ten the following morning. I was suddenly tired, as if the day had been too long and too full of surprises for my mind to absorb. I slipped off to sleep easily, but it was not a restful sleep. And then, at two in the morning, the sound of a quarrel awoke me.

I lay quietly in bed in the darkness, the only light the illuminated dial of my clock on the bureau turned so I could see it without moving. The voices were coming through the closed door to the bathroom that connected my room with Wendy's. I could not hear the words that were being said, but there was no mistaking the tone of complaint in Wendy's thin voice. Nor could I hear the words of the man she was arguing with; I could only hear enough to recognize his voice. After a few moments the voices stopped and I heard the door to her room being closed quietly but firmly and the sounds of careful footsteps disappearing down the hall. I lay as still as I could, trying to forget the questions in my mind.

Why was Jeb Reives in Wendy's bedroom at two o'clock in the morning?

And why had they quarreled?

I fell asleep finally, to toss restlessly, haunted by dreams I could not quite remember when I awoke the following morning. It was a steaming-hot day, the sun partially obscured by haze, but the energy was so strong among the company when they gathered for breakfast the heat seemed unimportant.

I couldn't help looking at Wendy closely that morning at breakfast, but she seemed much the same. It was Julie who looked as if she had spent the night in tears. She wore dark glasses throughout the meal, as if the sun coming in the windows was too bright for her to face. But I could see that behind the glasses her eyes were red and puffy. I wondered to myself if she knew that Jeb and Wendy were in some way involved, but her manner toward the young girl was as cool and impersonal as always. Perhaps loving a man considerably younger than herself had taught her restraint.

Jeb himself was not present, having gone on to the theater before the others. I avoided Corin's questioning face, going quickly to Lionel's study after breakfast and locking the door firmly behind me.

But through the days that followed I found it almost impossible to be alone at Vail's Point. Even during the long hours I spent on Lionel's papers (for there was still much to put in order, quite apart from the last mysterious months of his life), I was never out of the sight of others. May had appropriated the widow's walk that faced the sea to rehearse Wendy in her pantomime as the mute Emily. It was almost directly over Lionel's study, jutting out to the left above the room where I was working, and without raising my head I could see the two women at work.

The house itself hummed with activity. Furniture was constantly disappearing from the main rooms, to be carried down to the theater by sweating young boys and girls in paint-stained blue jeans. Their faces were always creased with serious, intense expressions, and all of them were clearly having the best time of their lives.

After the first day of rehearsal, Haidee took to walking along the side of the house that faced the water. From then on, when she was not rehearsing in the theater, she would pace back and forth, her head down, her step as methodic as a prisoner in a jailyard, muttering her lines over and over again. Behind her waddled Esme, rather like a cow trying to keep up with a whippet. She held the now dog-eared sides for Haidee's part close to her shortsighted little eyes, speaking only when Haidee, forgetting a word, would snap her fingers.

With many a groan, Oliver settled on the front porch as his place to learn the play. He would sit there hour after hour poring over his script, lifting his eyes only when he sensed someone passing that he thought might be trapped into cuing him. I tried to question him about Lionel once, but he brushed it away impatiently and I did not persist. For of all the company he was the only one to have large parts in all three of the plays planned for the season.

Julie seemed to be everywhere at once, cutting sandwiches at midnight after an evening rehearsal, on the phone to New York a dozen times a day trying to pry loose more equipment for the theater or checking on the arrival of the costumes.

What was strange was the way the Vails took to rehearsing Lionel's play about their family. If certain words that Julie said to Haidee were words that once Haidee herself had used in real life, I saw no sign that either actress was concerned about it. Haidee's performance grew slowly. Before my eyes she changed into a frail, pitiful old woman, heartbreaking to watch as she gradually realized her greedy family intended to force her into an insane asylum.

It was Julie who surprised me the most. Gone was the warm and lovely woman I sat down with each night at dinner. Instead, she became a subtle, cruel monster before my eyes, so realistically that I found myself wondering each time I saw them at work . . . who are these people? Which is the *real* Julie? The *real* Haidee?

The constant presence of people around me made it impossible for me to search for what I was now hopeful still existed: the lost play of Lionel Vail. My only consolation was that if the person who had carried a candle to Lionel's dressing room the night of my arrival was also searching for the manuscript, he was as out of luck as I. For the house was never still and no room empty for long.

In the daytime I continued my work in Lionel's study. Obviously I had had all the luck I was to receive, for I found no more lost pages that related to the final months of his life. After supper I would inevitably find myself wandering down to the theater to watch the evening rehearsals. At first I was shy about it, creeping into the theater as quietly as I could, taking my place in the very last row. But after a day or so, Jeb seemed to sense when I was in the auditorium, and occasionally he would shout at me to move around the theater and tell him if the scene he was directing looked "all right" from various parts of the house. It was a pleasure to have even this small share in the work the company was doing, for quite soon I realized not only was I about to see a superb production of Lionel's prize-winning play, but that a major part of the success would be due to Jeb's direction.

The only member of the cast who failed to improve was Wendy. She had few words to say. Lionel had written only three short scenes for the character: one at the beginning of the play, when the greedy relatives arrive; one in which Helen (the part Julie played) tempted the nearly mute girl with her jewels; and finally the renunciation scene in the last act, leading to the girl's accepting the glass from her grandmother and running off up the great staircase.

But Wendy seemed indifferent to the part. She would either forget her few lines or the places where she was to move, or else she would speak too early or too late. Since two of her scenes were with Haidee, her mistakes destroyed the rhythm of the older woman's performance. After Wendy made three such mistakes in a row one evening, Haidee shot her a steely look, clamping her mouth shut in a thin hard line. But with more patience than I would have expected of her, she left it to Jeb to correct the girl.

Even Wendy's appearance was against her. Her delicate features seemed to fade out on the stage, and she moved awkwardly, tripping over the long piece of sheeting tied around the waist of her skintight slacks. All the women dragged the same material through rehearsals to accustom them to the long dresses they would be wearing. Only Wendy seemed unable to handle her "costume."

The opening night was to be the following Tuesday. The actors urged me at supper to attend the dress rehearsal the night before the opening, but I decided to save the pleasure of seeing them in full costume and makeup, acting in front of the sets Jeb had designed and lit, until the opening performance. Eager to have someone in the auditorium, Jeb insisted that Yvonne and Frankie come down to the theater. So after supper that Monday I was alone in the house, and I allowed myself the luxury of a long hot bath, shampooing and then drying and brushing my hair, knowing it would be a long time before anybody would be back to disturb me. My hair had turned lighter from the sun in the past weeks, and while I spent too many hours in Lionel's study to have acquired a tan, there was more color in my face than when I arrived at Vail's Point.

I wrapped a bandanna-blue cotton dress around me and tied the long sash securely. As I slipped a pair of sandals on my bare feet I heard footsteps coming down the hall. Without bothering to knock, Wendy banged open the door and came into my room. She was in the tight orange shorts and blouse she had worn at supper, but her face was thickly smeared with theatrical makeup, and heavy false eyelashes weighed down her eyelids. She looked smudged and tired, and I could see that she had been crying.

"Wendy, what on earth . . . ?" I started to ask, but she paid no attention, just flung herself on my bed, her lower lip trembling indignantly.

"He yelled at me," she said, and I could see she was ready to cry again. "Right in front of everybody. Just because I couldn't remember those dumb words! I never wanted to act in his old theater, anyway."

"Who yelled at you?" I asked quietly, although I knew the answer before she spoke.

"Jeb, of course! He thinks he's God Almighty up here. He wasn't like that in New York, I can tell you. Oh, no, nothing was too good for me then. Coming in every night, hanging around the bar till all my regulars thought he was some kind of husband or something. Serve him right if I got a train out of here tonight and left him with his old show."

I knew as she said it she was seriously considering the possibility. I also knew exactly what it would do to the carefully planned structure of Jeb's production. Wendy's part was not large, but she was on stage during three of the major scenes of the play and it would be impossible to replace her before the opening the following night. Rather than give in to my first reaction of irritation, I made a determined effort to calm her down.

"Wendy," I began tactfully, "everyone's on edge tonight. It's only natural. Even I can understand that about a dress rehearsal. If Jeb was impatient, or even angry . . . well, I'm sure he didn't mean it."

She snorted and then, sitting up on my bed, began to peel off her false eyelashes. "You don't understand as much as you think, Alison. There's a lot more going on here than just some dumb play."

I stared at her. That sly look I'd seen before had come back to her face, and I found it hard to speak to her patiently. "I don't know what you're talking about, Wendy," I said as calmly as I could. "But I do know this could be a wonderful opportunity for you. There'll be New York critics here tomorrow and through the week. And producers. Haidee and Julie are big names in the theater, not to mention reopening the Vail's Point Theater after all these years with one of Lionel's plays."

She broke in then, looking at me with an odd expression in her pale eyes. "Especially that, right? The dead Lionel Vail you're so curious about? Well, I could tell you a few things about him you don't know!" She said it triumphantly, her eyes studying my face to see if I would show surprise.

"And what do you know about Lionel Vail?" I asked, without quite as much control as I had managed before.

She tilted her head saucily. "I know Julie hated him."

I must have made some sound of surprise, for she smiled a little. "That's right. The sainted Julie Vail, everybody's favorite soap-opera queen. Miss Goody Two-shoes herself. She hated Lionel enough to want to kill him. She even tried it once. No wonder he called this play about his family 'The Monsters.'"

My lips felt suddenly dry. I ran the tip of my tongue over them nervously, knowing that Wendy was watching every movement I made. "Where . . . where did you hear that?" I asked. I could barely say the words loud enough to be heard.

"Jeb let it slip one night. He told me lots of things. Like what makes May Vail so crazy." She looked at me shrewdly. "She is, you know. She goes off into the woods almost every night. I've seen her from my window."

I thought of the first night I came to Vail's Point and how I had watched May disappearing into the forest. So Wendy had seen it as well!

"That's something to do with Lionel, too," Wendy went on, smiling a little. "Julie told Jeb that. Only, nobody knows why." She pouted again, sticking her lip out sulkily. "A lot I care!"

I turned to the window. Through the dark trees I could see the lights twinkling from the theater. "Is rehearsal over?" I asked.

For some reason I felt strangely alone at that moment, even though I knew Wendy was still behind me, sullenly playing with the false eyelashes she had ripped off. The sky outside was dark by now; a few stars had already come out, and the roof of the porte-cochere and the empty concrete driveway below were silver from the moon rising on the far side of the house.

"No, they're going over the last scene again. But when he yelled at me, I left. I don't take that from anybody!"

I looked at her. Whatever secrets she had been told, she had obviously not understood. Or perhaps she just didn't care. I wanted to be by myself now, without having to listen to her thin, complaining voice.

"Maybe, Wendy, if you practiced by yourself you'd feel more comfortable in the part." She gave me a quick glance and then went back to studying her long nails.

"'Never! Never!' . . . how do you practice that?" she said sullenly, quoting her last words in the renunciation scene.

"You could try moving around in your costume. Till you felt comfortable in it." I sensed her first anger was gone and that she was looking for a way to stay with the company that would satisfy her pride.

"My costume's at the theater."

"Haven't you got a long skirt to practice walking in? That would do just as well. Then, by the time everybody comes back from the theater, you'll feel better . . . and you'll find everything's been forgotten."

"I don't have a long skirt." The sulkiness was still in her voice, but at least she was being more reasonable than when she had first come into my room.

"I do." I went over to the closet and pulled out the patchwork skirt I had worn my first night at Vail's Point. It had stayed at the back of the closet, not only because I still associated it with the unpleasantness of that evening, but because it had been too heavy to wear on the warm nights that followed. I pulled it out and offered it to Wendy, who held it up, her eyes appraising the design and material. She was obviously not impressed.

"Why not take it up on one of the widow's walks? There'll be enough light with the moon, and it'll be cooler than down here." I was determined not to spend the next hour with Wendy, alternating between complaints and veiled references to secrets. She seemed to sense my feelings, for she got up off my bed, the skirt still in her hands, and started for the door that led to her own room.

"Might as well," she said. "It's not as if there was anything else to do." She slung the full folds of the long skirt over her shoulder sulkily and slammed out of the room.

146

I took a deep breath. I didn't really think she would have made good her threat and deserted the company the night before the opening, but she was just angry enough to want to cause trouble. The room was stifling. I went over to the heavy glass lamp by my bed to turn it off. But I hesitated by the open window. There was the beginning of a breeze; it moved the leaves of the trees between the house and the theater softly, like a voice whispering. As I stood, half hidden by the curtains, I could see someone moving out of the woods below.

It was a tall figure, wearing even on this hot night a long cloak. I knew as it drifted closer to the house it must be May. If she had left the theater, the rehearsal must be nearly finished. She came out of the dark shadows of the trees, and for a moment I could see her face under the full hood, the deep eyes, the strong lines of her cheekbones and chin.

She stopped for a moment, not staring at the house as if she expected anyone to be watching her, but, rather, as if she were making up her mind about something. Then, her decision made, she swerved and started back into the dark woods, but in another direction, away from the theater, along the path she had taken that first night.

What Wendy had said was still in my mind. Which is the only excuse I can give for following May. I left my room quickly, practically running down the long corridor to the main staircase. Where did the old woman go that was not the theater and not the house?

I hurried down the great staircase. The drawing room was empty; only a few of the smaller table lamps had been lit, and most of the huge room was in shadows. Slipping out one of the open French windows, I ran across the driveway. The moon was not full, but there was enough to see the forest path ahead that led to the theater. But May had not gone that way. I started toward the section of the woods into which she had disappeared. Somewhere among these thick trees there must be a path. I knew the old woman would not be able to break her way through the bushes that filled the forest without something to guide her.

The path was easier to find than I thought, perhaps easier to find in the moonlight than it would have been during the day, for the silver light touched the trees at an odd angle, showing a deep cleft where there was an opening. Once past the first low bushes I could see a gravel walk, long fallen into disuse, but as clear as the one to the theater down the hill.

The path led upward through the woods. I had to move slowly, for I could not see my way except from time to time when the moonlight broke through the branches overhead. And I wanted to move quietly, for I had no wish for May to know that I was following her. Oddly, it never crossed my mind that I might confront her in the middle of the woods, that she might have finished her walk and already be starting back for the main house. If I had thought about that, I might perhaps have hesitated. But I do not think it would have prevented me from going on.

All along the path I could see the lights of the theater winking through the darkness to my left. But I could hear no voices or sounds of the company at rehearsal; I was too far away. Gradually the path grew wider and the trees not so close to the path, and I could move more quickly. The hill was steeper now, and up ahead I could see the crest. There seemed to be a cleared space at the top.

I stepped off the path then, moving cautiously from the shadow of one great tree to the next, for I had the feeling that May was directly ahead, up on the edge of the hill where the trees had been cleared away. Finally I was close enough to see the reason for the clearing.

The top of the hill had been leveled slightly and once, long ago, all the trees and bushes had been cut away. But the years of neglect that showed wherever one looked at Vail's Point were in evidence there as well: scrub brush was pushing up in the clear area, long grass weaved itself around the rusting iron fence that surrounded the clearing, and wind-blown branches covered the once-neat walks between the gravestones.

I had come upon the Vail family cemetery.

I stood there in the shadows, remembering what Lucy Treble had said that first day I had gone into town: that Lionel was buried in the family graveyard. Weeks had gone by since then, and I'd not even thought to look for it! Moonlight painted the top of the hill a silver white. Some of the old gravestones had settled into strange angles, like jagged black teeth against the sky. And in the very middle of the cemetery, her back toward me, her arms stretched out toward the stars, stood May.

She was motionless for a long moment. Then, as I watched, her thick figure in its long robes began to sway. I almost stepped forward, afraid she was about to fall, but I soon saw there was a pattern to her movements. Her arms held out the deep folds of her cloak like butterfly wings, and slowly she began to step from side to side, forcing her old body into a strange and unreal dance. Something stood in the middle of the area that she circled again and again, always with the same slow rhythm. It took me a few minutes to realize what was the center of her dance. I had been too far away at first to recognize it was an ancient stone sundial.

A sundial . . .

For a second I stopped breathing. What was a sundial but . . . *recorded time?* My mind was racing now, thinking of what Wendy had said about May and Lionel. Could this be where he had hidden the script, that summer so many years ago? And was May dancing, like some priestess at a forgotten temple, the dance of guardian?

Standing there in the shadows, I found myself thinking of something even more important than Lionel and his work. May, too, was an artist, even though her tall, aged body could no longer move with the grace she yearned to convey. How tragic her life must have been, I thought. Never able to fit into the conventional images of the dancers of her day, she had had to watch her talent and life decay without ever having the chance to express the art she felt as passionately as Lionel had felt about writing, or Haidee did about acting. No wonder May had closed a wall of silence around her—to retreat from the world and its people, who could never understand the agony she had suffered all her life.

For I could feel, as I watched May silently move in the moonlight of that summer night, her body no longer young, her steps no longer sure, that of all the Vails, May perhaps had been the greatest artist.

As tears filled my eyes, I heard from somewhere behind us a scream that split the silence of the night.

CHAPTER FIFTEEN

I knew, even as I turned, that the scream had come from the house. Without looking back to see if May had heard it as well, I started down the hill. I wasted no time in trying to move quietly; the scream still echoed in my ears too full of pain and terror for me to worry about precautions. I could see in the darkness lights moving through the woods. The scream must have been heard by the people at the theater, too.

By the time I reached the foot of the hill, two or three of the actors had gathered in a circle in the open area between the porte-cochere and the deserted garages beyond. They had their backs to me, their flashlights trained on something that lay silent on the cracked concrete that stretched along this side of the house. As I pushed through the last bushes, I could see more people hurrying from the theater, the lights in their hands throwing the shadows of the actors who stood in the silent circle high against the walls of the house.

And still the figure on the driveway did not move.

I came closer then, slipping between Rita and Oliver. They did not turn to look at me, but just silently stepped aside to allow me to join them.

There on the driveway in front of me, her body twisted in such a strange angle that I knew at once she was dead, lay Wendy.

The next hour was a confused blur of voices and questions and people moving in and out of the house like frightened animals. Jeb quickly took charge, sending Esme for a sheet to cover the broken body on the ground, stating that nothing should be touched before the police arrived. He assigned some of the young men of the back-stage crew the duty of guarding the body. The rest of the company grew quiet, obviously relieved to have someone giving orders.

But until they brought the sheet to cover Wendy, I could not move away. She had put on my long skirt; it spread over the concrete pavement where her body had landed. Only, now there were red patches in the blue-and-white material: blood seeping through from her dead body. How did it happen? I thought, but I could not make myself speak. Julie swung her flashlight up along the walls of the house. High above us we could see a broken railing on the widow's walk.

"She must have gone up to the roof, Jeb," Julie said quietly. "And if she leaned against the railing . . ." Her voice broke, and when she forced herself to speak again the words came out as soft as a whisper. "That wood's been rotting for years."

"But why was she wearing Alison's skirt?" said Jeb. He turned to me, as if for the first time he was aware I was standing next to him. Even in the darkness I could see a strange glitter in his green eyes.

"I lent it to her," I said. "I . . . I thought she might want to practice, using it like her costume. She was upset about what happened at the theater tonight." He made no answer, just continued to stare down at me. "It was I who sent her up to the roof. I thought it might be cooler there . . ." I could hear my voice growing thin and shrill, and I started to tremble. Jeb quickly put his arm around my shoulders and moved me toward Julie, turning me so I could no longer see the body on the ground.

"Take her inside, Julie," Jeb ordered. "There'll be time enough for questions when the police get here."

Julie led me into the house, and as soon as I was settled on one of the sofas in the drawing room, Haidee appeared with a large glass of brandy and insisted I drink it down. It burned my throat, but the warmth it gave stopped me from trembling. I noticed as I lay back on the sofa that May had joined the silent actors clustered around me. She started to move forward, her dark eyes steady on me, as if there was a question she wanted to ask. I wondered if she knew I had followed her up the hill. But before she could speak we all fell silent, listening to the police siren far off in the distance coming closer and closer.

I knew, of course, even before we heard the car screech to a stop outside, that Ed McNaughton would be in charge of the investigation. He was the only police officer in the town of Westaven, and whatever his feelings might be about the house and the people of Vail's Point, he could hardly refuse his official duty. But there was no tension as he questioned us. He looked at us impersonally as if we were total strangers, and there seemed to be no particular reaction from the Vails when they answered him. The tall young doctor that McNaughton had brought with him confirmed that Wendy had broken her neck in the fall.

The state trooper and some of the others then went up to the widow's walk to examine the railing. The wood was, as Julie had said, rotting. If Wendy had tripped while wearing my long skirt and had fallen against the railing with all her weight, the weakened balustrade would indeed have broken. Even if she had merely leaned against it or rested on it for a moment, it could not have supported her.

McNaughton made no comment, but quietly jotted down the answers to his questions in a small notebook he had pulled out of the pocket of his freshly starched blue uniform. He kept his face expressionless even when he questioned his own children. Yvonne and Frankie were unable to give him any answers; they had both been at the theater watching the rehearsal. The rest of the company had as little to offer. They had all been at the theater taking off their costumes and makeup.

Only Jeb admitted to having been alone. He was in the box office, he said, going over notes he had made during the runthrough of the play. McNaughton made no comment about this.

By the time the state trooper got around to asking me where I had been, I was prepared. I had already told him about lending the dead girl my long patchwork skirt and suggesting the widow's walk to her. Now when he asked me where I was when I heard the scream, I looked him straight in the eye and told him I had decided to walk down to the theater after all. I had been in the woods, I said firmly, which was not exactly a lie. But I was not going to sit there in front of May and reveal that I had followed her. Not until I had a chance to find out if the sundial in the graveyard was the hiding place that Lionel had chosen for his last play.

McNaughton seemed to accept my story. But when he turned to May, she answered him honestly, her voice deep and hoarse.

"I was up at the family cemetery," she said. And then she added, "I go there sometimes at night. When I am . . . disturbed."

We all fell silent, realizing how much pain it must have been for May to relive through the long rehearsals Lionel's bitter history of her family and her own tragedy.

The state trooper looked at her for a long moment, but then he carefully wrote down her answer and closed his notebook. He glanced at the young doctor who had just come in through the

French windows. The doctor nodded in answer to McNaughton's silent question, and I knew without asking that Wendy's body had been removed.

"There'll have to be an inquest tomorrow," McNaughton said quietly. There was a sound from one of the company gathered around us; not quite a gasp, but it broke the silence. Haidee moved forward, her shoulders stiff, a small frown pulling her eyebrows together.

"But it was an accident," she said. "The poor girl fell . . ."

McNaughton looked down at her, and though he continued to keep his face expressionless, there was no mistaking he was giving her orders. "There'll still have to be an inquest," he said. "The county courthouse. Tomorrow morning. I'll want all the people who are living at Vail's Point to be present." He looked at his children. Yvonne grinned back, but something in her father's face sobered her and she closed her mouth and nodded silently.

"The inquest," McNaughton added dryly, "will be at 9 A.M."

There was an audible groan from one of the actors. McNaughton paid no attention. He surveyed us all, touched the tip of his hat (which he had not bothered to remove) and strode out of the room. The younger doctor gave us all an apologetic smile, but followed him out without another word.

The company stood for a long moment in silence. But when we heard the police car start up outside and then move down the driveway to the main road, something like a collective sigh came from everybody in the drawing room. The circle of people broke up then, forming small groups, everybody talking at once, almost in relief. I forced myself to stand, moving through the actors toward the staircase. Nobody seemed to be paying any attention. But as I put my foot on the first step, I heard Corin behind me, his voice so quiet only I could hear him.

"I remembered you wore that patchwork skirt that first night," he said. I turned to look at him. There was something strange about his face; the restless excitement was gone, his eyes were very serious.

"Did you?"

"Funny, as I looked at Wendy out there . . . she reminded me of you. Now that you're wearing your hair loose. And your hair's lighter now, almost as light as hers." He moved slightly, and his

153

face was in shadows again. "For a moment I thought it was you on the ground."

I stared at him. For the first time since I had seen Wendy's dead body, I allowed myself to consider the thought that had been pressing the back of my brain.

"Yes," I said, keeping my voice low. "I thought of that too."

"Only, it was an accident," Corin whispered. "There isn't any reason for anybody to want to kill you. Or Wendy." He didn't sound convinced.

"Perhaps not. And perhaps someone's afraid I'm finding out too many secrets."

"You mean—Lionel's letter?" Corin frowned. "But nobody knows about that. Except us."

"I'm not so sure," I said. I remembered the curtain trembling behind us as we sat on the porch that night. "Someone *could* have heard us talking, somebody *could* have had the patience to wait until they knew I would be alone in the house."

I looked back at the drawing room. The others were still busy talking, the thin edge of hysteria that had been in all our voices gradually disappearing. Soon I knew the conversation would turn away from the death to what was really important: a detailed discussion of how the dress rehearsal had gone. For a moment I could almost hate them for their indifference, their selfish concentration on their own lives. Abruptly I turned away from Corin and started up the stairs to the darkness above. He followed after me, but he said nothing until we reached the landing.

"Alison? Are you all right?"

I turned around to look at him again. The lights on the second floor had been turned on and enough light spilled from the artificial little balcony above to show the concern in his face. He looked older than I had ever seen him before. And worried.

"I . . . I think so."

My shoulders were starting to tremble again. I stepped back into the shadows of the landing, away from the light, hoping that Corin would not notice. But he moved closer and put his fingers on my arms as if to hold me.

"Why did you lie to McNaughton about where you were when Wendy screamed?" I could feel myself grow tense, but his hands held me gently. "It's all right," he said. "I won't give you away."

"How did you know? That I was lying?"

He moved slightly, the light hitting the side of his face. There was none of the usual merriment in his eyes. "I was just coming out the stage door when I heard the scream. I was the first one up the path to the house. You couldn't have been coming to the theater. I would have seen you."

I would have liked to break free then, but he pulled me closer, holding me as gently as one might to comfort a crying child. "It's all right, Alison. You don't have to tell me where you were. I trust you."

And then the words came pouring out. I struggled to keep my voice low, although in the drawing room below the others were talking now and I knew we could not be overheard. I told Corin of May and the family cemetery and the sundial. And what I suspected. He listened without interrupting, still holding me close in his arms. Then, when I had finished, he released me and slumped down on the velvet-colored bench in front of the great organ that filled the wall of the landing.

" 'Recorded time,' " he said thoughtfully. "That *could* mean a sundial." And then he ran his fingers through his thick brush of dark red hair. For a moment he seemed young and vulnerable again. "God, I haven't been up there in years." He stood suddenly, as if he was ready to leave the house that moment. And then he stopped, letting his hands drop to his sides. "No point in going up there tonight. First thing in the morning . . ."

"There's the inquest," I reminded him.

He swore softly. "Right afterwards, then." He tilted his head and looked at me again, and for a moment he was the same mischievous Corin I had known the past weeks. "Why did you decide to tell me? Why tonight?"

For a moment I made no answer. He put his hands on my shoulders and turned me so that the light was on my face.

"You know why, Corin," I said finally. "There could be another 'accident.' And if what I suspect is correct, somebody should know. Someone else who cares about Lionel's work."

There was a sudden look of pain in his eyes, as if what I had told him were some sort of accusation. He pulled me close, and before I could stop him, his mouth was on mine. I could feel his body pressing me close, his legs shaking slightly. But his lips were firm and warm and insistent, and it was a long moment before he let me go. "There'll be no more 'accidents,' Alison," he whispered finally.

"We're in this together. I promise I'll stand by you, whatever happens."

I broke free from him, climbing the rest of the stairs without looking back. He did not follow me, or even say good night; nor did I expect it. His kiss had not startled me. I had been kissed before, and the days I'd spent in this house had taught me it was as common among theatrical people as handshakes in other circles. But a bond had been forged between us in that moment when we had stood together, a new feeling that neither one of us had quite expected and that I, for one, was not totally sure I wanted.

I went down the half-lit hall to my room. It was exactly as I had left it. I tried not to look at Wendy's cosmetics scattered around the bathroom as I bolted the connecting door to her room. Once more I found myself wishing there were a key to lock the door of my own room.

I sat down then on the bed and tried to calm myself, only to find I was going over all that had occurred since I had left this room. I pushed aside the thought of Corin and went back again to that long walk up the hill to the graveyard, seeing once more May and her strange dance against the night sky.

And then I thought about the poor dead girl crumpled on the driveway below my windows. There was no reason to whip myself with guilt because I had lent her my long skirt or suggested that she go up on the roof. She had been there every day this past week and nothing had happened. It was an accident, I whispered to myself.

Only, I could not convince myself.

The room was hot and airless, and I got up and went over to the French windows, pushing them wide. It would be hard enough to sleep as it was, with what I had to think about. I will not look up, I told myself as I stood by the window. I will not look up at the broken railing I knew was above me.

And yet, of course, I did.

The shredded pieces of wood hung loose over my head, jutting out at a strange angle like a gallows against the midnight sky. It was directly above the center of the narrow balcony that clung to the outside of my room. I felt my stomach twist as if I was going to be sick, and I leaned against the window frame for support.

It was then I saw something had fallen on my balcony from the widow's walk above me. It lay in the corner of the balcony, its pale lemon color bright in the dark shadows. I did not need to reach for it to recognize what it was. In the past week, while the company had been rehearsing, I had seen copies of that book at Vail's Point: thrown on coffee tables, held intently at breakfast as the reader went over the words silently, tucked into the back pockets of summer pants. The pale yellow cover had a distinctive design on it which I could see glimmering in the dark corner of the balcony. The script for *The Basilisks*. Wendy must have taken it up to the roof with her.

For the first time, I could feel genuinely sorry for the dead girl. I couldn't in honesty claim to have liked her, but there was something so . . . *pathetic* in her taking that book up to the widow's walk, to say her few words over and over again as she paraded around in my long skirt. In the moonlight she must have looked like a little girl dressed in her mother's clothes.

No, a voice inside my head reminded me. She must have looked like *you*.

Reaching out for the fallen book, I refused to let myself think about that. McNaughton and the others must have missed it when they examined the widow's walk earlier. It would have been easy; the top of the balcony railing was wide enough to hide it from anybody overhead, even if he had looked directly down.

I could reach the book from where I was standing, just inside the room; otherwise I would have left it where it was, for nothing could make me step onto that shaky balcony that night. The script was battered, the cover loose, and I remembered the words Jeb had used the night of the first reading, when he told the actors to put their names on their scripts and not to lose them. Wendy had held onto hers until her death.

Only, when I turned the copy over, it was not Wendy's name that had been scrawled on the cover.

It was Jeb's.

Chapter Sixteen

It took a long time to get to sleep that night. I lay in the darkness seeing Jeb's name scrawled on the cover of the script, hearing that terrifying scream that ripped from Wendy's throat as she fell. And when I finally managed to fall asleep, it was to dream again the dream I'd had the night before I first came to Vail's Point.

Again I was out on the stage of the theater, the hungry eyes in the darkness staring at me. The actors in the company surrounded me, only this time I knew they could see me. They circled me, smiling cold, evil smiles, their mouths moving; only I could not hear their words. And one by one, as I looked at them . . . Haidee and Julie, Corin and Oliver and Rita, their faces twisted and changed and each in turn became Jeb, until I was surrounded by a circle of leering Jebs.

And as they moved closer their hands reached out, turning into long, angry claws. But I could not scream, I could not speak, because somehow my silence was a part of the play and I dared not break the performance. Before they touched me, I woke up, my body damp with perspiration although I had no sheets over me in the hot night.

Outside the open windows, the sky was already growing light and the dawn breeze was ruffling the curtains.

I did not try to go back to sleep. Shortly before seven, I got up and bathed. I had no black dress to wear to the inquest, nor do I think I would have worn one if I had. I could feel no sense of mourning for the poor dead girl. I put on a navy blue shantung and my city shoes, now dry and cleaned, but still showing signs of that long walk I had had through the mud and rain the day I came to the house. And all the time the thought of Jeb was in my mind. Jeb and Wendy.

No. Jeb and Julie.

I was not the first down to breakfast that morning. Haidee was seated in solitary grandeur at the head of the table. She wore a black faille suit, and on the top of her upswept hair sat a thin black platter of a hat trimmed with white roses. It made her seem less like an actress on her way to an inquest than the lady of the manor about to open a bazaar. I noticed that for the first time there was a cane by her chair. But the moment that she saw me she gave me a smile of such radiant warmth that she looked as young and vital as always.

"You poor child," she said, patting the arm of the chair next to her for me to take. "I wanted to come to you last night, to see if I could help. Perhaps move you to another room. It must have been horrible for you to be there. But Julie said you'd probably gone to sleep and that I shouldn't disturb you."

"That was kind of you."

"We *could* find another room for you. Would you like that? Somewhere where you wouldn't be reminded of that poor girl all the time?"

"I'll be all right. Really."

Haidee looked at me carefully, her brilliant blue eyes searching my face. "You didn't sleep last night. I should have asked Julie to give you one of her little pills."

She smiled again and touched my arm gently. "Julie's having one of the apprentices clean out Wendy's things while we're gone. I understand from Jeb there's a sister in Pennsylvania who'll see about the burial. We'll send everything on to her . . ."

She must have felt me make some move when she mentioned Jeb's name, for she let her words trail off and then, when she spoke again, her voice was brisk and determinedly sensible. But there was no mistaking the compassion in her wise eyes.

"I won't let you worry about this, my dear," said Haidee. "When you reach my age you'll learn to accept these grotesque horrors Life calls accidents."

And an accident is what it was described as, officially. The inquest did not take place in Westaven, but in Conley, the county seat, twenty miles farther west and much larger than Westaven. It was strange to see how the people who had seemed so vital and important at Vail's Point were almost diminished in the middle of a bustling New England city. We had driven over in several cars, Haidee keeping me by her side in the family station wagon, Corin and Julie huddled together in Jeb's white sports car. Jeb looked older this morning, his face pale under his tan, his sturdy body uneasy in his dark blue suit. I could not meet his eyes.

But there was nothing for any of us to be uneasy about. The

coroner, a fat little man in thick glasses, read off his findings almost cheerfully, as if someone had once told him his grim reports would be more palatable if accompanied by a series of little smiles. The judge in charge of the hearing seemed impatient to get the whole matter over with, and the only person from Westaven called to give testimony was the state trooper, McNaughton. He read from his notebook in a carefully impersonal voice, giving all the statements he had gathered the night before. Neither the doctor, who sat alongside him, nor any of the people from Vail's Point were called for additional questions. The whole procedure was finished in less than half an hour. The judge's main concern seemed to be that Wendy would not have to be buried at the state's expense.

"Well, that's over," said Haidee cheerfully as we came down the courthouse steps. She stood for a moment in the hot morning sun, surveying the rest of the company as it pushed its way into the cars parked in front of her. Everyone seemed anxious to return to Vail's Point. "No reporters," she added. "Hmmm. I suppose it's a blessing." Then her eyes narrowed. "Or does it mean we're not news?"

"They don't know about it," said Jeb. He'd come down the courthouse steps behind us. "I asked McNaughton to forget about calling the papers. At least until after the opening."

"And he agreed?" Haidee seemed startled. She lifted a thin arm to straighten her hat. "Wonders never cease. It's been a long day since McNaughton did a favor for the Vails."

Jeb made no answer, but took me firmly by the elbow. "Haidee, Alison will ride back with me. We've a few things to talk about."

I felt myself stiffening, and Haidee's head rose imperiously. There was no question that what Jeb had said was not a request but an order. But before either of us could protest, Jeb went on in a more matter-of-fact voice. "After all, Alison is the principal backer of the company. We've got business matters to decide."

Jeb let the other cars pull out of the parking spaces before he turned the key of the ignition. We were alone in the front seat of the car. I made no attempt at conversation, and he busied himself lighting a cigarette during the silence. Finally, when the others had left moving swiftly down the highway back toward Westaven, Jeb turned his car out onto the road.

"You'll have to take Wendy's place tonight," he said as he shifted the gears. "You know that, don't you?"

I sat there absolutely stunned. I had not thought of the opening that night, or of the play or who would substitute for the dead girl. The cast for *The Basilisks* was small, and if I had thought at all about who would replace her, I suppose I imagined one of the young college students could be put into the part.

"I'm not an actress, Jeb," I protested when I finally realized he was serious. "Surely one of the young apprentices . . ."

"There isn't one of them who's right for it. Plus I need every member of the crew to run the show and start on next week's sets. No," he added, keeping his eyes fixed on the highway, "you're the only one who's free to step in. It's not too much to learn. Barely seven lines—I counted them. And you've probably paid more attention at rehearsals than Wendy did."

He said the dead girl's name as casually as if he were discussing the weather. Of course, I thought bitterly, nothing must disturb your precious play. Not the dead, not the feelings of the living, *nothing*. As if he sensed my thoughts, Jeb went on, his voice for the first time almost apologetic.

"I know what I'm saying sounds rough. Wendy was . . . all right. No actress, of course. I suppose it was my fault for trying to make her into one. But right now tonight's opening is the only thing I can think about." He glanced at me quickly, then went back to staring at the highway ahead of us. "And it should be the only thing you can think about, too."

"Not quite." As I sat there I saw again the book lying in the dark corner of my balcony.

"Listen, Alison, you've got to help us out." He swerved over to the side of the road, braking the car to a stop. The other cars had disappeared ahead of us, and the highway was empty in the warm July sunlight. He looked at me now, his eyes steady on my face, until I was forced to look back at him. There were shadows under his eyes, as if he, too, had not slept the night before. His Indian-black hair was no longer neatly combed; it stood up like a crest from the dark arrow of the widow's peak that grew on his forehead.

"We've got to open tonight, Alison. If we have the success I think we'll have, it can mean a lot . . . to the Vails, to theater, to everybody. Then, tomorrow, when the news gets out that a girl died in an accident . . . well, it'll be unfortunate, but it won't seem as horrible as it does now."

"My God, how selfish can you people be?"

The words were said before I had a chance to stop them, although I don't think I could have phrased it any differently. But Jeb seemed to understand my anger. He ran his fingers through his thick black hair impatiently, but when he spoke his voice was calm and reasonable.

"Alison, I'm not just thinking about the play, or myself. I'm trying to figure out what's best for everybody. The family, Haidee . . . even you—" I started to interrupt, but he silenced me with a wave of his hand. "You . . . and your family have got a lot of money invested in the season. It could all get washed right down the drain. Along with everybody's hard work. If the news gets out before we open . . . if we delay to get another actress up from New York, people will be coming to the theater for the wrong reasons. Like ghouls." He went on quickly, as if he was afraid I might break in, although I had no intention of trying. "I know what I'm talking about. There are enough mystery and rumors about the Vails already. It wouldn't take much for the cast to start thinking there's a jinx on the play . . . the theater . . . the whole family. You ought to know by now how superstitious theater people are. Everything we dreamed about will fall apart."

"Jeb, there must be somebody else besides me! Yvonne . . . somebody in the village." I thought with a sickening lurch of the dream that had haunted me, the dream I'd had again last night. "I can't do it, Jeb."

"Yes, you can." He started to put his hand out, as if he would comfort me, but then, obviously afraid of my reaction, he pulled it back again. "And there is no one else." His face sobered. "Haidee herself suggested you last night. This is an important night for her. She hasn't been on a stage in nearly ten years. Not to mention what she's going through having to act Lionel's version of her life. She said she'd feel . . . better if you were out there with her."

He battered down all my objections: the part was tiny, we could rehearse all afternoon; he even mentioned that I moved well in a long dress. It was when he made that last remark that I remembered Jeb, too, had seen me in the long patchwork skirt that first night. The thought silenced me, and I found my fingers

clutching my purse tightly. Jeb seemed to take my silence for
agreement, for he turned on the ignition once more, ready to start
the car. "I told the rest of the cast to assemble at the theater. We'll
start by walking through your scenes. Only, first we'd better stop at
the box office and see if we can find you a spare script. He frowned.
"Let's hope we can find two. I seem to have lost mine somewhere."

It was then I opened my purse and took out the script I had
found the night before.

And handed it to him in silence.

"Where did you get this?"

Even though I had been waiting for that question, it took me
by surprise. He said it so calmly, in such an ordinary tone of voice,
that for a second I could make no answer. It was hot in the front
seat of his car, even though all the windows were open and Jeb had
pulled under the shade of the old trees along the highway.

"I found it on the balcony. Outside my room." I forced myself
to look at him then. "I found it last night." His green eyes grew
dark and a muscle started twitching on the side of his jaw. But his
voice was quiet and controlled when he spoke.

"On the balcony? Wendy must have picked it up by mistake at
the theater."

"You told the police you were going over your notes when
Wendy died. Wouldn't you have needed your script for that?"

There was silence for a long moment, and then Jeb lifted one
of his eyebrows, thick and black against his tan face. It gave him a
look of skepticism; and something more, something hard and cold
was in his eyes. For the first time, I realized that if my suspicions—
my *half* suspicions—were correct, I could actually be in danger.

It was such an absurd thought my mind rejected it at once. I
was Alison Howard. I led a quiet life with my father in a university
town. I was sitting with a man I barely knew by the side of a public road on a warm morning in July discussing a summer-stock play.
Anything else was some sort of fantasy. But Jeb still stared at me,
his eyes cold and dark as emeralds.

"So you think I was up on the roof with Wendy. Do you also
think I killed her?"

"I—I don't know what I think." I couldn't bear to look at him
any more. His eyes seemed to be boring into my head, as if he
knew all I had considered through the long night.

163

"Is that why you took the book with you to the inquest? Were you going to bring it out as some kind of evidence?"

There was no mistaking the anger in his voice now. I looked down at my hands. I had gripped them together without thinking, and now I made myself separate them. But the fingers still felt stiff.

"I—I don't know what I intended to do." I made myself look at him. He had leaned back now, but his eyes were still steady on me. "I know you had a quarrel with Wendy. I heard you one night."

For some strange reason this relaxed him. He was not at all embarrassed by what I had said. "Did you hear what we were quarreling about?" he asked as he lit still another cigarette.

"No."

He snapped his lighter shut and shoved it into the pocket of his blue suit. "It was a good-by scene, Alison. One Wendy and I both knew was long overdue." He exhaled the smoke and reached forward to turn the key of the ignition. "And you don't kill girls after you've said good-by. Let's get to the theater. There's a lot to do before we open tonight."

"Were you on the widow's walk with her last night?" The question came out so abruptly, for a second I wondered if I had merely thought it. But then Jeb sighed. He did not turn to look at me.

"No," he said quietly. "But I can't prove it." Then he glanced back at me, a gleam of malice in his eyes. "Any more than you can prove that I *was* there. As you must have realized at the inquest, when you didn't tell them about finding my script."

He started the car then, moving it swiftly out on the highway, and for a moment I thought of that first afternoon when I had traveled this same road to Vail's Point and the white car had moved ahead of us so swiftly and deadly impervious to anything that might get in its way. Had Wendy been in his way? His and Julie's way? Once again the answers only brought more questions. I leaned back against the seat of the car, and there must have been something about my movement that told Jeb he had persuaded me.

"Good," he said. And then he added, so quietly I was not sure whether he was speaking to himself or to me, "God, how you hate me." Before I could protest, he said, more clearly, "And yet, you'd be better off with me than with some of the others."

I wanted to ask him what he meant, but he clamped his mouth shut in a thin line and did not say another word until we reached the theater.

Chapter Seventeen

Corin was waiting on the front steps of the theater. I remembered then for the first time since the drive to the inquest what we had agreed to do that morning. I checked the gold watch pinned to my dress as we drove up. It was already ten-thirty. But Corin was apparently resigned to wait still longer, for as Jeb stopped the car he came down the steps to meet us.

"The cast's all on stage, Jeb," said Corin.

"Good. Let's get started." Jeb hurried into the theater. I turned to Corin to explain, but he merely nodded and, taking my hand, said softly, "I figured Jeb would talk you into it. Don't worry. If that manuscript is up in the cemetery, it's waited thirty years. It can wait a few hours more."

We walked through the lobby of the theater. I'd not seen the actual set for the play before; the cast had rehearsed on bare platforms, under harsh work lights, while the crew built the scenery in the basement below the stage. Apparently it had only been completely assembled for the dress rehearsal the previous night, which I had missed. So when I opened the door from the lobby and saw the stage in front of me, it was a complete surprise. I must have tightened my grip on Corin, for he stopped and looked at me with some of the old wicked amusement in his eyes.

"I know," he said. "Dirty trick for Jeb to pull, wasn't it?"

Corin was right.

For Jeb had designed the set for *The Basilisks* to duplicate the drawing room of the house at Vail's Point. It was all there, barely smaller than the original: the great fireplace, the huge staircase at the back of the set leading up to the floors above, the French windows in the drawing room, the tall doors to the porte-cochere. Only the portrait of Viola and her children was missing. That still hung over the fireplace in the big house.

The play indeed demanded such an impressive room, and of course it was natural that the stage crew should borrow furniture from the house itself. But there could be no mistake that Jeb had deliberately worked to make the resemblance as accurate as possible. Lionel's play was a thinly disguised version of life at Vail's

Point and, maliciously or not, Jeb had chosen to duplicate the rooms exactly.

I turned to Corin. "What did Haidee say when she saw this?" I whispered, for the whole cast was gathered on the stage.

"Nothing." The doubt I felt must have shown on my face. "I mean it. If it was supposed to bring back unhappy echoes of the past, it didn't." Corin smiled. "You still don't understand actors, Alison. Gran's a star. All she wanted to know was if the spotlight outside the windows would hit her during her big scene. Come on, before Jeb starts yelling."

And he started down the aisle toward the stage.

The rehearsal lasted over two hours. As I knew from seeing the evening sessions, the part of Emily was small. I found I had already subconsciously learned the few brief lines from listening to Wendy agonize over them. In the first act, as the curtain rose I was to be discovered asleep. Julie and Corin arrive and I wake up and drift in silence into the garden. Later, Julie, as the cruel Helen, lures me into her plot by tempting me with her box of glittering jewelry.

But most of the time all I was required to do was to sit quietly and listen to the others. The only important scene I had was in the last act, when I turn on the villainous Helen and her attempts to get me to sign the commitment papers for the old lady. Then I drink the glass of milk that Haidee has brought in and dash up the great staircase and off the stage.

We rehearsed the first scenes several times. If I had expected to feel the strange dream of appearing on stage unprepared come true, I did not have time to think about it. The others were most helpful, especially Haidee.

"So much easier to work with you, my dear, rather than the other one," she whispered. She gave me a wink. "To pretend I cared about her—that took *acting!*" And without missing a beat, she picked up her cue from Julie and swept into her long speech.

It was not difficult in the last act to shrink back in fear as Julie (in the part of Helen) glared at me malevolently. But the exit up the long flight of stairs seemed endless, even though Jeb stopped me before I reached the top.

"Alison, first I had better show you where to go," he said, and

166

came up the steps from the auditorium. He walked across the stage and up to the landing of the staircase, which I had reached before he stopped me, and went on ahead up the rest of the stairs. At the top of the flight, which was practically under the rafters of the theater, he turned to the left, disappearing behind the scenery wall. I followed him carefully, and when I reached the top of the stairs I could see the reason for his caution.

The staircase ended abruptly offstage with a narrow platform bordered with a skinny railing. Bare wood steps nearly as steep as a ladder led down to the stage floor over twenty feet below.

"Be careful," said Jeb, as he reached out a hand for me. "It's a little tricky up here." I held back, somewhat hesitant. "You afraid of heights?" he asked.

"A little," I answered. There was no point in pretending otherwise. I stepped forward gingerly onto the platform, Jeb continuing to hold onto my hand. I was grateful for the strength of his grip.

"It's a fairly sturdy unit," he went on, his voice calm. "The wheels are blocked and it's more solidly braced than it looks." He glanced around at the ropes that hung from the rafters straight down to the heavy sandbags below, keeping them taut. "We'll practice your exit a couple of times until you feel comfortable." He yelled down to one of the college boys standing below. "Bradley, be sure there's white tape around the edges so that Alison can see just how far she can go." The boy nodded and made a note on his clipboard. "I would have liked to have built the whole escape-stair unit right into the walls, but we've got to keep it mobile. The stage has to be clear of scenery as of tomorrow morning." He grinned, and I could see his white teeth gleaming in the shadows where we stood. "That's summer stock. Big opening tonight, and tomorrow we start all over again with another play." He released my hand. "Okay, Alison, let's try the exit again."

Jeb made me run up the long staircase several times until I was confident I knew what to do. When at last we were finished I sat down beside Haidee and ventured my first look out at the dark auditorium. It seemed enormous from where I sat, full of shadows, the rows of seats rising like a wide staircase to the back of the theater. From the lobby the phone kept ringing in the box office, reminding me that tickets were being sold and that tonight every one of those empty seats in front of me would be filled.

"I'm not sure I can do this, Haidee," I said quietly as we sat together on the satin love seat that had been brought down from the big house on the hill to fill the stage.

"Of course you can, my dear." Haidee put her fingers on my shoulder. It was a gentle touch, as if a bird had landed there, but I could feel the warmth of her hand through the thin material of my dress. "You're going to do it splendidly," she went on, as Jeb rehearsed the rest of the cast in their curtain calls. I looked at Haidee's incredibly blue eyes. There was a softness in them now as if she truly did understand what I was feeling. "We—I need you here."

She glanced quickly at Julie, who was deep in conversation with Jeb at the far side of the stage. "I never really appreciated having a daughter, I'm afraid," she went on quietly. "My fault, I'm sure. I was too involved in my own career when Julie was young. We . . . grew apart. Having you here has been like having a second chance." She smiled again, rather wistfully. Then, as Jeb called her name, she raised her chin and rose grandly to take her place with the others in the line along the footlights, leaving me oddly touched and comforted by what she had said. I had to go through with it, I realized. For Haidee's sake.

When we were finally dismissed from rehearsal, I started instantly for Corin; only, before we could reach the stage door, Haidee swooped down on us, Esme directly behind her.

"Costumes, child," she said briskly, tucking her thin arm in mine and starting us toward the iron stairs that led down to the Green Room. She moved so quickly I almost tripped over one of the hinges of the closed trap door directly beneath the stair platform. Corin glowered and opened the stage door.

"Couldn't we do costumes later?" I asked hesitantly. I snapped the watch pinned to my dress open, but it was too dark in the wings to see the time. Haidee moved me toward the stairs without stopping.

"Now, my dear," said Haidee firmly, "you're slightly taller than Wendy. Esme will need the whole afternoon for alterations. And

May will want to work with you later on movement." She seemed to notice Corin then for the first time. "Corin, go away! Alison has to be fitted." She made the dismissal sound as if she were telling a small boy to go out and play in the sunshine.

"I'll wait," he said, looking directly at me. And he leaned back against the iron railing of the stairs and folded his arms deliberately.

The costume fitting took less time than I had anticipated. I took off the navy shantung in one of the dressing rooms and stepped into one of the costumes sent for Wendy's first appearance. Even before I had it fastened I knew that it would not do, but I opened the door of the dressing room and came out into the Green Room area for the others to see.

The Green Room was crowded now that rehearsals were over. Two of the apprentices were stapling new material over the love seat. Esme, down on her knees on the flagstone floor, was pinning up the hem of Julie's long gown, while Haidee and May stood at the long mirror examining a rusty black taffeta gown.

"Never," said Haidee as I came out of the dressing room. "Mother would never have worn anything like that." It was the first time I had heard Haidee admit that the play—and her character— were based on reality. She flung the dress down and turned to me.

"Absolutely impossible!"

Haidee's brilliant eyes narrowed. "Pink sateen for the part of Emily? What were those costumers thinking of?" she said, moving closer. "Too short . . . much too tight at the bosom and too loose at the waistline. No wonder Wendy didn't want to wear it last night." She glanced at Esme, who was holding the dress Julie had discarded.

"Esme," she said firmly, "Alison's got to look young and innocent. Not like one of those dreadful dolls they used to put on guest-room beds." I noticed Julie and Rita had disappeared tactfully into their dressing rooms, leaving only the two apprentices to stare up at Haidee with open-mouthed awe.

"We'll have to get something from one of the trunks in the attic," Haidee said firmly.

"I've got a million things to do this afternoon," grumbled Esme, but Haidee dismissed that with an airy wave of the hand.

"Nonsense," she said firmly, not even bothering to look at her former dresser. "You're going to have to go up there anyway to get the tea gown for me and an evening gown for Julie." Haidee turned to me. "You can just as well find something for Alison. She'll join you in the attic after lunch." It was a command and Esme knew it.

Five minutes later I had changed back into my own clothes and had met Corin at the stage door. Around us, apprentices were still fixing the last of the scenery. A girl was tacking curtains over the French windows. Two young men were high up on the bridge above the stage focusing the lights, and a couple of others were taping down a brilliant carpet. I felt a sinking moment of panic when I realized the next time I saw the theater there would be people in the auditorium beyond and my worst nightmare would be about to come true.

But seeing Corin waiting for me on the wide veranda reminded me of my real purpose at Vail's Point.

"If it's any consolation," he said cheerfully as I came out the door, "I think you're going to be damned good in the part."

Then he took me by the hand and we started across the grass for the edge of the forest.

Corin knew of another path to the top of the hill, so that we did not have to go back to the house and start up the way May had taken the previous night. The path was not easy, for I was still wearing the shoes and dress I had put on for the inquest, but Corin was impatient to reach the graveyard and so, I'll admit, was I. Corin pushed aside the branches and helped me over some of the rockier parts of the climb up the hill, never letting go of my hand. Finally we could see the clearing ahead of us.

The hill and the forest were different in the daylight, and by the time we reached the graveyard the clearing seemed almost cheerful in the summer sun. But one thing was the same as the night before. The place was not deserted.

Frankie stood in the middle of the Vail family cemetery, a shovel in his hands, his T shirt, soaked with perspiration, sticking to his thin shoulders.

And all around the sundial in the middle of the open space was a freshly dug trench.

"What—what in the name of heaven are you doing?" Corin's face had gone deathly white, his eyes blazed with anger and his grip on my hand was so tight I wanted to scream.

"Oh, hi, Corin . . ." Frankie smiled cheerfully, completely unaware of Corin's reaction. He wiped a dirty hand over his wet forehead and plunged the shovel into the earth by the trench. "Your mother said I should dig this up. Right after we came back from the inquest."

Corin made a move toward the boy, but I managed to step in front of him, freeing my hand from his grip as I did.

"Let me handle this, Corin," I said quietly. I walked closer to the sundial. It stood like a miniature island in the newly dug earth. I could tell in a glance that if anything had been buried in the ground surrounding it, Frankie would have discovered it by now. "You said Julie told you to dig up the earth around the sundial?"

Frankie was by now beginning to realize that something was wrong, for he gave us both a puzzled stare. "Sure. She said with folks coming to see Lionel's play, somebody might remember about him being buried here. You know, might want to make a sort of visit to his grave."

"His grave's over there someplace." Corin was still behind me, but I didn't need to see his face to know how he felt. His voice was as cold as steel.

"I know that," Frankie replied. I could see he was now thinking over his instructions. "But she made a point that the first thing I should do is dig up around the sundial. She said it three times. Then I'm supposed to go into town and get some geraniums to surround it. Then I'm to clear off the graves, and after that I should try to do something about the path down to the theater."

He sighed heavily, shrugging his boyish shoulders at the vagaries of adults. "I sure wish she'd got this idea before today." He turned back to pick the shovel out of the ground. "There's enough to do before the opening tonight. And the party afterwards."

I stepped closer to the sundial. It looked naked and out of place in the middle of the fresh black earth. "Was it difficult work, Frankie?"

"Not too bad. But I don't think anybody's cleaned up this place in years." He glanced around at the angled gravestones baking in the dry dirt. It was past noon and the sun was hot on our bare heads. There were no clouds in the sky today and not even a faint rustle of a breeze in the bushes that grew between the headstones.

"You . . . didn't find anything?" Corin asked the question, but I could tell from his voice he didn't really expect Frankie to be of help.

"You mean, like buried treasure?" Frankie's freckled face broke into a wide grin. "I'd have to dig up one of the old graves for that." He pointed toward the far end of the clearing. "There's some over there that go back to the 1600s."

I moved away from the center of the clearing toward Corin. He had turned his back to us, his shoulders rigid. When I was close enough to him so that Frankie would not hear, I said, "I'm sorry."

Corin made no move.

"I suppose it was a silly idea," I went on. Suddenly I felt very foolish. "It's just that . . . well . . . 'recorded time' . . . and May coming here last night. And something that Wendy had said about May and Lionel being close . . ."

"You tried, Alison." He sounded almost cheerful. "I suppose it was too much to expect we'd find it the first time out."

"Then you haven't given up?"

"No." He looked away from me now, across the gravestones in that quiet cemetery, past the tops of the trees that straggled up to the clearing where we stood to look at the green valley that stretched to the west of us. "I suppose I'm being foolish. All we know for sure is that Lionel finished his last play. And I know the chances are that whoever destroyed him, destroyed the play as well." His face was serious. "Only, I can't give up! Not until I at least know what he meant by 'recorded time.'" A small line appeared between his eyebrows.

"Only, why would Mother, of all people, want the sundial dug up? And why today?"

They left soon after that, Frankie having persuaded Corin to drive him into town for the plants that Julie wanted for the grave-yard. I was not sorry to see them go; I still felt embarrassed. The idea that Lionel might have buried a copy of his manuscript here in the cemetery seemed more and more ridiculous as I thought about it.

It was quiet up there after Frankie and Corin went down the hill, and I was happy to be alone. I forced myself not to think about what lay ahead of me before the end of the day. The idea of appearing on a stage still seemed so alien and unreal; I suppose some part of me believed the evening would never really come.

I walked along the overgrown paths of the graveyard. To my right a mausoleum dominated the clearing. It was large and ugly, of the liver-colored stone popular in the early years of this century. I knew this must be all that remained of Matthew Patch, and probably the only place on the whole of Vail's Point where his name appeared. Looking at the grotesque hut, I wondered about the man who had married Viola so many years ago and fathered that strange trio, Lionel and Haidee and May.

Somewhere in the trees that circled the graveyard a bird whistled. The sun was very hot now, and I stopped to rest on a small stone bench on the other side of the path. Almost directly behind it was a plain low gray marble marker. From where I sat I could see the name inscribed on it:

LIONEL VAIL

I got up and moved closer to the stone. The ground was clear around his grave, unlike the rest of the plots in the cemetery. May, I thought. All these years, she must have kept her beloved brother's grave free of the straggling grass and wild bushes. I stood for a moment in silence, looking down at the stone. Perhaps I thought I might feel that strange chill that had touched me in the dressing room of the theater or when I stared at the family portrait in the drawing room of the big house.

But it did not happen. All I could feel was the July sun on my back.

By now my curiosity was aroused and I began to wander among the older gravestones that filled this section of the cleared land. Viola's grave was near Lionel's, which surprised me, for I would have thought she would have lain in the dark mausoleum beside her husband. But, seeing the grave, I had a feeling she had chosen her final resting place herself. A small willow tree draped its branches becomingly over the pale pink stone, and rosebushes had once been planted around the plot. Another small stone bench was placed in the shade of the tree so that one could visit Viola in death with comfort.

There were no dates on the stone. Her name had been traced gracefully in what I suppose was a facsimile of her signature. It looked almost as if the actress were giving one final autograph to the world. Below it her full name was spelled out in smaller but clearly carved letters: "VIOLA VAIL PATCH." I noticed with interest that May had not given the graves of her mother and father the same attention she had given Lionel's.

My curiosity led me on through the rest of the stones tracing the family back through the years. There were indeed graves that dated back to before the American Revolution, and others that might be even older; but the years and the New England weather had erased the carving on the thin stone slabs. There were other names now, stern, uncompromising New England names: Janes and Abigails, Joshuas and Calebs, all ending with sturdy family names such as Dale and Pickett and Hopkins.

And then, in a far corner of the cemetery, I found a small stone with a name on it I had not expected:

REIVES

I looked at it again carefully. It was spelled exactly the way Jeb spelled his, not the conventional spelling with two E's in the middle. It was the gravestone of a young woman, a Phoebe Reives. I knelt and pushed aside the grass that grew long about the stone. This marker was set somewhat timidly apart from the others, just inside the wall, as if even in death Phoebe had realized she did not quite belong.

Dead leaves had protected the carving somewhat, and when I brushed them aside I could read the inscription clearly:

PHOEBE REIVES
1820–1838
"Go and sin no more"

I stood and stared down at the little marker. The quotation was from the Bible, of course, as most gravestone inscriptions were in those days, and I knew it came from the story of the woman taken in adultery. But Phoebe would barely have been eighteen when she died, and early death in that cold Puritan world of over a century ago seemed far more likely than illicit passion. She would hardly be buried here unless she was in some way part of the family, and yet none of the other stones bore that singular last name.

Reives.

I glanced at the watch pinned to my dress. It was time for me to be getting back to the house. But even as I walked away, I kept seeing the name carved on the old stone. Could I have been wrong about Jeb? Could he be in some way related to the Vail family? That could mean he had more of an interest in the Vail family fortunes than he had in Julie. And the Vail family fortunes included Lionel's plays, both the known and the unknown.

Nearly a month I've been here, I thought as I left the cemetery. And how much actually do I know about the family history? It's time to start learning a few facts, I muttered to myself as I started down the hill.

Esme, I thought as I walked. If anyone knows the truth, it's Esme . . .

CHAPTER EIGHTEEN

Although it was long past the lunch hour by the time I reached the house, I was not hungry. The drawing room was quiet, cool and empty, the rest of the company having probably retreated to their rooms for naps. At least I saw no one as I made my way back to the kitchen. Yvonne was working over a long table already half covered with platters of food for the opening-night party.

"If you want something, I can make it for you," she said. "But Esme's waiting in the attic." The young girl seemed oddly subdued.

"No, I'm fine," I said. "But I'm not exactly sure how to get up there."

Without saying another word, Yvonne wiped her hands on her apron and started for the swinging door to the butler's pantry and the dining room beyond. "This way," she called over her shoulder. She did not speak again as we climbed the main staircase to the floor above. Turning down a hall that led to a part of the house I had not explored, she finally stopped in front of a small door and opened it quietly. Ahead of me I could see dusty stairs angling upward. "I don't envy you," Yvonne whispered as she opened the door. "Esme's in a funny mood." Then she scurried back down the hall and out of sight.

The steps were narrow, but sunlight was coming in from somewhere above and I could see clearly. Apparently the attic had not been invaded for a long time, for there was a clear footprint in the middle of each tread of the stairs where Esme had climbed before me. By the time I reached the top, the heat of the attic was baking me as if I had walked into an oven.

On the top step I took a deep breath. The attic was under the great shingled bubble that dominated the roof of the house. I realized now the huge onion-shaped dome had not been designed for decoration alone, but as a primitive method of ventilation, shutting off the hot summer sun as well as allowing space between the high, curved roof and the floors below, which kept the house relatively cool even during the middle of the day. All around the edge of the great swell of the roof were thin slots of windows. The glass had not been washed in years, but there was still enough light to see the attic clearly.

It was an enormous area, covering as it did most of the house. And it seemed to me, as I stood there catching my breath in the airless heat, that almost every inch of the floor was filled. Great pieces of heavy Victorian furniture were stacked one on top of another around the walls, reaching in places well up under the curve of the roof above. Shabby mattresses lay piled directly ahead of me, rusting bicycles leaned against each other next to them, and the rest of the floor space was crammed with cardboard cartons tied with twine; with boxes and suitcases and hampers, all in different sizes and all of them thickly covered with dust.

And trunks.

There must have been at least twenty-five trunks, some tall and solid, pasted with faded labels of theaters; some graceful reminders of a time when the only way to cross the ocean was by steamship; some were even humpbacked antiques. The trunks were all massive, belonging to that era when people dressed elaborately and traveled leisurely, supremely confident that there would always be porters to haul the great boxes and docile maids to tend to the clothes that had been packed so carefully inside.

In the center of the attic, Esme knelt on the floor. She had pushed aside some of the clutter to create a little island of space. One thin shaft of light pushed through the slit of a window behind her, sliding down past the dark shadows of the discarded furniture and dusty cabinets to light the area where she worked. She straightened as I reached the top step, and the sunlight touched her improbably dyed red hair, making it glitter metallically.

For a second I felt I had walked into the cave of a witch.

"There you are," she said cheerfully, showing no trace of her previous crankiness. "I've found some petticoats . . . you'll need them if this white organdy fits." She nodded toward a full-skirted summer dress she had spread over the top of one of the open trunks. "Slip out of your clothes, dearie, and let's see if I've guessed the sizes right."

I managed to find a path through the cartons to where Esme stood (and I had thought Lionel's study was cluttered!).

"Are all these trunks filled with clothes?" I asked, as I made my way toward her. "Didn't anybody ever throw anything away?"

"Oh, no, dearie," said Esme, preparing to plunge back into the depths of the trunk again. "Actors don't. Never can tell when you might need something . . . for stock or the telly. Regular magpies they are. And, of course, everything ends up here. Being built as a summer house, they didn't think to put in a cellar." She held up an armload of ivory cotton. "Slip one of these on, ducks. Just so I can get an idea of the length."

Esme paid no attention as I took off my navy blue shantung and pulled the full petticoat up to my waist. She had gone to still another trunk, banging the lid back loudly and rummaging through the contents. Then she lifted something out of the depths of the box and twisted around to face me, holding a long gown up in front of her.

In that moment, for the first and only time, I saw Esme as she would have wanted to be: a pretty young woman with a slim waist and delicate features.

But as she took a step forward, the cruel sunlight touched the pudgy hips behind the cloth she held in front of her, turning her dyed hair into a hard purple, revealing every line and wrinkle behind the white powdered mask of her face. Only the gown in her hands remained beautiful, and her fat little fingers trembled as they stroked the soft silk.

"It's for Haidee," she said gently. "Do you like it?"

I nodded. It was a long, soft rose crepe tea gown with incredibly delicate cream lace at the neck and the cuffs of the full sleeves. Esme took another step forward, holding the dress out.

"You can touch it if you like. They knew how to make gowns in those days. See?" She lifted the hem of the robe carefully, almost pushing the cloth into my fingers. I could feel something like a cord sewn into the hem of the dress. "Little metal chains to weight the train, so that it will flow right." She took the dress back from me, running her fingers carefully along the skirt. "Yes, all intact, all along the hem. Just as perfect as when Viola put it away years ago . . ."

She wasn't looking at me any longer. She stood there in the harsh sunlight, touching the filmy crepe with her hands, remembering the past. After a moment she went on, as quietly as if she were talking to herself.

"Viola . . . ," she said, "wasn't the way Lionel saw her in this play. Not really." She gave a little sniff and went on, as briskly practical as always. "Still, it's a good part for Haidee. With a little touch of the iron, she'll look ever so well in this."

She glanced at me, as if suddenly remembering she wasn't

alone. I had managed to finish fastening the tiny pearl buttons on the sleeves of the dress she had found for me, and the cloth, soft and fine as handkerchief linen, flowed gracefully around my body down to the floor.

"Yes, that'll do," said Esme, looking at me with a shrewdly practical eye. "I've some blue taffeta downstairs somewhere for a sash and a hair ribbon." She draped the tea gown carefully over a broken chair and started opening another trunk, paying no attention as I started to remove the dress. "You can handle a long skirt, too, which is more than that other one could do."

I realized suddenly Esme also remembered my first evening at Vail's Point and the patchwork skirt that I had worn. It was time now to get answers for some of the questions that puzzled me.

"Tell me more about the family, Esme," I said, trying to keep my voice casual. "There's still so much I don't know." She turned quickly, a small frown cracking her dead-white face, her eyes suspicious. I smiled at her innocently and continued fastening my dress.

"What do you want to know?" Her voice was cold now, and she kept her tiny eyes fastened on me.

"Corin took me up to the family graveyard this morning," I began, moving to keep my face away from Esme's sharp eyes. "Or was it the graveyard for the whole town?" I glanced at her, safe now that my face was in the shadows. "There were so many different names on the stones."

"No, it's all family as far as I know." Esme resumed searching through the open trunk, and while she may have been pretending, it seemed to me the question had calmed her suspicions. "Lord, I haven't been up there in years," she muttered, half to herself. "Not since Lionel was buried."

"I still seem to know so little about him," I went on cautiously. I could see there was no point in asking Esme about the forlorn little gravestone I had found. Phoebe Reives obviously would mean nothing to her.

"After all this time?" Her words were sharp, but not her voice, and I decided to try again.

"I'm curious about the play . . . *The Basilisks*," I began tentatively. Esme's back stiffened at once. There was dignity in her fat body now and strength in that puffy face.

"Lionel was vicious." She said it quietly. "Oh, I know," she went on hurriedly, as if she was afraid I'd try to defend him.

179

"Everybody thinks him the great playwright. But he was nothing but a nasty drunk—jealous of Haidee, always was. And a thief . . ."

I must have made some sound that she took as protest, for she repeated the word. "A thief! *He* was the one who was always after Viola for money. Not Haidee, the way he's written it. The whole family knew that and hated him."

I thought of what Wendy had told me the night before. "Even Julie?"

"Why do you ask about Julie?" She was holding a small cotton pouch she had plucked from the trunk in front of her, and now she began to shift it from hand to hand, almost as if she were weighing it.

"I . . . I just meant . . . well, you said the 'whole family.'" It sounded lame even to me. Esme's eyes stayed fastened on me and the look in them was as cold as the winter ocean.

"I suspect we all had our own reasons to hate Lionel," she said finally. Little beads of sweat were breaking through the thick makeup on her face, but she did not brush them away. Her fingers kept tugging at the little bag she had pulled from the trunk.

"You should never have recommended *The Basilisks*," she went on, her voice very quiet. "It's bad luck. I warned you, that first night. The theater should have stayed closed and Lionel forgotten. He was evil. He made evil things happen. They say he haunts the theater. Maybe he does."

"I've heard the superstitions . . ." If I'd hoped to change the subject or soften Esme's intense stare, I was unsuccessful. She sniffed and started to untie the knot that fastened the cloth sack in her hands.

"I'm not talking about superstitions!" There was energy in her voice now, and her fat fingers were untying the string deftly. "That girl dying last night—that wasn't superstition, was it? And there'll be more. You mark my words. As long as people listen to Lionel's poison." She took a short step forward, not exactly toward me, but still closer than I liked. I found myself fumbling nervously with the watch pinned to my navy blue dress, wondering how I could get away from this strange old woman without incurring more of her anger.

"Corin tells me he's sure Lionel *did* write a last play," I said, trying to be tactful. I thought of the phrase Lionel had used in his letter: "to avenge a terrible wrong." "Perhaps he made up in that for what he'd said about Haidee in *The Basilisks*."

"Corin's full of nonsense." Esme stretched the opening of the sack in her hands and bent her head to study the contents. Without looking up, she continued talking, her words clear and firm in the dusty silence of the attic. "Don't let Corin fool you into some kind of a crazy search."

She raised her head very slowly. There was a strange look in her eyes. "Or Lionel's evil might spread to you. His evil . . . and his bad luck."

I wanted to step back, to break away from the steady gaze of her tiny eyes, dark as raisins in the fat dough of her face, but there was no room to move; the trunks surrounded me like a wall. Esme smiled, her mouth grotesque as the painted smile of a clown. Slowly she began to draw out a long string of tiny beads from the bag in her hands. They were a thin metal cord, and she twisted them among her fingers as if testing their strength.

"Look," she said, holding them up so the sunlight glittered along the length. "I've found some more dress weights. I'll sew them into your gown, if you like." The smile still on her face, she began to move closer.

"Alison? Are you up there?"

Esme froze, her eyes flickering toward the stairs. Jeb was climbing up into the attic, his head already in view. "Sorry, ladies. Everybody decent?" he said. I turned back to Esme, but she was already busy collecting the gowns in her short arms. The moment before might never have happened.

"We're all through, Mr. Jeb," she said, her voice ordinary again. "I thought this rose for Haidee's first act; what do you think?" She held up the material of the long gown and Jeb nodded absently. Esme started for the stairs; then, just as she reached the top step, she looked back, her eyes holding mine. "Mind what I told you, Alison," she said, and started down the stairs.

When we heard the last of her footsteps, I found myself suddenly weak and sat down on the top of the trunk behind me. "You're going to get your dress dirty," said Jeb, but he wasn't really looking at me. He was gazing at the attic the way he had examined Lionel's study that first night I had come to Vail's Point.

"What was that all about?" he asked abruptly, glancing down at me. Something in my face must have startled him, for he knelt on the floor beside the trunk where I sat. "What's happened? You look like you've seen a ghost."

I took a deep swallow. The attic was still now, so hot and airless I felt I could hardly breathe. "She was so . . . strange," I added, looking at Jeb.

"Esme?" He frowned a little, but there was none of the cold sarcasm in his voice that I usually heard.

"Jeb, it was as if—I know it sounds mad, but . . . I thought for a moment she might . . . kill me."

He considered it for a moment, instead of laughing as I might have expected. "You're having quite a day, aren't you?" he said, his voice dry as usual. "First you think I'm a killer, now you think Esme's one."

I got up and moved away impatiently. Even that slight movement seemed to intensify the heat of the attic. "You think I'm talking nonsense." But even as I said it, I realized I couldn't very well blame him. Esme as a killer *was* absurd. Only, he hadn't seen the look on her face as she held the thin metal cord . . .

"I think you believe it. Which keeps it from being nonsense." He walked around me so that he could stare at my face. "Only, . . . why would she want to kill you?"

"Because of Lionel. She hated him."

"So? He's been dead thirty years."

"It doesn't matter." He was standing very close now, looking so strong and solid that for a brief second I wanted to move closer, into his arms, like a frightened child hoping to be comforted. He *would* think me mad if I did that, I knew, and the thought almost made me laugh.

"Good, you're smiling," he said, and there was a twinkle of amusement in his green eyes. "You must be contemplating putting me in my place again."

I blushed. Better he believe that than what I really had been thinking. "I'm not joking about Lionel."

He ran his fingers through his crisp, black hair. "My God, woman, I think you're obsessed with the man." He stepped away. Perversely, I felt sorry I had been the one to break the moment between us. "Even if Esme hated Lionel," he went on, "why on earth would she want to threaten you?"

"For prying into his life, his secrets." He snorted at the idea, and I continued, somewhat defiantly. "*I* was the one who made the theater season possible; *I* was the one who suggested opening with *The Basilisks—*"

"Giving Haidee the best part she's had in years," he added in that maddeningly reasonable voice that always infuriated me. "And giving us all a lot of publicity. Considering how Esme worships Haidee, she should be down on her knees thanking you for what you've done."

"Well, she isn't." I stood there trying to reason out what I was feeling. It was then that the thought came to me. "Besides," I added slowly, "I think she's afraid."

"Of you?"

"Of what I might find," I added thoughtfully. "Of what Corin and I might find."

He made an impatient gesture, "You're not talking about that damned lost play again, are you? I told you, it doesn't exist." He turned away from me deliberately, so I could not see his face. But just for a moment I felt he was not so sure of himself as he wanted me to believe and, stubbornly, I wanted to prove him wrong.

"It *does* exist. Or at least it did."

He looked back at me, but now his face was guarded, as if he was determined not to show what he was thinking. For a second I thought of the small stone half hidden in the graveyard on the hill. Phoebe Reives. What do you know about her? I wondered. But I was determined to give him no further opportunity to mock, to laugh at my conjectures or dismiss them with glib talk of "coincidences." I touched the watch pinned to my dress. This time I would argue only with facts.

"There *was* a last play," I went on stubbornly. "You've seen how Lionel treated his family in *Red Mountain* and in *The Basilisks*. Do you really think he would have turned lovable about them in the third play of the trilogy?"

"Probably not." His face had not changed, but he was listening to me with more attention than he had before.

"And isn't it possible that what he wrote might have been so . . . vicious, so slanderous even, that somebody might have had a very good reason for destroying the play and him as well? And anybody who tried to find the play, even now?"

"It's possible." The cynical smile appeared on his face, and I knew he was about to walk into my trap. "Only, there's absolutely no proof there *was* a last play."

"Yes there is," I said, and for once I allowed my voice to take the same superior tone he so often used. "I found part of a letter in Lionel's rooms. Would you like to see it?" I asked, fumbling with the pin of my watch.

"We haven't got the time," he answered abruptly and started toward the stairs. "I only came up to tell you that May is waiting for you in her studio. To rehearse."

"The letter's right here." The antique watch was in my hands now, and I started to open the back of it. "Perhaps you'll believe me when you've read it."

"Perhaps." He watched me fumble with the catch. "Have you been carrying it around pinned to your bosom? How very Victorian!"

"I couldn't get into town to have it copied," I said, knowing I was losing my temper again. Why didn't the catch open? "And it was too valuable to risk losing . . ."

The back of the watch came free then. I stood for a moment looking down at it silently, knowing the color was rising again in my cheeks.

I will not cry, I told myself firmly. I will not give him that pleasure.

For the page Lionel had written was gone.

CHAPTER NINETEEN

"Alison?"

I will not cry, I told myself. I will *not* cry!

Jeb took a step closer, his eyes almost sympathetic. "You don't seem to have much luck with evidence, do you?" he said. And while he may have meant it kindly, that was more than I could bear.

"Go away . . . *please!*" If only I could get out of the attic without having to pass him. If only I could be by myself to think . . . the Green Room that morning, trying on the costumes! They had all been there, it could have been anyone . . .

But Jeb was speaking again.

"Alison, I'm not laughing at you. The greatest actress in the world couldn't have faked that look on your face when you opened the watch."

"There *was* a letter, Jeb!" I broke in angrily. "Corin saw it! I showed it to him!"

"Corin . . . ," he said, his voice drifting off. "I'm afraid that wouldn't be much proof, not for the rest of us. Corin's had an obsession about this last play for years. Nobody even listens any more."

"But he's right!" At least Jeb wasn't sneering now. "I found the page in Lionel's desk," I went on more calmly. "Oliver had said something . . . strange that first day at lunch."

"Oliver?" Jeb broke in. "Is he in on this, too?"

"I—I don't know." The whole affair was beginning to sound ridiculous as I tried to explain it. "But he asked if I had found any papers from the last year of Lionel's life, the winter he spent here. It started me thinking. I didn't remember any, so that afternoon I went through all my files. And there was nothing." Jeb stared at me silently, his eyes skeptical. "I mean it, Jeb. Nothing from all those months. And yet, Lionel was like the rest of the Vails . . ." I gestured at the boxes and trunks that surrounded us in the attic. "None of them ever threw anything away. Not any of them. Not clothes or books or papers or *anything*. And certainly not letters or notes."

"That still doesn't prove . . ."

"Listen to me! The page I found was the carbon of a letter he had written. If it hadn't been pushed in behind a drawer, I think it would have been missing, too. It was very clearly about the last play . . . about having finished it."

I looked him straight in the eyes. "Do you know what the title of the last play was?" His green eyes revealed nothing. "It was *All Our Yesterdays.* That puts another meaning on the page from *Macbeth* they found in his hands, doesn't it?" I said the quote quietly: "'And all our yesterdays have lighted fools the way to dusty death. . . .'"

He considered this for a moment. "Possibly," he said, and then his eyes were suddenly shrewd. "The page you found was the carbon of a letter?"

I nodded. "Typed on Lionel's typewriter. I checked that myself."

He nodded slightly. "Still, that doesn't prove *Lionel* typed it, does it? It *could* have been planted there by Corin, couldn't it? Or by somebody? To keep you interested?" A thin smile twisted his lips. "You . . . and your family's foundation?"

I didn't decide what I did then; I didn't think about it or choose to do it. It was an automatic reflex. My hand went out swiftly to claw that superior smirk off his handsome face. But he must have sensed what I was going to do, for he grabbed my wrist effortlessly before it was even near him.

"Steady, my dear," he said. "I haven't got much of a face, but I prefer it intact." We stood for a moment, glaring at each other. But my anger was already leaving.

"You can let me go," I said finally. "I won't do that again."

He dropped my hand and smiled wryly. "For a proper young lady, you have a very short temper."

But now his face was thoughtful. "Alison, you *could* be right about all this. I don't know. I've laughed at the idea of the 'missing masterpiece' for so long, maybe I'm the one who's being stupid and stubborn. Maybe being a director makes me too practical. But you have to admit that lost plays and fat old Esme as a menace and stolen letters . . ."

"And candle wax that only I saw," I added. "And *your* script below where Wendy fell. Let's not forget that."

"I explained that." Jeb sighed. "Didn't you believe me?"

"I don't know what I believe any more," I said. Or whom, I added to myself silently.

"Alison, be sensible!" Jeb said explosively. "This is all too theatrical and melodramatic! Real life just isn't like that!"

186

"Only, when have any of the Vails been like real life?"

I walked past him then, with as much dignity as I could, and started down the stairs.

A month in this house had at least taught me the value of a good exit line.

I started for my bedroom, forgetting why Jeb had come up to the attic, but in the center area above the great stairs May stood waiting, her hands folded in front of her long, tan linen robe, her back straight. I remembered then what lay ahead of me that evening.

"I'm sorry," I stammered. "I forgot you were waiting." I barely managed to finish the sentence before she beckoned me to follow her.

She moved majestically down the corridor toward Lionel's study. But we were not to go to his rooms. She went past them to a door on the other side of the hall and went in without even looking back to see if I had followed her.

I stood in the open doorway, a little hesitant. Ahead was a great sweep of windows facing the sea. The room itself was large and, in comparison with the rest of Vail's Point, almost bare. Plain straw mats covered most of the floor. Two simple wooden benches stood in front of the windows, and there was a long narrow bed placed so that whoever lay upon it could see the sea and the sky outside. The bed had a thin mattress, the headboard and footboard low and ebony black and carved in an intricate oriental design. Beside the bed stood a huge antique armoire, the front and sides covered with a design of gold dragons painted centuries before and now dim with the years. There were no shelves in the room, no pictures or paintings or books: it was as severe as the cell of an abbess.

May stood in the center of the room. She was not looking at me. She faced the wall opposite the bed, and as I stepped into the room I turned toward it also. This wall was completely mirrored from floor to ceiling, broken only by a narrow bar that stretched across it at waist height. There was no mistaking this was the room of a dancer.

"You move well." May did not face me; she said it to my reflection in the mirror, as though it was easier to speak to me that way.

"Thank you." Now that I was there I was not sure exactly what was expected of me. The part I was to play that evening had no dancing in it, and there seemed to be no specific pantomime required. The silence between us stretched as we continued to stare at each other in the mirror. Finally, May looked away from our reflections and faced me directly.

In the past weeks I had seen little of May. In daylight she shielded herself behind dark glasses; in the evening she sat quietly in corners, silent as a shadow. Only occasionally would I see in her dark eyes that flicker of light I had noticed the first night. It seemed to come from somewhere deep inside her imperious head, but if she noticed anyone watching her she would instantly drop her eyelids and glance away. It was as if she were afraid of what people might see.

She glided closer, her appraisal as matter-of-fact as if I had been a statue or a piece of furniture. "You could have been a dancer," she said. "Did you ever consider it?"

"No." Since that sounded like a rejection of what she clearly held most dear, I added somewhat hesitantly, "I know that you were one—"

"I taught." The soft caramel linen swept the floor gracefully as she moved away. "I was never allowed to perform. I was too big. I was too ugly." It was a statement. She did not expect contradiction. Her face was still expressionless, but a dull flush had crept into her sallow skin.

"You're playing me, you know. Tonight." She said the words coldly, but somehow I sensed behind them years of pain. "The only difference is you are beautiful."

"But that's how Lionel saw you," I said quietly. It was the only answer I could think of to break the silence between us. "He must have loved you very much."

"Lionel . . ." For a second her thin red lips trembled. Then her head went up and her wide shoulders straightened and she looked once more as regal as a Chinese empress. "Let us get to work," she said.

And work we did. For the next two hours, as the sunlight faded from the ocean outside and the first dark blue of twilight came into the sky, May drilled me over and over again on each moment I would spend on stage. Nothing was too insignificant for her attention—the curve of my fingers as I touched the jewels in the second scene, the way I was to seize the glass in the last act, even to how I was to awaken and drift from the stage in silence at the beginning of the play. We went over and over what I was to do, and instead of making me feel restricted or self-conscious, it seemed to free me. Whatever Fate may have denied May as a performer, she was undoubtedly a superb teacher.

"You'll do," she said finally. And there was something very close to a pleased smile on the tight mask of her face. "Not too much makeup," she added. "This girl lives most of her life in dreams. Indoors. Quietly."

So we're back to talking about the character as something separate from your own life, I thought. I was wrong. May walked over to the giant armoire and opened the doors of the chest, saying as she moved, "Would you like to see how I looked at that time? The time Lionel was writing about?"

She did not wait for an answer, and from where I was standing I could not see the inside of the chest. After a moment she moved back to me in that same smooth, gliding walk that seemed at such variance with her rawboned body. I knew May must be an old woman, as Haidee was, and yet it was hard to think of either of the sisters being aged. They had both forced time to stand still, Haidee with humor and vitality and warmth, May with the stiff, disciplined rigidity of a primitive icon.

She held out a small photograph, sepia brown as they used to be many years ago, and I could see now why my father had thought May gentle and kind in her youth. The girl who had seemed so dim in the painting in the drawing room had grown into a tall young woman, perhaps not conventionally beautiful, but there was a vulnerability about her in her simple white dress, her hair hanging straight to her shoulders, that made one think of flowers touched by a spring breeze.

May took the photograph back, studying it for a moment as if she were seeing it for the first time. "She was a very simple girl," she said quietly.

"I'll remember."

"She wanted to bring beauty into the world."

May raised her eyes from the picture and stared again at her reflection in the mirrored wall. A look of almost pure hatred came

189

over her face. Abruptly she looked away and silently took the picture back to the armoire.

I could see her place it on what must be a high shelf. But her hand was shaking and it brushed against something. A loud mechanical ticking broke the silence of the dim room. It was a ticking I'd heard before: that first afternoon on my balcony; during some of the quiet nights; but it was not the ticking of a clock. I moved closer out of curiosity. May still had her back toward me, but she must have sensed that I was nearer, for she twisted her head over her shoulder to look at me, her eyes suddenly dark with suspicion. The ticking stopped abruptly. I could see now it had been coming from the large wooden object she held in her hands.

It was a metronome, obviously an expensive one, large and heavy and inlaid with ivory. I should have recognized the sound earlier, I thought. I should have known that dancers use it to beat out time while they practice their exercises.

To *record* time . . .

I do not think I gasped, or even made a sound, but what I was thinking must have been in my face, for May smiled, her thin lips barely curving. "Do you like it?" she asked, holding the metronome forward for me to examine.

It was growing dark in the room and it was hard to see the tiny, perfect details of the wooden pyramid she held. It *could* be big enough to hold the manuscript of a play, I thought. It *could* fit into the back of it.

"Lionel gave it to me many years ago," May said, her eyes never leaving my face. "It's quite valuable. The person he bought it from said that it had once belonged to Pavlova."

Let me touch it, I thought. Let me just have a chance to examine it. "Recorded time" . . . what else could Lionel have meant? To leave his last, his most dangerous manuscript with his trusted sister, of course that would be the "precautions" he had taken! I reached out for the metronome, and even in the dimness of the room I could see my hands were trembling.

"It's very beautiful," I said. May gave it to me without protest. There was still enough light to see that there was a tiny door in the back of the instrument, fastened with a metal catch. If I could just get it open . . .

"No."

May's voice was clear and firm as she stood watching me. She made no move. "It isn't there."

I looked at her, not even trying to hide my feelings. "I thought . . ." My hands began to tremble again, and May swiftly took the precious antique away from me.

"I know," she said quietly. "You thought the last play was hidden in the metronome. "Recorded time . . ." She laughed dryly. "It's the sort of thing Lionel would have liked. He loved secrets, mystery . . ." She slid back the catch of the panel and opened it, turning the antique so that I could see inside. The space was empty, or, rather, it was full of cogs and weights and wires. "You see?" said May. "No manuscript."

"You must think me a fool," I said. Suddenly I was very tired. I sat down on the low bench by the window, my hands still shaking. To be disappointed twice in one day was too much. May put the metronome back in the armoire carefully and closed the great, carved door. "It's just that phrase . . . the one he'd underlined . . . I felt it meant something." I had no reason now not to tell May of the page of the letter. Now that it was gone, it didn't really matter who knew about it.

"I found a copy of a letter," I said, picking my words carefully. I realized suddenly how much I wanted May to believe me. "It's the only thing I've found from that last winter, and it was only by accident I found it. It said he had finished a last play, that it might cause trouble, that rehearsals were to begin on Monday—"

"And it was time 'to avenge a terrible wrong,'" said May quietly. "That it didn't matter what the family thought. Or the town."

I stared at her. She was quoting it exactly. Lionel had written that letter to her!

"'I have taken the usual precautions . . . ,'" she went on. And then she looked down at me, her eyes no longer fierce and dark but shining with tears that had not been shed for a very long time.

"Yes, my dear. Lionel wrote that letter to me."

"Then there *was* a last play! You believe that, too, don't you?" She nodded. "I not only believe it, I *saw* it."

She was taller than I, but for once I felt the stronger, the more powerful. I think if she had not gone on speaking I might physically have shaken her to learn the truth. But she sank down on the low bench and continued talking in her quiet, somber voice, her ugly hands hiding themselves in the soft folds of her robe.

"Yes, I saw the manuscript," she said. Perhaps it was the twilight, or perhaps remembering that long-ago summer softened her so that for the first time I could see traces of the young girl in the photograph. "Lionel spent that whole last winter up here. Most of the time he was alone. I think he knew in some way it was his last chance to save himself.

"So he came up here," she went on. "He said he was working on a play. I think we all expected it would be about the War. He'd been in the Army, he'd seen cruel things. It was logical that this would be the obsession that would make him want to write again." The room was getting darker. I could barely see her face in the fading light.

"But something happened after Christmas . . . whatever he'd been working on he decided to abandon. Perhaps the War was still too close for him to write about. At any rate, about the end of February he wrote me that he had stumbled on something, something he *had* to write. I had the feeling that it was to be the third play to complete the family triology . . . to follow *Red Mountain* and *The Basilisks*, although he never said so specifically."

"But the 'usual precautions'? What did that mean?"

She smiled, but she was not looking at me. It was if she were seeing Lionel and that rare, shy smile was for him. "That came out of the past . . . long before the War. When he was first starting as a writer. He'd throw all of himself into whatever he was working on, all his passion and energy, all his genius. And then, when he was finished, he'd go off on a great, glorious drunken spree. He'd be gone for days sometimes, we'd never know where he was. Unless he got into a fight and it made the papers. Mama was still remembered by her public, Haidee was making a name for herself . . . the Vails were always good copy for the newspapers."

Her voice grew sad. "Only one time when he'd finished a new play, he didn't leave the house. He got drunk here . . . and he reread what he had written. And he hated it. Everything he wrote always seemed when he finished it so far from what he meant it to be."

She shuddered a little. "So he tore it up, that play. His only manuscript. Burned it in the fireplace downstairs. We were alone here that night. I tried to stop him, but it was useless. He was so much stronger than I. I had to stand and watch the flames burning. Knowing that it might be a masterpiece . . ."

When she began to speak again, her voice was tired. "Of course the next day he bitterly regretted what he'd done. So we made an agreement. I would keep a copy of everything he wrote, so that never again could he destroy his work completely." She looked at me, almost as if she were pleading with me to understand. "You see, he could never write a thing a second time. It was his greatest talent and his greatest curse. He could never repeat something. Once the passion was spent, the work completed, he could never go back to it again."

"Then you have a copy of that last play? The 'usual precautions'. . . he sent you the manuscript?"

Her stiff shoulders slumped a little, and even in the twilight shadows I could see she was an old, tired woman. "No," she said finally. "He didn't want me to read it. He never wanted anybody to read his work until it was completely finished. In the letter you read, the letter he sent me that last month, he included the key to that armoire." She nodded toward the great chest behind her. "He had put a copy of the manuscript there while he was polishing the final version, locked it safely away and sent the key to me in New York."

"And after his death . . . ?" But I knew before she answered that somehow the "precautions" had failed.

"I came up from the city the Saturday before rehearsals were to begin," May continued, as if she had not heard my question. "The way he had talked about the play, something in his letter had frightened me. Lionel could be . . . cruel at times. It's in all his work, especially the plays he wrote about the family. He'd told none of us what to expect, just writing to Haidee rather grandly about the number of actors he would need and who they should be.

"Haidee was rather afraid of him in those days." She smiled again, a little sadly. "Perhaps we all were." She fell silent for a moment, turning to stare out the window at the twilight blue sky and the sea below it.

"Surely you weren't? Afraid of him, I mean," I said, trying to prompt her back to that last weekend.

"No," she answered. "Lionel never made me fear him. Even in his wildest rages . . ." She looked at me again. "When I came up that Saturday, Lionel was . . . different than I'd ever seen him before. There was a wild gaiety to him, as if he couldn't stop laughing over some enormous private joke. I thought he might have started drinking again, but he swore to me that he hadn't, and finally I believed him. He showed me the manuscript, all carefully typed, even to the booklets of sides for all the actors. But he wouldn't let me read it."

She frowned a little, as if it still puzzled her after all these years. "And he asked for the key to the armoire back. He wanted that copy as well. I argued with him, something I never did. I said I'd give it to him Monday. But it was no use. He promised me over and over again that there was no chance that he might destroy this play, it was too good, too important. But he was to meet someone the following day, that Sunday before the rehearsals. He wanted them to read the play before anybody else."

"Did he say who it was?"

She shook her head. "No. It seemed to be part of his pleasure, that it was a secret. I had a feeling whoever it was knew about our arrangement, knew that a copy of his work was always locked in the armoire." She forced herself to stand then, her big body stiff with age. "So I gave him the key, finally. And he sent me back to the city." She looked out at the evening sky.

"I never saw him alive again."

The shadows were dark in the room now, and I had to strain my eyes to read the expression on her face. It was no use; she was in control of herself once more.

"And that is the end of it?"

"Not quite."

She continued to stare out at the ocean below. "We found him dead in the theater that Monday, the page from *Macbeth* clutched in his hand. I knew, of course, what it meant, but what could I prove? Then, later, when the reporters and police and ambulance had gone, I came back here to the house. I think I was the first one. It was summer, remember. The fireplace downstairs had been empty Saturday when I left, completely clean. But now it held a pile of ashes."

I felt for a moment almost physically sick. To have come this far, only to find at the end *nothing!*

"So he'd burned the play after all." I could not hide my disappointment. It's all over, I thought. The whole fool's game of clues and mysteries and family secrets, all pointless nonsense. Jeb had been right all along. I stood. It was getting late. Soon I would have to think about the evening ahead. And the theater.

"Not quite." May turned to face me now, letting me look deep into her eyes for the first time. "The *original* of the manuscript was burned. I could see that from some scraps that had been left. And the sides. They had all been stapled together very carefully." Her lips twisted again, but without amusement. "Staples don't burn."

"And your copy of the play?" But it was a foolish question to ask, for who could tell from a pile of ashes whether both copies of Lionel Vail's last play had been burned or not?

"I'm not so sure."

May walked over to the armoire and swung the two painted doors open. "When I finally came up here to my room that morning I noticed that the lock to the chest had been broken. See?" She swung the doors back together again and beckoned me nearer. "I've never had it fixed. There wasn't any reason for locks with Lionel dead."

A thought began to pick at my brain. "But why would anyone break—?" I began, but May interrupted me, her voice clear in the shadows.

"Precisely. Why would anybody break into the armoire if they had found *both* copies of the play?" She put her strong, ugly hands on my shoulders so that I could not look away from her. "But suppose they never found my copy? Suppose Lionel was too clever for them after all?" Her voice was hushed, barely louder than a whisper, although no one could have overheard us. "Suppose the play still exists? And whoever murdered Lionel has been searching for it for these last thirty years? And is *still* searching for it?"

Her voice was very cold, but I heard something else surging through her: a feeling of hope reviving. The search wasn't over, not for her or me or Corin . . . and not for the person who had tried to block us every step of the way, who had tried so desperately to erase every trace of what Lionel had written, who may have killed him to do it.

From the great hall downstairs we heard the slow chimes of the grandfather's clock toll off the hour. May dropped her hands.

"It's late," she said. "This is not the time for the past. Now we must get you through tonight."

ACT THREE
(THE PERFORMANCE)

CHAPTER TWENTY

For the rest of my life I will never be able to remember clearly all that happened between the time I left May's room and when the curtain finally rose at the theater.

May stayed by my side nearly every moment. Somehow, the confession she had made seemed to have broken the stiff façade she had preserved since I had come to Vail's Point. She saw me to my bedroom; then, while I was bathing she went to the kitchen and prepared a small tray and brought it back to me. Having missed lunch, I was famished. But the nervousness I was starting to feel had reached my stomach, and I wasn't sure I could swallow anything.

"A cup of hot soup," said May, lifting the silver lid from a small bowl. "And some plain bread and butter, a slice of chicken, a little salad—nothing you can't handle." She pulled a chair over to the bureau and sat down. To my surprise, I managed to eat it all.

I know now how much effort it must have been for the always-silent old woman to have kept up a constant stream of conversation while she was with me. Perhaps I even realized it then—that it was solely to keep my mind off the performance ahead. At that she was successful. Not that we discussed Lionel further; May was determined I was to forget him for the evening, and after the few attempts on my part to get more information failed, I gave up and simply listened.

This was a different May from the one I had seen before, telling anecdotes of the dance world with a wry and caustic tongue. It was as if she were consciously trying to be as charming and witty as Haidee. And while she would never have the humor and warmth of her older sister, she was excellent company. The clock ticked nearer and nearer to the moment when I knew I would have to leave for the theater.

May had us start earlier than I expected, walking right along with me as if afraid that if left alone I might take it into my mind to run—away from the house, the theater and the evening before me. She carried the starched brown-and-white-striped cotton dress I had picked for the party after the performance. Seeing it in her hands was almost like a talisman that somehow eleven o'clock must come.

We were not alone on the path through the woods to the theater. Ahead was Esme, with Haidee. Esme, too, was carrying a long dress as well as various boxes and bags Haidee had obviously decided at the last minute were essential. We made no attempt to catch up with them, and they did not wait for us. Behind, Rita walked with Oliver. She held his script in her hands, and we could hear her cuing the old man as they made their way along the path.

The sunset was in my eyes as we approached the theater. But even with the fresh paint and frame of bright flowers it did not look as cheerful as it had before; it seemed ominous now, the way the big house did. A couple of the apprentices stood in the cleared area in front of the theater, waiting to park the cars that would arrive only too soon. Another apprentice, a serious-faced young girl, was tacking a paper onto an easel. I knew what the paper said.

"The part of Emily will be played tonight by Alison Howard."

May would not let me look at it. She took my arm firmly and directed me toward the rear of the theater. "We'll go in the stage door," she said.

I had expected noise and confusion backstage. That is what is always shown in movies and books about theatrical opening nights. Instead, the whole area was quiet, except for the distant sound of someone using a staple machine to fasten one last bit of décor more firmly.

For me that sound will always be the symbol of an opening night in summer stock.

Because the cast for *The Basilisks* was small, there were sufficient dressing rooms on the stage level for all of us. I noticed that mine (a card had been carefully tacked to the door) was next to the one where Lionel had died. There seemed to be something odd about that locked door, but I had no time to think of that, or him; for May was already inside the dressing room, opening the window and the small door to the porch beyond. On the makeup shelf that stretched the short length of the little room there were flowers—a large bunch of long-stemmed yellow roses from Oliver (how he managed to have them delivered this far out in the country I couldn't imagine!), a single red carnation (and a romantic card) from Corin, and a strikingly beautiful arrangement of simple field flowers that I knew had been put there by May. There was nothing from Jeb.

Before I could thank May, I noticed in the center of the makeup shelf a small box and a note: "My dear child," Haidee had written, "the pin enclosed is of no great material value, but my mother gave it to me the night I made my debut in the theater. I think she would want you to have it and I find it right for Emily to wear. All good luck to you, dear Alison . . . and all my gratitude . . . for being your own sweet, courageous self . . . and for helping us this important night."

The pin inside the box was small, a simple circle of silver. "I must thank her," I said, starting for the door. But May stopped me, her face a frozen mask again. "Not now. Haidee doesn't see anybody before a performance," she said.

And then it was as if I were on a great, long slide that I could not get off until the curtain fell at the end of the play. Every movement I made, every breath I took, was pointed toward that final moment, and I knew the others of the cast in their separate dressing rooms were feeling the same way.

May began by brushing my hair until it shone. From the pockets of her deep robe she pulled out various pots and sticks of makeup. I looked at her questioningly. "No," she said. "They aren't Wendy's. It's bad luck to use other people's makeup without their permission. It's the one unbroken rule of the theater."

Time seemed to be going much faster than before. I could hear cars pulling up outside, the chatter of voices of the audience arriving. The night was warm, and I knew that all the doors and windows of the theater were open; and yet the voices seemed very far away. I should be out there with them, I thought dully, not sitting here. But May was powdering my face carefully, and I had no time to think. Someone tapped on the closed dressing-room door and said, "Half hour," and then, in what seemed seconds later, "Fifteen minutes." May paid no attention.

By now she had helped me into my dress, fastening the tiny white pearl buttons at the wrist of each full sleeve. Esme had performed some magic with my costume. It seemed soft and fresh, billowing over the petticoats down to the flat ballet slippers she had found for me. I touched the thin, pale blue silk ribbon that caught my hair back from my face, leaving it to fall free from the crown of my head in soft curls. As May finished tying my long sash, I took my first look at myself in the mirror.

I was no longer the woman I thought I was: sensible, adult, modern. The long, white muslin dress, the hair hanging loose behind my shoulders, the pale face May had given me, made me someone completely different. Young and fragile and, perhaps, for the first time in my life, even beautiful.

"Oh, May," I said, "do I really look like that?"

"You're a very beautiful girl," she said, her eyes meeting mine in the mirror. "Didn't you know?"

Before I could think of an answer, the door opened abruptly and Jeb stuck his head in. "Good luck—," he started to say, and then he stopped cold and whistled softly. "My God, Alison! You're gorgeous!" I could see May smile slightly, but Jeb was standing directly in front of me, studying me carefully.

"Yes, yes," he said half under his breath. "Perfect for the part." He glanced at the old woman behind me. "Good job, May." I felt a strange glow of pride, although I had done nothing.

"How's the house?" asked May practically.

"Packed. We've put up folding chairs and the standing room's almost gone." He looked at me now and smiled. "You may even get your money back on the season." Then to May: "Two critics from New York are here. All the local newspapers, of course. A couple of magazines have made reservations for later in the week. The executives from the network are out front and rumor has it there is even a Broadway producer. And they've parked more Cadillacs than you'd find at a state funeral."

May broke in, her voice crisp and businesslike. "What are you trying to do, Jeb? Frighten the girl?"

"Nope." He looked straight into my eyes, and for once I saw something that was neither amusement nor anger nor the cynicism he hid behind so often. There was something almost warm and trusting in the way he looked at me, as if for one moment he was letting me look deep, deep through his green eyes into himself.

"Alison," he said softly. "You're going to be wonderful tonight. Just let it happen."

They led me out onto the stage then, May on one side, Jeb on the other. Haidee stood waiting—looking, even under the harsh overhead lights, calm and beautiful. She wore the rose gown Esme had found, soft lace at her wrists and throat, silver hair piled high, her back straight, like a queen about to receive her courtiers. Behind her was the heavy velvet curtain. I could hear, more clearly than I wanted, the sound of the audience settling into their seats. Oh, God, I thought, it'll be like the dream! That terrible nightmare. I can't go through with it. *I can't!*

My shoulders started to tremble, but I think only Haidee noticed.

"Go away," she said to the others. Her voice was low so that no one but those of us on stage could hear it, but there was no mistaking the authority of her tone. Haidee had come back to her own world, and no one would dare contradict a great star on her opening night. Jeb and May left without protest, May giving my cold fingers a gentle squeeze before she went. Then we were alone on the stage, Haidee and I.

"I won't tell you this isn't a frightening experience," she said, her voice soft as a whisper. "But you can do it. Just keep your mind on this stage and what is happening here. Don't worry about them out there. They don't exist. Only this room and the people in it and the story we have to tell matter now."

The imperiousness disappeared and she leaned forward, a giggle in her voice like a schoolgirl. "Besides, you're nearsighted, aren't you?" I nodded dumbly.

"Good," she said. "So am I. It's the best gift an actor can have. Makes them all look like rows of white balloons out there." She gave my shoulder a gentle pat and led me over to the sofa where I was to pretend to be asleep when the curtain rose.

"Thank you for the pin," I whispered, clinging to her hand for one last moment.

She nodded and took her hand from mine. "I should get some applause for my entrance," she added. "Don't let it throw you." With grandeur she swept off through the main doors of the set.

I was alone on the stage now. I leaned back, forcing myself to close my eyes. Thank God I had nothing to say in this first scene. My mouth was so dry I knew no words would come. You're asleep, I thought. Emily is asleep. I made myself think about the play. It's a warm summer afternoon, I told myself. I'm a dominated, timid girl, no longer a child but very like one still, in my dependency.

A blaze of lights flashed across my closed eyelids, and I could hear whispers from the stage crew beyond the scenery walls as they turned on, one after another, the great spotlights of lavender and rose and amber. In a second it will happen, I thought. The curtain will rise and I'll be out here alone . . .

A great swoosh of cloth, and the lights on my closed eyelids as I lay on the sofa became suddenly brighter. For a moment silence, and then I heard polite applause for the set. Before that could quite die out, there was another swell of applause, and I knew that Haidee had made her entrance carrying the glass of milk that was the symbol of the love between Lavinia and her cousin Emily.

But the applause didn't die down. It continued to grow, a huge surge of noise as if the audience couldn't bear to end demonstrating the love they felt for a great star who had dominated the theater for most of her life and now at last had come back to them. Then Haidee must have done something, for the audience stilled their applause as if she had snapped a whip, and sat back to listen.

The first performance of *The Basilisks* had begun.

Then, incredibly, as if there were no such thing as time, the play was over, swept by in a jumble of lights and colors and words.

I know somehow after the applause the audience had given Haidee, all my fears disappeared. I never thought again about the dream that had haunted me, not even at the beginning of the last act.

I managed to leave the stage when I was supposed to in the first act, but even in the comforting shadows behind the scenery I still felt somehow as if I were still in the play, walking in the garden as Emily was supposed to be doing. Julie made her entrance, sleek and tailored, completely opposite from the vague, rather sweet-faced woman I had seen for so many weeks. She, too, received applause on her entrance. It was almost but not quite as explosive as that they had greeted Haidee with, as if the audience knew instinctively the gradations of approval they wished to give.

"It's going well."

Jeb whispered it quietly in my ear. He had tiptoed up behind me, but I was not startled. Nothing could frighten me now. I nodded. Oddly enough, all I wanted to do was to get back on that stage, start my next scene. I had no fear now; my mouth was not dry and I had no desire to run. I was part of the company.

I belonged.

The intermission was a blur of conversation, as if the actors had been holding their breaths all through the first act and were now wildly, pantingly eager to talk. The curtain had fallen to still more applause. But I could hardly wait for it to rise again.

My second scene went by, over before it seemed to begin. I could tell the audience could hear me, for there was no coughing, no restlessness. Julie's eyes were bright and glittering as she played the jewel-box scene with me, moving carefully around the table so that the audience could be sure to see my reactions. I won't say I wasn't aware of people watching, but they didn't frighten me—they *wanted* to hear what Emily had to say. And later, in the last scene, I could feel their eyes again on me, willing me to fight the villains as they tried to persuade this timid girl to sign the commitment papers on the old woman.

Haidee appeared. No longer a grand and gracious lady in her soft gowns and laces, her silver hair was straggling, the dress she wore made her look like a tired ladies' maid. Only the tray in her hand was steady.

I could hear a gasp from the audience. Lionel had set the scene melodramatically perhaps, but without her saying a word we could see what evil the villains had achieved. I could feel my eyes filling with tears as Haidee came closer. She looked so pitiful, so frail.

I turned to Julie, and it took no acting to hate her for what had happened. I sprang up and took the glass from Haidee and swallowed the contents quickly. With all the anger in my heart, I ran up the stairs crying out the defiance Lionel had written. "Never!" I screamed.

And then I was off stage, high up on the dark platform. Someone was holding me, and there seemed to be a roaring in my ears.

"Listen to that, Alison," whispered Jeb as he held me. "They're giving you an exit hand." As my head cleared I could hear the audience applauding. "They like you."

"Did I do all right?" I said to Jeb. For some reason it seemed natural to stand there in the shadows with his arms around me.

"All right? You were perfect!" His face was dark in the shadows, but we were standing so close I could see he had the same expression he had worn that last moment in the dressing room. I think it was at that moment I stopped fearing him.

Curtain calls and flowers and people standing and Haidee bowing as the curtain rose and fell. Once she even made me come out with her, and we stood there hand in hand, bending to the pale circles in the dark auditorium who would not stop applauding. Finally, the curtain came down and stayed down.

People began pushing their way in backstage, voices high and excited; Haidee and Julie, their eyes glistening, greeted their friends; the other actors chattered among themselves. I made my way through the crowd to my dressing room. Several people tried to talk to me, but I couldn't seem to hear them. They appeared not to notice. A smile was all they wanted. I saw the librarian, Lucy Treble, in the crowd. She looked at me strangely, but she was hemmed in by other people and I could not reach her.

May was in my dressing room, waiting like a quiet sentinel. I sank down into the chair in front of the dressing-room shelf. Suddenly I felt exhausted. "Thank you, May," I said quietly. "Thank you for everything." She nodded.

"Lionel would have been proud of you," she said and began to help me out of my costume.

It was half an hour before I was ready to leave the theater. May disappeared after hanging up my dress and petticoats. I felt it was the first time I had been alone all that day, and it was good to be alone. As I used the cold cream May had provided, gradually my own face began to reappear. But somehow it was different, as if a little of Emily still remained that could not be wiped away.

I slipped on the crisp brown-and-white-striped jumper I had brought for the opening-night party. I wasn't tired any longer. I felt happy and warm and confident in a way I had not felt for a long, long time.

And *very* hungry!

When I came out of the dressing room, the backstage area was nearly deserted. I could hear a chatter of voices in other dressing rooms, Rita teasing Oliver about twisting a line of dialogue in the last act, Oliver rumbling back with good humor. It made me happy just to stand there listening for a moment. The actors were jubilant; you could feel it through the building. Grim play though it may be, *The Basilisks* had stunned the audience thoroughly, and though I did not know it then, that night marked the beginning of the revival of interest in all of Lionel Vail's work.

The thought of Lionel reminded me. I turned in the half darkness to look again at the closed door to his dressing room. Something had puzzled me as I passed it on my way into the theater, but I'd not had time to think about it. Now I did.

I looked at the closed door and carefully tried the handle. The door was still locked, as it was a month before, when I had turned the one key that fitted all the locks to Lionel's rooms. The key, at least, I had managed to hang on to. Bending over to examine the lock, I noticed now there were scratches on the metal plate near the keyhole. Those scratches weren't there before, I knew. Even the wood at the edge of the door had been nicked; tiny bits of wood were shredded as if someone had tried with force to pry the door open. Tried and not succeeded.

Oddly, this last discovery was the perfect ending of the evening. I found myself singing as I went through the stage door onto the veranda that circled the theater. May and I were not wrong. Someone *was* still searching for the copy of Lionel's play.

Corin stood waiting, smiling cheerfully. The veranda had been strung with Japanese lanterns. They swayed a little in the evening breeze, changing the light on his face.

"Congratulations, love," he said, hugging me tight, his eyes dancing. "That's the theater for you! Here I come from a long line of actors, I'm specially trained, I've worked for years at my trade . . . and the first time out, you walk off with the play!"

I laughed. It was good to relax now, to feel part of what the others had shared so long. "It's a great part, Corin," I said. "Nobody could fail in it."

"Wendy could have."

His mentioning her name sobered both of us. As we started

through the woods I told him all that had happened—the disappearance of the letter, what May had revealed to me, even about the scratches on the door to the dressing room where Lionel had died. We had almost reached the great house by the time I finished. Corin hesitated for a moment, holding me back in the shadow.

Ahead, Vail's Point blazed with light. Lights were strung on all the porches down to the beach, where the younger members of the crew were having a clambake. Cars had been parked at odd angles on the driveway, and I could see through the open windows people moving back and forth, their hands full of plates and glasses and cigarettes. It seemed as if the whole audience had come up the hill to praise Haidee for her performance.

"Be careful, Alison," said Corin as we stood there on the edge of the path into the forest. "Whoever destroyed the original of the play thirty years ago must think we're getting close. It could be dangerous."

Almost automatically we both looked up at the broken railing of the widow's walk above the balcony of my room. It was only twenty-four hours since Wendy had died, and yet so much had happened it seemed as if it had been a month.

"Try to sound out Oliver tonight," Corin whispered. "He'll be less on guard with the show over, more relaxed . . . he was a good friend of Lionel's in those days. I'll bet he knows more than he's said."

I nodded, and together we crossed the driveway and went into the house.

But what Corin asked was impossible. Each member of the cast, even I, was quickly surrounded by people with flattering words to say, all of them eager to get drinks and plates of food or anything else that might make us happy. Esme (with the help of Yvonne and Frankie) had achieved miracles.

I had never tasted a real New England clambake before . . . the cherrystones and littlenecks in cheesecloth bags baking on their bedding of seaweed, to be topped by layers of grilled chicken. Then more seaweed and big fat lobsters, red and crackling. There was also hot corn on the cob, golden as the melted butter dripping over it, and thin, crisp, salty fried potatoes.

For the more delicate, lobster Newburgh and chicken à la king bubbled in separate silver chafing dishes, ready to be poured over slivers of toast. And a great turkey stood at one end of the long dining-room table, half of its plump white breast already carved and served.

Every dish in the house must be in use tonight, I thought as I struggled through the crowd searching for Oliver. Haidee, in scarlet silk, was already enthroned on one of the long sofas in the drawing room, regaling an audience of middle-aged gentlemen (executives from Julie's network) with theatrical stories, her voice twisted in mimicry. Julie herself held court on the far side of the room, deep in a great wicker throne. Jeb sat at her feet, his profile sharp against the green of her skirt. But when he saw me he got up instantly and pushed his way through the noisy crowd. I saw Julie's eyes following him.

"Just the girl I want to see," he said when he reached me. "I've been talking it over with Julie and Haidee, and we don't see any reason to replace Wendy with somebody from New York. You were great tonight. So why don't you take over the other part she was to do . . . Lady Agatha in *Lady Windermere's Fan?* It's not any bigger than Emily. He grinned. "Or will you only accept leads now?"

"Thank you," I said. Where *was* Oliver? "But I'm not sure I'll still be here then. It's a couple of weeks away," I added lamely. "I may be finished with Lionel's papers by then."

The smile disappeared from Jeb's face and his eyes grew cold again. "Lionel," he said softly. "He's the only thing that matters, isn't he?"

"Couldn't I decide later? Please, Jeb," I said.

"Of course." His voice was formal. "Could I get you something to eat?"

"Actually, I was looking for Oliver."

"He's gone to bed," he said. He turned away abruptly and plunged back through the crowd to Julie. She had been watching us as we talked, I noticed, a curious smile on her face.

May also had disappeared, and I wondered as I climbed the great staircase later, moving between the people seated on the steps finishing the last of the supper, if she had gone up to the cemetery. What pleasure it would give her to visit Lionel's grave tonight, I thought. To whisper to him that once more his work was alive, once more he had stunned his audience, held them fascinated.

It was quiet on my side of the house. I opened the windows wide to let the breeze in. By now the driveway was empty of cars.

Far off, down on the beach, I could hear Bradley and some of the crew singing old college songs.

I should call Father, I thought as I looked out at the forest in the moonlight, the room dark behind me. I should tell him what has happened. But I knew I wouldn't. He would want to drive up to see me, and it was hard enough appearing on the stage in front of strangers without worrying about what his reaction would be. Later, I thought. I'll tell him later, when it's all over.

Something glittered in the dark woods below, something small and metallic. Someone is down there, I thought, part of the dark shadow of a tree at the edge of the forest, staring at the house.

The breeze was stronger now. It twisted the branches of the trees below me, and for a second I could see the silhouette of the person who stood watching so silently. I saw first the wide brim of his hat, then the metal that had caught my eye: a shield pinned to his shirt.

The man who had sworn never to set foot voluntarily here was below in the darkness, standing almost as though he was on guard.

Why, tonight, was Ed McNaughton watching Vail's Point?

Chapter Twenty-one

If our production of *The Basilisks* had opened in New York (I was to find out later), the next day would have been one of endless congratulatory phone calls from friends. There would have been dozens of copies of the newspapers scattered through every room, all turned to the theater page. Telegrams and still more flowers would arrive constantly at the front door, and inside the house excited meetings would go on for hours between the cast and the press representatives over the exact wording of the huge ads that would be taken to proclaim our triumph.

But Vail's Point was deep in the country, we were playing summer stock and our success was known only to the people who had actually been in the theater the night before.

The house was quiet when I finally came down for breakfast. Yvonne and Frankie must have been at work early, for there was no sign of the celebration of the night before. The drawing room was as it had always been, and there was only one place set at the long table in the dining room.

"The ones in the new play are already at rehearsal," Yvonne said as she brought in my orange juice. "Miss May and Miss Haidee are having breakfast in their rooms."

I felt in an odd way disappointed, as if somehow I had expected the magic of the night before to have changed the house in some permanent way. Instead, all the excitement, the applause, the crowds of people, the flattering words seemed a dream—something I had heard about but not really experienced.

I should go up to Lionel's study, I thought after I finished my solitary breakfast. It was time to start the bibliography of Lionel's library. But we were having another really hot day and anything more energetic than lying on the beach seemed beyond me.

The hours slipped by slowly, and I found myself impatient for the evening ahead. Through the long afternoon I found my mind returning again and again to the problem of the lost play. There were simply too many people whose lives had been affected by Lionel who were still alive and living at Vail's Point. May and

Haidee, Julie and Esme, even Oliver. Not to mention the people in the town of Westaven who had their own feelings toward him. I remembered Lucy Treble's strange look at the theater. And Ed McNaughton standing silent vigil outside the house the night before.

There may even be others, I thought glumly, that I don't know about. I lay back on the warm sand. I was the last person to be involved in a mystery, I decided, and yet, surely this was all evidence that Lionel's lost manuscript still existed, somewhere.

But *where?*

Shortly after five I came back up to the house to bathe and prepare for supper. I slipped on the lightest dress I owned, a thin lilac-and-blue-striped voile, and skewered my hair up on the top of my head in a knot. My hair had grown longer since I had been at Vail's Point. It was well below my shoulders. I must see about getting it cut, I thought. When I leave here. That will be soon, for Lionel's papers were almost completely in order now, ready for whoever would be his biographer.

I'll be leaving soon, I thought as I went down the hall to supper. The thought seemed unreal. When this week is over, I decided as I started down the stairs. When *The Basilisks* is finished, Saturday night.

Except I knew I wouldn't. I knew that I would stay to do the second play that Jeb had mentioned. I knew I would stay until the season ended. It was not as if I no longer had a will of my own. It was because there was still too much unfinished, too much that was important waiting for me in the days ahead.

The company that assembled for supper that evening was curiously divided. The actors who had started rehearsals that morning for the second production were in high spirits, energetic and preoccupied with the Ibsen play, while the rest of us—Haidee and May and I—found ourselves eating in silence, feeling (or at least I did) rather like children who had not been invited to a party. Jeb did not appear at dinner.

Later, when we were in the theater, May cautioned me about this evening's performance of *The Basilisks*. "Don't let down," she said as she brushed my hair smooth. "Don't grow careless." The theater was completely sold out again. Even without newspaper reviews, word had spread quickly through the nearby towns and vacation areas. Rita, passing by the dressing room, stuck her head in to report that most of the seats for the rest of the week had been sold as well.

The heat continued even after the sun had set, challenging us to give less than we had the night before. Beads of perspiration seeped through our makeup, and even my light dress seemed unbearably heavy. But halfway through the evening something happened that made me forget the weather.

Bradley, the earnest young stage manager, had warned us that most of the crew would not be present that evening, as they had been working all day on the set for *Ghosts* and Jeb had given them the evening off. In consequence, whoever was not on stage was to be useful to the actors who had to make quick changes of costume. Corin held Oliver's stiff dinner shirt off stage, ready to help him change into the white tie and tails needed for the last scene. Julie had brought Yvonne down from the house to help her dress for the same scene. Throughout the play, I could see the young girl, her bright eyes wide, staring out from the darkness at us when we were on stage, obviously fascinated to have such an intimate look at the people she had seen only as the difficult employers and guests of the house on the hill.

It was just before the last scene that something strange occurred. I was with Yvonne in Julie's dressing room, ready to help her make the quick change necessary for the last scene. Lionel had written *The Basilisks* in four acts, but we were playing it in two, with only one intermission. This meant that instead of having a leisurely ten minutes to remove her heavy taffeta afternoon dress and reappear in the ornate peach satin evening gown of the last scene, Julie had barely a minute while the curtain was down to switch costumes. May had disappeared after helping me get ready for the evening, and Bradley asked me to help Yvonne.

Her glittering evening jewelry was laid out carefully on Julie's dressing table. Yvonne stood quietly by the door to the veranda holding the long, rich gown (another contribution from Viola's trunks) Julie was to change into. Her high-heeled slippers had been carefully placed, her long white gloves—everything was set out as neatly as the instruments in an operating room.

We could tell from the muffled applause that the curtain had fallen, and a second later Julie rushed into the dressing room. She turned her back to me without a word, and I started unfastening the elaborate hooks that held her green silk dress together. She slipped out of the dress before I had the hooks completely open and, standing there in her heavy petticoats, took a swipe at her nose with a powder puff. Then, still in silence, she stepped into the satin gown as Yvonne held it for her. I was still trying to straighten out the dress she discarded when she whispered violently, "Forget that! Hook me up!" and turned around once more.

But before I could reach her, something metallic fell to the linoleum floor of the room. Instantly Julie pulled free from Yvonne and scooped up the long skirt of her costume. Her eyes glittered in the harsh light of the room, and the heavy mascara and blue eye shadow gave her the look of a wild animal.

"Find it!" she whispered. "It's down there someplace!" She was bending over, searching the bare floor carefully, twisting away from me and Yvonne. The young girl stared at her, panic-stricken. The whole rhythm of the change of costume had been broken. Whatever had fallen to the floor was clearly more important to Julie than getting the curtain up again.

"Find it! It must be there!" she said again, still in the same fierce whisper.

Bradley appeared at the open dressing-room door, a frown creasing his young face. "You ready, Julie?" he asked. And then he hesitated, staring at the three of us all searching for whatever it was that Julie had dropped.

"Not yet," Julie flung over her bare shoulder. She stood straight, shaking the peach satin material of her dress as if whatever it was she had lost might still be caught in the material, even though we had all heard it hit the floor.

"Honest, Miss Julie, it wasn't . . ." Yvonne stumbled over the words, but Julie, her eyes wild, cut in before she could finish the sentence.

"It's a ring! Don't just stand there! Look for it!" This was a Julie none of us had seen before, violent as a tigress, her long satin train sweeping the floor of the room, her hands claws as she poked among the discarded tissue and empty shoes below the makeup shelf.

"But it wasn't yours," Yvonne managed to stutter. She straightened, holding out a heavy ring for Julie's inspection. "See? It's just my class ring. It fell off, it's kind of loose."

As Julie faced the young girl, Yvonne took a hesitant step backward. I have never seen such violent anger in anyone's face as

I saw in Julie's that moment. Without a word she snatched the ring from the girl's hand and held it up to the lights around her mirror to study.

"It's almost two minutes, Julie," said Bradley quietly from the doorway. I think I was the only one to hear him. "Will you be ready soon?"

Neither Julie nor Yvonne seemed to hear him. They were staring at each other in the mirror, Yvonne's face frightened, confused; Julie with her back stiff, her eyes full of rage.

"It's mine!" Julie said it quietly, but the anger seemed to be seeping out of her as she turned away.

"Julie! For gosh sakes, we've got to get the curtain up." Bradley took a tentative step into the dressing room, and then, thinking better of it, stayed in the doorway. Julie did not move.

"Honest, it isn't yours, Miss Julie," said the girl, still frightened, but obviously trying to be helpful. She raised her hand for the ring, but Julie closed her fist and glared at her. "I mean it," said Yvonne, her eyes more puzzled now than afraid. "Look at the year. It's on the side there. I got it this last June. For graduation."

Slowly Julie opened her hand and studied the ring. For a long moment no one in the quiet room moved. Then the actress moved her hand to her waist as if feeling for something. Her head went up and there was a sudden look of pain in her deep blue eyes. Abruptly she flung the ring down on the makeup shelf and, scooping up her stage jewelry and gloves, swept out of the dressing room, her dress still unfastened.

"Get the curtain up, Bradley," she said as she passed the stage manager. "I'll be ready in time for my cue." He turned to follow her, and we could see Julie snap her fingers to Esme standing in the shadows by the iron staircase. The old woman waddled forward to finish preparing Julie for her entrance. Yvonne and I were clearly to stay out of the way.

The young girl retrieved her ring from the clutter of the dressing table and now she held it up, a puzzled look still on her usually cheerful face.

"What was all that about?" she said quietly. Outside we could hear the curtain rising. Soon it would be time for my last entrance.

"I don't know," I said. No time to go back to my own dressing room now. I smoothed my hair in Julie's mirror. I could see Yvonne's reflection as she studied the ring in her hand.

"It's just the Westaven High School class ring," she said, half to herself. "It's not like it was rubies or diamonds or something."

If Julie behaved strangely the night of the second performance, by Friday she was totally unlike the woman I had known through the long weeks I had been at Vail's Point. The weather continued hot, there was no chance that it might grow cooler without a summer storm, and the heat was making all of us nervous and on edge. We might have reasonably expected temperament from Haidee; she was, after all, far from young, and her part was both long and demanding (not to mention that it reopened ancient family wounds).

Instead, Haidee remained calm and serene, never letting her performance vary by so much as a word. It was Julie who became highly erratic, playing some scenes faster than Jeb had directed, cutting into other actors' lines, bringing a wild violence to her major speeches as if she were no longer pretending to be the cruel Helen but was actually becoming the character. It took no talent to shrink back in fear from her in the last scene of the play. I had to use all the strength I had in me to defy her on stage before I made my last exit.

I found myself remembering again what Wendy had told me. "Julie hated Lionel." I wondered, not for the first time, how much of what the dead girl had said was the truth.

Friday night was when the anger that seemed to fill Julie finally erupted. May and I had come to the theater early as usual, and we could hear the argument from my dressing room.

"I don't want them backstage," Julie was insisting stubbornly. We could hear the low rumble of Jeb's voice and the higher sounds of Bradley as they tried to calm her.

"I don't care!" shouted Julie. "I can see them staring at me from the wings, whispering among themselves. As if I were some kind of freak. I can't concentrate out there."

There was a loud bang, as if she had slammed her dressing-room door shut. After a moment Jeb appeared in our doorway. He looked tired, as if the heat and the argument had drained him of all energy.

"Sorry to bother you, ladies," he said quietly, "but there'll be nobody to help with the changes tonight. Julie finds the crew back-stage . . . distracting."

May nodded, keeping her silence.

"Esme will help her with the quick change for the last scene. Everybody else is to stay out of the way." He looked at me, his eyes weary. "I understand you told Bradley tonight that you'll stay for the rest of the season?"

"If you still want me," I said. I felt sorry for Jeb. He looked be-wildered and very tired.

"Thanks. It'll make things easier." He hesitated, as if he wanted to say something more, but finally just muttered, "Keep up the good work." Without another word he left the doorway.

I looked at May. She stood very still, her head tilted as if she were listening to something only she could hear.

"There'll be a storm soon," she said. "Let's hope it clears the air." Then, more practically, she picked up my hairbrush and added, "Speak up tonight, Alison. You have no idea what a clatter rain can make on the roof." And she started in again to brush my hair.

The storm held off during the first act, but even on stage we could hear the wind tossing the trees that surrounded the theater. There was a curious hushed feeling inside the building, as if both the audience and the actors were waiting for the thunder and light-ning. During the intermission (which Bradley deliberately made longer that night) we could hear the constant slamming of car doors in the parking lot as careful owners rolled up the windows against the rain one could almost feel in the air.

There were crackles of lightning during the first scene of the second act, and even on stage we could hear the low rumbles of thunder as it came nearer and nearer. Just before the curtain rose on the last scene of the play, the storm broke in all its fury. It sounded as if the center of it were directly over the golden knob high on the roof of the theater. The wind was wilder now, banging the loose doors and shutters on the veranda that circled the build-ing, and I could hear the apprentices on the crew scurrying around to fasten them securely.

On stage it was hard to pretend we were in a quiet house on a peaceful evening. Overhead the rain slashed at the roof, and I was thankful I had only a few words to say. I felt I was shouting when I did speak. The others in the cast perceptibly raised the volume of their voices and doggedly continued with the play, ignoring the steady drip of rain that fell on the left corner of the stage from a leak in the old roof.

We were in the middle of the most important scene by now, a scene usually played quietly with growing menace until Haidee's entrance with the last glass of milk. But now, with the storm raging directly overhead and the actors trying to overcome the noise, it was as if I were on stage during the most savage of Greek tragedies. Everyone seemed larger than before, the makeup harshly artificial under the stage lights.

Try as I could, I found myself forgetting that I was supposed to be Emily . . . I was only Alison Howard on a stage with people staring at me, not able to relate to the others, the storm pushing in around us, crackling with thunder and lightning and the wild rain. It's like . . .

It's like that horrible dream, I thought. But only for a second, for Julie had made her entrance and I could see off stage in the shadows Haidee picking up her tray from the prop table, ready to bring in the glass of milk that would lead to my exit.

Let me get through it, I thought. Let me just get through this. Haidee came on, and as always there was the same gasp from the audience, clear to us over the sound of the rain beating on the roof of the old theater.

I drank the milk, shouted my word of defiance as I started off stage (although I doubt if anyone, including the actors on stage, could have heard me), and continued my frantic run up the great staircase.

As I had the other nights, I turned on the landing. For once my eyes were glazed by the spotlights almost directly over my head, and when I ran off out of the light into the darkness of the escape platform, I could not see.

Only, I *knew.*

Even before I reached the darkness I knew something had been changed. And I knew what it was. But I was powerless, I was running too fast, there was no way to stop.

Tonight there was no safe, carefully marked platform off the grand staircase to hold me. The darkness in front of my feet was

217

empty. I could not stop. I could feel a scream forming deep inside me as my feet toppled off the edge.

I do not know if the scream ever came out. There was a crash of thunder that last moment as I teetered on the end of the scaffolding that led from the staircase. And then I felt myself falling forward, into the empty darkness. Down below was a great, lighted square. The trap door was open! All that was below me were the cold gray flagstones of the cellar beneath the stage.

I reached out into the darkness. There was nothing. I was falling, falling through empty time to the stone floor far below . . .

Chapter Twenty-two

Pain . . .

I could feel it in my fingers, all the way up my arms to my shoulders. I knew the skin was raw on my knees, and I felt dizzy even with my eyes closed. There were voices around me, fierce whispers. Somewhere beyond my eyelids there was light, but I could not make my eyes open.

"She's moving. Maybe she's coming to . . ." Haidee's voice. Thin, frightened.

"Sssh . . . let her rest." Someone else. Jeb? Where am I?

I forced myself to lift my eyelids. I was in my bedroom at the house in my own bed. They were all around me: Jeb and Haidee and May and Corin. Behind them, Oliver and Rita were half supporting Julie; but they were not looking at her. They were all staring down at me. Seated on the bed beside me, his hand holding my wrist, was the young doctor who had come to Vail's Point the night Wendy died. His eyes were gray, I noticed, and worried.

Then it all came back: the long fall into the darkness, the great square of light where the trap door should have been, and I twisted my head as if that would make the memory go away. Only, it didn't. It only hurt more.

"Lie still," said the doctor. He looked at the others. "She should be x-rayed tomorrow. I'll arrange for it at the County Hospital." Even as he said it I knew nothing in my body was broken, and I struggled to sit up. "Don't move!" the young doctor said quickly, but it was too late and I could feel the pain grow less.

"Please, Doctor, there's nothing really wrong." I flexed my fingers gently. The skin on my hands was torn under the bandages that had been placed across the palms. I saw I was still in my costume. "What . . . how did I get here?"

"Jeb carried you. All the way from the theater."

Haidee's voice was quiet, her great eyes dim for once, and I could see tears had made streaks through her heavy makeup. She, too, was still in the costume she wore at the end of the play. She seemed very old as she studied me, her head trembling as if she could not control it.

"How did the accident happen?" The young doctor's voice was cold as he looked at the people gathered around my bed.

"She must have missed her footing. Fallen off the escape-stair platform." Bradley was at my left by the windows. The face of the young stage manager was drained of color, his eyes wide. "That's the stairs that lead off the grand staircase on stage," he explained to the doctor.

"It wasn't there!"

The others stared at me, the young doctor leaning forward, his eyes suspicious.

"The platform wasn't there?" he asked. "You mean it had been moved?"

I hesitated. Haidee's beautiful old head was still shaking slightly from side to side, almost like a signal to deny the truth.

"It was moved," I said stubbornly. "The whole platform. I could even see the open trap door to the cellar below the stage."

"It couldn't have been, Alison!" Bradley turned to the doctor. "Sure, the platform gets moved after each performance. We have to strike the whole set each night so we can have a bare stage for daytime rehearsals. But nothing gets touched until after the final curtain. And I know the unit was in place before we started the last act. I checked."

"Could somebody have moved it? Quietly? During the last act?" The doctor's face was hard now, his questions more like a policeman than a medical man. At least *he* seemed willing to believe me.

"I . . . I guess so." Bradley was not so positive now. "I'm over on the other side of the stage so that I can handle the curtain."

Jeb stepped forward. "Except the stair unit was exactly where it should have been when we found Alison. And the trap door closed." He looked at the others. "Remember? When we went looking for her after she didn't show up for the curtain call?"

They don't believe me, I thought. No one will ever believe me. Not even the one policeman I could call; Ed McNaughton wouldn't lift a finger. The others in the room were nodding in agreement with Jeb.

"How . . . how did I manage . . . ?" I lay back again. It was too hard to finish the sentence.

"You must have grabbed one of the guy ropes holding the sandbags." Instinctively I closed my torn hands. Jeb's voice seemed very near, as if he were whispering in my ear, but when I opened my eyes again, he was still standing where he had been before at the end of the bed.

"The ropes broke her fall," he explained to the doctor.

"Otherwise she might be dead. Or permanently injured," said the doctor. He pursed his lips. "It all sounds very . . . peculiar." His words were still cool, but I could see he was beginning to be persuaded.

"You *did* say you were shaky about heights, Alison. And with the storm making so much noise . . ." Corin let his voice trail off. He gave the doctor a look of such innocent frankness that only someone who knew him well would have been able to tell he was acting. Even *you* are against me, I thought bitterly.

"It's easy to lose your footing up there in the dark, Doctor," Corin added. "And if heights make you dizzy . . . well, accidents *do* happen." Carefully, Corin did not look at me. "After all, Doctor," he went on, "it's not as if anyone could possibly have a reason to harm Alison."

As they all turned to the doctor I realized the truth had been settled for good—by the Vails.

"I think we had better leave Alison alone now." Julie made a gesture to the others and, picking up something that lay out of my sight, said, "I'll see Alison takes the pills, Doctor. That's what she needs most, I think. A good night's rest."

Then they were gone, Julie closing the door behind them. I could hear the doctor asking more questions, Jeb's voice answering calmly as they walked away from the room. Julie disappeared into the bathroom to get a glass of water, and I made myself sit up straighter. The storm had passed. There was not even the dripping of rain on the balcony outside. Suddenly everything that had happened came rushing back, filling my head, and I began to tremble.

"Here. Drink this. Take one of the pills." Julie had moved swiftly to my side and put her arm around me as I leaned against the tall headboard.

"No. Not yet. I don't want to go to sleep yet. There's too much I don't know," I said, pulling away from her. I'd not meant it cruelly, but I could see her wince at my reaction.

She stood and put the glass of water on the marble top of the bureau. "I suppose I'm to blame," she said.

"You?" I couldn't look at her. I kept my eyes on the skirt of my dress. It was ripped and soiled with dust and dark brown stains of blood.

"I was the one who insisted there should be no one backstage. Nothing could have happened, accident or not, if the crew had been there." Her voice was bitter with recrimination. She stared out the dark windows at the silent evening sky, hugging her arms.

"Then you believe me?" I said. "That the platform was moved?"

"It could have been." She sighed. "With all the thunder and lightning we wouldn't have heard it, even on stage." She shifted so she could look at me. "But I didn't move it, if that's what you're thinking. What possible reason could I have?"

There could be reasons, I thought. I saw Jeb's face and suddenly I felt very tired.

"Of course, there's Lionel," she added thoughtfully, as if trying to see what had happened from my point of view. "Lionel and that lost play you and Corin keep searching for."

"You hated Lionel, didn't you?"

She nodded. Then, as if she had made up her mind not to avoid something, Julie came back to the bed and sat down next to me. "I had good reason to hate him. Surely you must have found that out from the papers in his office?" I shook my head. Julie frowned a little. "That's not like him—he always kept copies of his letters." She let her voice trail off. "He was once very cruel to me," she added after a moment.

She wasn't looking at me now. Her eyes were studying the fireplace, seeing something that had happened many years before. I was forgotten. "Maybe that's why it's been such hell this week, saying his words, repeating his venom . . ." She looked at me, her face serious. "I'm sorry if I've seemed cruel. It's that damned part. It's haunted me all week."

"Only one more performance. " She nodded. "And then I'll be gone," I said.

She leaned forward to look at me directly. "Gone?" she repeated. "Why? Jeb told me you would stay for the summer."

"Wouldn't it be better if I stayed out of Jeb's way?" She stared at me, obviously not understanding. I began to feel foolish, but it was too late to hold back now. "Wouldn't you prefer that?" I said trying to keep my voice steady.

A breeze lifted one of the curtains, but other than that there was no sound, no movement in the bedroom. Julie's eyes lost their bewilderment, something very close to a smile tugging at her lips. "You mean . . . because I love him?" she asked.

"You do, don't you?"

"Yes," she answered. "Don't you?"

I felt myself beginning to blush. I had never really considered the possibility. From the first moment there had been nothing but antagonism between us. If anything, Corin had been more kind, more attractive.

Until tonight . . . when Corin lied to the doctor to save the family from scandal. With that I knew I could never be intrigued by him again.

"It's all right, Alison." Julie leaned forward and covered my hand with hers, her deep blue eyes searching my face, her lips smiling sympathetically. "I've wanted Jeb to have a girl like you to care for him, to love him . . ."

She gave my hand a brisk pat and leaned back once more. "Still, I see what you're thinking. The older woman, jealous of her young lover . . . yes, that *could* be a reason to wish you harm." Her face grew very serious. "But it isn't true, Alison. Jeb and I aren't lovers."

Tears formed in her eyes, but her lips were still curving in that same gentle smile.

"Alison, Jeb is my son."

I stared at her. She made no attempt now to stop the tears that rolled down her cheeks. Her lips were trembling, but she continued to smile. "It's a long story. I thought you'd guessed by now. I'm sure Haidee has, and Esme. May's known from the beginning."

"I . . . I didn't . . . I saw the way you looked at him. With love in your eyes. I didn't realize . . ."

"I've not been very careful, have I?" she said wryly. "But there were so many years when I couldn't look at him, couldn't see him . . ." She broke off, turning back to me. "He doesn't know. I don't want him to . . . not ever." Her voice was far from steady. "He might hate me if he knew."

I could think of nothing I could say tactfully. Once again the answers had only brought more questions.

"It's all right," said Julie soothingly. "I wanted you to know. Maybe it'll explain why I hated Lionel so much." Her mouth was thin, the smile gone. "And I *did* hate him, Alison. It took me to the last minute even to have his grave cleaned up. I think at one time I might have killed him. Only, I didn't." She didn't glance at me. "You can believe that or not."

"Go on."

She took a deep breath and started to talk, her face down, her eyes studying her hands twisted in her lap.

"It was at the beginning of the War. I was just sixteen. Mother was on tour. May was in New York teaching. Lionel hadn't joined the Army yet. He was drinking heavily." She hesitated. "He wasn't very kind when he was drinking.

"It was decided by Mother and Lionel that I should finish high school in Westaven. The house was too big to keep open, even if we could have found somebody to look after me. So I was to board with a couple in town, a brother and sister. She worked at the library . . ."

"The Trebles? Lucy Treble?"

She was startled by my question. "Yes. Have you met them?"

"Just Lucy," I said. "That first day, at the library. She warned me about all of you, about this house."

"She has good reason." Julie sighed. "I think she and Lionel had an affair years later, that last winter he spent here. Not that he ever thought to marry her."

Julie sat up so she could look at me. "Alison, that year here at Westaven, finishing high school, was the happiest year of my life."

"Away from the theater?" My astonishment sounded naïve even to me, but Julie paid no attention.

"I *hate* the theater," she said vehemently. "I always have. All those years as a child being shunted around, hearing nothing but talk about plays and costumes and rehearsals, always knowing as a child I was merely in the way."

The anger faded from her voice. "You can't imagine what that one year in town was like . . . to be the same as other girls . . . to go to dances and parties. To giggle over movie stars and have homework to do and wonder who would take me to the senior prom." Her voice dropped so low I could barely hear the next sentence. "To fall in love."

She smiled quickly, as if embarrassed about what she had said, but then went on. "And it *was* love. We were very young, of course, but he was *real*. He made all the other people in my life seem so artificial."

She hesitated.

"What happened?" I prompted, for I knew she wanted to talk, was desperate to talk after all these years.

"We wanted to get married," she said finally. "The War was on, he was a few years older. He was about to enlist. Time was very short, very precious." She sighed. "Haidee was halfway across the country, so she left me to Lionel's authority. He wouldn't answer my letters; when I tried to call him he was always drunk. And abusive. He said he knew—had proof the boy was only after me for my money, for my position. It wasn't true, of course, but Lionel wouldn't listen. He said he would come up and take me by force back to the city." She smiled ruefully. "Just as melodramatic as something out of one of his plays."

I could see tears forming once more in her deep blue eyes. "I was a minor, so I couldn't marry without the permission of the family. But there was one thing I could have those last few days. I could have love." She raised her chin even as the tears spilled down her cheeks. "And I took it. Greedily. Defiantly. I didn't care about morals or conventions or anything. I don't regret it. And I haven't for one moment all these years."

"You became pregnant?"

She nodded. "I couldn't tell the boy, of course. He had enough to face without worrying about me."

"Did you never tell him?"

"How could I? That I had had his baby and Lionel had made me give our son away? That I was a frightened coward and a fool?" Her lips twisted in bitterness. "The only thing I could do was save our child's life. I didn't tell anyone until it was too late to have the baby destroyed. I couldn't have taken that. So when Jeb was born, far from here where no one knew me, I gave him the one last name that seemed right—the name of a poor girl who, over a hundred years ago, the family also betrayed. She's buried up in the graveyard. Phoebe Reives. She, too, had had a son. I used to sit by her gravestone all those long months of waiting, thinking about her and her baby. And the Vail she had once loved who didn't or wouldn't marry her. A poor, frightened girl. Like me."

"And . . . afterwards?"

"May helped. She knew some actors who had retired, bought a small business out in Ohio. They had no children. They raised Jeb. When he was older and I had some money, I helped him through school, through college. Watching his reports, seeing his interest grow in the theater . . . but always having to stay at a distance. Never letting him know. Never seeing him. Never being able to touch him or hold him . . ."

"Where does Corin fit into all this?"

She gave me a strange look, as if she had not expected this question but something else. "I married the following winter, just as soon as I could. I would have married anyone to get free of the family. Only, this time they approved. Grayson was rich, sensitive; it was considered the perfect match. We had three months together before he was shipped out. He never came back." She rubbed her forehead wearily. "I can barely remember now what he looked like, Corin is so much a Vail."

"And Jeb's father? Did he die in the War, too?" But I knew the answer.

"Of course not," she said, looking me straight in the eyes.

"You know who Jeb's father is, Alison. That's how Jeb got his name. J for Julie, E for his father, B for their boy. That's why I carry his father's ring with me everywhere . . ." She pulled a thin chain from around her neck. A heavy class ring hung at the end of it, identical to the one Yvonne had claimed as her own. "It's the only thing I have left of the one happy year in my life. Jeb's father will never speak to me again. I can't say I blame him."

"It's Mr. McNaughton, isn't it? Jeb's father?"

She nodded again, holding the ring tight in her hand. "Julie and Ed's boy," she said softly. Then she turned to face me, and there was no sorrow in her eyes now. They flickered with cold anger. "Now do you see why I hated Lionel? Why I'll always hate him?"

She left soon after that, her eyes dry, her face tired. She looked old enough now to be Jeb's mother. I had tried to tell her about

226

McNaughton and his curious vigil outside the house the night be-fore, but she would not listen. She only wanted to speak of Jeb.

"He's fallen in love with you," she said as she helped me get ready for bed. "You should have seen his face when he found you, all crumpled up in the shadows backstage. And when he carried you up here to the house."

"Until this week we've done nothing but argue." My protest seemed weak, even to me.

"That's Jeb's way," Julie went on, with a hint of a smile. "Very like his father. Jeb's fighting himself. It would be so much easier for him to go through life with a series of Wendys."

She must have seen the question forming in my face, for she laughed lightly. "No I didn't push her off the roof, if that's what you're thinking. It wasn't necessary. He'd broken with her. I heard him go to her room one night. I cried that night, I was so afraid the affair was continuing. But it wasn't. It was over."

She smiled at me. "I think it was over the day he met you."

"But . . ."

"Try to sleep, Alison." She smiled once more and went out and shut the door.

I lay back in bed. The pain was beginning to fade, even with-out medicine. What I had suffered from the fall was more shock than anything else, but still my hands trembled. It *could* have been an accident, I tried to tell myself. Some careless apprentice *could* have moved the platform and then been afraid to admit it. It was possible the Vails all genuinely believed the platform was there and that I slipped.

Only, I knew I hadn't.

The stairs had been moved deliberately. Whether whoever had done it had really expected to kill me or whether he had only hoped that the accident would be serious enough to send me to a hospital and away from Vail's Point, I could not know.

Still, it was only tonight the others had heard I would be stay-ing on for the rest of the summer.

It was time to take the pills, I knew. Time to try to sleep. One more day in this house, one more performance . . . for I knew I would have to do that for Haidee's sake, if danger waited for me wherever I set my foot. Then I will leave I said to myself. Jeb can find himself a more placid girl, Corin can continue his search for the manuscript alone.

Only, I could not dismiss what Julie had guessed of my feelings. Jeb was attractive, certainly. Not the way I had found other men attractive, the quiet scholars and teachers at my father's university. Or even Corin, with his intensity, his flickering, malicious wit. There was a roughness about Jeb, a strength, a vigor, an impatience that was often close to cruel.

And yet . . . as he had reminded me so often, how much of that cruelty was my own fault? From the very first day, my short temper, my stiff-backed pride had made us seem in some sort of competition. Strange to think of his jealousy of Lionel; strange, now that I knew Lionel's blood ran in his veins.

The Vails, I sighed wearily. I'm surrounded by the whole complicated family.

And one of them is trying to kill me.

CHAPTER TWENTY-THREE

I awoke late that next morning, the beginning of the most terrifying day of my life. The skin on my hands still throbbed, and my shoulders and arms still ached; but there was no sign, under my light suntan, of the restless night I had spent.

If only we could have some warning of what lies ahead in a day (I was to think later), so that we might prepare ourselves for it. Not that I had much choice in what to wear, for Esme had not brought up the laundry and there was only one clean summer dress left in my closet: a lime-green cotton with thin, spaghetti straps that left my shoulders and arms bare. Still, it was loose and comfortable, with deep pockets.

The sun baking the grass outside was promising another scorchingly hot day. We might never have had the storm, I thought as I tied my hair back with the thin green string I usually wore as a belt for the dress, not worrying how it looked, only happy to have my long hair back from my already warm face.

I had breakfast alone, or, rather, I sat alone at the table. Yvonne kept darting in with specially prepared dishes and an avid curiosity about the "accident" I had had the night before. I found myself studying her, wondering how she would feel if I told her that Jeb was her half brother and that once, long ago, Julie and her father had been lovers. But because she wanted to talk, I did allow myself to ask about her mother . . . and when and how her father had married.

"It was after he came back from the War . . . I guess about five or six years after. He sent for her. She was French. I think maybe he'd known her family during the War. She couldn't have been much more than a child then. That's how we got our names—Yvonne for me, François for Frankie."

She grinned. "My brother always hated that. So when he started school he asked Dad if he could change it. Mother was dead by then and Dad didn't care." She shrugged, a teen-aged caricature of amused helplessness. "Unfortunately, there isn't one darn thing you can do with a name like Yvonne."

"Were your parents happy together?" I asked, knowing it was none of my business. But I was curious to hear the other half of Julie's romantic story.

229

Yvonne regarded me seriously. "No, I don't think so," she said after a moment. "You saw how Dad is, so grim and determined about everything."

A small frown appeared on her freckled face. "And yet, you know something, Alison? Folks tell me that before the War Dad was the most popular boy in town." She giggled. "And the best-looking. Would you believe it?"

After breakfast I went up to Lionel's study. There was still time to start a bibliography of his books even though I told myself firmly that I would leave the next day, after *The Basilisks* was over. I had thought as I dressed that morning that maybe the clue to "recorded time" might be among Lionel's books—what else would a history book be, perhaps? Or an almanac?

But I knew even as I started up the stairs the idea was foolish. Lionel was not the sort of man to scoop out pages from a book to make a hiding place, or tuck a manuscript behind the long rows of volumes. Nothing that simple would have satisfied his devious nature.

Still, it wouldn't hurt to look . . .

I had been in the library several hours when Jeb came to the door. My search had been as useless as I had expected. There were books of history on each shelf. And almanacs. I had examined each of them, opening them carefully, flipping through the pages for clues, looking behind them on the shelves. They were, as I suspected, simply what they seemed to be—part of the dusty library of a man with many interests.

I was replacing them on the shelves when Jeb appeared at the door. It was hot in Lionel's study; the early-afternoon sun scorched the grass on the lawn below, the trees were still, even the waves along the shore came in slowly, barely seeping up over the flat dry sand.

"What are you doing here?"

Although I recognized his voice, I was still startled. Jeb had a way of approaching in total silence, moving as quietly as an Indian. He stood, hands on hips, in the open doorway. "Accidents" or not, I'd left the door open deliberately in the hopes of catching a cross current of air. "Sorting Lionel's books." I kept my face away from his sharp eyes. I still had not decided what I felt about what Julie had told me. "Why aren't you at rehearsal?"

"Lunch break." He moved into the room. "I thought you'd be gone by now. Packed and on your way to safety."

"So you finally think I might be in danger?"

He wore a curious expression, guarded, but something more. His eyes seemed to be searching my face as if they were looking for an answer to some unspoken question. I could feel a flush rising in my cheeks as he stared.

"Danger . . ." He said the word thoughtfully. "I don't know." He sat down wearily in the chair at Lionel's desk, stretching out his long, sturdy legs. "Maybe I don't know anything any more. What happened to Wendy—well, I still believe that could have been an accident. But last night . . ." He let the sentence drift off. "I checked with the crew, by the way. They all swore none of them had touched the escape platform." He sighed. "And I believe them. Sure, the whole platform's on wheels, it wouldn't take any strength to move it a few feet to the side, but . . ." He got up and came closer, taking me by the shoulders as if by touching me he could convince me of his argument. "Alison, the platform *was* in place when we found you. The trap door *was* closed."

I made no effort to break free. "And it's so much easier to believe that I was mistaken. That I just slipped." I said quietly, but he must have heard the anger I felt in my voice, for he released me and stepped back, running an impatient hand through his dark hair.

"God, I don't know," he said. "I know you don't lie. I know you wouldn't make up a story like this . . . but everything that happens, *you* seem to be the only witness."

"Or victim."

Then, as if he were happy to have some way of expressing his frustration, he turned on me almost in anger. "Then, why are you still here? Why haven't you gone? My God, do you think I want you killed?"

I stared at him silently. His anger disappeared as suddenly as it had come. He did not move, nor did I.

"What *do* you want, Jeb?" My voice was so low I was not sure he could hear me, even though he stood only a few feet away.

"You know what I want." He moved closer, his strong hands

231

reaching out again and resting on my bare shoulders. "I'm in love with you, Alison. You know that, don't you?" He stepped still closer. I could feel his hard body press against mine, but he made no effort to bend down and kiss me. "You do know that?" he repeated.

I nodded. I couldn't trust myself to speak.

"And you?" His voice was hardly louder than a whisper.

I tried to step back, but his hands were strong on my shoulders. "I—I don't know what I feel." It was a weak answer and I found myself trembling. I couldn't take my eyes off his face. "Up until just a few days ago I thought you were cruel and . . . and selfish . . ."

"I am." But there was a beginning of a smile. "I'm also bossy and bad-tempered and sloppy around the house. And up to now I've only wanted placid, easy ladies."

"Like Wendy?"

He stopped smiling. With one hand he tilted my chin up so he could continue to stare at me. "I didn't love her," he said quietly. "I didn't love any of them. At least not enough to marry them." He had said the word very deliberately. "I never wanted to get married at all. Certainly not to a strong-minded girl like you." He grinned then. "You're stubborn, Alison. Just as much as I am. We're going to have a very stormy life together."

It was incredible to stand there, his arms holding me, listening to him discuss the future, so sure that I couldn't possibly turn him down. But I found myself relaxing. For he was right. Perhaps what was happening between us was sudden; perhaps what I felt as he held me was far from what I expected of love. But I knew that whether or not I left Vail's Point, Jeb was now part of my life.

And would be forever.

He kissed me then, and for a long time afterwards we were silent. I think each of us must have been thinking of the other people we had kissed and how little they meant now that we were together.

"You must go," he said finally.

I broke away from him, startled by the casualness with which he had spoken. "Go?" I asked. "Go where?"

"I'll get you a room at the inn in town. We'll lock up Lionel's belongings, his papers—that should keep you safe. If somebody *is* trying to stop this search."

"And what am I to do in Westaven?"

"We can see each other. I'll move out of here as well. Mother will understand."

He said it so quietly my gasp sounded even louder than it was. He looked at me, raising an eyebrow. "You knew, didn't you? That Julie was my mother? I figured that going through the family papers you must have learned that."

"She told me last night. But how did . . . ? She never wanted you to know."

"Poor Julie . . ." He rubbed his chin thoughtfully. "All these years trying to keep it a secret . . . as if it mattered any more whether an actress has a child, in or out of wedlock."

"When—when did you find out about it?"

"Years ago." He smiled sadly. "She wasn't very subtle—the expensive toys and clothes that always arrived for Christmas and birthdays, the Julie Vail scholarship at college that was practically handed to me. Even my first jobs in the theater, Julie was always somewhere involved in the productions."

"Why haven't you ever told her? Why haven't you ever talked to her about it?" Once again I found his coolness inexplicable.

"It was her secret. Not mine." His face froze, and I wondered suddenly how much anger and resentment he had suffered through the years. I reached out to touch him, but he moved away and stared out the window at the flat blue sea below.

"And your father? Do you know who he is?" I was glad at that moment he could not see my face, for I'm sure it would have told him that I knew.

"Some soldier on a weekend pass, I expect." His voice was cruel. He had become again the Jeb I had disliked all these weeks. Then he looked back at me, a cynical smile on his lips. "So it turns out that you won't be able to escape the Vails after all . . . even if I *am* on the wrong side of the family blanket."

He looked around the room and then came over and took my hand. Once more he was the warm, strong man who had asked me to marry him. "Let's leave here, Alison," he said quietly. "Just the two of us. Let's leave the Vails and all their secrets and all their tragedies and have our own life. I want that so much."

And yet even with his hand in mine, I hesitated. He could see the doubt in my eyes.

"Is it me?" he asked. "Is it that you don't trust yourself to love me?"

"What about tonight?" I knew I was still evading him, and he knew it, too. "There's still one more performance of the play."

"I'll be backstage every minute. And there'll be no grand exit up the stairs. Emily can run off into the garden just as well." He set his mouth in a grim line, and for a moment I could see his father in him. "I'm not letting anything more happen to you. By accident or not. And tomorrow you move out. Agreed?"

He pulled me closer and kissed me again. With that kiss my doubts disappeared. There was another world outside of this house, a world where Jeb and I could live and be happy. It would be no hardship to leave the Vails now.

He left shortly after that to go back to rehearsal. I looked around Lionel's study. It's over, I thought to myself. Some scholar years from now might decipher the clues and find the lost play, if it still exists, but I had something else to think about.

I closed the windows carefully. The cards I had worked on were all neatly in place on Lionel's desk. The boxes that had covered the floor that first day were gone. Lionel's letters were now in the long row of filing cabinets I had bought. The room was clean and cheerful, suitable as the repository of a great writer's work. The job I had set out to accomplish was finished. And if once I had been intrigued by mysteries and family secrets and the thought of what might have been, that time was over.

I stood at the doorway and looked at the room one last time.

And then I closed the door firmly and locked it.

I spent the rest of the afternoon walking along the shore, content to watch the calm water ripple over the sand like white lace, to feel the sun hot on my shoulders, to let my mind wander into the future when Jeb and I would leave Vail's Point and this strange summer far behind us. I felt free for the first time in weeks, perhaps for the first time in my life.

I could think about my life now—the years with my father at the university—as quiet and uneventful as if I'd slept through them. And the six weeks I'd spent here, vivid and overcolored, like the makeup we wore on stage.

Tomorrow it would all be over. I would move into the placid town of Westaven, and the focus of my life would no longer be Lionel Vail but the great-nephew he'd never known.

It was after six when I came back to the house, I would have to hurry if I was to be ready for the theater. I could hear voices behind the closed doors to the dining room, but I was not hungry and I hurried up the great staircase, eager to get to my room, to bathe and change and prepare myself for the last performance of *The Basilisks.*

But I felt something different when I reached the landing of the staircase. Someone was watching me. I twisted my head and looked up at the artificial balcony built so many years ago. A wisp of mauve silk disappeared instantly, as whoever had been standing there stepped back out of sight. I came up the rest of the stairs slowly. The lamps had not been lit in the hall. It was as dark as it had been that first afternoon I had come to the house.

"Who's there?" My voice sounded as loud as a shout. There was no answer.

In the shadows the hall seemed empty. But I had seen someone, I knew it. "Who's there?" I said again, keeping my voice as controlled as I could.

"Over here! Quickly!" Haidee's voice. I recognized it even in a whisper. I stepped forward through the gloom toward a dark doorway at the far side of the hall.

"Quickly!" A thin white hand appeared around the edge of the doorway, summoning me forward. I walked through the shadows boldly, and when I was close enough the fingers grasped my wrist and pulled me forward into the room beyond. Haidee closed the door behind us and, with her fingers still fastened to my wrist, turned me to face her.

There was not much more light in her room than in the landing behind us. I barely had time to notice thick curtains had been half drawn over the long windows. From somewhere there was the slow whir of an ancient air conditioner, but the room was no cooler than the hall outside.

"What are you doing here?"

I could barely see Haidee in the shadows, but I could hear the fear in her voice. "Haidee, what is it? What's wrong?"

"Where have you been all afternoon?" She released my hand and moved past me, brushing back her straggling white hair with her hand. Her hand was shaking, I could see that in the gloom. "I went to your room. You were gone. I thought you'd left for good." She sank down on her bed and then, almost absently, reached out and pulled the cord of a small lamp beside her.

The lamp, a confection of pink satin and lace ruffles, gave enough light to see Haidee's bedroom. The room was all in pink: the long drapes, the skirt around the huge dressing table, a sweep of dusty satin forming a canopy over the peeling gilt of her swan bed. The room was as much a curio as the bedroom of a silent-film star, all faded silks and musty perfume and mirrors. Only the sound of the air conditioner with its faint pulse of air reminded us that time had not stood still, that it was no longer the years of Haidee's youth.

For she was an old woman. I could see that now as I came closer to the bed. She had leaned back against the lace pillows, her great eyes closed, as if she were exhausted. And not even the soft pink light or the careful powder on her skull of a face could hide the marks of her seventy years.

"What is it, Haidee? What's the matter?" I said again.

"Why didn't you go?" It was almost a moan. "Why have you come back here?" She opened her eyes then, the clear aquamarine clouded with tears. I realized suddenly what had made the ravages in her face.

For the first time, I was seeing Haidee afraid.

"I had to come back, Haidee," I said as calmly as I could. "There's still one more performance to give."

"We could have canceled it," she moaned. "I would have said I was sick . . . *anything!*" Her mouth twisted in bitter humor. For a second she was as I had always known her. "The show doesn't *have* to go on, Alison. That's only a myth started by greedy managers who don't want to return the money."

I sat down beside her on the bed, although she had not asked me. She seemed unable to stop her clawlike hands from trembling. I took them in my own, forcing her to look at me.

"Haidee, what is it? What are you so afraid of?"

"Not me, child. *You!*" Even in a whisper I could feel the force

236

of her words. "Why didn't you run away today? Anywhere . . . to your home, to your father!" The words, barely murmured, burst forth in a torrent: "My God, I thought when I found your room empty you had been smart enough to leave. Then to see you strolling back along the beach as if you hadn't a care in the world . . . Don't you know what they're trying to do to you? Don't you *care?*" Her hands gripped mine. I could feel her long nails clawing into my skin.

"'They'? Who do you mean?" Some of her fear was beginning to soak through my skin.

"The killer. Or killers." Her eyes were not looking at me now. They moved from side to side as if she expected something unseen to appear at any moment from behind the long satin folds that framed the bed. "Or is it this family?" Her thoughts were rambling now, as if she were talking to herself. "Is it all of us? Are we doomed? I've never really known."

She looked at me again, her eyes clear, her voice quiet and controlled. "There was a girl once, she's buried up in the graveyard . . ." For a moment she paused, and I knew we were both seeing the small stone that covered all that remained of Phoebe Reives. "One of the family had ruined her, she died in childbirth." She sighed heavily, but it barely moved the chiffon ruffles on her thin chest. "They say she cursed us. All of us. I've often wondered . . ."

I forced myself to smile, as calmly and soothingly as I could. "Haidee? I'm not a Vail. No curse can touch me."

"Don't be so sure." Her voice was stronger, but the heavy false eyelashes that rimmed her eyes still fluttered nervously. "You've been searching through our lives, through our secrets . . ."

"And found nothing," I broke in, holding her hands firmly, willing her to look at me. "Nothing, Haidee. And tomorrow I'll be leaving." I thought it wise not to mention that I would only be moving into town. The family could learn that when I was settled.

"Tomorrow," she said quietly. For a moment I thought she might repeat the word, and again I thought of the opening lines of the speech that had started my search: "Tomorrow, and tomorrow, and tomorrow, . . ." But Haidee had fallen silent. She sighed once more, and I could feel her hands relax.

"I'm so tired, Alison," she said. "I've fought so long to keep the evil from this family and I've lost." She looked at me then, her great blue eyes clear and direct. "For there *is* evil in this house. You've felt it, I know. I couldn't bear it if anything happened to you."

"Nothing will happen," I said soothingly. "I'll be gone tomorrow."

"There's still tonight." Her fingers tightened around me. "Be careful, Alison." She took another deep breath, her clear eyes still fastened on me.

"I heard the platform being moved last night, when I was on stage. I didn't know what it was at the time, but I *did* hear it. You were telling the truth." Her voice sunk to a whisper again. "That means somebody was lying. Somebody *was* trying to kill you."

But before I could question her further she pulled her hand from mine and raised it to her mouth, her head twisting toward the doorway. Someone was standing quietly in the shadows.

Chapter Twenty-four

"Who . . . who's there?" said Haidee, her hand gripping mine tightly.

The figure moved forward and we could both see Yvonne, standing rather awkwardly just inside the circle of light from the bedside lamp.

"I'm sorry to bother you," she said. "I *did* knock."

"I didn't ring for you." Haidee had control of herself again, but there was still a faint tremor, as if the roles of mistress and maid had suddenly been reversed.

"I know. But Esme sent me up . . ." Yvonne took another tentative step forward, her eyes on me. "We've been trying to find Alison. Esme had us looking all over the house."

Yvonne giggled nervously. I had a feeling she had never been in this room before, for even as she spoke her eyes flickered around it curiously. "Esme thought you might just have gone . . . what with the accident last night and everything."

"What does Esme want with Alison?" Haidee's voice was sharp.

"It's not Esme." Yvonne's fingers were twisting the cloth of her apron nervously. "Alison has a visitor. He's very anxious to see her."

"Who . . . ?"

"Honest, I never saw him before." The young girl turned to Haidee. "And Esme told me I'm to help you get started, Miss Haidee. It's almost time for the theater. Esme will be up as soon as she's finished feeding the others."

Without waiting for instructions, Yvonne went to the windows and started pushing back the pink drapes. Haidee sank back against the pillows, her eyes closed again. But she was still breathing rapidly and she was still afraid. I patted her hand and stood. I would learn no more from Haidee, not with Yvonne on guard.

My mind was still going over our conversation as I hurried down the great staircase. At first glance the drawing room seemed empty. The sunset was coming through the long French windows, and the lamps had not yet been lit. And then I saw someone standing in front of the fireplace, staring up at the Vail family portrait as I had the first afternoon I came to the house. It was a tall man in a dark suit, and as I walked down the last steps he turned to face me. I did not recognize him in the shadows of the room, but something about the way we were standing seemed vaguely familiar. Then he moved forward, a smile breaking his narrow face, and a second later I knew him.

But there had been one second, and I must admit it, when looking right at him I had no idea who he was.

"Alison," he said, and took my hand.

"Peter, how good to see you." My voice sounded thin and strange to my ears. "What are you doing here? And why didn't you let me know you were coming?"

I pulled my hand free and walked farther into the room, knowing he was following me. My mind was a jumble at that moment, still stunned to realize that the man I had thought I'd loved six weeks before was now so much a stranger I had almost forgotten what he looked like. But he was speaking.

"Not a long journey," he was saying. "Only a few hours by car."

I smiled politely. "How's Dilys?" I asked, thankful I had not had to stumble over her name. "Is she with you?"

"No." He looked at me curiously and then he came closer. Taking me by the arms, he moved me into the sunlight still coming through the windows so that he could study my face. His fingers felt cold. "Let me look at you," he said, and then, as if suddenly aware of his hands on my bare skin, he dropped them. "You look . . . different."

"Better or worse?"

"Beautiful," Peter said solemnly.

"That's just suntan," I said. His skin was pale, I noticed, as if he had been indoors through the summer. He frowned, bringing his thick eyebrows together until they were almost a straight line across his forehead.

"No, it's more than that," he said, still frowning.

"You haven't told me how you happen to be here." A thought chilled me. "My father . . . is something wrong?"

"No, he's fine," he said hastily. "As a matter of fact, Alison, it was his suggestion that I drive up to see you."

"I don't understand." He's not really handsome, I thought. Not compared to Jeb, or even Corin. I remembered the nights that past spring I had cried myself to sleep over him, and smiled ruefully. "And how is Dilys?" I asked, trying to fill the silence between us.

240

"That's . . . why I'm here," Peter said. He ran a long hand over his forehead. "I thought perhaps your father might have written. It's . . . over between us, Alison." He continued to stare at me, but there was nothing I could say to help him. "We've decided to break the engagement."

"I'm sorry."

"I'm not." He smiled, and for the first time since I had entered the room he looked like the man who had charmed me for nearly a year. "Dilys and I didn't belong together. I was just something to . . . amuse her, I think." He shoved his hands into his pockets. For a moment he looked rather like a small boy hoping to avoid punishment. "After a while we didn't even amuse each other any more."

"I see." Suddenly the whole thing became clear. For a moment I was able to leave Vail's Point and go back to the Alison I had been at the university, to think like her, to feel as she had. "I suppose there's been a great deal of gossip about the break-up." I could see the small university campus during the summer months, the reduced faculty, the whispers. Only, now it all seemed very far away. And unimportant.

"You should be thankful it ended now, Peter," I said as tactfully as I could. "Before marriage."

"God, Alison, I've been such a fool!" He sounded more annoyed than angry. "How could I have been so wrong about Dilys? It was you I loved, it always was."

He's going to propose, I thought, and I felt my heart sink. Six weeks ago it would have been the most perfect ending in the world. Now it was simply a nuisance. Covertly I pulled my watch from my pocket and snapped it open. Ten minutes to eight. I would be late for the theater! "Peter, perhaps we can talk about this some other time . . ."

He moved closer, frowning slightly. "Alison, I love you," he said, with a thin edge of irritation. "Didn't you hear me? I want to marry you."

"Peter," I began, trying to pick the most diplomatic words, knowing what a blow it would be to him to be turned down by two different women in one summer. "It's very kind of you to say this, but it's really impossible."

"Why?"

My attempt at tact was not going to succeed. He stepped still closer, blocking my path to the open windows and the theater beyond. "You loved me once, I know you did. People don't change their feelings that quickly."

"You did."

As soon as I said that, I regretted it. It sounded as if I were taking some sort of revenge on him, and nothing could have been further from the truth. Actually, I felt rather sorry for him standing there, hot and uncomfortable in his dark suit, finding everything he had (perhaps rather complacently!) believed real crumbling about him.

"That was unkind," I said to fill the awkward silence. "I didn't mean to throw that at you."

"You have the right." He looked suddenly older. There were lines on the sides of his mouth, lines that had not been there when I had seen him last. "Alison, I want us to start again." He smiled a little tentatively. "I think even your father would like that."

"We can't, Peter." I forced myself to walk past him toward the open French windows. I must end this, I thought. I'll be late for the first act. I could hear from where I stood the sound of cars pulling up in front of the theater, doors slamming . . . "Peter, I really have to go now. I'm terribly sorry, but it's late."

"Go?" He walked over to me, clearly puzzled. "But I thought . . . can't we find someplace to have dinner? To talk?"

"I can't tonight, Peter." I realized now that I would have to tell him the truth. "I have a performance to give."

"You're . . . an actress?" His tone implied this was simply one more incredible surprise in a world that had suddenly turned upside down.

"It's a long story, Peter. I didn't want to tell Father . . ." Peter was staring at me now as if he had never seen me before. "You know I'm here to work on Lionel Vail's papers? Well, there was an accident; they needed someone in a hurry. Tonight's the last performance. I really have to get to the theater or I'll be late." Then, as if it might make it more plausible, I added somewhat lamely, "It's only a small part."

"But surely that's not as important as us? Our future?"

"I don't think we have a future, Peter."

He reached forward then, trying to hold me, but I stepped back and he stopped where he was, his hands falling limply to his sides. "Alison, if you want to hurt me, if you want to take your revenge, I understand," he said wearily.

"That's not it . . ."

But he wasn't listening. He went on as if I had not spoken. "But don't leave me without any hope at all."

"Peter, I'm sorry." He looked so beaten I wanted to comfort him, but only as I might a stranger who had tripped and fallen on a sidewalk ahead of me. "I wish I could explain, but I'm so terribly late. Perhaps after the performance tonight . . ."

"Is there someone else?" His face was hard now, his voice harsh, forcing me to look at him.

"Yes, Peter," I said quietly.

He was angry now, that slow, quiet anger I had seen before when he found he wasn't going to get his own way. "Is it one of these theater people?"

I nodded, not trusting myself to speak, not even wanting to mention Jeb's name.

"Alison, that's impossible!" A vein stood out on the side of his forehead. "It's only been six weeks! You can't be in love with some theater vagabond!"

"Don't talk like that!" My voice came back and I found myself growing angry. "They're wonderful people, Peter, I never realized that before. Talented, hard-working, dedicated . . ."

"They're children." His voice crackled with contempt.

Suddenly I was furious. "And what about people who elect to spend their lives in a classroom, repeating the knowledge that everybody else has learned centuries before? Just how adult are they?"

"You can't compare my life . . . your father's life with . . ." He sputtered, trying to think of a phrase strong enough to quell me. "Spending half their time out of a job . . . dressing up to be somebody else . . . penciling wrinkles on their faces to pretend they're older or younger or some damned thing . . . as if life could be changed that easily . . ."

And then, standing there in the last of the sunlight, I felt a cold chill on my shoulders. For I knew now where Lionel's manuscript was.

Peter had told me.

It was hard to make him leave. I was frantic with impatience, knowing that it must be after eight, knowing I would have to race

243

to be ready on time, and that I would have no chance to prove what I had guessed about Lionel's hiding place. It was so obvious, so simple that I never had the slightest doubt that I had finally deciphered the clue that Lionel had left for the world thirty years before.

Eventually Peter realized nothing he had to say was making any impression, that in fact I was barely listening. He slammed out of the house. I remembered later I did not even ask if he had a room at the inn in town or if he would be driving back to the university that night. He quite simply no longer mattered.

Even as he turned in fury for the door, I was out the open windows, running across the concrete driveway for the path through the woods, hurrying between the blue shadows growing along the way, until I reached the stage door of the theater and had to stop, gasping for breath, before I climbed the steps of the veranda. The screen door in front of me opened and Bradley came out on the porch, a troubled look on his young face.

"Gee, we were beginning to worry, Alison," he said. "It's almost quarter past."

"I'm sorry to be late. I had a visitor." I climbed the steps and walked past him into the darkness of the backstage.

"I'll check you in on the sign-in sheet," he said as he followed behind me. "Careful—the crew's moved in the scenery for the next play. Makes everything a little crowded backstage."

I stood still for a moment, took a deep breath and let my eyes adjust to the gloom. Since the set for *The Basilisks* was so enormous, there had never been a great deal of free space backstage. Now what little space there had been was filled. Large canvas flats were stacked carefully against the theater walls, and furniture for *Ghosts* was piled in every available corner: between the stage braces, behind the black velvet curtains that masked the exits, underneath the spotlights that stood like thin metal sentinels facing the stage.

"This way," said Bradley, offering me a hand. "Go slow—it's a little tricky through here."

Guided by him, I made my way through the clutter toward the dressing rooms. It was then, for the first time that day, I thought of the performance ahead.

"Bradley! My costume . . ."

"It's all right," he answered reassuringly. "Esme got you another dress from the attic. And Jeb has told everybody you won't be making your last exit up the stairs."

"Is he here?" Suddenly I needed to see him. If I could tell him what I knew, if only we had one minute to ourselves so that someone else might know what I did . . .

"When you didn't show up he went out front to call the house."

Bradley led me to my dressing-room door. It was hard to see his face in the darkness, but I could see he was smiling proudly. "We're a real hit tonight, Alison! Standing room, folding chairs—there's even people who've bought seats out on the side verandas. We told them they can't see all of the stage, but they don't seem to care." His voice was quietly triumphant, as if he had written the play himself, designed the scenery and was playing all the parts. I couldn't blame him. I felt the same.

But neither of us had a second to savor the moment, for the door to my dressing room opened and May stood there, tall and grim. "Quickly, Alison!" She pulled me inside the room. "Where have you been?" She didn't wait for my answer, but began to untie the band that held back my hair.

"You've only got ten minutes, Alison," said Bradley, the triumph gone, once more the nervous stage manager. "Will you be ready?"

"She'll be ready," said May firmly, closing the door in his face.

And I was.

But there was no moment to speak privately to Jeb, who passed from actor to actor wishing us all well. The packed house beyond the heavy velvet curtain had infected all of us with a kind of fever. We were like animals ready to race, impatient for the curtain to rise, for the play to begin. Even the knowledge that I had untangled the secret that Lionel had left seemed unimportant now, something to enjoy for a moment as May brushed my hair smooth and helped me into my new costume. It was a pale blue organdy, prettier than my original costume, and I couldn't help feeling pleased that Jeb would see me at my best this triumphant night.

May walked me out to the stage, stepping carefully among the hulking furniture and canvas flats that crowded in around us. Bradley was with Haidee at the far side of the stage. The prop table had been moved closer to the entrance to the stage; a hastily hung black velvet drape would barely hide it from audience view. Haidee did not seem to see me. She was listening intently to the stage manager, the glass of milk that she brought in on her first entrance already in her hands.

For the last time I stretched out on the antique sofa, alone on stage. The spotlights on each side and high above me blazed into light. I could hear the audience beyond the curtain grow quiet. I closed my eyes and leaned back on the pillows.

Silence . . .

A hoarse whisper from Bradley: "Curtain!" A rush of air as the curtain rose, and the last performance of *The Basilisks* began.

If I had thought the opening night exciting, this final performance was magic. Haidee's entrance was greeted with a salvo of applause that almost stopped the play completely. Julie was once again in control, playing surely and steadily, her voice like ice, her body lithe, her timing perfect as she added layer upon layer to the evil character that Lionel had written. The audience on that hot, airless night sat as though hypnotized; there was no rustling, no coughs, no rattle of programs. They knew they were seeing two superb actresses at the peak of their careers, and it was a night to be remembered for the rest of their lives.

The first act ended with deafening applause. It continued long after all of us had left the stage. For the first time since I had arrived at the theater, I had a moment to think. I hesitated outside the door of my dressing room. The dressing room where Lionel had died was next to mine, but because it was not in use, the crew had piled the heavy canvas flats for the next play against the door. I thought of what I had at last discovered. Later. The second half of the play was all that mattered now.

Suddenly I was aware of someone behind me. I whirled around, thankful the shadows hid the expression on my face; my thoughts would be only too easy to read. But it was only Corin standing in the darkness.

"Alison," he said quietly. "I have to talk to you, I have to explain about last night . . ."

For a moment I didn't understand what he was talking about.

"The doctor," he explained, sensing my bewilderment. "I

should have been on your side, instead of all that talk about you being afraid of heights."

"That doesn't matter, Corin." I remembered then the feeling of disillusion I had felt. But that was before I had talked to Julie, before Jeb . . .

"It *does* matter," Corin persisted. "It's just that . . . well, after Wendy's death, we couldn't afford another suspicious accident. McNaughton would love to close the theater down, splash our names all over the papers."

"Corin, it's not important." He made a gesture as if he would interrupt, but I went on, keeping my voice low. "I'll be leaving tomorrow anyway. It's all over."

"But the play . . . Lionel's manuscript . . . ?"

That's all that ever mattered, wasn't it? I thought. All the laughter and flirting, even his one kiss . . . it was simply to make me want to help him in his search. I had meant nothing else to him. I felt a curious sense of relief, as if the last barrier between me and Jeb had finally been removed. "I know now where Lionel's play is, Corin," I said quietly.

"But . . ." Even in the shadows I could see the stunned look on his face.

"Later." And I went into my dressing room.

May was there, which was unusual, for generally after she had finished making me up for the performance she would disappear to watch the play from the front of the house, or stand on the quiet veranda, content to hear the words her beloved brother had written so many years before. But this night there would be no place in the building where she could be alone except in my room backstage. She retied my hair ribbon and brushed my hair smooth once more. Neither of us felt like conversation.

The second act began, moving steadily toward the climactic moment of Haidee's appearance. I was on stage, mute witness to a scene between Oliver and Corin, my face carefully blank, leaving the audience to wonder how much Emily understands of what is going on around her. Usually it was easy to hold the position, staring at the door where Haidee would make her dramatic entrance.

But tonight it was different. The clutter of furniture for the next play had forced them to move the prop table near the doorway. I could even see the glass of milk on the silver tray that Haidee would bring in for me to drink.

And then as the scene continued around me, I saw the black velvet drape masking the prop table move, and through the drape came a hand.

I could not tell from where I sat in the bright lights if the hand belonged to a man or a woman; all I could see was that the fingers were clutching something like a small bottle. And slowly, steadily, as if whoever belonged to the hand had no fear of being discovered, was perhaps indifferent to the fact I might be watching, the bottle tipped and a whitish powder poured into the glass from which I would have to drink.

"Emily, you agree with us, don't you?"

That was my cue to turn back to Corin, to stare at him blankly. But something of what I had seen must have shown in my face, for while Corin continued smiling blandly as he was supposed to, I could see a flicker of puzzlement in his eyes.

Julie, opulent in her peach satin evening gown and glittering with stage diamonds, swept into the room from the back of the set. We were approaching the climactic moment of the play. Thank God I had nothing to say until my exit. My lips were stuck tight, my mouth dry . . .

They circled me now: Corin and Oliver and Julie. From the corner of my eyes I could see a blur offstage: Haidee picking up the tray with the glass of milk. In a moment she would come on stage . . . the audience would gasp at her striking appearance, and I would have to seize the glass and drink it.

Only, what was in it?

Was it my imagination? Had I *really* seen a hand pour something in the glass? Pour *what?*

Poison?

Spotlights hot on my head and face . . . the voices of the others unnaturally loud. I looked at them as they moved closer and closer. I was no longer Emily now. I was Alison Howard and one of them might be trying to kill me.

No. *Was* trying to kill me!

But who? Julie, with her face an evil mask as she said the vicious dialogue Lionel had written for her? Oliver, a bemused smile on his old face—Oliver, who had never told any of us all that he knew about Lionel's death? Or was it Corin, his cold eyes flickering as he stared at me? Or the others . . . May . . . Esme . . . even Haidee?

How much of the evil that I felt that moment was acting? And how much was real?

It seemed to me then that all of this had happened long before. It had been in my dream, from the very beginning, from the night before I had come to Vail's Point. I'd been through it all: the terror, the panic, the absolute helplessness I felt there on the stage. The faces, cruel and sardonic, circling me, the audience waiting and watching in silence.

There was no way out. The play would collapse into insane farce if I as Emily refused to drink the glass Haidee was about to bring in.

And I knew as I sat there, the tension of the scene growing thicker and thicker, there was nothing else I *could* do.

A sharp hiss: the audience caught their breath. Haidee had entered, the glass in her hand. Attention was on her for that moment, and even as I sat there in panic, unable to move, I remembered what I had said to Corin at the intermission.

Someone must have been listening, I thought dully. Someone has always been listening. And because of that I am to die.

Haidee came closer, the tray steady in her hand. There was no sound on stage, none in the crowded dark auditorium beyond. Every eye was on me.

For one second I hesitated. *Help me! Somebody please help me!*

But then I had to reach out for the glass.

CHAPTER TWENTY-FIVE

The curtain has gone up on the last act . . . I can hear the voices of the actors on stage . . . I can see the black velvet drapes. There is silence now, endless silence as the actors wait for me . . .

The lights are bright.

My mouth is dry.

What is nightmare and what is real?

My fingers curve around the glass, lift it from the tray that Haidee holds. I must have imagined the hand, I *must* have! I must drink what is in the glass . . .

Suddenly Julie, swift as a tigress, lunged forward, her arm raised. With a swift swipe she slapped the glass from my hand. "You're too old for milk now, Emily," she improvised. The glass splashed to the carpet. The others stared at Julie, stunned, but I could see Oliver was already improvising another line of dialogue. The words being spoken were no longer Lionel's. Even Corin added something that sounded vaguely right. Only Haidee stood there silent, her eyes glazed as if she were not aware of the change in the play.

One glance at Julie's dark blue eyes and I no longer saw the evil villainess, but a conscientious professional, forcing me to keep the scene going, inventing a tirade of angry words to make me stand and defy her. Only when I was offstage could they return to the script.

I don't remember exactly what I said. The one word "Never" would no longer be enough. Bradley told me afterwards I had added a sentence, something like "I'll never give in to you, never!" And turned and ran off through the French windows to the "garden."

Then at last I was safe, the dark shadows hiding me, Jeb's strong arms around me, holding me. My legs gave way and I sagged against him.

"Alison!" he whispered, "what the hell happened out there?"

He pulled me back farther into the shadows, still holding me firmly. I looked back at the stage. They had returned to the words of the play now, the audience still and quiet, the dialogue as I remembered it. The moment of improvisation—the moment when Julie had stepped forward and broken the spell and saved my life—had been missed by the crowded theater. Only those of us who had been on stage knew what had happened.

Before I could answer Jeb, Julie swept through the French windows. She would only have a minute before she had to return to the stage and the end of the play. She came directly toward us, her long satin train rippling behind her.

"Are you all right?" she said to me softly. I still could not speak, only nod. "Good." She turned to Jeb. "Somebody tried to kill Alison out there," she whispered. I could feel Jeb's arms tight around me.

"What . . . ?"

"Ssh!" hissed Julie. She grabbed his arm, her fingers as clawlike as Haidee's. "I saw somebody tampering with the glass she was to drink from—I couldn't see who it was from where I was standing. But I think if there's any of that milk left we'll find it's been poisoned."

Jeb straightened and even in the shadows I could see the anger in his eyes. "This is a matter for the police, Julie." His lips were tight; they barely moved. Julie nodded and then looked back at the brightly lit stage. Her cue to re-enter was coming closer and closer.

"Get McNaughton," she whispered quickly. "Alison will be safe now. Nothing more can happen until after the curtain calls."

"Not McNaughton," said Jeb, frowning. "He's trouble, Julie . . ."

"McNaughton," she repeated. She drew herself up and looked her son levelly in the eyes. "I know what I'm doing, Jeb," she said. She smiled, but I could see her eyes under the heavy stage makeup were glistening. "It'll be all right," said Julie. Then she added, and there was no mistaking her meaning, "After all, he's . . . family."

Oliver, on stage, spoke her cue. Julie gave a bitter laugh in answer, whirled around and went back onto the stage.

Jeb watched her leave, and I knew even with his arms around me I was no longer in his thoughts. In that one look he had exchanged with Julie they had acknowledged their relationship.

And he had learned the identity of his father.

He left then, after placing me carefully alongside Bradley, who stood by the ropes that would lower the curtain at the end of the

251

play. Bradley barely glanced at me. I knew he must be curious about what had happened on stage, but the swift change of dialogue had brought him conscientiously back to studying each line of the script that lay open under the small lamp on his stage manager's desk. Obviously something had gone wrong and he would have to be prepared to prompt if it happened again.

On stage the play was driving forward to the climax—the final revolt of the old lady that Haidee played—and the heart attack that would lead to her death on stage and the bitter triumph of the villains. Julie was playing coolly and with strength, and I think no one who had not seen her act the scene before could have known that her attention was no longer on the part. Only her technical skill as a professional kept her going. The fine bright edge was off Oliver's and Corin's performances as well. Only Haidee seemed unchanged; no, more than unchanged. Brilliant.

Through the weeks, I had often watched Haidee work on this scene. She had always been incredibly moving in the last speeches as the vague old lady fights back to reality for one last stinging moment before her death. Only, tonight there was something extra, something so unbelievably touching about her. The words had become *her* words, what the character was feeling was what *she* felt; and as I watched her I felt tears burning my eyes.

Finally the curtain descended slowly, quietly, on the last tableau: the dead woman, Julie the villainess triumphant; only, now the other conspirators stared at her with loathing. I could barely see the curtain reach the floor for the tears in my eyes. For once, there was no applause. For one endless moment the entire building, actors and audience, was frozen in silence.

When the applause began it was not just louder than any we had heard during the week; it was a roar, like the sea pounding, like a mob set free, as if it were not just hands clapping that were making the noise, but feet stamping, voices crying "Bravo!"

"What happened out there?" asked Bradley through the noise, but he didn't wait for an answer—just shoved me through the narrow space between the wall of the theater and the edge of the scenery to take my place for the first curtain call.

The curtain came down for the last time on Haidee alone, curtseying deeply, her head high, with a dignity an empress would have envied. Julie stood at my side offstage, watching her mother receive the tribute she deserved. "It's over," she said quietly. "And you're safe." She looked at me. "But this means all the other things that have happened weren't accidents either. Can you ever forgive us?"

Julie's face was tired now; even the heavy greasepaint could not hide the fine lines around her deep eyes. "Only, . . . why? Why?" she insisted.

"Because Lionel's killer knows I've found the lost manuscript," I answered, and taking her arm I led her toward the dressing rooms.

She said nothing further, but moved past to her own room. May was waiting at the open door to my dressing room, her face empty of expression as always, but something curious in her black eyes: that glint of fire I had noticed the first day that I had only seen when she was deeply moved or excited.

I sat down in front of the dressing table. Suddenly I felt exhausted. But there was still one thing more to do tonight.

Before Jeb returned with the police.

Usually after the performance the theater was crowded with people who had watched the show: theater friends of the Vails up from New York: townspeople from Westaven who had known the family over the years, standing back a little shyly, hoping to be recognized, wanting to tell the cast how moved they had been; tourists wanting autographs. But tonight there was no one; even the crew had been barred from backstage by Jeb's orders. So when Corin tapped on my door ten minutes later, I was out of costume and makeup and the theater was dark and quiet.

May stiffened when she heard the hesitant rapping on the dressing-room door. "Who is it?" she asked, her voice barely a whisper. The doorknob turned. Without answering, Corin came in.

"Let's keep this quiet, although I think everybody's left," he said. My hair was still loose about my shoulders, but I didn't waste the time to tie it back. The same curiosity, the same eagerness that Corin was feeling, filled me, too. "Are you sure?" he asked. "What you told me?"

I stood up from the dressing table then, fingering the key to Lionel's rooms that had hung about my neck all these weeks I had been at Vail's Point. "I'm sure," I said. I moved toward the doorway, Corin stepping aside to let me pass. "I'll need your help, Corin," I added.

The theater was very quiet, the doors to the other dressing

253

rooms closed. Where we stood was very dark, filled with furniture and flattened scenery that tomorrow would become the set for the next play. I turned to my left and stood in front of the panels of scenery that hid the door to the room where Lionel had died.

"Help me move this, Corin," I said.

He was right beside me, his clever face serious for once. He looked older as he frowned; an aging boy. "But there's nothing in there, Alison," he said. "You saw that the first day. You told me!"

I made no answer, but began to push the heavy canvas structures to one side, and after a second he joined me. May stood behind us, saying nothing. When the doorway was free I took the chain from my neck and fitted the key into the lock.

"Lionel was very clever," I said as I fiddled with the lock. "Even that last night with the pills and the alcohol working in him, he knew how to leave a message that would fool the world for thirty years." The lock turned and I pushed the door open.

The tiny room beyond was dark, the dirty windows in the far wall letting in only a few flickers of light from the lanterns on the veranda outside. Standing on the threshold, I could feel the coldness of the room beyond, that coldness I had felt the first day I walked in there, the coldness I had felt when I stared at the family portrait in the great house. The coldness of evil. Haidee had been right. There *was* evil here.

There were no lights in the room; the dusty bulbs had worn out years before. But I needed no light to find what I knew was there. I signaled the others to wait where they stood and, shivering slightly, walked purposefully into the shadowy dressing room. "Lionel's message was quite clear," I said over my shoulder. "Only, we forgot there were *two* parts to that message."

Good. I had found it, just where it was that first day. I picked it up and turned back. Corin and May were framed in the doorway. The work lights, high up under the roof and always left on, cast strange shadows across their faces: Corin's was twisted into a clever smile, May's high forehead and deep-set eyes turned her into a skull. For a second I thought of the symbols of the theater, the tragic and comic masks. They both stood there in the open doorway watching me.

I walked back to them, holding what I had found carefully.

"I don't get it . . . *two* parts of the message?" said Corin. He peered at what I was holding in the shadows, not understanding. I felt frozen just from the few seconds I had been in the room, the skin prickling on my bare shoulders.

"Yes," I said, stepping back over the threshold. "The *words* he underlined."

Slowly I raised what I held in my hands. "And what he used to underline them *with*."

I was holding Lionel's makeup box.

They stepped aside in silence as I moved past them back into the lights of my own dressing room, the box still in my hands. I placed it carefully on the table in front of the mirror. May came to my left and Corin to my right, and the three of us stared down at the open box in front of us.

It was of plain wood, the size of a shoe box or one that might contain shoe-shining equipment. The cracked old lid was open. We could see odds and ends of stage makeup that might have been used before: stubs of pink greasepaint, still with the faint odor of cheap perfume; flat, round containers of rouge, dried and cracked with age; braids of crepe hair; tiny bottles and jars. I took them out one by one, knowing I must find somewhere in the box the one thing I was looking for . . .

"I never saw the actual 'suicide' note," I said.

"None of us did, after that morning," May broke in. "McNaughton took it."

"Exactly. All I ever saw was the photograph of it in the newspaper clippings." I was reaching the bottom of the box now. Where was it? "I knew the words had been underlined with a coarse pencil . . . but only after someone said something to me today did I realize what sort of a pencil Lionel must have used . . ." Yes, there they were. Several of them. Gray and white and brown, several shades of brown, coarse-pointed pencils used for drawing wrinkles and changing eyebrows, all jumbled together in the bottom of the shallow box. I held them up to the others. They stared at me, still puzzled.

"Don't you see?" I said, my voice rising a little in excitement. "This was the *other* part of the message. What he used to write it with. Maybe it was the *only* message after all. The idea of 'recorded time' being the wrinkles that actors draw on their faces is a little fanciful, even for Lionel."

"But the manuscript . . . where is it?" Corin moved closer and looked at the box in front of us. He could see the bottom of it.

"It's here," I answered patiently. "Lionel knew actors wouldn't poke through a makeup box, not one that belonged to someone else." I turned to May. "You told me that the night of the first performance. But someday, some scholar might. Somebody who didn't know about theater traditions. Lionel always knew he would be important to scholars someday."

Corin lifted the box and dumped out the rest of the makeup. "But it's empty!" he said.

"No, it isn't."

I took it from him. Oddly, I had no hesitancy, no doubt; it never crossed my mind I could be wrong. I held up the empty box to May and Corin with one hand and placed a finger down the inside of the box, and then against the outside. The outside of the box was, as I was sure it would be, deeper by almost an inch.

Corin grabbed the makeup kit from me. We will never know whether there was a secret panel to the box or whether over the years the top shelf holding the bits of makeup had become stuck, for Corin slammed the box down on the table with all his might and the three of us could hear the thin old wood splinter. As savage as if he were ripping apart an animal, Corin tore at the shredded wood at the bottom of the makeup, and the rusty nails squealed as they were pulled loose. A pile of thin white pages fell onto the table in front of us.

For a second, no one moved. The pages had been folded in half, lengthwise. Slowly, as if some unseen hand were smoothing them flat, they fell back to their natural width and we could see the words on the first page.

ALL OUR YESTERDAYS
A new play
by
Lionel Vail

I think we were all afraid to touch it, to pick it up. Finding it had been the passion of Corin's life, its loss the bitterest regret of the past thirty years for May. For me, it was as if I had finally proved my right to be there, to be part of the Vails. At last, May, with great grace and dignity, moved. She took me by the shoulders and kissed me gently on each cheek.

"I thank you for Lionel, my dear," she whispered softly.

Corin had picked up the white pages now and was flipping through them quickly. "It's all here," he said, more to himself than to us. "The whole play."

"What play?"

The three of us could not have been more startled if we had heard a gunshot. Our heads turned together toward the doorway. Standing there, still in her heavy stage makeup and opulent evening gown, was Julie. She stared at us, puzzled. "I thought you'd all gone," she said, that funny little break in her voice making her sound like a deserted child. "I thought I was alone in the theater."

"Alison's found it, Ma," said Corin. "She found the copy of Lionel's last play."

Julie did not move. "I thought everyone had gone up to the house," she said, paying no attention to the papers Corin held in his hands. "I was going to stay here and wait for Jeb and . . ." She broke off and glanced at me. "And . . . well . . . who he was bringing back. I felt sure they would come here first."

"I've got to read this!" said Corin. The color had come back into his face and his voice was strident with excitement. "Right away!" He glanced at Julie and then back at the pages in his hands. "Get out of your makeup, Ma. This is a history-making night. A new play by Lionel Vail!" Once again he said it with the same quiet awe as he had the first afternoon in Lionel's study, so many weeks before.

"Not . . . tonight, Corin."

A muscle on the side of Julie's face twitched a little, and I knew she could think only of what lay ahead—the meeting with the man she had loved and the knowledge that he would be coming here to search for a murderer. Then she froze, her head turning swiftly to the side as if she had heard something. She raised a hand to us for silence and called off into the darkness, "Is someone there?"

There was no answer.

She turned back to us instantly. "Get out of here!" she whispered. "Take the play up to the house! Quick!" She pointed at the door to the veranda behind us. "Someone's on stage searching for that glass. Someone who knows what was in it."

Corin moved swiftly to the screen door and held it open for May and me. May moved past him, but as I looked at Julie I saw she was trembling. Whatever was to happen, she needed me here.

"Go on!" I whispered to May and Corin as they hesitated in the doorway. "Go up to the house!" Corin nodded, and the door closed quietly behind them. I turned back to the dressing-room doorway, but it was empty now. Julie had left.

"Julie?" I whispered, looking out at the dark shadows of the backstage. Somewhere outside a wind was moving the trees. The theater was cooler now. There was very little light. I had to feel my way carefully through the clumps of furniture toward the stage beyond. I could hear neither Julie nor anyone else now; it was as if I were alone in the dark building.

I thought, perhaps for the first time, of how old the building was; as old as the house on the hill, and as haunted with memories, haunted with actors and audiences who had been dead for years, of plays long forgotten, of triumphs and tragedies.

Haunted with the Vails . . .

I managed to reach the great double doors that opened onto the stage. The curtain was not down now. When the last of the audience leaves, the stage manager always raises it; I never knew why. Ahead of me, standing motionless, was Julie, her long stiff satin train and her bare shoulders lit by the one working light on the stage. The light, a thin metal rod with a bare light bulb on top of it, was placed in the middle of the stage, throwing a weak glow on the furniture, all carefully covered with sheets.

Julie paid no attention as I came onto the stage. She was looking up at the great staircase that had dominated the stage as it did in the house on the hill.

"Come down," said Julie quietly, speaking to someone I could not see. "It's time we had a talk."

Chapter Twenty-six

For a long moment Haidee did not move. She was still wearing the dressing gown she always changed into for her curtain calls, a long black velvet robe with cuffs of white fox. She did not look down at Julie or me; she continued to stare out at the empty auditorium as if she could still see the crowds who had applauded her, not just tonight but for the decades she had been a reigning star.

"The house is so dark," she muttered to herself. "I need lights for my exit."

"Come down," said Julie again.

This time Haidee heard her. She tugged at the mandarin collar of her robe and said, "Who is it? Who's down there?"

"It's me, Mother. Julie. Come down. We have to talk."

Slowly, very slowly, Haidee started down the stairs to the stage, one shaking hand on the railing, the other holding up the long skirt of her velvet robe. "For a moment," she said, her voice strangely distant, "seeing you there in Viola's dress, with your hair the way she always wore it, I almost thought . . ."

She came down the last steps and hesitated. "I never realized how much you look like your grandmother." She shook her head gently, as if trying to clear it of old memories.

Julie made no effort to come closer to Haidee, but remained where she was in the middle of the shadowy stage. "Something happened this evening during the play," she said. "Remember? I knocked the glass out of Alison's hand."

"That was wrong, I remember that." There was enough light on her face for both Julie and me to see Haidee's eyes. They were narrowed, as if she were trying to peer through a fog. "Or was it last night that things went wrong? Something about the stairs?" She let the hand that had been clinging to the newel post at the bottom of the railing drop to her side, and for a moment she swayed a little as if she might fall. "Oh, Julie," she said, "I'm so tired."

"Sit down, Mother." There was no pity in Julie's voice; it was almost stern. She pointed toward the covered love seat in front of Haidee. The old woman moved to it slowly and sank into it, one quavering hand covering her eyes again.

"I knocked the glass out of Alison's hand because someone had put something in it." Julie went on, her voice controlled. "It may have been poison."

Haidee looked up then, her brilliant eyes sharp once more. "Who was it? Did you see?"

"No," said Julie. She moved a little closer. "But I've kept the glass. It's locked in my dressing room. I'll have to give it to the police."

Haidee's head snapped back, her eyes opened, and we could see her face become blotched with anger. "Nonsense!" Her voice was shrill. "Who would want to poison Alison?"

"There are reasons," said Julie. For the first time since I had crept onto the stage, she indicated me. "Alison saw it, too, didn't you?"

I stepped forward into the circle of the work light. Haidee looked at me as I nodded, but she was frowning slightly. "That's not Alison," she said. "Alison's a prim, white-faced old maid. Poking her nose into things. I don't like that. I don't like her." Then, as if something had clicked in her brain, she looked up at her daughter.

"Julie, what on earth are we doing here?" Haidee said in her usual crisp manner. "The performance is over. It's time to get out of costume and go up to the house."

Julie placed her hand on the back of the love seat where Haidee sat. "Let's stay here, Mama. Just for a little." There was that intriguing little break in her voice now that always sounded as if she were close to tears. "There are things I want to know . . . before the police come. I've had to send Jeb for Ed McNaughton."

Haidee's back stiffened. "I won't have that man here," she said. "Cheap, vicious oaf!" She spread her arms wide, indicating the stage. "I won't have him here in my house!" Clenching her thin hands into tight fists, she pounded her knees. "You're not to see him again, Julie. Do you hear me?"

The violence of her anger startled both of us. Julie stepped back from the little sofa. "I had to send for him, Mama," she said. "Too many dangerous things have happened. They must be stopped."

Haidee rose, moving as swiftly as when I had first seen her, crossing the stage to the windows. She stood there looking out—as if she were seeing the gardens around the great house, not the backstage clutter that lay in the dark shadows beyond.

"It's all Lionel's fault," she said slowly. "This whole last week

260

. . ." She looked back at us, that same puzzled little frown on her face, as if she had lost her place in a speech. "Or was it always?" She nodded then, making up her mind. "Yes, it's always been Lionel's fault. All the way from the beginning."

She started toward us, but something strange was happening to her face now. Behind the fine web of wrinkles, something young and sly seemed to be peering out, and her voice became that of a wheedling little girl. "Lionel's bad. He likes to hurt people." She reached out a tentative hand toward Julie.

"You know that, Mama," she said in her little-girl's voice.

Julie shrank back, her eyes wide and frightened. "Mother, look at me!" she said. "I'm not Viola! I'm your daughter! I'm Julie!"

Haidee looked at Julie, a strange little smile on her face as if she were trying to humor her. "Why do you say that? My daughter's a little girl."

She began pacing back and forth like an animal confined to the boundaries of a cage, her clawlike hands twisting together, her voice harsh with rage. "The only thing that wretched Geoffrey ever gave me, my daughter! And then he wouldn't touch me again. Any other woman, yes. But not me."

Her voice was a shout now. "Well, let him walk out! See if I care!" She whirled around, but whether she was seeing us or someone else I could not tell. "They're all alike. Men!" She said it with contempt. "Papa, Geoffrey, Lionel—all cruel! All vicious!"

Julie's hand clutched the back of the love seat as if she would fall without its support. Haidee had come closer, that strange, crafty, young look in her face now. "But you could have trusted me, Mama." She reached out and caressed Julie's bare arm. "I wouldn't really have committed you, Mama," she said softly, coaxingly. "I was just teasing. I needed money for my career. So that I didn't have to take just any play that came along."

Julie pulled herself free. Her face was in the light now, and I could see the horror in her eyes. Haidee drew herself up as well, the fake humility disappearing. "But no . . . you wouldn't do anything for me. Everything had to go for Lionel, to pay his debts, to get him out of trouble. All I'm to get are your diamonds . . . and I can't even sell them! Everything has to be for Lionel . . . so he can write his filth, his trash! *The Basilisks!*"

She practically spat out the two words. "That's what he thinks of me! That I'm a monster." She grabbed Julie's arm, sinking her nails into the skin. "And he's still doing it!"

Julie seemed frozen, unable to move, unable to free herself. I stepped forward close enough to put my hand on Haidee's, hoping it would startle her enough to let her daughter free. She glanced at me, her head twisting swiftly as I touched her, but I could feel her fingers become soft. I grasped Haidee's hands in mine as Julie stepped back. There were red marks from Haidee's nails on her skin.

"Who . . . who are you?" said Haidee, looking at me with a polite smile on her face. "You're very pretty." Then her wide blue eyes seem to focus for a second. "I remember now. You're Alison . . . something." A frown creased her face. "I thought I'd frightened you into going this afternoon."

She looked around the empty stage, and I knew in her mind she was not here but in the drawing room of the house on the hill, the room that Jeb had so cleverly duplicated at the theater. "Everything seems changed." She shook herself free, and I could see her becoming angry and bitter again. "All except Lionel. He still wants to hurt me."

"Lionel's dead, Haidee." Almost as if she were picking up her cue in a scene, Haidee turned back to me, her thin body stiff, her hands curling once more into claws.

"No! Lionel isn't dead," she said. "He's written a new play . . . didn't you know that? It's to be the last about the family."

Where was Jeb? He should be back by now! Perhaps if we keep her talking . . .

"Tell us about the play, Haidee," I said as gently as I could.

Haidee's face turned grim; the last of the little girl disappeared with the tightening of her lips. "He found out about what I did— through him—to Julie . . . some woman in the village told him," she said. "He put it into his play . . . terrible things about me. It mustn't ever be performed!"

At this, the fear left Julie. Her face grew hard, the way a duelist might look. "What did you do to Julie?" she said quietly.

"I gave her a career!"

Haidee faced her daughter, but there was no sign that she recognized her. "She wanted to marry some good-looking local boy. Well, I broke that up!" Her lips twisted in a bitter smile. It was the first time I'd ever seen Haidee look ugly. "Julie never blamed me, she blamed Lionel . . . because I was clever. They never knew the truth. None of them. The fools." She moved slowly away from us down toward the auditorium, looking out at the empty blackness, no longer paying us any attention.

"She would have thrown it away—the Vail name, her chances, her talent—all for a man. Well, I stopped that!" She swayed a little, her voice fainter now. "Only, somehow Lionel found out I'd tricked him.

"I came up that Sunday." She hesitated, looking at us as if we could help her. "When was it? A week ago? I had suspected something, so I drove up in the rain. I didn't tell anybody."

She looked away suddenly, and when she spoke again it was to someone standing by the windows, someone only she could see. "I want to read that play, Lionel! You're not going to pull any surprises on me tomorrow at rehearsal." She held out her hands. "Don't you laugh! You give it to me!" She reached out as if she had grabbed something from an unseen hand.

For a second, no one moved.

"*All Our Yesterdays,* it was called," said the old woman absently. Her hands dropped to her sides once more. "I read it that evening. I got Lionel to start drinking. 'You should celebrate,' I said. I'd even brought a bottle with me. Luckily, by the time I finished he was drunk."

She looked very old now, all the anger and strength drained out of her. "He called it 'murder,' what I'd done to Julie. Only, what was he trying to do to me but murder? Murdering my reputation, my life, my whole career?"

"So you killed him?" Even Haidee could feel the hatred in Julie's voice.

"No . . ."

But her voice wavered. "I don't think so," said Haidee. "Maybe. There were powders . . ."

She looked at us, her eyes stricken. "Just to knock him out. So the play could be destroyed." Then, more humbly than I could have believed, she went on. "Because it was a great play, you see. It would have been done all over the world. The whole world would have known about me . . . my secrets, my life. They would have despised me." Her wide, pale blue eyes were filled with tears now. "You can't live if the whole world despises you."

She moved away toward the imitation fireplace that dominated the set as it did the great hall at Vail's Point, her black velvet robe whispering softly as she crossed the floor. "So I burned it here, with

263

him unconscious down at the theater, before driving back through the storm. That way no one could know that I'd been here. And the next day it would all be a bad dream to him."

"Only, he never had a next day." I doubt if Haidee had heard what I said, but the old woman looked back at us as if she had the proper answer.

"I didn't burn all of it."

"There was a copy," I said. Haidee glanced at me as if she had never seen me before.

"Was there?" she said absently. "Usually he made one, but I couldn't find it. Not in his papers or in May's room or in his dressing room. I searched a long time. Now somebody else is searching . . . but who?" She sighed. She did not really expect an answer.

Then, very simply, "The only thing I kept were my sides." She smiled at us gently. "You see we knew it was a great part."

"'We'? Was someone with you?" Julie stared at her mother, but before she could ask again, suddenly the stage blazed into light— the long rows of floodlights glowing high above us, the great spotlights on each side of the stage, even the thin row of lights in the footlight trough. For a moment I was blinded as I think Julie was, and then in the open windows that led to the "garden" backstage I saw a dark silhouette, thick and solid.

"Of course there was someone else, ducks," said Esme as she came onto the stage.

I suppose I knew all along she must be somewhere in the theater, for when had I ever seen Haidee that Esme wasn't close by? She moved across the lighted stage slowly, her fat figure finally dignified, and stood just behind Haidee. If I had expected the evil that they had done over the long years to show at last, I was to be disappointed. Esme looked the same as always, her clown face smiling complacently, her plump little hands folded over her stomach.

Julie stepped back and put an arm around my shoulder. "The police will be here any moment, Esme. Don't try anything more."

"You found the play, didn't you?" said Esme to me. Her tiny eyes were cold and unpleasant. "Oh, yes, I heard you. I've kept an eye on you from the beginning." She started to move forward, but Haidee raised her arm, blocking her.

"We never meant to kill," said Haidee. "Not Lionel or that Wendy. We just wanted everybody to go away. To forget." She swayed a little, as if she might faint. Esme put her strong arms about her and led her back to the love seat carefully.

"That doesn't matter any more, Haidee," she said gently. "The only important thing is to rehearse the new play."

Esme looked back at us, her face ordinary as always. "You'll have to go now," she said to us. "I have to hear Haidee's lines. The way I always do." She looked down at the old woman and smoothed her white hair with her hand. "Oh, luv, you're going to be wonderful in this new one. It's a great part."

Haidee looked up at her, bewildered. "'Part'? I . . . I don't remember."

"Of course you do," said Esme. She pulled out a wad of pages from the pocket of her dark skirt. "It's a new play called *All Our Yesterdays*. It's going to be the triumph of your career."

"I—I can't rehearse now. I'm too tired." But Haidee was staring at the pages in Esme's hands, fascinated.

"You always feel better once you've run your lines." Esme spread the pages flat with her fat fingers. Even from where Julie and I were standing we could see the pages were gray with age. "I'll cue you, luv, just like always."

"You won't go? Like the others?" Haidee pleaded.

For one second the placid mask of Esme's face cracked. There were tears in her eyes, and again she smoothed Haidee's silver hair, her hand hesitant and gentle, as if she were touching something very fragile, something that might shatter at any moment. "No, luv, I won't ever go.

"We'll be here when you want us," Esme said calmly, once more in control. She opened the pages in her hand, squinting at the typed words. "The cue for your entrance is 'Sit down, Charles. Sit down now.'"

"It's a great part. I must be perfect in it."

Haidee struggled to her feet and moved away from the love seat. She stopped, squared her shoulders and turned to face the dark auditorium. She was smiling brightly, her head high, and for a moment she looked as young as the first day I had seen her.

Nodding gracefully to an unseen partner, she glided forward as if entering a drawing room. "Mr. Fields, I think you're trying to comfort me," she said lightly, looking to her left.

"Oh, God! Mama!"

Julie would have fallen if she had not been leaning on me, but

Haidee paid no attention. She started pantomiming the arrangement of flowers in an invisible vase. Esme shot us a look of anger.

"Get out!" she whispered. "This is *our* time. Get out!"

Julie crumpled now, the tears streaming down her face. "Take me away, Alison. Please! I can't bear any more," she sobbed.

I led her from the stage, away from the lights into the darkness beyond. "They're mad!" she whispered, clinging to me. "Did you hear them? They're both mad!"

"Hush! Hush!" I started toward Julie's dressing room, but she held back.

"No! I can't stand to be here . . . not one minute more!" Her thick dark red hair had pulled loose and was straggling down over her bare shoulders. She brushed it aside impatiently. "We've got to get out of here," she muttered, and pulled me with her toward the stage door.

And behind us we could hear Haidee's voice, high and artificial, with the low murmur of Esme as she cued her.

The stage door closed, the lock clicking automatically. Julie moved forward alone across the veranda and down the steps to the grass beyond. She stood gulping in the evening air as if it had been hours since she had been able to breathe. As I came to her side she looked back at the dark theater.

"Alison, what am I going to do? They'll have to be locked up." She took my hand. "I don't want to wait here. We can wait for Jeb on the road." She looked once more at the dark, closed building behind us. "God, all those years of hatred!"

She pulled me forward, her free hand holding up the long skirt of her gown. Together we crossed the cleared area in front of the theater. The full moon turned the trees and grass silver and a strong wind had risen; it felt cool on our faces.

Before we could reach the side road that led through the trees to the highway beyond, we saw the lights of a car coming toward us. Julie stopped dead. "Ed . . . ," she whispered. "What can I tell him?"

The car swerved into the driveway, the headlights illuminating us like two great spotlights. It braked to a stop, the doors on each side bursting open, and Ed and Jeb came running toward us.

I missed the moment when Ed approached Julie. Jeb had moved faster, and his arms were around me, holding me as if he would never let go.

"Are you all right?" he whispered in my ear.

I started to speak, but then I saw the expression on McNaughton's face. He was looking beyond us, back at the theater, and there was horror in his eyes.

"My God . . . ," he yelled, "look!"

We all turned, and for a moment I didn't know what the state trooper had seen. The building was dark and solid as always against the night sky. But then I noticed something that looked like a gray fog swirling around the closed doors and shutters. At almost the same instant there was a flicker of light on the roof of the theater, as if a flame had climbed high in a chimney. Only, there were no chimneys in the theater.

"Jeb, it's on fire!"

Without waiting for us, Ed raced across the driveway and up the wide steps. We followed after him, Julie half stumbling in her long skirt. By the time we reached McNaughton, he had tried all the front doors of the theater and stood looking at us, balked with frustration.

"Locked," he said. "Is there any other way to get inside?"

"The stage door," said Jeb, and started for it.

"That's locked, too," I cried after him, and he stopped.

Julie was clinging to Ed's arm. "They're in there," she pleaded. "Esme and Haidee."

He nodded. "Is there an ax around someplace?" he asked Jeb, his face grim.

"Maybe in the shop." They raced off then into the darkness. I reached out to Julie. She was swaying as if she were about to faint.

"Did they plan this?" she whispered to me. I could make no answer. Even with the smoke we could smell the unmistakable odor of gasoline. Esme, I thought. She'd had time to prepare this if the poison failed.

The smoke was thicker now, finding its way out through the cracks and crevices of the old wooden building. I half-dragged Julie down the steps and across the driveway. There were fires in three places on the roof now, yellow-red flames growing like flowers among the cheerful wooden curlicues that decorated the building.

Even from where we stood we could feel the heat of the blaze, hear the crackle of burning wood . . .

Ed and Jeb came running back. They each had an ax and together they started on one of the shuttered windows on the side veranda. Julie pulled free and ran toward them, her eyes wild, her long, red hair hanging thick about her bare shoulders. By the time we reached the two men, we could hear the roar of the flames inside the building.

There was a shatter of wood as Jeb and McNaughton crashed through the shuttered window, and a great wave of heat swept out, scorching our faces. Beyond, the whole theater was ablaze, the old dry wood from the long days of the hot summer feeding the fire as if the building were made of matches. Breaking open the window seemed to spur the fire; I could see fingers of flame climbing up the seams of the walls inside, etching row after row of seats yellow, as well as the outlines of the far windows.

"Get back!" shouted Ed. He pushed us as something that looked like a burning chariot fell directly in front of us, blocking the window.

"The balcony's coming down," said Jeb. There was no way we could get past the fiery rubble in front of us.

"Mama!" Julie pointed beyond the smoke and flames. There was a steady roar of noise now as the ceiling came crashing down before our eyes, and Julie had to shout.

But the two people in the theater did not hear her.

They were still on the stage, Esme and Haidee. I think that the crackling flames and crash of burning wood that surrounded them must have seemed by now no different to the two old women than brilliant spotlights and the sound of applause. Indeed, it may have been a trick of the fierce light, but it seemed to me that Haidee was curtseying deeply again and again to the flaming auditorium, Esme watching her, her fat little hands clapping steadily.

I need lights for my exit, I remembered.

There was a great, long ripping sound as the heavy velvet curtain burned loose from the metal bar that held it. It fell, a brilliant orange of flames, over the stage, and after that we could see them no more.

FINAL CURTAIN

CHAPTER TWENTY-SEVEN

The day of the funeral was one of those August days that happen only in New England. The sky was a clear blue, and by the time we started for the plain white church in Westaven it was already summer hot. But there was still a crispness in the air that seemed to warn of an early fall, and along the road into town a few leaves on the deep-green trees had already turned red. They reminded me of flames, and I shuddered a little.

May had decreed the women were to wear black. She sat in the first car, straight-backed and dignified, wearing a conventional dress for the first time since I had known her. Beside her sat Julie, neat in black linen. Not surprisingly, Ed McNaughton sat next to her. He was not in uniform but in a well-cut dark blue suit and tie. He looked strong and very handsome.

Corin, Rita, and Oliver were in the long station wagon, with Yvonne and Frankie quietly subdued in the back seats. Jeb and I brought up the end of the short procession. But we were not alone. For the day after the fire my father had arrived unexpectedly. The news of the disaster had reached him the same evening that Peter returned to the college to inform him that his daughter was planning to marry a stranger. Hiding his curiosity behind an air of mild amusement, he appeared at Vail's Point the following afternoon just as we were all straggling down to the dining room, all of us still shaken by the incredible night we had been through.

May greeted my father cordially and insisted he stay at Vail's Point. With the death of her sister and Esme, May had come into her own, rather like a queen who has spent years of exile planning every detail of her reign and now was determined to forget nothing.

I watched with some amusement that afternoon as Jeb and my father talked politely, rather like two diplomats from enemy countries. But my father soon started Jeb on a discussion of the theater, telling him of great opening nights he had seen before Jeb was born and questioning him skillfully about his own plans. By the time supper was ready the two of them were close friends, and I had a deep suspicion that if I had any quarrels with my future husband, my father was going to be on *his* side.

The relationship between Jeb and his own father was not so easily established. They had worked together through the long night, trying to help the volunteer fire department of Westaven, but now that it was over they seemed to have little to say to each other. They would look at each other covertly when they thought nobody was watching, rather like two dogs from different kennels who have been brought to live together in the same house. It was only when they looked at Julie that their faces seemed alike and one could recognize that they shared the same blood.

Julie seemed to float on a cloud of happiness. Somehow, during that long night, she had found the time to explain to Ed what Haidee had confessed. At any rate, sometime before dawn, when I had come up to the house to get more coffee for the firemen, I had found them together on the porch, hand in hand, looking at each other with that silence that belongs only to two people who are deeply in love. They made a handsome couple, no longer young, but beautiful in their strength and maturity. I suspect that the world of the theater and television will see very little of Julie Vail in the future.

The theater was completely destroyed. Shortly after the first light of day, the flames had subsided enough for one of the firemen to hack his way through the smoldering rubble to where the stage had been. It was he who found the bodies of Haidee and Esme. They would not allow any of the family to view them. But I did hear one of the firemen tell McNaughton that when they found them, the two old women were lying together, hand in hand.

They would be buried side by side as well, May stated.

Sunday evening after supper, McNaughton called us all into the drawing room. "We'd all better get our stories straight," he said when we were finally settled around the great fireplace.

Newspapers all across the country had been full of the Vails that day, with front-page accounts of the fire and long, laudatory reviews of Haidee's career. There was also an eerie postscript: a glowing review of the play we had presented. The Vails were definitely news again.

"So we . . ." Ed glanced quickly at Julie, who gave him a dazzling smile. "That is, *I*," he went on a little awkwardly, "feel we ought to get everything settled now."

Oliver from his corner on the couch muttered, "Hear, hear."

"As a police officer, it's my duty to make a full report on what has happened. It's fairly clear that Esme, either with or without Haidee's open approval, killed Wendy, thinking she was Alison. And made several other attempts on Alison's life."

My father, sitting next to me, put his hand on mine. I had never seen his face so grave.

"But what do we do about it?" said Ed, looking once more at Julie. "There doesn't seem to be much point in destroying the old woman's reputation." He sighed heavily. "God knows Julie and I have more reason to hate her than anybody."

"That's over, Ed," Julie broke in quickly.

"Yeah. She made fools of everybody, if we can believe that play Alison found." He rubbed his forehead as if hoping to wipe away the memory of all the bitter years when he had thought of Julie as having deserted him.

"What I suggest is this," he went on, looking directly at me. "Let's leave it as the newspapers and television people have reported it. The two old ladies stayed behind in the theater to rehearse, somehow the fire started . . ."

Corin shifted in his chair. Ed gave him a look. It suggested that whatever the future held, Ed and Corin were never going to be friends.

"Yes?" said Ed, his voice once more that of a policeman.

"I was just thinking," answered Corin, mildly for him. "The next play was to be *Ghosts*. That ends with a fire," he explained to McNaughton. "There were smoke bombs backstage at the theater to make the effect. I saw them. That could be an explanation," he added, somewhat lamely. McNaughton nodded curtly and turned back to me.

"It depends on what *you* want, Alison. You've been through a bad time here." He walked over to Julie and rested his hand on her shoulder. Together they looked at me, waiting.

"We'll do whatever you wish," Julie said.

I studied them all for a moment. Julie and Ed together. May in her deep, hooded chair. Oliver and Corin and Rita on the long sofa opposite me. I was seated between my father and Jeb, and I reached out and took a hand from each. "There's no point in creating more scandal about the Vails," I said firmly. I looked at Jeb and smiled. "Especially since it seems I'm going to be one of them."

Jeb squeezed my hand gently and grinned. "Definitely one of them. There's no question about that." I could feel the others relax.

And then my father, who had said nothing during this meeting, leaned forward and, tapping the tobacco out of his cold pipe, said mildly, "And what about Lionel?"

I looked at him puzzled, as did the others.

"You all seem to have forgotten that Alison came here to prepare Lionel's papers so that a proper biography could be written," he went on. "What is to be told about Lionel's death? Or is that to be hidden as well?"

There was a moment of silence. Then May stood and, moving slowly and with great dignity, came over to where my father was sitting. "Grant, I want you to write Lionel's biography," she said. "Write what we know—that Haidee *did* try to destroy his play. Whether she actually meant to kill him or not, we can never be sure."

Her face was as cold and merciless as a judge. "But that part of Haidee's reputation can't be saved. And shouldn't be."

There was no sound in the room now. She looked at each of us in turn, her mouth grim. "Haidee dedicated her life to the theater. By trying to destroy Lionel and his finest play," she announced slowly, "Haidee betrayed that dedication. It is fitting that the theater killed her."

Monday was spent in preparations for the funeral. Cablegrams and telegrams arrived every hour, and the flowers not only filled the church and the cemetery but made huge splashes of color throughout the house. Nearly every major figure in the theater had sent something. And not just for Haidee; Esme was remembered as well.

Again we assembled in the drawing room after supper. But this time we sat quietly as Corin read the manuscript of *All Our Yesterdays*. He had found time that afternoon to have the manuscript duplicated, and there was a high pile of copies of the play at his side. There would be no further chances taken with Lionel's last work.

It was, as Lionel had predicted so many years before, his greatest play. Haidee had been right that the leading female role was magnificent. She was also right that it revealed more about her than anyone could be expected to face. It showed a cold and selfish woman who hated and envied her daughter for the love the girl had found, and the mother's determination to destroy that love if only to prove her own barren life was justified.

Julie was in tears at the end of the play, sobbing bitterly on Ed's shoulder. All of us were stricken by what we had heard, but there was no mistaking that the play would be a triumph when produced.

"Jeb will direct it, of course," said Corin briskly after he had finally closed the manuscript. "With Lionel's reputation, especially after all the publicity we got for *The Basilisks,* I shouldn't have any trouble raising the money."

My father looked at me, and I nodded. "Alison and I had a little talk this afternoon," he said, smiling quietly. "We feel the Howard Foundation would be interested in helping finance Lionel Vail's last play."

"There are also the family diamonds," added May from her chair. "With Haidee's death, there are no more restrictions on them. You'll inherit them, Julie," she said, looking at her niece.

Julie, her eyes still red, spoke out angrily. "I don't want them! I don't want anything that was Mother's. Take them, Corin. Sell them or do anything you want. I never want to see them again!" She dried her eyes with a handkerchief Ed gave her.

"I suppose there's no chance . . . ?" Corin let the sentence end in silence, his eyes on his mother.

"That I might play it?" Julie's voice crackled with anger. "Never! Live through the worst unhappiness of my life every night of the week and two matinees? I'd go insane!" She smiled a little ruefully. "No, Corin. Some other actress will make the hit of her career next season in the part. But it won't be me."

The gathering broke up shortly after that. The funeral would be in the morning and we were all aware of what an ordeal it would be. Television units from all the networks had already staked out the places for their cameras to cover the funeral and the burial in the family cemetery afterward. The town of Westaven was enjoying a tourist boom it had never expected when the Vails first suggested reopening the theater. The inn and all the nearby motels were crowded. Yvonne reported that there was almost a carnival atmosphere in the quiet New England town.

Jeb left me with a hasty kiss to drive into town to confer with the cameramen from his network who would be working the next day. He is determined to have me as his assistant when the new play is produced, and I have agreed that will be his wedding present. He also threatens to turn me into an actress in the future, but to that I merely smile. I can only hope after our marriage he will forget.

So finally I was alone, moving about the great drawing room turning off the lights. Without the furniture that had been destroyed in the theater fire the room was less cluttered. It had dignity now, and peace.

The last light in the room was the spotlight over the family portrait. I hesitated for a moment and looked up at the huge painting. There they all were as I had first seen them—Viola and Haidee, May and Lionel. But I felt no chill now, no cold sense of evil. Perhaps it had disappeared with the burning of the theater.

"I wonder if I could have prevented any of this?" Oliver stood in the doorway to the dining room, one last glass of brandy in his hand. He came over to where I was standing and looked up at the painting over the fireplace.

"I always meant to ask you if you knew something that was important," I said. "About the lost play, I mean. Something you said that first day was what really made me suspicious."

"I meant it to," said the old man. He sighed. "I knew there was a play. I even suspected what it was about. But I had no proof, nothing that would stand up in court." He took another sip of his brandy and went on thoughtfully. "Lionel had called me, the week before his death. He was full of the new play . . . He kept saying how Haidee would loathe it. He seemed to take pleasure in that."

"Oliver, you've known them all these years, all of the Vails. What *is* the truth? Was Haidee a cold, vicious woman or a struggling actress cheated by her brother of her inheritance? Was Viola a victim? Or a selfish miser?"

"Was Lionel a genius or a monster?" he added, finishing my question. He shook his head slowly. "I don't know, Alison. I suspect like most people they were somewhere in between." He looked at me, his shrewd old eyes twinkling. "But you haven't asked *why*

Lionel called me that last week. He said he was finally going to be married. Some local girl he'd met that winter. He wanted me to be his best man."

Tomorrow, I thought, I must see that Oliver and Lucy Treble have a chance to talk tomorrow.

The funeral service was short; the minister contented himself with reading some of the obituary that had appeared in the New York *Times*. It was a full account of Haidee's career, her contributions to the theater, her great performances and the praise and honors she had earned for them. The old New England church was packed with people—actors of Haidee's era from New York, sightseers and residents of the town—all of them crowded together. Even the back of the church was filled with people willing to stand through the service.

"Haidee would have liked that," said Oliver as we waited to get into the cars that would take us to the cemetery. "A sold-out house."

The final burial at the graveyard was mercifully brief. Below us we could see through the trees the great, black, scorched circle that was all that remained of the theater. Soon souvenir hunters would remove the last bits of rubble.

Because the cemetery was on private property, McNaughton was able to keep most of the crowd out. May had been to the top of the hill early that morning and had cleared away some of the more lavish of the flower arrangements. She had placed the flowers that remained all through the graveyard so that when we reached the crest of the hill it seemed almost as if the summer had never started, that we were still in spring. She stood talking quietly with Lucy Treble. Between the two lonely women, I suspect Vail's Point will become a public shrine to Lionel.

It may bring them some happiness in the years that lie ahead.

I waited until the others had left, Jeb not questioning me but standing quietly at my side. Then, when we were at last alone I took the small bouquet of white flowers I had bought in the village and walked past the two new graves to the far corner of the cemetery. May's work had not extended this far, and the old, angled stones in the August sunlight wore no decorations but the shadow of dark green moss.

Jeb stood as I knelt to put my flowers on the small white stone. Rest in peace, Phoebe, I prayed.

May all the Vails rest in peace.